D0464850

RECEIVED

OCT   2018

By

NO LONGER PROPERTY OF
SEATTLE PUBLIC LIBRARY

The
PASHA
OF
CUISINE

The PASHA OF CUISINE

A Novel

SAYGIN ERSIN

Translated by Mark David Wyers

Arcade Publishing • New York

Copyright © 2016 by Saygın Ersin
English-language translation copyright © 2018 by Mark David Wyers

All rights reserved. No part of this book may be reproduced in any manner without the express written consent of the publisher, except in the case of brief excerpts in critical reviews or articles. All inquiries should be addressed to Arcade Publishing, 307 West 36th Street, 11th Floor, New York, NY 10018.

First English-language Edition

First published in Turkey in 2016 by April Yayincilik under the title *Pir-i-Lezzet*

This is a work of fiction. Names, characters, places, and incidents are either the products of the author's imagination or used fictitiously.

Arcade Publishing books may be purchased in bulk at special discounts for sales promotion, corporate gifts, fund-raising, or educational purposes. Special editions can also be created to specifications. For details, contact the Special Sales Department, Arcade Publishing, 307 West 36th Street, 11th Floor, New York, NY 10018 or arcade@skyhorsepublishing.com.

Arcade Publishing® is a registered trademark of Skyhorse Publishing, Inc.®, a Delaware corporation.

Visit our website at www.arcadepub.com.

10 9 8 7 6 5 4 3 2 1

Names: Ersin, Saygın, 1975- author. | Wyers, Mark, translator.
Title: The pasha of cuisine : a novel / by Saygın Ersin ; translated by Mark Wyers.
Other titles: Pir-i Lezzet. English
Description: First English edition. | New York : Arcade Publishing, 2018.
Identifiers: LCCN 2018012759 | ISBN 9781628729610 (hardcover : alk. paper)
Subjects: LCSH: Cooks—Turkey—Fiction. | Sultans—Turkey—Fiction. | Turkey—
    History—Ottoman Empire, 1288-1918—Fiction. | GSAFD: Historical fiction |
    Adventure stories
Classification: LCC PL249.E75 P5813 2018 | DDC 894/.3534—dc23 LC record available
    at https://lccn.loc.gov/2018012759

Cover design by Erin Seaward-Hiatt
Cover photo courtesy of iStockphoto

Printed in the United States of America

The
PASHA
OF
CUISINE

1

The Lord of the Mansion

ZÜMRÜTZADE HÜSNÜ BEY, one of Constantinople's most eminent merchants, was hosting an evening banquet for a guest who was as imposing in stature as he was in name: Siyavuş Agha, the Chief Sword Bearer to the sultan, who had agreed to grace Hüsnü Bey's humble mansion with his presence.

The feast was being held in the mansion's magnificent selamlique. Four massive trays had been carefully spaced out along a long low table which was covered in a tablecloth that was mustard yellow in hue and embroidered in silver. The cushions laid out on the floor around the table were, like the divans that lined three walls of the room, covered in plush blue velvet. The goldwork of the guests' garments shimmered in the glow of twenty-one silver candelabras, each of which made the crystal glasses on the table gleam, casting a flickering shine over the porcelain serving dishes adorned with ornate designs of blue and green.

The servants of the mansion, who for weeks had been busy preparing for the feast and enduring the endless instructions and admonitions of their masters, were carrying out their duties with artfulness and grace worthy of a palace. Under the direction of the mansion chamberlain, the servant boys padded, catlike, across a Persian carpet which covered the length of the selamlique as they placed bowls on the trays. Their movements were so nimble that nary a clink of porcelain could be heard. One particularly young servant boy who had gray-blue eyes filled the drinking glass of the guest of honor with such decorum and deliberateness that when the Chief Sword Bearer murmured in deference, "By the grace of God," the sound of his voice mingled with the musical tones of the water as it splashed into his glass.

Seated to the left of Siyavuş Agha, whose fame and notoriety as the Chief Sword Bearer were known throughout the lands of the empire, was a member of the Imperial Council, a man by the name of Halil Pasha, who happened to be the Chief Treasurer. Decorum prescribed that a guest of his standing should add yet more grandeur to such a banquet, but Halil Pasha was feeling out of sorts in both mind and body that evening. His heart, which had grown weary after years of keeping records of the thrice-monthly payment of the Janissaries' salaries, was no longer able to bear even the slightest of squabbles. For Halil Pasha, the banquet was little more than an irritating necessity. Sweating profusely and short of breath, he looked like he might give up his soul should the slightest provocation arise.

Halil Pasha was of the opinion that, even if heavenly ambrosia were to be served, dining with Siyavuş Agha was a situation that should be avoided at all costs. Of course, it was undeniable that Siyavuş Agha was a man of great influence. He was just one of four distinguished personages who could visit the sultan at Edirne Palace unannounced. A single word from his lips had the power to bring prosperity and good tidings, but not once had a single soul been touched by the goodwill he had at his fingertips.

Siyavuş Agha had acquired an unprecedented reputation for being cranky and peevish. For centuries, the palace had bore witness to the rise and demise of the surliest of sultans, imperial consorts, and wives of sultans, but none could have rivaled that cantankerous old man. The agha could not tolerate the slightest imperfection. The muslin windings of his massive turban had to be unwound and washed every single night regardless of whether or not they were dirty, and every morning he expected his turban to be wound afresh, smelling of soap. When he went to the hammam, the water for bathing had to be heated to just the right temperature, and if it wasn't, the consequences were dire. When he had to stay overnight outside the palace, mere candles were insufficient for illuminating his presence; only lamps filled with scented oils would do. His moustache and beard had to be anointed with almond oil, and his hair and skin were to be cleansed by the finest soaps and softened with the purest of olive oil. Intolerant of mistakes, he meted out punishments that far outweighed the crime. Once, the agha had a servant boy beaten to the point of death just because the lad had folded his kaftan incorrectly, and that was just the last in a long list of such incidents.

When it came to pleasures of the gastronomic sort, the agha's capriciousness was a source of despair throughout the Ottoman lands. The most skilled chefs would slave over dishes just to find that he turned his nose up at them, and to make matters worse, he actually knew nothing of the culinary arts. The agha was pleased or displeased based on mere whims, so in the end the cooks simply prepared dishes as they saw fit and left the rest in the hands of God. The agha once heaped praise on an undercooked dish of grilled dove that had been carelessly prepared by an inexperienced young chef, whom he went on to lavish with gold. Another time he was presented with a dish of lamb served on roasted aubergine puree which would have made a king swoon with delight. But what did he do? Tossed it to the ground without a second glance.

Despite all the gossip, stories, and speculation, there was one thing about Siyavuş Agha's taste in food that was known for certain: he despised leeks. His hatred of that particular vegetable was so rancorous that the sultan himself, though he might be craving it, would refrain from having it brought to the table when he was dining with the agha just to avoid his Sword Bearer's displeasure.

So for Halil Pasha, a banquet with Siyavuş Agha promised to be about as enjoyable as bedding down for the night in a sleeping bear's cave. He feared that in his heart he would curse Hüsnü Bey, the host of the banquet, every time that a dish was served and Siyavuş Agha's face darkened with displeasure. And he wasn't unjustified, as he would find out. The only reason he was invited that night was because Hüsnü Bey had personally requested his presence. Yakup Efendi, one of the four guests seated around the tray beside him, was Hüsnü Bey's brother-in-law and, like many of the others at the feast that night, he was a wheat merchant. It had been a scorching summer and famine was engulfing the empire, so the Imperial Council had forbidden the export of certain goods, including wheat. Yakup Efendi (who would swear up and down that he didn't have an ounce of flour despite the fact that his storehouses were brimming with wheat) was hoping to obtain an export concession from the sultan. Siyavuş Agha, who was known for his ability to pull strings with the sultan, was promised that he would pocket a hefty commission in return.

Zümrützade Hüsnü Bey was thereby forced to invite Halil Pasha to the banquet, since, as the Provincial Treasurer, he was the only person on the Imperial Council who could possibly object to the granting of the concession. Despite his somewhat timid disposition, Halil Pasha was a skilled statesman with extensive experience and he wielded notable influence especially in matters of finance. Still, making a speech at an Imperial Council gathering was one thing; openly objecting to a motion made by the Chief Sword Bearer was another. And that's why Hüsnü Bey had invited Halil Pasha to his mansion that night; he knew that while Halil Pasha was a clever statesman, he would refrain from publically drawing the wrath of Siyavuş Agha upon himself.

A devout man, Halil Pasha stoically accepted his lot in life and all that might befall him in the future. At the moment, however, there was one thing that was making him uneasy: there was a tension in the room which he knew would prevent him from properly enjoying the fine dishes that had been prepared for the evening.

Halil Pasha wasn't much of an epicurean. Because of his mild-mannered nature, religious devotion, and humble background, he would eat whatever was placed before him without a word of complaint. He had spent his childhood years as a servant at a countryside manor, and the first lesson he had learned in life was thankfulness for all that God provided.

But something was about to change all that.

The food that was being brought out smelled so exquisite that the Provisional Treasurer was, perhaps for the first time in his life, becoming aware of the fact that he, too, could indulge himself in the enjoyment of food, and that eating was about much more than just filling one's belly.

When the mansion's chamberlain gave the order, the serving boys removed the lids of the bowls, at which time the quiet conversations at the table abruptly ceased. The dish that was about to be served may have merely been rice topped with black pepper, but the scent of the pepper was so enticing that it sent all of the men into reveries. If Hüsnü Bey hadn't enjoined his guests to partake in the feast, none of them would have deigned to pick up their ebony spoons inlaid with mother of pearl and dig into the masterpiece that had been laid before them.

While savoring the rice on the tongue was a pleasure in itself, swallowing it was an altogether different delight. The soft rice soothed the zing of the peppercorns, and, fused in fresh butter, the spice and rice gently glided down toward the stomach.

After the guests had polished off the first dish, the chamberlain signaled for some of the servant boys to clear away the spoons and bowls. As they backed toward the door with measured steps, three other servants approached, placing hot bowls of soup on the trays while a fourth meticulously placed a large spoon made of an antler on the table in front of each guest, beginning with the Chief Sword Bearer.

This next dish was *makiyan* soup, and it made the peppered rice seem as if it had been but a paltry introduction.

Every flavor in the soup had been perfectly orchestrated. There wasn't a trace of flavor from the egg that had been used to thicken the soup; as if under the firm control of a master conductor, it duly performed its task of bringing out the scent of the lemon and the richness of the chicken—nothing more, nothing less. Not a single person reached for the salt or pepper on the table because the soup fell into flawless harmony with the palate of each guest.

Each new dish that the servants brought in was even more delightful than the previous.

As Siyavuş Agha was taking his last bite of *me'muniye*, a sweet dish made with chicken breast and milk (and reportedly named after Caliph Me'mun), Halil Pasha caught himself glaring at the man, and quickly pulled himself together and looked away. He surprised himself. Throughout his life, which had been marked by constant struggle, he had glared at only a handful of people with such hatred, and envy had pierced his heart just as few times. Even stranger, however, was the fact that after he was served *me'muniye*, his mind started wandering to more pleasant thoughts. He found himself thinking of the woman he had married six months earlier but had not yet taken into his arms, and, after taking a bite, he felt a stirring in his loins for the first time in years. As for the Chief Sword Bearer, he was oblivious to the thoughts of the Treasurer sitting beside him. Eyes closed, he was chewing his last bite of *me'muniye* slowly, as if he wanted to savor every last buttery morsel before swallowing.

The guests were left with a pleasant prickle in the backs of their throats, brought on by rosewater thickened with caramelized sugar. All eyes were now on the next round of dishes being brought out. Since the third course had been sweet, the next course would, per the terms of tradition, consist of a pastry or vegetable dish. Halil Pasha found himself wondering, *What will be next? Pastries with cheese and cream? Or maybe stuffed quince or stewed courgette? But surely the real surprise will come with the final course. The chef, whoever that master may be, must be holding out on his grand finale for a kebab or something of the like.*

The guests closed their eyes as the servants approached, eagerly anticipating the scents that would soon fill their nostrils. When the Treasurer heard the gentle clink of a porcelain lid, he breathed in deeply and a smile spread across his lips. The scent brought back to life some of his oldest memories, whisking him nearly seventy years back to his childhood. Carrying a heavy basket on his back which was nearly as large as himself, he was following the chamberlain of the manor where he'd been taken in as a servant. They were walking to the market, and they had to travel a long way. Still, while the chamberlain was in a foul mood, young Halil's cheer knew no bounds. Going to the market meant that for a few hours he would be saved from his humdrum work at the manor, and he always reveled in the scents and sounds that greeted him there. First, they passed by a stand that was stacked with bundles of green onions, and up ahead there was a vendor selling the freshest of butter. Halil Pasha's eye lingered on orange carrots and the reddest radishes, and his nose was filled with the scent of dill carried on the breeze. The chamberlain started haggling over the price of a bundle of leeks.

The Treasurer pulled himself from his reverie just as he was imagining the scent that had arisen from the leeks as the chamberlain loaded them into his basket. When he opened his eyes, his heart was pounding and he prayed that the scent lingering in the air was just a remnant of that journey into his memory.

But when he looked up, his worst fears came true. In the center of the tray, there was a copper pan filled with stewed leeks neatly arranged around a steaming mound of chopped, roasted lamb.

Halil Pasha groaned to himself, "And so the merry times end! Zümrützade Hüsnü Bey, you've done us in! Your brother-in-law is done for, and so are you."

As he gazed sadly at the leeks, his left arm and lower lip suddenly were numb. He knew that when Siyavuş Agha realized what had been served, he would take it as a personal affront and bring everyone at the banquet to rack and ruin regardless of their station in life. Halil Pasha had always been fond of leeks, so this was doubly tragic because, depending on what happened, there was a chance that he may not be able to enjoy a single spoonful. But he resigned himself to this turn of events, telling himself that nothing could be done, and he sat back, waiting for Siyavuş Agha to unleash his fury. A deathly silence hung over the table, the silence before a storm.

When Halil Pasha could bear it no longer and cast a glance to his right, his eyes widened in disbelief. The Chief Sword Bearer was muttering a blessing and slowly reaching for his spoon. His eyes were open, yet seemed to be blind to the world. Everyone at the table was watching in horror, but Hüsnü Bey was in the most woeful state of them all. He opened his mouth to warn Siyavuş Agha, but thought better of it at the last minute. His eyes were bulging in their sockets, giving him the appearance of a gray mullet just hauled out of the sea, the hook still in its mouth.

Siyavuş Agha brought a spoonful of leeks to his mouth. As he chewed, he appeared to be on the brink of ecstasy. After he swallowed his first bite, a smile appeared on his face, the likes of which no one had ever seen before, almost a childish grin. Judging by the look in his eyes, he seemed to be lost in a world of daydreams.

If Hüsnü Bey hadn't said, "May it bring you good health," the agha would have perhaps never returned from that land of daydreams, nor would the order in the host's house have been upturned, the Treasurer wouldn't have been discharged from his post, and the other guests at the table wouldn't have remembered the dinner as a dark turning point in their lives.

But Hüsnü Bey did speak those words.

Immediately Siyavuş Agha's smile vanished and his usual ill-tempered, vindictive, calculating stare returned. Slowly he turned to Hüsnü Bey and hissed, "Are you mocking me?"

Those words seemed to wind around Hüsnü Bey's neck like a greased noose and his eyes widened in terror. He wanted to say, "By no means, your Highness," but he could manage naught but the faintest of whispers.

Siyavuş Agha didn't say another word as he glared at each of the guests at the table one by one. They knew what that stare meant: the scene they had just witnessed was to be a secret they would keep till the end of their days. That is, aside from the Treasurer.

Treasurer Halil Pasha's left arm, which had been tingling for some time, now went completely limp and his lower lip hung slack. He was unable to get to his feet when Siyavuş Agha stormed away from the dinner table, nor was he able to stir when Hüsnü Bey and his brother-in-law trailed after him stammering apologies, or when all the other guests scampered off. He was completely paralyzed on his left side, unable to move or talk. Silently he began to curse, reserving his most bitter curses for Zümrützade Hüsnü Bey, who he blamed for bringing him to such a state, and for Siyavuş Agha. Then he heaped curses on all the state officials he had ever met, starting from his childhood. Swearing brought him some small comfort. *So, this is my fate*, he thought, hoping that his staunch faith, which had taken him far in life and given him the patience to deal with every trying situation, leading him to believe that God was behind all that was good and mankind was the source of all evil, wouldn't abandon him. Slowly and with great difficulty, he reached forward, plunging his spoon into the dish on the table, and stuffed his half-open mouth with leeks. Ignoring the oil and bits of vegetable dripping down his chin, he smiled; his half-paralyzed lips twisted into a crooked grin as he tried to chew. The pleasure he felt was beyond words. He felt as though an entire autumn—with its leaves, wind, and rain—had been transformed into the taste that was now tantalizing his palate. Treasurer Halil Pasha addressed his only blessing of that night to the cook who had prepared such a wondrous dish.

As the Treasurer sat there relishing the taste of the leeks, down in the courtyard silence reigned, hanging so thickly in the air that the crackling of the torches carried by the servants seemed to be a roar.

Even though he begged and pleaded, Zümrützade Hüsnü Bey was unable to keep Siyavuş Agha from storming off through the gate, bristling with spite and calculations for revenge. After the agha left, the other guests quickly and noiselessly followed suit.

Hüsnü Bey was plunged into thought. He wondered how the Chief Sword Bearer would settle accounts, knowing he would do so even over a mere dish of leeks. After all, he was Siyavuş Agha, a man who took revenge no matter how big or small the offence. He was pitiless, and that cruelty was what propelled him up through the ranks of the state's hierarchy.

His name had echoed through the halls of the palace on the night the sultan ascended to the throne. Everyone knew about the new sovereign's orders and the murders that the agha had committed with his silk noose, and he made no effort to keep them a secret. After having a few drinks at banquets and revelries, a vicious gleam would come into his eyes and he would begin to talk, a lascivious grin twisting his lips as he spoke about the atrocities he committed, sparing no detail.

The other guests, unable to close their ears to his tales of the slaughtering of women and children, would feel gloom pressing down upon their hearts. But he was Siyavuş Agha, after all, so they had no choice but to join in with his deranged laughter.

That was precisely what concerned Zümrützade Hüsnü Bey. Siyavuş Agha would take that dish of leeks which had been set before him as a personal affront and mete out his punishment accordingly. Hüsnü Bey decided that the next morning he would send some of his slaves to the palace bearing trunks filled with gifts, as he knew that gold and jewelry soothed the soul of the Chief Sword Bearer, and then he would quietly ride out the storm. His greatest fear was that he might have to deal with Siyavuş Agha in the near future, in which case the Chief Sword Bearer would unleash his rage with exacting precision.

Hüsnü Bey heaved a sigh and turned to his butler, who appeared as unsteady as the flickering flames of the torches in the servants' hands. Hüsnü Bey's eyes, which had been heavy with grief just a moment before, suddenly filled with anger. "Summon the cook," he snapped.

The butler's expression fell, as if he'd been expecting that command but praying it would never be uttered. "Yes, Master," he murmured and shuffled off, disappearing into the shadows of the courtyard.

Soon after, the butler reappeared in the light of the torches, a thin figure following a few steps behind him. The butler stopped and stepped aside. The man behind him took a few bold steps forward until his face and figure were well within the glow of the torches. He stopped two paces from Hüsnü Bey and greeted him.

Hüsnü Bey could only bring himself to glance at the young face shining before him as the cook's piercing green eyes bore into his own. A few brown curls of hair fell onto the cook's eyebrows from beneath his turban, and his moustache with its curled ends lent his face an expression of mild, composed nobility. He not so much walked as glided, spoke little, but was eloquent when he did so, and worked at a calm, steady pace, never saying a harsh word even when the kitchen was at its busiest. Throughout his life, Hüsnü Bey had known dozens of aristocrats and for many of them, their elegance, just like their reputation, was a veneer, their actions mere imitations of refinement. But this young man was different. He carried nobility in his soul, not only in his body.

"Haven't I told you a thousand times?" Hüsnü Bey growled. It occurred to him that the forced anger in his voice probably wasn't very convincing, but he brushed aside the thought.

With a hint of a smile on his lips, the cook asked, "About what?"

Hüsnü Bey raised his voice. "The leeks, the cursed leeks! Hadn't I told you that the Chief Sword Bearer hates leeks?"

The young cook thought for a moment and then smiled again. "Ah, yes, Your Grace, you did mention that . . ."

By now Hüsnü Bey actually was starting to get angry. The flames of a nearby torch seemed to be blown back by the force of his breath as he bellowed, "Then why on earth did you cook them?"

A somber silence fell over the courtyard. The smile had fallen from the cook's lips but his gaze was still fixed on Hüsnü Bey's eyes. Just as Hüsnü Bey was about to berate him further, the cook calmly asked, "Did he not enjoy them?"

Hüsnü Bey's jaw dropped.

The cook asked, "Did he not eat them? Was something wrong?"

The master was at a loss for words. He couldn't bring himself to say, "No, he didn't eat them," because the image of the Chief Sword Bearer raising the spoon of leeks to his mouth still lingered in his thoughts. Desperately he shouted, "You watch your tongue! I told you that the agha hates leeks. All of Constantinople knows that!"

"Well, the whole of Constantinople is wrong then. Including His Highness the Agha himself," the cook coolly responded.

Hüsnü Bey was trembling from head to toe, not so much out of anger but because he was flustered. Still, he was one of the gentry, a man of influence; if he so desired, he could kill the cook on the spot and no one would dare question him about it. He could send him into exile for the rest of his life. But in the face of the young man's coolness and the exquisiteness of his cooking, Hüsnü Bey felt helpless. For months, ever since that green-eyed menace had first stepped through the door of his mansion, that was how it had been. Hüsnü Bey had sensed that feeling of helplessness before, but that night, for the very first time, he admitted it to himself, and that was why he was trembling.

Drawing on all his willpower, he gestured toward the main gate as he prepared to say, "Get out!" but the words stuck in his throat because of a taste that inexplicably appeared on his palate just at that moment. It was the taste of *medfune*. He imagined the slow-cooked aubergine dissolving in his mouth, the smell of braised meat, and the sharpness of sumac. Slowly he licked his lips and gulped. Still pointing at the gate, he glanced at his servants and the butler standing nearby with their torches. At that moment, Hüsnü Bey realized what a delicate position he was in. The eyes of his servants weren't just filled with concern but also anger. For a second, he wondered about the dishes the cook had prepared which now held them spellbound.

Hüsnü Bey knew that his hand mustn't remain aloft any longer, pointing at the gate. At last he broke free from the grip of the tastes he was imagining and pulled himself together. Pointing at the cook, he snapped at the butler, "Take him away and give him forty lashes."

The butler motioned for two servants to take the cook to the cellar, which was at the far end of the courtyard. Hüsnü Bey watched the young man as he walked, head held high in the light of the flames; it was as if he wasn't being led away but rather leading his captors. Glancing up at the windows of the mansion's harem, Hüsnü Bey saw a sudden movement of shadows. He surmised that the women of the harem were also curious about what would happen to the cook.

"God, protect my sanity," Hüsnü Bey muttered. He was in a sticky situation indeed, one that would appear to be sheer lunacy to anyone on the outside. The fact of the matter was that the cook had bewitched his entire household, from the harem to the servants, and everyone did his bidding. Early on, Hüsnü Bey had sensed that something was amiss; in the beginning he had cast his unease from his thoughts but as the situation became graver, he realized that he was trapped. Dozens of times he had decided to fire the cook but each time he put off doing so "until the next meal," and ultimately all his firm decisions softened in the presence of a dish of *kapama* or the scent of stuffed vegetables. He wouldn't have minded so much if he could have discovered the cook's secret, but that proved to be impossible. The cook worked alone, without an apprentice or assistant. Whenever Hüsnü Bey sent his servants into the kitchen to keep an eye on him, they would return babbling about the wondrous scents there. The cook's past was just as puzzling for him. Hüsnü Bey had searched high and low but been unable to discover anything about who he was. In the end, Hüsnü Bey felt like he was on the verge of losing his mind.

He breathed in the cool evening air and sighed. Thinking that Hüsnü Bey had said something, the butler sprang forward and said, "Yes, master?" Guessing that the butler had also been lost in thought, Hüsnü Bey ordered him away with a snap of his fingers.

The butler led the servants back into the mansion. Hüsnü Bey lingered in the courtyard a while longer, taking comfort in the darkness and quiet, which helped clear his mind. He knew that he had to come up with a solution, but he also knew that sending the cook away wasn't an option. He wasn't about to make another firm decision only to be brought to shame because he went back on it. He thought, *Only wisdom and science can sort this out.* He considered asking a religious scholar for help, someone with extensive knowledge and pious insights who he could treat as a confidant. He knew that if the Council of Elders caught wind of his troubles, or even worse the Shaykh-al Islam, it would spell disaster. He already had enough trouble with the Chief Sword Bearer, and he knew that if word got out about his current plight, he would be endlessly ridiculed.

Feeling more at ease now that he'd come up with a solution, Hüsnü Bey decided to make his way to the harem, but just as he was about to walk through the door he turned around, deciding that it would be better to go to the men's quarters, smoke half a pipe, and think about who he could speak with as a confidant. Before going inside, he listened at the cellar door. After every lash of the cane, he could hear a muffled groan. Hüsnü Bey smiled, wondering if forty lashes had been too few. Then he thought about lunch the following day, worriedly realizing that if the cook couldn't stand, he wouldn't be able to prepare anything. Since he hadn't been able to enjoy dinner that night, he hoped to make up for it the following day. A broad smile on his lips, he walked toward the staircase.

However, matters weren't going to unfold as the unfortunate Hüsnü Bey hoped. Not as he hoped at all.

As Zümrützade Hüsnü Bey puffed on his pipe in his room, the young cook lit the stove in the kitchen and started making a pot of semolina halva, humming a tune as he listened to the sounds coming from the cellar. There was another crack of the cane, followed by a groan. A voice said, "Easy, easy! For heaven's sake, you're not caning an enemy here."

"As if your hide were so precious!" another voice responded. "We're not even halfway done yet."

"What do you mean? That made eleven."

"You fool, it's not like I've hit you in the head! You still know how to count, right? We've only done nine so far."

"But the soles of my feet are already bruised. Please, show some mercy."

"Look, you gave me twenty lashes. Now it's my turn. Plus, the Master is next door, and he's keeping count."

He was right. The cook was stirring the contents of the pot, counting each blow. The page boys had agreed to get twenty lashes each in exchange for the semolina halva that the cook was preparing.

When he heard the last crack of the cane, he took the pot off the stove. Not every cook could make halva so quickly without burning it, but for our young cook, it was as easy as breathing. The sweet smell of caramelized sugar that filled the kitchen was a testament to the perfection of his work.

Shortly afterwards, he heard the sound of two pairs of feet scuffling along the floor and then a knock on the door. "Come in," the cook called out. As the two boys stumbled inside, the cook glanced into the courtyard to make sure no one was watching.

When they breathed in the scent of the halva, the boys forgot all about their pain. Eyes fixed on the pot, they were eager to get their hands on their reward. "It's done, Master," one of them said. "Forty lashes."

The other one added, "Maybe more, but certainly not less than forty."

The cook looked at the boys with a mixture of anger and pity. They were the most wretched residents at that wretched mansion. They washed Hüsnü Bey's laundry and in return they were allowed to be vile to their heart's content. They had gone through so much in their short lives that they could no longer tell pain from pleasure. The cook was well aware of the fact that such people always had a fondness for sweets, particularly syrupy desserts. The rich taste of the sugar, which went straight to the brain, mingled with a pleasant burning sensation in the throat, creating a sense of delight.

The cook made his way toward a wicker basket of spoons hanging on the wall. He chose two large spoons, held them out to the boys, and left the kitchen, as he couldn't stand to see his halva devoured with such haste and savagery.

If there was one thing that had escaped the attention of the servants who had been scouring the mansion from top to bottom since the morning call to prayer for the feast that night, it was the cook's attire. The butler, who had an eye for the smallest of details, and even the mansion's owner, hadn't noticed that he was wearing his outdoor clothes. Like many things that escape notice, it was an important detail.

After withdrawing to his room, which was next to the kitchen, the cook started packing his belongings. He didn't have much. Of the two outfits he owned, he was wearing the newer one, and the other was at the bottom of his bundle. On top of those he placed his work clothes, which consisted of two burgundy shirts, a pair of knee-length *shalwar*, and shoes with low heels. He wrapped his set of knives, which included a small knife, a larger one, and a meat cleaver, in a leather case which he packed beside his shoes. Before placing his red silk apron—which was a symbol of his rank as a master cook—in his bundle, he pulled two books out from under his bed. One of them was bound in black, and the other in green. He placed the thicker green book on his apron, and, after glancing over a few pages in the black book, he placed it on top of the other one and wrapped the apron around them.

He was almost ready. He sat cross-legged on the bed and stared at length at the single oil lamp illuminating the room. Then he closed his eyes and whispered one word. That word was from a language that was either unknown or had been forgotten long ago. At that moment, a scent wafted into his mind. The cook breathed it in, the scent of apple with cloves spreading in waves from his mind to his senses.

Nights of loneliness and yearning had taught him that if he breathed in deeply enough, so deep that he was filled with memories and dreams as well as the scent he conjured up in his mind, a beautiful figure from his past would appear in a corner of his mind, even if fleetingly. That moment, which was briefer than the flash of a flint spark, was the sole source of his love for life and his desire to keep fighting to stay alive.

The cook sat and waited, trying to relax his body and mind. His journey was beginning. The next day, nothing and no one would remain the same, not in his life nor at that mansion he was leaving behind, nor at the place to which he was going.

Zümrützade Hüsnü Bey woke up quite late the next morning.

The previous night, when the servants found the poor Treasurer still sitting at the dinner table, they informed Hüsnü Bey as well as the neighborhood physician, who confirmed that Halil Pasha was paralyzed. After placing Halil Pasha in the back of a coach, they sent him home to be tended to by his wives.

As he smoked his pipe, Hüsnü Bey had some coffee to clear his mind. Then he filled another pipe and had another strong coffee, at which point the possibility of sleep completely abandoned him, so he went to his harem, hoping a little vigorous activity might bring on sleep. Afterwards, he went to the mansion's hammam for his ablutions and finally got into bed well after midnight.

When he woke up, he quickly did his morning prayers, even though it was well past morning by that time. He noticed that there was a commotion in the mansion. He wasn't surprised, however, that no one had let him know what was happening because he was always in a foul mood when he woke up, and unless there was pressing official business, no one would dare knock on his door, not even if the mansion was burning down.

Once downstairs, Hüsnü Bey saw that everyone was gathered in front of the kitchen. Yet again, shadows were darting about behind the latticed windows of the harem. After casting a stern glance up at his wives and odalisques, he walked across the courtyard. Everyone was staring at the kitchen door and the door to the small room beside the kitchen, which were still closed. The fact that no one had noticed his arrival infuriated Hüsnü Bey.

"What in God's name is going on here?" he thundered, making everyone jump. Anxious eyes turned toward him. The butler looked up at the kitchen's chimney. There was no smoke.

"Speak!" Hüsnü Bey bellowed again. But the fear he saw in their faces was already working its way into his soul.

The butler said, "He should have lit the stove hours ago. It's been ages since the morning call to prayer. Something must have happened to him."

The thought of that possibly being true caused a few people to gasp. "Have you looked in his room?" Hüsnü Bey asked. The butler merely shook his head.

Normally it would have been out of line for someone to answer his master like that, particularly when that master happened to be the head of the Zümrützade family, but Hüsnü Bey was in no state to give any thought to the matter. The flavors and scents of all the dishes the cook had ever prepared glided through his mind like the verses of a farewell sonnet.

One of the younger servant boys, known at the mansion for his thick-headedness, muttered, "You were too hard on him last night and tried to send him away. His feelings were probably hurt and he ran off."

Blinded by rage, Hüsnü Bey imagined banging the boy's head against a rock. The fact of the matter, however, was that Hüsnü Bey was powerless to do anything. Because if the boy was right and the cook had fled in the night, Hüsnü Bey knew that he would be held responsible, and he didn't want to be one of those rare Zümrützade's who went down in the annals of history as a paragon of ineptitude.

"Open the door," he snapped at the butler. Mumbling a prayer, the butler knocked on the door. His first three knocks went unanswered, and the tension in the courtyard became almost palpable. The butler knocked on the door once more. After a few seconds, which felt like an eternity for everyone standing there, they heard the jangling of a lock and the door swung open.

Relief spread through the courtyard when the cook appeared in the doorway. But it did not last long, as everyone saw that the cook was holding a bundle and was dressed in his outdoor clothes.

The dim-witted servant boy began to softly weep, which irritated Hüsnü Bey to no end. He slapped the boy with the back of his hand and proceeded to walk toward the door. He was in no state to notice that everyone present was glaring at him. He stopped in front of the cook, and after looking the young man up and down, asked in a quiet yet stern voice, "What's going on here?"

As usual, the cook didn't reply at first. He merely looked at the master of the mansion, head held high. Hüsnü Bey said more loudly, "Where do you think you're going?"

Again the cook didn't respond.

"Now you listen to me," continued Hüsnü Bey. "Go back in there, put on your apron, and get back to work."

The cook again said nothing.

Hüsnü Bey took a step toward the cook and shouted, "What insolence is this! What brazenness! Do you know whose mansion this is? Get out of my sight and change back into your cooking clothes! Straight back into the kitchen with you! Now!"

Hüsnü Bey's rant was interrupted by a loud knocking on the outside gate. He turned to the butler and said, "See who it is."

The butler nodded at one of the servants standing nearby. In turn, the servant relegated the duty to someone his junior both in position and age, who did the same, and in the end the two youngest boys were left with the task. When they started kicking each other because they couldn't decide who should open the gate, Hüsnü Bey grabbed the butler by the collar and shoved him, saying, "Go see who the hell is here!"

The butler was an elderly, well-respected man, and anger flashed in the eyes of the others in the courtyard when the master of the mansion shoved him.

As Hüsnü Bey continued shouting, the cook stood there motionless, holding his bundle. Hüsnü Bey's threats progressed from "I'll ruin you! You won't find a place to work, a home to shelter in, or a bite to eat in all these lands!" to making him a galley slave, imprisoning him in dungeons, and having his head cut off.

The butler returned, out of breath. "Master . . ." he wheezed.

But Hüsnü Bey didn't hear him. The butler called out to him again. "What is it?" Zümrützade Hüsnü Bey snapped, turning around. His face was blotchy and dripping with sweat.

"Men from the palace, sir," the butler said. "They're asking for you."

As soon as he heard the word "palace," Hüsnü Bey's face drained of color. "God protect us," he muttered. Then he turned to the cook and said, "Don't you dare move an inch."

The cook watched Hüsnü Bey walk toward the gate with the butler by his side. After a while, he began to slowly walk toward the gate and the servants followed behind him.

Outside the gate, a page from the Imperial Court was waiting with his hands respectfully folded in front of him as Hüsnü Bey read a letter. The silver embroidery on his golden cap and the silver kaftan he was wearing indicated that he was in the service of the Privy Chamber. Standing behind the page were two palace guards, their formidable figures almost blocking the entirety of the mansion's broad gate.

For someone who was educated, Hüsnü Bey was taking far too long to read the letter. In fact, he was trying to keep his hands from trembling as he read each sentence over and over.

The letter was from Siyavuş Agha, the Chief Sword Bearer, and as far as Hüsnü Bey could tell, in essence it said that the agha was ready to forget what transpired the previous night. Furthermore, the letter said that he would personally speak to His Highness the Sultan himself about the concession that Hüsnü Bey's brother-in-law was seeking.

In exchange for all that, Siyavuş Agha wanted just one thing: the cook.

Hüsnü Bey read that last sentence, which spelt out the Chief Sword Bearer's demand in no uncertain terms, and looked up at the page. A myriad of tastes and smells swept through his mind as if bidding him farewell. His heart sank. He tried to think logically, telling himself, *Compared to all this, what importance is a cook?* Still, the knot in his throat grew tighter. He knew what would happen if he were to turn down the offer. Even the slightest hesitance would increase Siyavuş Agha's wrath a hundredfold, while an outright refusal would spell disaster. Hüsnü Bey thought about his wives and his children. . . . A single tear slid down his cheek as he softly replied, "So be it. I'll send him along first thing tomorrow."

He wanted to enjoy one last dinner prepared by the cook, but the agha was cruel and his demands were clear.

"His Highness wants him now!" the Privy Council Page responded.

Another tear slid down Hüsnü Bey's cheek. Hopelessly he shook his head and turned around. The cook, who had been standing in the middle of the courtyard, walked toward the gate and strode out without saying a word. As he disappeared into the distance with the page and guards, whispers from behind the harem windows echoed in the deathly silence of the courtyard.

Nothing would ever be the same again at the Zümrützade mansion.

2

The Great Kitchen

FLANKED BY THE palace guards as he walked behind the page
boy, the cook was led toward Horses' Square, a slight smile still
on his lips. He had taken the first step in his plan, and that
pleased him. However, when they arrived at the square, the smile fell
from his lips and a chill ran down his spine.

He looked up and saw the Hagia Sophia, its imposing dome and
minarets looking as if they could come toppling down on him at any
moment. Behind it the Tower of Justice rose into the sky like a white
arrow. The cook could hear his heart beating in his ears. Few things in
life could move him, and there was but one emotion that could make
him feel truly alive, but that had made his heart feel like it had stopped,
not beat wildly as it was at that moment.

As they walked from the square toward the Hagia Sophia, he tried
to calm the pounding of his heart, but when he saw the Imperial Gate
on the right, it started racing again. Suddenly out of breath, the cook
slowed his steps, forcing the guards to slow down as well. The page
looked back and offered a smile, likely thinking that the cook was nervous about going to the palace. He wasn't altogether wrong. But if he

knew the real reason why the cook felt so uneasy, he would have started feeling uneasy as well.

For the rest of his life, the cook would not be able to remember how he walked the distance between the Hagia Sophia and the Imperial Gate. His heart was gripped by terror and his entire body felt like it was going numb—he couldn't even feel the ground beneath his feet. When he saw the Janissaries standing guard on each side of the gate, his strength left him. He was drenched in sweat and the bundle he was carrying got heavier with every step. His legs refused to budge, and though he thought the only way to free himself of the stifling feeling weighing on his heart was to shout, his throat had locked up. He leaned over, placing one hand on his heaving chest and the other on his knee. One of the palace guards rushed over to support him. The page stopped the guard with a gesture, leaned toward the cook and whispered, "Are you feeling well, Master?"

The cook managed a groan in response. As he struggled to shake off the thousands of thoughts and memories swarming through his mind, he tried to remember the phrase he'd whispered the night before. He thought that if he could, he'd be saved by the scent of apple and cloves which stirred in him a desire to live. But the situation seemed hopeless. The cacophony in his mind grew louder with each passing moment until it enveloped his entire being.

Just as he felt that he was about to lose consciousness, he clutched at the slight scent of apple that was lingering in the deepest recesses of his memory, which helped his mind slowly started to clear. "I'm fine," he finally managed to say. He straightened up and glanced at the page.

"We should hurry," the page said. "The Chief Sword Bearer awaits us."

The cook struggled to hang onto the scent he'd captured so he could control the pounding of his heart and the shaking of his knees. They reached the Imperial Gate, and as he stepped across the threshold, he held his breath. Their footsteps echoed in the arched passageway as Janissaries whispered to one another under swords hung on the wall.

An Imperial Gatekeeper standing guard at the entrance of the palace was loudly berating two young men as they approached, but when they drew near, he turned and ordered the men to stand at attention. The page responded with a salute and they passed into the palace grounds.

Once they were out in the sunlight again, the cook exhaled, noticing with relief that his heart was slowing down. As he walked beside the page, he glanced around. About three hundred paces in front of them was the second gate, the Gate of Salutation. Around half a dozen palace servants were trudging through the gate with large sacks on their backs, making their way single-file toward a coal shed.

No sooner had they passed the palace hospital when a sweet scent assailed their nostrils, meaning that they were getting close to the Royal Bakery. Well aware of the effect that the scent of freshly baked bread had on the human mind, the cook breathed it in. Unlike other scents, the scent of bread didn't incite wild desires or passions, and it wasn't for nothing that the Sufis referred to the smell of bread as being prophet-like in nature. For them, bread was sacred; its scent alone was filling, bringing on a feeling of comfort and peace. And at that moment, the scent swept away the last remnants of the foreboding feeling that had been tormenting the cook. By the time they reached the Gate of Salutation, the young cook was standing tall as the two towers on each side of the gate built by Suleiman the Magnificent.

The page stopped the cook and guards a few paces from the door, and, stepping forward, greeted the guard on duty.

"And peace be upon you, Agha," the gatekeeper replied. Nodding toward the cook, he asked, "Who is he?"

"He," the Privy Chamber Page replied, "is the new cook. I'm here to take him to the kitchens."

The gatekeeper sneered, "The palace has got more cooks than guards already. Hell, we may as well have the guards cook, too."

The two guards standing behind the cook bristled at his comment. As the gatekeeper gleefully watched them grind their teeth, the page cut in, hoping to stave off a confrontation. "It's an order."

"Well," the gatekeeper replied, "do you have an order from the Head Steward?"

The page muttered a prayer for patience. "No, Agha. I was told to bring him on the orders of—"

The gatekeeper cut him off, pointing at the gilt inscription over the gate. "This is the gate to the palace. Edicts first, subjects second."

Just as the guards standing behind the cook were reaching for their swords, the page went on: "It's an order from the Chief Sword Bearer."

The gatekeeper's eyes widened in confusion at first and then narrowed as the gravity of the situation became clear. He knew that mundane tasks such as bringing a cook to the palace would only be entrusted to someone of low rank, a lieutenant at most, so if a page from the Privy Chamber was ordered to do so with two armed guards, it was clear that the order had come from high up. The blood drained from his face. He called inside, "You! Find me the Head Gatekeeper, and be quick about it."

As they waited for the Head Gatekeeper, the cook looked up at the towering gate. Most of the time, entering it meant hope and prosperity, while leaving was a sign of disappointment and ruin. Many proud people had passed through the gate with pompous ceremony, and just as many had left without even being noticed—in most cases as headless corpses.

Like the other gate, the Gate of Salutation was a passage, but much longer. The light at the other end seemed to be far, far away, as though symbolizing the plight of those who passed through. Living at the palace was a journey, the end of which was unknown as you walked through the Gate of Salutation. That held true for everyone, from the youngest page to His Highness the Sultan himself. You walked toward the light, yet it seemed that you'd never reach it. Your life spilled onto that infinite road moment by moment, hour by hour, and day by day; you were filled with the fear that you may be plunged into darkness at any time. And in the end, your life would be extinguished either at the hands of an executioner or by a natural death, at best becoming a few lines in a dusty history book. The light at the end of the passage became a mere dream. But the cook was not bothered in the least. The light he sought to reach lay not beyond that gate but the next, the one that he had not yet seen. But he was determined to find it no matter what the cost and illuminate the deepest darkness of his world.

The cook stared into that spot of light ahead of the gate. From where he was standing, he could only see part of the wall separating the Harem and Inner Palace from the Second Courtyard, the wall that lead to the Gate of Felicity. What he wanted lay past those walls, but he knew that except for the sultan himself, no man could ever get in with his testicles intact. But he also knew there was always more than one way to scale a wall or pass through a gate.

Soon enough, undoubtedly prompted by the mention of Siyavuş Agha's name, the Gate of Salutation's head gatekeeper rushed up, panting for breath. As he approached, he was in such a hurry that he was holding aloft the staff that he would normally strike against the ground with every step he took and holding his cap on his head with one hand so it wouldn't fly off. After the page greeted him by bowing down to the ground, the Head Gatekeeper said, pointing to the gate, "You may enter." The mere mention of Siyavuş Agha's name precluded any need for an explanation.

The cook and the page passed through the Gate of Salutation. The palace guards left, having fulfilled the tedious task that had been thrust upon them so early in the morning, and withdrew to their rooms to rest until they were summoned again.

When they stepped into the Second Courtyard, the page let loose the curls he had hidden beneath his embroidered golden cap while outside the palace. Without waiting to be guided, the cook set off in what turned out to be the right direction. It wasn't a conscious decision. Like a child, he followed his intuition and started walking toward the place where he knew he would feel safest. He was walking toward the kitchen, where his life—or to be more accurate, his second life—would begin and most probably end.

Even though he understood the young master's excitement, the page was offended by the fact that the cook had walked off, almost breaking into a run. The page tried to quicken his steps, but the long kaftan he was wearing made that impossible and, in any case, it was frowned upon in the palace to have one's curls bounce.

The page called out to the cook, whose eyes were fixed on the porticos further ahead between the ancient trees. The kitchens were right behind the porticos, extending to the right along the side of the massive courtyard. Not only were they the largest buildings on the palace grounds, more people worked there than anywhere else in the palace.

There were more than a thousand cooks and apprentice cooks working in the kitchens, and that didn't include the nearly four hundred confectionery cooks who prepared desserts, sherbets, and pickled foodstuff, nor the apprentices of the Head Grocer, the Chamberlain of the Royal Cellar and his scribes, the sifters, mixers, and bakers of the Royal Bakery and Commons' Bakery, the water-bearers, the fire-stokers who lit the stoves when the morning call to prayer sounded, the cheese and yogurt makers, the herbalists who collected healing herbs, the ice-makers, the butchers, or the poultry-men.

On any given day, the Imperial Kitchens prepared two meals for the four thousand residents at the palace. On special occasions such as ceremonies, banquets, and the Sovereign's Feast, up to twenty thousand people were served. Every year nearly forty thousand sheep, eighty thousand chickens, one million *oka* of rice, and two million *oka* of sugar were used at the kitchens.

And that is why it came to be known as the *Matbah-ı Azam*, The Great Kitchen.

When the page caught up to him, the cook asked, "Is something wrong?"

The page, who was unused to hurrying, was out of breath. "There's no need to hurry, Master Cook. The Chief Sword Bearer eats his supper late. We still have a lot of time."

The cook shook his head. "But the kitchen is large and always so busy, and I need to be able to find my way around. As a cook, you can't rush things. I wouldn't want to disappoint His Highness on my very first day."

"God bless," said the page. "How dedicated you are, even though your shoes are still dusty and you haven't even picked up a knife yet. God bless! You are right, the kitchens are busy, but don't concern yourself about that. You'll be cooking only for the Chief Sword Bearer. Everyone has been informed, including the Head Cook and Kitchen Custodian. No one will ask anything more of you."

The cook bowed his head. "I will pray for the health and prosperity of His Highness the Agha. I'm grateful to him. May I ask, who is the Head Cook?"

The page scowled. "Master İsfendiyar. He's an old man, very good at what he does, but infamous for his bad temper. Try to stay away from him if you can."

"Don't you worry," the cook said with a smile.

The page pointed toward the path. "Let's continue. After you."

Soon they passed through one of the three entrances to the Royal Kitchen.

The Imperial Kitchens consisted of two long rectangular buildings that ran parallel to each other. The area at the front was set aside for the lodgings of the apprentices and servants who ran errands, as well as the Tinsmiths' Lodge. The broader section at the rear was where the actual kitchens were located, and the two buildings were separated by a narrow, open-ceilinged corridor called the Kitchens' Passageway.

The kitchens had six doors in total. The one located furthest to the left was the entrance to the Confectionery. There, all the desserts and sherbets of the palace were made, vegetables were pickled, and medicines were prepared. It was separate from the rest of the kitchens physically as well as administratively. The Chief Confectioner was lower in rank than the Head Cook but he was just as respected, and no one else could order the people working under him to do anything.

The other five doors opened onto the beehive, that is, the seven kitchens which were the heart of the Imperial Kitchens. Unlike at the confectionary, these kitchens there were closely connected. Walls separated them so that the scents of cooking wouldn't mingle, but they were open in the front.

The Kitchens' Passageway passed under a small vaulted gate and opened onto yet another section of the Imperial Kitchens. To the left of this area were the cooks' masjid and the hammam. Next to those were the cellar, the oil storeroom, and the lodgings for the masters and the Kitchen Chamberlain.

The cook and page stopped in the middle of the Kitchens' Passageway and looked around. It was quiet, and no one else was present. The page, either out of fear of the Head Cook's wrath or out of habit, didn't want to go inside without someone to accompany them.

As the tedious wait dragged on, they eventually heard the tapping of a cane coming from behind the rightmost door. A small, elderly man appeared in the doorway, walking quickly but with a limp. He was wearing a green apron over his white attire, and a large knife was tucked into the sash tied around his waist. Irritably he cocked an ear to listen for the sound of work being done and straightened his cap, which was similar to that of the palace guards. In a voice that was unexpectedly loud for someone of his stature, he shouted, "Everyone at their posts! Now! It's almost time for the noon prayers but not a single cauldron is ready! Be quick about it!"

That was none other than the Head Cook, Master İsfendiyar himself.

His voice echoed through the Kitchens' Passageway and then faded away. After a few moments, however, hasty steps could be heard coming from the front building, becoming louder and louder with each passing second, and then the cooks, assistants, and apprentices began pouring through the doors. Soon enough, the narrow hallway was bustling with people.

Cooks with silk aprons of green, red, and blue, assistants wearing aprons embroidered with designs, and apprentices dressed in white crowded into the kitchen. The page and the cook pressed themselves against the wall to avoid being trampled underfoot. Master İsfendiyar disappeared from sight in the swarm of people. Only his cane could be occasionally seen rising into the air, punctuating an order or tongue-lashing.

As they rushed into the kitchens, the cooks, assistant cooks, and apprentices left the hallway as swiftly as they'd filled it. The only thing that proved to the cook that he wasn't dreaming was Master İsfendiyar, who was still standing in the same place. After listening to the sounds coming from within and making sure everyone was hard at work, the Head Cook entered the kitchens. When the cook and the page followed him into the kitchens, they saw that Master İsfendiyar was already inspecting the Royal Kitchen.

The two huge halberdier guards standing in front of the door to the Royal Kitchen would not let the page inside, as that was where food for the sovereign's household was prepared, including dishes for his mother, the Valide Sultan, as well as for his wives and sons, so he had to wait outside for Master İsfendiyar.

The cook caught a glimpse of the Royal Kitchen through the doorway. Compared to the other kitchens, this one was larger, as well as more orderly. Around a dozen cooks were quietly working at wooden tables and stoves, some of them with young assistants standing by their left shoulders, waiting to do their masters' bidding. A few of the more experienced apprentices were standing at a table dicing onions and peeling carrots. The master cooks gave order after order, but never raised their voices. Their knives didn't clatter and even the apprentices quietly bustled about doing their tasks. On the wall across from the doorway were shelves of row upon row of china. Patterned porcelain plates, bowls embellished with gold, enameled soup pots, and crockery made from the whitest Chinese porcelain all gleamed in the flames from the stoves. The cook could tell that the ingredients used in that kitchen were of the highest quality, and he gazed with envy at the bright green leaves of two celery roots waiting to be peeled and the perfect orange of a bunch of carrots. The purest of oils sizzled as it was poured into heated pans and the scent of the richest cumin lingered in the air.

However, based on what the cook could hear, the Head Cook of the Royal Kitchen was unimpressed by the present state of affairs. A rather short person, he caught up with Master İsfendiyar near the door and started complaining about the quality and the quantity of the ingredients he had been given.

"I am quite afraid, Master İsfendiyar," said the Head Cook of the Royal Kitchen. "You know that His Highness is a man of simple taste and he wouldn't turn his nose up at anything. But his chief consort, Haseki Sultan? You know better than I do, Master, that it is simply impossible to please her with what we've got here. The meat isn't fresh. The other day, they brought me a chicken that looked like it had died of old age. I had planned on making stuffed chicken but had no choice but to make kebab instead. I'm at my wit's end. If it were only me bearing the brunt of it all, that would be fine, but Haseki Sultan will bring the whole kitchen down over our heads."

Master İsfendiyar nodded, listening intently as he watched the others working inside. "Let me speak with the Kitchen Chamberlain," he said, approaching a table to inspect two lamb chops brought in by an apprentice.

As the cook pondered what he'd just heard, he was startled by voices coming from farther back in the kitchen. He turned and saw two cooks arguing over a small sack of butter, each trying to drag it away. "Let go!" the larger cook shouted. "The boy brought it for me. I've been saving it for a week!"

The other cook was clearly not as strong but he showed no signs of giving up. "Look at you, this is shameless!" he snapped. "You've used up all the rice in the whole cellar. You hide everything away like a magpie. This isn't your father's kitchen, you know!"

The argument was becoming increasingly heated. As insults turned into swear words, an elderly cook who had been muttering "God give me patience" put his knife down, picked up a huge meat cleaver that was wedged into a rack of lamb on a table and approached the two

31

cooks. Without saying a word, he split the sack of butter in two with a single swipe of the cleaver and cast them both a dark look.

The two cooks fell silent, as did everyone else in the kitchen. As they backed away, each holding half a sack of butter, silence gave way to the usual hustle and bustle of the kitchen.

The page laughed as he explained the situation to the cook. "The bigger man is the Chief Gatekeeper's cook and the other cooks for the Chief Eunuch. Everyone is used to their arguments. They're always bickering."

The cook smiled and continued watching the work of the kitchen, trying to understand who prepared dishes for which part of the palace and memorizing their faces.

In the Imperial Kitchen, the second most important area after the Royal Kitchen was the Aghas' Kitchen. As the Chief Sword Bearer's personal cook, the cook surmised that he would be working there, which he knew would be a boon for him. By the very nature of their work, the aghas' cooks were in constant communication with the various chambers of the palace. Sometimes a disgruntled page would confide in an apprentice his own age, telling him things that were supposed to be kept secret, and inexperienced servants would let ill-advised comments slip. That was precisely why the cook considered himself lucky—he knew he would learn much in the Aghas' Kitchen.

The page's voice saved the cook from the barrage of thoughts swirling through his mind: "Here he comes . . ."

The cook saw that Master İsfendiyar was leaving the Royal Kitchen. Taking a few steps toward the door, the page waited, his hands folded in front of him. Master İsfendiyar told the halberdiers standing guard by the door to step aside and he left the kitchen, coming face to face with the Privy Chamber Page.

"What do you want?" he asked.

The page stepped aside and gestured toward the cook. "This is the Chief Sword Bearer's new cook. They told me—"

Master İsfendiyar cut him off. "Very well! Come with me."

He had already started walking away, tapping his cane. He made his way toward the area where the cook who'd settled the dispute a few moments ago was working. When they realized that Master İsfendiyar was passing by, the cooks and assistants immediately stopped what they were doing and turned to face him. Only one cook seemed to be oblivious. He was gazing at cubes of meat on the table in front of him. He was stocky, but his shoulders sagged as if he was bearing a great burden. His eyes seemed lifeless and his face was ashen. One by one he was picking up the pieces of meat and inspecting them, and whenever he found the slightest discoloration or trace of sinew, he cut it away with the utmost care. But it was the twitching of his face which most clearly revealed the tormented state of his soul; his left eye kept blinking and occasionally the left side of his mouth worked up and down.

Master İsfendiyar quietly approached him, as if he was afraid to startle him. But the cook was so engrossed in his inspection of the meat that he didn't even notice the master's presence.

"Master Bekir," Master İsfendiyar called softly. The corner of the man's mouth twitched three times in a row. Master İsfendiyar called his name a little louder, finally getting his attention.

"Yes, Master," he stammered, trying to keep his wildly twitching left eye under control.

Master İsfendiyar placed his hand on the man's shoulder and nodded in the direction of the cook, who was standing behind him. "Do you know who this is?"

Master Bekir turned to look at the cook, while also keeping an eye on the Privy Chamber Page. "No, I do not," he managed to stammer.

Master İsfendiyar smiled and said, "He's the Chief Sword Bearer's new cook."

It took a while for those words to sink in. Master Bekir's eye twitched one last time, and then a smile spread across his face. He stared at the cook as if bearing witness to a miracle. "Do you really mean what you say, Master?" he asked in a quivering voice. "Does this mean that I am . . ."

Master İsfendiyar finished the question for him. "Free to go? Yes, that is precisely what it means. You are no longer the Chief Sword Bearer's personal cook."

Master Bekir started trembling, not out of fear, but joy. "Do you really mean it?" he asked. Master İsfendiyar smiled and nodded. Siyavuş Agha's old cook tossed his knife onto the counter and raised his hands toward Heaven. "God, thank you!" The color returned to his face and his shoulders seemed to suddenly straighten up.

After murmuring a prayer of thanks, Master Bekir hugged the cook and kissed him on both cheeks. The cook was unaccustomed to such displays of affection and he was not fond of them, but there was nothing to be done—the man's joy was boundless. At last he had been released from enduring the Chief Sword Bearer's habitual displeasure and incessant demands, which had almost driven him to the point of madness.

"My brother," said Master Bekir, firmly grabbing the cook by the shoulders. "May God give you strength and grant you patience. I can't wish you good luck, because there's nothing about luck in the kitchen. But since you saved me from my woes, may the merciful Almighty save you from yours as well."

The cook looked at him for a few moments, and, at a loss for words, softly replied, "Amen."

After embracing the other cooks, Master Bekir quickly began to pack his knives. He gave the impression that he was leaving Constantinople to start a new life in another land rather than just leaving the kitchen.

Master İsfendiyar asked, "Where are you going to go, Bekir?"

Master Bekir, who was busy rolling his knives into his apron, paused. His expression resembled that of a man who had been caught committing a ridiculous crime. "I don't know, Master," he replied, smiling sheepishly. "As long as I get out of here."

Master İsfendiyar said, "There's a place waiting for you in the Royal Kitchen. You've suffered a great deal; you deserve it."

The eyes of the other cooks in the kitchen widened not just in incredulity but also jealousy, since working in the Royal Kitchen was every cook's dream. Master Bekir looked at Master İsfendiyar with a pained expression on his face. "Master, you do me a great honor. You think me suitable for such a job, and I'm grateful for that. But . . . I no longer want to cook for royalty. I'm tired of it. Why don't you have me work at the Outer Palace Kitchen? I'll cook rice for the servants and make soup."

Master İsfendiyar shook his head. "That I cannot do. I cannot squander the talents of someone such as you like that. Go to the Councilors' Kitchen. There's less work there, you'll get some rest."

Master Bekir bowed his head. "Please don't, Master. Working for aghas brought me to ruin. Don't make me deal with pashas next. I don't have the strength."

The Head Cook thought for a while. "The Odalisques' Kitchen, then. They're not too well off. They'll get some proper food thanks to you."

Master Bekir's face brightened. "That, sir, I can do!" Working there meant he would be cooking for the lowest in rank in the Imperial Harem and he would not be harangued by complaints or picky demands. At the same time, regardless of whom he was cooking for, he'd have to maintain a certain level of sophistication since his dishes were going to be sent to the Harem.

The Chief Sword Bearer's old cook left the kitchen after being promised two days' rest. Naturally, he wouldn't spend his time off at the palace. He would head straight for Galata, enjoy himself at Banyoz's tavern in the evening, and think about the next day when it came around.

Everyone turned to look at the new cook, curious about who he was. He, however, was little inclined to reveal any details about his identity. When the Privy Chamber Page introduced him to the other cooks, he merely greeted them with a nod. As he brushed off attempts at small talk with a polite smile, he was also trying to ascertain his position in the kitchen. The personal cooks of the six most important aghas of the

Inner Palace worked there, and their positions were based not only on their rank and ability, but also on the title of the person for whom they cooked.

That was why the cook wasn't surprised to discover that the man who'd broken up the argument a few moments ago was the personal cook of the Chief Privy Chamber Page. Named Asım, he was the highest-ranking cook in the kitchen, as well as the oldest. The fact he was the Chief Privy Chamber Page's cook further bolstered his authority.

With one look at Master Asım, the cook saw that he was a somewhat fatherly, sweet-natured man, despite the first impression he gave of being something of a despot. Still, the cook knew that he had to be careful around him. The Chief Privy Chamber Page was the highest-ranking agha in the Inner Palace, followed by the Chief Sword Bearer, and just as influential. It was a well-known fact that the two of them vied for power, but the cook hoped that would not spill over into the kitchen. The cook had to quickly make sure that Master Asım realized he had no ambitions to climb higher on the social ladder. Even though he had just arrived and was less experienced than the other cooks, the fact that he was the Chief Sword Bearer's cook made him second-in-line in the kitchen hierarchy. He knew that the other cooks—that is, the personal cooks for Rikabdar Agha and Çuhadar Agha, the Chief Chamberlain and the Chief Treasurer—might see him as competition, which could be a source of ill will. The cook was aware that he was going to have enough on his plate without such wiles.

After introducing him to the other cooks, the page requested permission to leave. At the same time, however, he seemed to be rather reluctant to go and kept looking the cook in the eye as if insinuating something.

Finally the cook understood what he'd been waiting for, and in a tone of voice no less polite than the page's, said, "Let me see you out."

As per custom, the page replied, "Don't trouble yourself," but started walking out. Together they stepped out into the Kitchens' Passageway, avoiding the apprentices who were dashing around with sacks on their backs and carrying pots and cauldrons. The page whispered, "I'll visit you this evening, before prayers. His Highness the Agha has a personal request. He wishes it to be kept secret. Master İsfendiyar will know, but you should take care. Make sure you're alone in the kitchen."

The cook responded with a smile. "Not to worry. His Highness the Agha's secret is my secret."

The page nodded. By this time they were at the door and they saluted each other one last time. Just as he was about to leave, the page turned around and with a meaningful glance told the cook, "My name is Firuz."

The cook was embarrassed to realize that he hadn't thought to ask the page boy his name even though he'd been with him all morning. He stammered, "Pleased to meet you, thank you."

Firuz Agha from the Privy Chamber smiled and walked away.

At last the cook was alone. He quickly realized that he had to make up for his untoward behavior, seeing as the page would likely be one of the most useful people to him at the palace.

He walked back into the kitchens and made his way toward the Confectionery. As he got farther from the Aghas' Kitchen, there were more people rushing around and small pots gave way to massive cauldrons. In the other kitchens, the cooks prepared food not just for one person, as he himself did, but for the other residents of the Palace who numbered in the thousands, such as the Inner Palace pages, concubines, halberdiers, and palace guards.

In the neighboring Gate of Felicity Kitchen, the Chief Gatekeeper's personal cook, one of the two cooks who had fought over a sack of butter, was leaning over a table preparing food. The other cooks and assistants were standing over large pots, preparing food for the White Eunuchs, or the White Aghas as the palace residents called them, who worked under the Chief Gatekeeper.

In the next kitchen, which served the Imperial Harem, the situation was similar. The Black Eunuchs, who oversaw the training of novice concubines, served the sovereign's consorts and sons, and also ensured the safety and order of the Harem, were fewer in number than the White Eunuchs, which meant the kitchen was quieter. The highest-ranking member of the Black Aghas was known as the Girls' Agha, or the Agha of the Harem, and his personal cook held the highest rank in the Odalisques' Kitchen. The quarreling cooks of these neighboring kitchens were not only responsible for a single master but also dozens of eunuch aghas, each pickier than the next, who had to be served twice a day.

The cook stopped to watch Master Hayri, the Chief Eunuch's personal cook, who was inspecting pots of food to be sent to the Harem. The cook had learned his name when he overheard an apprentice address him. Master Hayri was thin and of medium height. He had a thin moustache, bushy eyebrows, and a proclivity for glancing spitefully at people as he rained orders down upon then.

The cook had had his sights set on the Odalisques' Kitchen weeks before he'd even arrived at the palace. He hoped he'd quickly take his first steps toward that goal, which led to the heart of the Harem. But he knew that even the slightest altercation with Master Hayri could lead to problems and be more trouble than it was worth.

As he gazed at the kitchen, the cook was going over ideas he'd formulated long before when he noticed that one of the younger apprentices was watching him. Not wanting to be the center of attention on his very first day, he smiled at the boy who was suspiciously eyeing him and went on his way. As he did so, he realized that the boy hadn't been the only person watching him—he almost ran headfirst into Master İsfendiyar.

"What's the matter?" Master İsfendiyar asked in a low but stern tone. "Why are you wandering around?"

Tongue-tied, the cook tried to say something but merely ended up stammering incoherently, so he gave up. The Head Cook went on to say, "If you have nothing to do, don't go around getting in the way. Go to your lodgings and get some rest."

"Yes, Master," the cook replied and turned around to leave.

Master İsfendiyar called after him, "Ask one of the boys to show you where you'll be sleeping."

Trying to suppress a grin, the cook entered the Aghas' Kitchen. He picked up his bundle and, tapping the shoulder of an apprentice who was about to take out the slop bins, asked where the lodgings were.

"I'll show you, Master," the boy replied. When they stepped outside, the apprentice turned left and, after passing through the Kitchens' Passageway, went through the vaulted gate, stopping at the entrance to a narrow rectangular courtyard. Pointing at the rear entrance of a two-story building which extended lengthwise along the courtyard next to the kitchen, he said, "That's the place, Master. Go in and climb the stairs. The lodgings are above the masjid. There should be a guard on duty inside; he'll show you an empty bed." Without waiting for a word of thanks, he dashed back inside.

The cook briefly listened to the silence of the courtyard and then went in through the door the boy had showed him and proceeded upstairs. The cooks' lodgings consisted of a spacious room filled with rows of beds lined up along the walls. Next to each bed was a small chest with a lock and there were recesses in the walls for storing items. The room was silent. The cook glanced around, but there was no one to be seen.

"Peace be upon you," he called out. His voice echoed along the walls. He heard a rustling in a dark corner of the room and then a voice: "And peace be upon you."

He surmised that the guard on duty had been napping. A few moments later, the guard appeared in the rays of light shining through the high windows in the middle of the room. Despite his youth, he was quite large, and he seemed to be relieved to find that it was not one of the master cooks who had come.

"What do you need?" he asked.

The cook introduced himself. The guard pointed to a bed near the middle of the room under a window. "That one over there is empty," he said.

The cook walked over to the bed. He placed his bundle in one of the recesses in the wall and, as he pulled the blanket back, the guard called to him from the other side of the room. "Which kitchen do you work for?"

"The Aghas'," replied the cook.

The guard's expression fell. "Which agha?" he asked.

"The Chief Sword Bearer."

The young guard rushed over, saying "Wait, wait," and as soon as he removed the cook's bundle from the niche in the wall, he walked to a corner of the room. "You'll be more comfortable here," he said, pointing to a bed in the corner. "It's quieter here. You'll sleep better."

"Thank you," the cook said.

The guard was still standing beside the bed. "Is there anything else you need?" he asked.

"No, thank you," the cook replied. Pulling back the blanket, he sat cross-legged on the bed and opened the lid of a nearby chest, which contained the key to the lock. Unrolling his bundle, he first removed the books he'd wrapped in his apron and opened the black book. After pensively perusing a few recipes, he closed the book and placed it at the very bottom of the chest along with the green book. After putting in the rest of his possessions, he locked the chest, tucked the key into the sash tied around his waist, and lay down.

The cook thought about how he should proceed. He knew that he had to find another way to put his plan in motion that did not involve the Odalisques' Kitchen while also remembering to be wary of the people around him.

Since he was Siyavuş Agha's cook, he could count on winning the affections of certain people, such as the guard of the lodgings. But there was also the possibility that such affections could arouse feelings of enmity among others, a situation that was bound to create problems for him. What he sought was not clout in the kitchens, a post at the palace, or gifts from a pasha. He was interested in something else entirely, and while the Imperial Kitchens were impressive, for him they would only serve as a means to an end.

Heaviness tugged at his eyelids as he lay there thinking. He hadn't slept at all the night before, and he slipped into a deep sleep.

When he opened his eyes, he heard a low whisper: "Master, Master . . ." It was already dark. He looked over and through the gloom saw that it was the assistant from earlier calling him. "There's someone here from the Privy Chamber asking for you."

The cook sat up in bed. He glanced at the boy and whispered, "What's your name?"

"Mahir," he responded with a smile. He seemed pleased that someone had asked his name.

The cook got out of bed and looked around. Overcome by exhaustion, most of the cooks were lying in their beds, fast asleep. Only here and there did he see the glow of oil lamps. A few cooks chatted in hushed voices, passing pitchers of wine around.

Trying not to catch anyone's eye, the cook tiptoed through the shadows and slipped down the stairs. The courtyard was just as silent as the stairwell. When he reached the small gate that opened onto the Kitchens' Passageway, he saw a few flickering lights up ahead, illuminating several people. He could tell the person standing in front was Firuz Agha. When he got closer, he realized that the large silhouettes behind the page were actually palace guards.

"A pleasant evening to you," said Firuz Agha.

"To us all," the cook replied. He glanced at the sack that the page was carrying and then looked at the tense expression on the page's face.

Just then, a fourth palace guard emerged from the kitchen, along with a halberdier. "Everything is ready, Agha," the palace guard said.

"After you," the page said, gesturing toward the door. When they walked inside, the three guards took their places, each standing in front of the doors to the kitchen.

The page and the cook made their way to the Aghas' Kitchen. When the cook looked inside, he was surprised to see that two of the hearths had been lit. A large piece of cloth had been spread over one of the tables, on top of which were two small pots, bearing the seal of the

Cellar Wing, and a large frying pan with a lid. Carefully diced meat had been placed on paper next to the pots, along with two large yellow quinces and a few carrots. All was at the ready, including oil and salt. At the end of the night, the cloth would be rolled up and returned to the Cellar Wing. Clearly, Siyavuş Agha didn't want anyone to discover a thing about the dish he was about to devour in secret in a few hours.

The Privy Council Page placed a bag on the table and said, "His Highness the Agha desires the same dish he had at the Zümrützade mansion."

Smiling, the cook opened the bag, revealing bright green stalks of leeks. He ran his fingers over the stalks and said, "If I were to choose the ingredients, I could please His Highness the Agha even more."

"Of course, Master," the page replied. "I'll have a word with the Market Steward."

The cook took the leeks out of the bag and started cooking half of the diced meat in a pan. He put the rest of the meat into another pot with some water to make broth and started chopping the leeks. Once they were all chopped, he peeled and cubed the quince, and then grated two carrots. While they were fresh and crisp, the quince had been picked too late after surviving a cold, sunless winter. The cook knew that it was going to be difficult to make the dish palatable. Still, he was pleased that the Privy Chamber Page hadn't brought any onions as he was able to choose them himself from the kitchen stocks. Emptying out a sack of onions, he carefully selected the most fragrant ones, knowing that onions were the secret to cooking a good dish of leeks. Although he knew that they hadn't bathed long enough in the light of the full moon, he would have to make do.

As he sliced the onion, he watched the page from the corner of his eye. The page seemed intent on watching his every move, as if he'd been entrusted with the task of finding out the cook's secret—but ultimately his efforts would prove to be in vain.

When the mouth-watering scent of roasted meat began rising from the pan, the cook added the onions together with a tablespoon of butter, releasing a symphony of scents that rose into the air. It smelled neither of meat nor of butter, and not of onion either. It was something else altogether, a blend of scents and flavors, unique in itself.

The cook whispered peculiarly, prompting the page to ask, "Did you ask for something?"

"No," the cook said, adding the quince and carrot and letting it all stew until the onions became transparent. After breathing in the scent, the cook removed the pot from the stove, whispering a phrase over it. He placed the meat mixture in the center of a large copper pan and surrounded it with the leeks. When he was satisfied with the arrangement, he drizzled broth over the dish and sprinkled on a little sumac, salt, and red pepper flakes. Only one step remained: covering it with a lid and letting it simmer over low heat. As he placed the pan on the stove, he whispered one last time.

It had taken him less than an hour to prepare the dish. The cook removed the pan from the stove, holding it with the hem of his apron, and placed it on the table. "It's ready," he said.

The page looked uneasy. The truth of the matter was that he was concerned he would not be able to take the tray all the way into the Privy Chamber without falling victim to his appetite. Not once had he dared touch anything that belonged to his masters. But taking that dish to Siyavuş Agha without tasting a single morsel struck him as being an impossible task.

Sighing, he picked up the pan, praying to God to give him restraint.

The cook walked with the Privy Council Page to the entrance of the kitchen. After bidding him a good evening, he stood under the portico and watched as the page departed with the guards and made his way toward the Gate of Felicity. The light from their torches cast an eerie glow in the pitch darkness of night. Quickly they reached the stone landing by the gate and disappeared.

The cook gazed after them, envying how easily they passed through the gate. He knew full well who had gone through that gate and the price they paid to do so. There were odalisques whose fates changed by the minute, pages who devoted their lives to the palace, dwarves who entertained, guards with their hands constantly on the hilts of their swords, a mute executioner, an heir apparent kept in a cage, a sultan on a throne . . .

The cook had always been grateful for what fate had given him, recalling with thanks all the memories he had of that great sacrifice which had saved his life, every clamoring voice, every shout, every tear, every hand reaching out toward him, and even that overwhelming fear and terror that had swirled through in his mind. But life was a matter of games. Until a short while ago, every time he'd thought of that gate, fear and anger had rushed through him, yet he was thankful that he'd been saved. It had seemed that he'd never see that gate again for as long as he lived, let alone pass through it. But here he was, gazing with envy after the page, who passed through it with such ease.

Silence filled the courtyard when the sound of their echoing footsteps died away. The cook locked his eyes on the Tower of Justice, where imperial council meetings were held. Although he couldn't see it, he knew the Harem was right behind the Tower. He stood in silence, listening for one particular sound, a melody or note that would show that he was on the right path, but he heard nothing.

The cook knew it was too early to expect anything and that he would have to work much more before he'd get the chance to hear it. But still, he listened intently to the stillness of the night. Just as he was on the brink of bursting into tears, someone behind him asked, "What are you doing here?"

The cook turned around and saw Master İsfendiyar standing near the door, shrouded in shadow.

Master İsfendiyar took a step toward him. "What are you looking at?" He took one more step. "What are you listening for?"

When Master İsfendiyar had drawn quite near with his limping gait, the cook bowed his head like a child who had been caught red-handed. Then he looked at Master İsfendiyar with his piercing green eyes and said, "Let me explain."

Master İsfendiyar nodded. They both looked around to make sure no one was eavesdropping on them.

When the cook looked back at his master, a somewhat mysterious yet friendly smile spread across his lips. Master İsfendiyar smiled in return.

"Master?" the cook said.

Master İsfendiyar responded by opening his arms.

They embraced.

Master İsfendiyar's thoughts had turned to a night twenty years earlier.

The cook was thinking of the same night. That night when he had first stepped through that door.

3

Deaf Night, Mute Dawn

MASTER İSFENDIYAR REMEMBERED . . .

He remembered every second of that night.

It was late and he was in the Royal Kitchen. There was no one else around, not even the halberdiers who were usually standing by the door. He was preparing an ill-timed meal, as the morning call to prayer would ring out in a few hours. As usual, he was cooking for the young princes and the older princes' children. But that day he'd gotten started early. He knew that when it was time for the children to eat, their food would be cold, but that didn't matter because by the time dawn broke there wouldn't be a single child left in the entire Imperial Palace.

Master İsfendiyar worked relentlessly, and he cursed relentlessly as he worked:

"A plague on your reign!"

"May your throne bring you nothing but sorrow!"

"May the mute executioner lay his hands upon you!"

The master cursed out loud because he needed a distraction from the sounds coming from outside: the screaming of women, the crying of children, the wailing of nannies, the weeping of mothers. . . . He needed something to drown out the sounds that pierced the Harem's walls and reached all the way into the kitchen.

He was also weeping. Tears dripped into the pots in front of him, into dishes the young princes would never taste.

He had known since the day before that something was going to happen. The new sultan had been sworn in shortly after the morning call to prayer. After the evening call to prayer, he had signed an edict ordering the murder of all his siblings and his siblings' children in the palace.

The palace corridors echoed with screams, but the night was deaf.

Master İsfendiyar knew all the young princes and the princes' sons. Many of them he had never met but he knew what kind of food each one liked. But there was one among them, a delicate boy with green eyes, who was a world apart. He was the son of one of the new sultan's younger brothers. His mother was fourteen when he was born, and his father was sixteen. Everyone thought him to be a sickly, fussy boy. He was picky and often complained about the dishes that were served to him. Sometimes he would even start to cry when the lid was taken off the serving tray.

The previous cook had gotten tired of the complaints made by the boy's mother and nanny, so he decided to quit, and Master İsfendiyar took his place. He was intrigued by the strange behavior of the child. It wasn't that he was fussy or didn't like certain foods. It was about the food itself. Take lentil soup, for example. He would gulp down a bowl of soup with relish one day and spit it out the next.

When the master realized the truth of the matter, he was so surprised that he could have swallowed his own tongue. The child wouldn't eat something if the slightest mistake had been made when it was cooked, such as if the heat had been too high, if there was too much of a certain spice, or if the butter was rancid. In short, his palate was extraordinary. To test his theory, the master began to deliberately make mistakes when he was cooking. The experiment never failed. The boy noticed the mistakes of even the most experienced cooks and would refuse to eat what he was served. After making that discovery, Master İsfendiyar started to pay more attention to the young prince's food, choosing the highest quality ingredients and cooking his food in separate pots. He cooked for him like that for three years, putting an end to his constant crying fits. The dishes he prepared helped the boy grow, bringing color to his face and making his eyes sparkle a brighter shade of green.

That night twenty years earlier, the child had just turned five years old.

The cook also remembered that night . . .

He remembered the silence more than anything. The hardened silence under whose weight the Harem had been buckling since early morning.

Then he remembered his father: how, on that day, he had hugged him tightly dozens of times, and performed prayer after prayer.

He remembered how Güldeste, his nanny, who had been his father's wet-nurse, wept silently from dawn till dusk, reading the Qur'an.

How cruel it was for a person to watch his own death being mourned.

There was a knock on the door shortly after the evening call to prayer. One of the Black Eunuchs handed his father a summons. His father received the edict with a deep bow, kissed it, and placed it over his head.

When his father hugged him for the last time, he was sitting in his mother's lap. His father placed his hands on each side of his face and kissed his cheeks. He never forgot how his father's thin moustache tickled his skin.

His father kissed his mother one last time on the forehead, whispering something in her ear. "Of course," his mother whispered in return.

He looked at his mother's clear features and eyes, which were green like his own. From that day on, the word "resolute" always made him think of his mother's face at that moment.

His father walked out without looking back. When the sound of his footsteps could no longer be heard, Güldeste broke down in tears. Women from the neighboring rooms joined in one by one, all of them weeping for the wet-nurse who had to send the boy she'd raised to the executioner's noose.

Nineteen princes, nineteen brothers, walked into the hands of their executioners as the edict demanded, out of obedience to ancient law and respect for the peace of the land.

The cook remembered falling asleep in his mother's lap. When he awoke to the sound of screams, his head was under the covers. Doors were broken down and furniture upturned. The screams of women echoed through the halls:

"My son!"

"My Mustafa!"

"My Mehmed!"

"My Bayezid!"

"My Murad!"

"My Korkut!"

The sultan's thirst for blood was still unquenched. Another edict was issued, one that ordered the killing of the princes' children and pregnant wives. There weren't enough executioners to carry out the killings, so the new sultan set his royal dogs from the Inner Palace upon the occupants of the Harem.

The rest was darkness. He remembered burying his face in his mother's breast, her heart beating like a dove's, her scent, her breathing, the tumult.

"Stand behind me," Güldeste whispered to the boy's mother. This time there was no trace of sorrow or fear in her voice. They heard the sound of swords being unsheathed, the door being broken down, and the grunts of men. Güldeste whispered again, "We must go."

He remembered running, his mother's breathing becoming more labored, and the shrieks of horror that lodged in her throat.

They made it to the landing, Güldeste right behind them. She stopped and called out to them one last time: "Run!"

They stopped only once when they heard Güldeste let out a scream.

The cook remembered passing through narrow passageways and climbing up stairs, and then feeling the cool night air on his face. He looked up from his mother's breast to breathe in the fresh air and glanced around. They were on a roof surrounded by minarets and towers. His mother ran toward one of the towers but their way was blocked by a wall. Two figures were running after them, one of them brandishing a dagger while the other was clutching a noose.

"Climb onto my shoulders," his mother said. "Climb up . . ."

The boy clambered onto her shoulders and managed to climb on top of the wall. His mother jumped, trying but failing to get a grip. On her second try, she held on, but she slipped and fell to the ground. The figures were getting ever closer. She jumped again, catching hold of the edge of the wall, but she was too tired to pull herself up. With his tiny hands the boy held onto his mother's arm and pulled with all his might, but he didn't have the strength.

Their pursuers reached the wall and started pulling his mother down by her waist but she refused to let go, and the boy held on as tightly as he could. As her fingers slipped, she looked at her son's face one last time, her tear-filled eyes gleaming in the light of the moon. She smiled and whispered, "Go."

He started running. He passed two large domed buildings, and then the ground slipped out from beneath his feet. He remembered tumbling downwards into a void, letting out a short scream as he fell before hitting the ground. After a moment of silence, his nostrils filled with the scent of freshly cut vegetables. He got up and looked around, rubbing his aching arm. It was dark. He didn't know where he was or where he would go. Then he noticed another smell, one that he knew well—the smell of chicken, which he loved. He began to follow it. As he got closer, he caught the scent of pepper. He quickened his steps as he caught the scent of rice boiled as soft as his mother's hands. His fear started to fade and he broke into a run.

Master İsfendiyar was stirring a pot, thinking about the mute dawn that he knew would break in a few hours' time and wondering how many coffins would be carried out through the third gate. There was one thing, however, that he knew for certain: No one would ever speak about what had happened that night or its victims. The palace had condemned those who remained to certain death.

When the cook walked into the kitchen for the first time in his life that night, Master İsfendiyar was removing the pot of soup from the stove.

Master İsfendiyar saw the boy standing by the door. His face was a mask of horror as he clutched his arm, his green eyes pleading for help.

The master's surprise quickly gave way to fear for his life, as he heard the sound of footsteps echoing outside and he knew what would happen if they caught him helping the boy. His conscience told him to find a way but his fears held him back.

He stepped out of the kitchen, still unsure of what he should do. He hid in a dark corner near the gate of the confectionary and saw the torches looming near. Palace guards, pages from the Inner Palace, and Black and White Eunuchs were pouring into the courtyard, which was now aglow in the light of torches. He imagined the cold blade of a sharp dagger pressed against his neck.

Knees shaking, he returned to the kitchen. All the curses he had been heaping upon the sultan moments ago left his thoughts. He knew that if he didn't help the boy he would come to despise himself, but fear was greater than all else, and fear was always right.

However, what he saw when he walked back into the kitchen would save both the boy's life and Master İsfendiyar's conscience.

The boy had climbed onto the counter and sat next to the pot of soup, and he was trying to get a spoonful with a ladle that was as long as he was tall.

In itself, that may have not been surprising as every cook knows that fear can be one of the best ways to whet the appetite. What caught his attention was the scent of the soup, as he knew it wasn't his own handiwork.

It was overwhelming enough to make him forget all his fears. There were open earthenware jars on the counter beside the boy and his tiny fingers were covered in spices.

The master stuck two fingers into the pot and tasted the soup. He found himself unable to stop licking his fingers, feeling as though he might faint from joy at any moment. While he'd been a cook for years and risen through the ranks to be stationed in the Royal Kitchen, he'd never heard of such a recipe nor recalled such a taste. The soup had hints of clover tinged with a perfect combination of cumin and pepper. Although he used the same spices day in and out, he was unable to figure out how the boy had come up with such an ideal blend—nor would he ever.

When he heard footsteps approaching the kitchen, he picked up the boy and placed him in a large pot under the counter. Before putting on the lid, he told the boy, "Don't make a sound." The boy nodded, still clutching the spoon.

What saved them from the wrath of the palace guards who burst into the kitchen was partly the prestige of the Royal Kitchen and partly the soup. No one in their right mind would ever want to run the risk of being blamed for the simplest case of food poisoning or the smallest stomach cramp that anyone in the sultan's household might get as the result of the food cooked there, and the palace guards were smart enough to know better. They only took a few steps inside and were content with asking Master İsfendiyar a few questions. Soon enough, however, they began to sniff the air. The master realized that the scent of the soup had enchanted not just himself but the guards as well. The guards gladly accepted the bowls of soup he offered them and even said "God's blessings be upon you" as they left.

Master İsfendiyar waited until dawn to whisk the boy out of the kitchen. After asking the head cook for two hours' leave, he took the boy to the home of a childhood friend. He asked him to take the child to Master Adem, who had trained them both. Upon hearing the name of their master, his friend agreed without saying a word.

His hands trembling, Master İsfendiyar wrote four words on a scrap of paper which he placed in the boy's palm.

Those four words had the power to set anyone's heart aflutter:
"The Pasha of Cuisine."

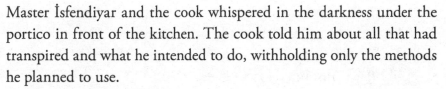

Master İsfendiyar and the cook whispered in the darkness under the
portico in front of the kitchen. The cook told him about all that had
transpired and what he intended to do, withholding only the methods
he planned to use.

The master's face knotted in a frown.

"Look," he said, chuckling, "it's not like I can hide you in a cauldron
this time, you won't fit."

The cook laughed. "God willing, there won't be any need for that."
Then his expression became grave. "But if anything goes wrong, you
must pretend that you don't know who I really am. Promise me that.
You risked your life for me once already."

Master İsfendiyar nodded and glanced at the Tower of Justice,
thinking of what he could do to help. "I can't have you taken on at the
Royal Kitchen," he sighed. "That's above my position."

"There's no need for that," the cook responded. "I have no business
there anyway."

The master's eyes remained on the Tower. "But I will ask around. I
know people there. I can find out where she is and—"

The cook cut in, "No! I don't want anyone mentioning her name.
Not a single whisper."

"Hear me out," Master İsfendiyar continued. "I'm just thinking of
your well-being. But . . . are you sure this is worth it? You know what
kind of place this is. No one ever leaves the way they came in.
Afterwards . . . well, I don't want to see your dreams crushed."

The cook laughed, but there was a bitter edge to his voice. "This has
nothing to do with dreams, Master. It doesn't matter what she may say
to me. But I have to do this. It is the only thing I truly want to do."

Master İsfendiyar heaved a deep sigh, looking into the cook's determined eyes. "Very well, but tell me what I can do for you."

"Do you know the boy Mahir? I want him to be my assistant."

Surprised, the master asked, "The one who watches over the lodgings?"

"Yes, him."

"Don't be fooled by what he's called. His name might mean 'wise,' but he's not much help at all."

"I know that. Why else would you have him watch over the lodgings?"

"And I don't trust him."

"I know that."

The master searched the cook's eyes and realized that it was pointless to ask too many questions. "Consider it done. Mahir will be your assistant. But don't rely on him too much."

"I know what I'm getting myself into," the cook replied. "But there's something else."

"Yes?"

"I need to spend some time alone in the Odalisques' Kitchen tomorrow. Could you arrange that?"

Master İsfendiyar thought for a few moments. "I'll find a way."

"Then that's all for now." The cook embraced Master İsfendiyar. "Thank you."

"No, son, it is you who I must thank. Now go on, off to bed with you. Tomorrow you'll get up along with everyone else. Don't expect any special treatment from me just because you cook for an agha. I care nothing for the Chief Sword Bearer or his ilk."

The cook folded his hands and bowed.

"Good night," the master said.

Everyone was asleep at the lodgings. The cook tiptoed to his bed like a shadow, mulling over his plans. He was sure. He had to be sure. Then he closed his eyes, cleared his mind of thoughts, and drifted into a deep sleep.

When he was awoken by the morning call to prayer, the sky was still dark. Mahir, who was on guard duty again, was dashing around lighting the oil lamps. Yet again he was late. One of the older cooks, no doubt tired of waking up to darkness every morning, snapped, "For God's sake, Mahir! Be a man of your name for once, why don't you!"

The cook chuckled to himself, realizing that he had indeed chosen the right person to be his assistant. He stretched, got out of bed, and joined the other cooks making their way to the hammam.

They performed their ablutions, taking turns according to rank, and prayed together. By the time they made their way to the kitchen, the stoves had been lit and the water-bearers had filled all the pitchers. The usual sounds arose from the kitchens: the whooshing of bellows, the jangling of cauldrons, the clatter of knives, the thudding of meat cleavers, the rustling of rice poured into bowls.

In one of the kitchens, the smell of burnt oil filled the air and a cook shouted, "You idiot, I told you to put in equal parts flour and oil for the *miyane*!"

The trembling voice of a young apprentice answered, "That's what I did, Master. I put in a spoonful of oil for each spoonful of flour."

Then there was the sound of a slap. "Since when is a spoonful of oil the same as a spoonful of flour? Don't you know how to use the scales?"

Someone else called out, "Bring some water!" and another cook asked for the fires to be stoked.

One assistant chided another, "Look, you're not giving water to a horse. Pour it in slowly," and a cook threatened his apprentice, "If you take your eyes off that stove for a single moment and burn those onions, you'll regret the day you were born."

The cook smiled as he listened to the sounds of the kitchen, but his joy was short-lived. Just as he'd been expecting, Firuz Agha from the Privy Chamber appeared in the doorway.

Over a pair of dark yellow *shalwar* he was wearing a long cream-colored shirt with a tulip pattern. The hem of his shirt was gathered in front and tucked under a sash tied around his waist, which was the same shade of yellow as his baggy pants. While Firuz Agha was meticulously dressed, there was unmistakable panic and anxiety in his eyes.

"Is something wrong?" the cook enquired.

The page tried to muster a smile. "His Highness the Agha must have got up on the wrong side of bed this morning. He summoned us all for a tongue-lashing, saying that his quarters were dirty."

"Well," the cook replied, "I hope you're not too troubled?"

"No, sir. It happens all the time. We're used to it now."

"I know that what you have to do is anything but easy. Perhaps I could help. A nice meal might calm the agha's anger. Do tell, what would His Highness the Agha like today?"

"That is most kind of you," the page replied, genuinely grateful. "His Highness the Agha would like fried eggs for lunch and stewed lamb for dinner."

The cook tried to conceal his surprise at the Chief Sword Bearer's request. Stewed lamb was a rather ordinary dish that novice page boys ate almost every day of the week and fried eggs were a quick lunch for inexperienced pages, because as soon as they climbed the ranks a little, they'd fry up eggs in their small kitchens whenever they got a chance and gobble them down in a quiet corner.

It was telling that Siyavuş Agha had chosen those two dishes, as they spoke of his own time as a novice working at the palace. The cook guessed that the internal wounds he'd spent years patching up had begun to bleed again, and the book of his conscience had fallen open. The cook knew that would happen but he was surprised at how quickly it had all unfolded. Either the stewed leeks had been a much more potent dish than he thought or the wounds in Siyavuş Agha's psyche were deeper than he'd assumed. Either way, he was certain of one thing: the agha's soul was in the grip of a mysterious dread. The agha didn't yet realize that his woes were bound up with his past, but he was seeking a remedy in the dishes of his difficult youth. Siyavuş Agha was wrong, however. There was no cure for his sickened soul. The unease that stirred in Siyavuş Agha's breast and stoked his anger would only get worse day by day because his rotten soul was now at the mercy of the cook.

The cook replied, "It would be my pleasure."

As Firuz Agha quickly made his way toward the Inner Palace, the cook took a sack from the kitchen to the cellar. The morning rush had not abated. Carrying bags and sacks, apprentices fetched ingredients for their masters and water-bearers carried pitchers of water on their shoulders to the kitchens. No sooner had the cook stepped aside to make way for an apprentice, carrying on his back a sack as large as himself when he heard someone shout, "Easy boys, easy!" Two fire-stokers were carrying a massive charcoal burner filled with burning cinders to the kitchens where they would feed the fires of the stoves. The charcoal burner was so hot that the cook had to back away when they passed by.

The cook walked out into the courtyard to escape the hustle and bustle of the kitchens. He thought about what he was supposed to cook for the Chief Sword Bearer. His Highness the Agha had requested just one dish per meal, leaving the rest for him to decide, and he realized that it was a perfect opportunity. He thought, *If the agha wants to revisit his past, then I'll help him.* When he walked through the huge door of the cellar, he knew what he'd be cooking that day.

He was greeted by a cacophony of angry voices. Some apprentices, assistants, and a few cooks had gathered by the sacks of rice, grain, and legumes, and all of them were shouting.

The cook made his way toward the crowd, passing a long table behind which the Chamberlain of the Cellar and his scribes were sitting. The Chief Cellar Steward, who was standing behind the sacks, was holding a basket woven from date palm leaves over his head as he begged, "Aghas, pashas! I swear to you, there's not one grain of *Dimyat* rice left. It all got sent to the Royal Kitchen. All that's left is Plovdiv rice. Please stop your bickering!"

But they were quite right to grumble—the most popular dish at the palace was rice. Everyone from the most inexperienced palace guard to the highest-ranking agha requested rice, and each day cauldrons of it were prepared with vegetables and fruit of all sorts. So naturally every cook wanted to use the best rice that soaked up the most water.

The cook turned right, avoiding the disgruntled crowd, and made his way to the butcher's room, grateful to find that there was no shortage of meat. Lamb, chickens, geese, and duck hung from hooks on the ceiling, and two cellar stewards were standing there with cleavers and knives tucked into their belts disinterestedly listening to the argument over rice.

The cook asked for a fat thigh of lamb and had the stewards cut out the bone. He placed the meat in a sack and took another right turn as he headed to the dairy room, where he got six eggs, a quarter *oka* of cheese, and fifty dirhams of pastrami. Then he got some pastry dough, carrots, spinach, dill, and parsley, as well as a few green stalks of celery. The bickering had died down in the grain room so the cook got in line. When his turn came, he asked for a quarter *oka* each of lentils, rice, and sugar, as well as fifty dirhams of vermicelli and ten dirhams of starch. As he walked out, wanting nothing more than to get out of the stifling cellar as quickly as possible, he suddenly stopped, realizing that he'd forgotten to get the ingredients for the dessert he'd planned on making. He was chagrined to realize that the dried fruits were at the farthest end of the cellar. For a moment he considered having the Confectionery Kitchen prepare the dessert, which he was allowed to do as a master cook, but he thought better of it. The cooks there were naturally quite skilled and he knew that anything they prepared would please the Chief Sword Bearer, but if his plan was going to work, he would need to handle everything the agha would eat. He made his way toward the sacks of dried fruit and selected ten dirhams each of dried figs and raisins, as well as twenty dirhams of dried plums. He then walked back to the long table behind which the Chamberlain of the Cellar and his scribes were sitting. He greeted the scribes, who were sitting on tattered cushions on the floor. From dawn till dusk they sat there with their inkwells and pens, keeping track of everything that left the cellar, the sparkle in their eyes long since dulled by keeping meticulous records. That was one of the oldest and strictest rules of the Imperial Kitchens. Everything that left the Imperial Cellar had to be documented, even a single clove of garlic. No one would dare dream of taking goods and selling them off because an inspection of the books would reveal the crime and the culprit would be accused of stealing from the sovereign's treasury and heavily punished.

The cook went back to the kitchen as fast as his feet could carry him. There was very little time, as he had to prepare eight different dishes, four for lunch and another four for dinner. However, when he walked into the kitchen he was surprised to see that Master İsfendiyar was waiting for him with Mahir by his side.

"You can't do all this alone," the master said. "What would we say to the Chief Sword Bearer if you couldn't finish on time?"

The master slapped Mahir's back and said, "Here's a strapping young assistant for you. He's yours for the taking." The other cooks in the kitchen sniggered. "He'll do as you say and bring you whatever you need."

"Thank you, Master," the cook replied.

Master İsfendiyar turned to Mahir and ordered him to kiss his new master's hand. Mahir dashed over to the cook and, taking the cook's hand, kissed it three times. Then he looked up and asked with sparkling eyes, "Is there anything you need?"

The cook realized that his new assistant must have been terribly bored watching over the lodgings and that he would do anything to please him, which was exactly what the cook wanted. The tastes and smells that arose in his thoughts when he first saw Mahir spoke of a slimy ball of greed and ambition buried deep down, traits that the cook knew could prove to be useful indeed. The cook wasn't yet able to fully understand the sensations that had appeared in his mind but he decided it was worth trying. He hoped the means—Mahir himself—would be worth the trouble.

He shot a glare at Mahir, who was still standing there with laughter in his eyes, and snapped, "First of all, you can take these things."

Chuckles echoed through the kitchen again. For an assistant to ask his master who was standing there with a sack on his back whether he needed anything was at best a laughable display of foolishness, and from what the cook could tell, Mahir had entertained the occupants of the kitchen once too often in the past with such displays. Everyone started laughing, from the apprentices to the head cooks, but a sudden bang cut their titters short.

The lid of a large pot had fallen to the ground next to Master Asım's feet and was still spinning in place. With eyes filled with fire, Master Asım glared at everyone around him and told his assistant to pick up the lid. Everyone fell silent and went back to work.

The reinstated solemnity of the Aghas' Kitchen pleased Master İsfendiyar. After wishing the cooks a good day, he started walking out, casting a secretive look at the cook as he stepped out the door.

Mahir was still standing there sheepishly holding the bag. The cook could see that his new assistant, stupefied by nervousness, could do nothing of his own accord.

"Empty it," he said, pointing to the bag. Mahir was just about to empty the bag on the table when the cook stopped him. "Slowly! There are eggs inside."

The other cooks in the kitchen were biting their lips to hold back their laughter as Mahir placed the items on the table.

The cook glanced at the pastrami he was going to use for the eggs. He sniffed the slice he was holding, and, noticing that Mahir was finished, said, "Go and fetch me an armful of onions. Also, put the lentils into a pot with some water and put it on the stove to boil."

"Yes, Master," Mahir responded. He thought for a moment and then grabbed a pot, filled it with water, poured the lentils into it, placed it on the stove, and set off to get the onions. The cook watched him out of the corner of his eye, thinking that if nothing else, his new assistant was quick on his feet.

Soon enough he brought the onions. The cook inspected them one by one, picking the ones he would use, when his assistant suddenly broke his concentration by asking, "What did the Chief Sword Bearer ask for?"

The cook cast him an annoyed look. "Eggs for lunch and lamb stew for dinner."

Mahir looked at the items on the table in confusion. "Who are all the other things for, then?" he asked after a moment.

Of course, it was unthinkable that Siyavuş Agha could do with only one dish per meal. At the palace, the number of dishes one was served followed certain rules. Even the youngest apprentice knew that for every meal the lowest-ranked residents—the odalisques, orderlies, and new page boys—would get two dishes, aghas four, pashas six, the sultan's favorite concubines eight, the sultan's chief consort sixteen, the sultan's mother and children eighteen, and lastly the sovereign would get between twenty-four to thirty-two dishes per meal.

He replied to Mahir with a question of his own: "Mahir, how long have you been working here?"

Mahir thought and then said, "A little more than two years, Master."

"And for how long did you look after the lodgings?"

"It would've been exactly eighteen months next week, Master."

The cook was now even more curious about the young man's past but decided he would ask later. "For His Highness the Agha's lunch we're going to make lentil soup, cup pastries, plum compote, and eggs," he explained. "And for his dinner we're going to cook green rice, vermicelli soup, fruit blancmange, and stewed lamb. Every day, for every meal, we're going to prepare four different dishes for him."

Mahir nodded.

The cook pushed a few carrots, along with the onions he'd selected, toward him. "Go on and start peeling these."

Mahir got to work and the cook finally got the peace and quiet he needed. He decided that he would make the plum compote first, since it would take time to cool down, and then move on to the eggs, soup, and pastries.

He dissolved some of the sugar in the water, added the plums, and placed the small pot on a stove to cook at a medium heat. In the meantime, Mahir had finished peeling the onions and moved on to the carrots.

"Cut four or five of the onions into small cubes," the cook said, "and split one in half and put it in the pot of lentils. Then slice the carrots and put them in with the lentils as well. Leave them to boil, and then mince the dill and parsley."

Mahir stared at him uncomprehendingly. At first, the cook thought he'd asked for too much, but the truth came to light when the boy asked, "What should I do with the dill and parsley, Master?" The cook realized that Mahir knew nothing about the terms that every apprentice learns. There was "halving," which obviously meant cutting something in half. Then there was "cutting," "chopping," and "shredding." Very fine cutting was referred to as "mincing." Then there was "grating" and "pounding" with a pestle and mortar.

At that moment, he had neither the time nor inclination to explain everything to his assistant, so he grabbed a large onion, sliced it in half, and threw it into the now-boiling pot of lentils. The he took the bunch of dill and minced it.

"Now you do the same with the parsley," he said to Mahir. The young man nodded, unable to take his eyes from the knife which his master wielded so expertly.

Mahir placed the bunch of parsley on a chopping board and began carefully chopping it up. To make sure they wouldn't be late, the cook began to work his knife ever faster, slicing four onions in the blink of an eye. After melting a generous amount of butter in the pan, he added the onions. Then he poured a little water into a smaller pan and, as he was putting in the pastrami, he noticed that the pan of onions was sizzling a little louder than it should have been.

He said to Mahir, "Reduce the heat."

Mahir crouched by the fire and sprinkled some ashes on the cinders.

The sizzling now satisfyingly quieter, Mahir went back to mincing the parsley, which was proving to be a challenge for him. The cook cast a disappointed glance at the green mound of mush in front of the boy. He knew that the amount of force used while mincing something was critical and that Mahir had pushed too hard, meaning that the juice of the parsley had been pressed out. The pastry would turn out a little tasteless, but there was nothing he could do at that point.

Just then the cook noticed with irritation that the pot of lentils was steaming. "Forget about the parsley for now," he told Mahir in a quiet but firm tone. "Put the carrots into the pot. Otherwise the water will boil away and they won't cook right."

Mahir set to work, peeling and cutting the carrots. The cook returned his attention to the pastrami. After placing the strips of meat in a pan over the lowest heat he could manage, he stirred the onions. The pastrami softened and the herbs on the edge of each slice dissolved into the oil, and when the onions became translucent, the cook slid the pastrami into the pan of onions and blew on the fire underneath the stove. After stirring the pastrami for a while, he added a dash of vinegar and a pinch of sugar. With a dash of salt the pastrami became even softer, approaching the consistency of a paste. The cook whisked the contents of the pan and five minutes later his work was done; the pan now contained a pungent light red puree. The onions had nearly dissolved, and all he had to do was to wait a moment before cracking the eggs into the pan. Before covering it with a lid, the cook whispered a mysterious word over its contents.

The cook took the plum compote off the stove and added a few cloves and a small piece of mastic to give it flavor as it cooled. He mixed the dill and parsley with some cheese in a bowl and then spread the mixture between the layers of pastry dough he'd laid out on the counter. After using up the mixture, he started cutting the dough into circles using a small bowl so that the pastries would be ready to be fried in olive oil and served up hot.

In the meantime, Mahir was straining the lentils. His surprising strength finally came into use as he worked the lentils, onions, and carrots through a sieve. The cook tasted a bit of puree on the edge of the sieve; just as he had guessed, the carrots weren't cooked through. He whispered another word and tasted the puree again. The carrots may still have been undercooked but their taste blended into the background. He could now move onto melting some butter for the soup.

The cook managed to prepare all the dishes a quarter of an hour before they were expected and was able to start working on the stew for the evening, adding the lamb to a pot of water along with two onions, half a bunch of parsley, and one clove of garlic. The plum compote had cooled down sufficiently and he poured the soup into a porcelain bowl. The eggs and the pastries were ready, being kept warm in copper pans with lids over coals.

All they had to do was wait. Soon enough, Master İsfendiyar's voice would ring out: "Time!" Then the bustle would begin anew as servants from all around the palace poured into the kitchens to pick up the dishes and deliver them to their masters.

As he waited, the cook watched the others at work in the kitchen. He'd only just met them, but he soon realized that all of the cooks were fairly proficient. Their mastery of the art of cuisine was evident even in the way they held their knives.

The cook was most impressed by Master Asım, the Chief Privy Chamber Page's cook. He was quiet and disciplined, and while he wasn't very fast, he used his time well. Most notably, he used a massive meat cleaver to perform almost every task that required cutting. This crude knife, which could split a leg of lamb in half with a single stroke, became the most precise of instruments in Master Asım's hands, and he could slice a shallot into the thinnest of slices.

He was also fascinated by the personal cook of Rikabdar Agha, who used the same table as him. He was a meticulous man, and the cook assumed that he'd learned his art in the kitchen of a wealthy household. He worked carefully with the various knives he lined up on the table and decorated his dishes so well that they were as elegant as they were delectable; that day he had adorned, for example, a tray of stuffed meatballs with roses he'd carved from radishes.

The cook suddenly realized that he couldn't remember the name of the cook with whom he shared a table—all he knew was that he was Rikabdar Agha's cook. It also occurred to him that the only person he knew by name was Master Asım and that the rest of the cooks were just titles and ranks to him. That struck him as odd, and he wondered if his mind was just focusing on what really mattered to him as he put his plan into motion.

As he attempted to figure out what the cooks of Çuhadar Agha and the Chief Treasurer were preparing by sniffing at the air, Master İsfendiyar's voice echoed through the kitchens. But instead of saying "Time!" as usual, he said, "All cooks are hereby summoned to the Stewards' Room! The Kitchen Council will gather."

Many of the cooks looked at each other and muttered, "Hopefully it's not bad news." The Kitchen Council only gathered to discuss matters of the greatest importance. Led by the Head Cook, all the cooks working in the kitchens and the confectionery, the cellar scribes, the Chief Baker, and the Market Steward would meet in the Kitchen Chamberlain's office to discuss whatever was at hand.

The announcement that the assistants would be expected to deliver lunch alarmed Mahir as he'd never had to deal with officials before. He looked at his master with inquiring eyes, too shy to question him directly.

The cook smiled. "It will be fine," he said. "Simply greet him and place his food on the tray. But if Firuz Agha has any instructions, listen well."

"Yes, Master," replied Mahir. "Is there anything you need?"

The cook thought for a few moments, stroking his chin. "After you take the agha his lunch, go to the cellar," he said. "I saw some apples there earlier. Get two *oka* of those and a handful of cloves."

"Of course, Master," Mahir repeated.

One by one the other cooks were leaving. The cook told Mahir to make sure that he cleaned up and started making his way toward the Stewards' Room, which was adjacent to the cellar. The large room was filled with people.

The cooks from the kitchens and the Confectionery were standing on the left side of the room in order of rank. At the front stood the Chief Confectioner and the Chief Baker, and Master Asım and the other high-ranking cooks were standing behind them. On the right were the staff of the kitchen and the cellar, headed by the Market Steward and the Chamberlain of the Cellar.

The cook stood at the rear. Master İsfendiyar and Şakir Effendi, the Chamberlain of the Kitchen, entered the room, and everyone fell silent, bowing their heads.

Master İsfendiyar and Şakir Effendi sat on a divan, leaving a space between them for the Chief Cellar Steward, who was responsible for reporting to the sultan about the kitchens and the cellar.

After a period of silence, the Chamberlain of the Kitchen said, "Aghas, effendis, brother cooks. As you know, we are running low on stock. But this is a temporary state of affairs. We must be more careful, and more considerate, during these difficult times—"

Without waiting for Şakir Effendi to finish, the Chief Confectioner interrupted him. Irritably he said, "And how long is this situation going to last? We're being more inconvenienced each day."

The Chamberlain of the Cellar patiently went on, "Not much longer. As you're aware, Treasurer Halil Pasha had to retire because of ill health, so there have been some delays in payments. But there's no need to panic. The Imperial Council will be meeting in three days. A new treasurer will be appointed, and the payments will continue as usual."

The Chief Confectioner nodded, but his frown indicated that he wasn't entirely satisfied. Şakir Effendi's explanation only made him feel more uneasy; Treasurer Halil Pasha had retired only the day before, but the troubles in the cellar had been going on for weeks. He surmised that if the Chamberlain of the Cellar was using the retirement of the Treasurer as an excuse, the problem ran deeper.

Şakir Effendi attempted to continue, but the Chief Baker interrupted him: "Please, Your Highness, find a solution to this problem as soon as you can. Otherwise we'll all be brought to ruin. I have less than a week's supply of flour in my cellar."

Şakir Effendi exclaimed, "What? How can that be?"

The Chief Baker took a step forward. "It is so, Effendi. For weeks no flour has been delivered. We're making do with what was delivered at the beginning of winter."

Şakir Effendi glared at the Market Steward. "Ömer Effendi, is this possible?"

The Market Steward, Ömer Effendi, had been responsible for the supply of goods to the Imperial Cellar for years, and years of haggling with vendors had etched a forced smile onto his face. He appeared as calm as ever. "There's no money," he said. "No one wants to sell goods on credit, and the few who do ask for bonds. And interest rates are high."

The Chamberlain of the Cellar roared, "How is that possible? What insolence! We," he said, pounding his chest, "buy ingredients for the Palace Bakery. What better debtor could they find?"

"This is how matters stand," Ömer Effendi replied, as patient as ever. "Ever since the famine, no one has sold a grain of rice or a dirham of flour without being paid in cash."

Silence fell over the room and Ömer Effendi bowed his head in contemplation. He knew that the famine wasn't the reason behind the dearth of grain; the real reason was that the Treasury had been broke for months. Merchants and bankers had sensed an oncoming financial crisis and were acting accordingly. Ömer Effendi, who had worked with the merchants for years, knew that they no longer trusted the palace's word when it came to promises of payment.

Şakir Effendi sighed. "Find a solution, Ömer Effendi. If need be, purchase your supplies from shopkeepers. Do whatever it takes. The day that the Royal Bakery doesn't produce a single loaf of bread will be the day of our doom."

The Market Steward replied, "Of course, Master Chamberlain." At the time, he was thinking, *You can't make a mill turn with buckets of water. Buy from shopkeepers, he says . . . and what am I supposed to give the shopkeepers in return? Beads?*

The Chamberlain of the Cellar looked down with a lost expression on his face for a few moments. "Do not worry, Effendis. In any case, that's not why we are gathered here today. God willing, our stoves will always burn and our soup will always boil. But, as I said before, we have to take certain measures to overcome these difficult times. From now on, all of you will choose what to cook based on what ingredients we have in the cellar."

The cooks in the room started murmuring to each other. Master Asım, who was standing toward the front, gave voice to the cooks' concerns: "Şakir Effendi, how are we supposed to do that?"

"Quiet, please, quiet!" the Chamberlain of the Cellar snapped. Then, attempting a smile, he said, "We'll take stock of what remains in the cellar. Everyone will cook accordingly. It's all very simple, you see."

The Head Cook of the Royal Kitchen, who was standing next to Master Asım, angrily objected, "It's not simple at all, Şakir Effendi. Suppose our sovereign desires fresh fava beans? There aren't any left in the cellar. What shall I say to him? Shall I tell him, 'There are no fava beans left, but we have string beans, would you like those instead?' That would bring shame on a well-to-do mansion, let alone the palace itself!"

The cook's concern was so legitimate that Şakir Effendi had to acquiesce. "Very well. We'll make an exception for the Royal Kitchen."

This stirred up an even greater uproar among the cooks. Çuhadar Agha's cook shouted, "Are we lesser men than the cooks of the Royal Kitchen? Do you not know how irritable the residents of the Inner Palace can be?"

The Chief Treasurer's cook leapt to the defense of his kitchen-mate: "He's right! Our heads are in the lion's mouth, too!"

Şakir Effendi was at a loss for words. He knew that if he were to grant the same privilege to the Aghas' Kitchen, the other kitchens would rebel as well. Master İsfendiyar stepped in and bellowed, "Enough! Are we at a council meeting or at the hammam?"

The murmuring quieted down. Master İsfendiyar used his cane to get to his feet and said, "You are cooks! Use your minds. A cook can create much out of little, little out of much, something out of nothing. Do I have to teach you your job at this age?"

The cooks fell silent. Master İsfendiyar continued, "We've explained to you that this is a time of shortage. Adversity creates wisdom. We'll work together and persevere. Is there anything else you don't understand?"

When no reply came, the master sat back down and the Chamberlain of the Cellar continued the discussion. Eventually it was decided that careful stocktaking would be carried out at the cellar and a group of senior cooks would decide on weekly lists of the dishes each kitchen would prepare, particularly those that served many people, and "important" kitchens such as the Royal Kitchen, the Aghas' Kitchen, and the Imperial Council Kitchen would borrow funds from the Cooks' Union for emergency supplies.

When the meeting was over, the cook slowly walked to the courtyard, keeping an eye out for Master İsfendiyar, who had been talking to Şakir Effendi. Their eyes had met during the meeting and the cook felt that Master İsfendiyar's gaze had been telling him to wait for him.

He decided to wait in a corner of the courtyard. Some of the cooks had gone back to their lodgings, while others had returned to the kitchen. Yet others had congregated in the courtyard and were talking amongst themselves. He eavesdropped on the conversation between two cooks on his left.

"What happened to the Chief Treasurer?" the younger one asked.

"Paralysis. God forgive me for saying this, but he couldn't have found a worse time."

"Who will be appointed in his place?"

"Either his scribe, Sadık Agha, or the Interior Minister, Lütfü Pasha."

"Neither would do. They can't take the place of Halil Pasha."

"You're right on that point. He's been Treasurer for so many years. Who could take his place? He was a great man. May God grant him a speedy recovery."

"Amen," the younger one said. They began to walk toward the kitchen. The cook watched them go, thinking that they were right. Particularly at such a tumultuous time, no one would want to take that position. The cook had heard the praises of the Pasha sung a long time ago. Under his sweet-natured facade lay an intelligent, capable man of state who loved his job. His word counted for legal tender not just in Constantinople, but in the whole of the empire. When he had led the Treasury, he'd steered the empire through many difficult times. Halil Pasha knew how much to borrow, from where and when, and how to pay it back when the time came. And he was brave. The time he secured an audience with the sultan prior to the sovereign's sister's wedding and told him in no uncertain terms that the money spent on banquets and her dowry should be cut was still the stuff of legend.

That was the sort of man Halil Pasha was, and the cook knew that his absence would make their financial troubles even more difficult to handle.

Just as he was getting tired of waiting, he saw Master İsfendiyar emerge from the building. He was joined by the Chamberlain of the Kitchen, the Chief Confectioner, the Chief Privy Chamber Page's personal cook, and a few other senior cooks, including Master Bekir, the Chief Sword Bearer's previous cook.

Master İsfendiyar looked around as he walked. The cook began to slowly walk toward the kitchen. After he took two steps, Master İsfendiyar's voice thundered behind him.

Quickly repressing a smile, the cook turned and gave him a questioning glance.

Master İsfendiyar called him over.

The cook folded his hands and walked toward Master İsfendiyar and Master Bekir. He bowed his head and said, "Yes, Master?"

"Master Bekir has matters to attend to. I need you to oversee the Odalisques' Kitchen."

The cook feigned surprise. "But Master—"

"No excuses! You think you can lie on your backside all day after cooking three dishes? That won't do here!"

The cook bowed his head. "As you wish, Master." He appeared so crestfallen that Master Bekir pitied him. "My assistants are very capable," he said gently. "They'll handle everything. You'll just need to check on them a few times."

Without raising his head, the cook began to murmur "Thank you," but Master İsfendiyar interrupted him. He was clearly enjoying the game. "What are you saying, Master Bekir?" he asked. "He can't leave the cooking to your assistants. A real cook would do the job himself. So let him see what it's like to really work. We'll have no layabouts here!"

Master Bekir looked at Master İsfendiyar with pleading eyes. It seemed there was a special place in his heart for the cook who had put an end to his toil trying to please the Chief Sword Bearer. "It is unkind to say such things," he said in a trembling voice. "His job is more difficult than everyone else's. You wouldn't understand unless you've been in his place. Don't push the boy too much."

Master İsfendiyar had no time for his entreaties. "Off to work with you," he said to the cook, pointing toward the kitchen with his cane. Then he turned to the other cooks around him and said, "And off to work with you, too."

As the Head Cook started walking toward the cellar, the cook remained for a moment, head bowed and hands folded. Then he turned and quickly made his way to the kitchens. Mahir was waiting for him by the table. He'd brought the apples and the cloves, cleaned up the table, and even prepared the ingredients for that night's dinner.

"Good work, Mahir." The boy beamed, but his smile fell when the cook explained that they were going to be working at the Odalisques' Kitchen. "What will we do, Master?" he asked anxiously. "Will we have enough time to handle both?"

"Don't worry about that," the cook replied. He seemed completely at ease. "Fill a large pot with water. Crush the cloves and put them in the pot, then bring it to a boil. Cut the apples in half, and when you can smell the scent of the cloves rising from the pot, add the apples. Count to one hundred, take them out, and place them on a plate to cool."

Mahir stared uncomprehendingly at his master. "Is this for the Odalisques' Kitchen?"

"Yes, Mahir!" he replied sternly. "It's for the Odalisques' Kitchen. Now do as I say. Remember, count to one hundred and then remove the apples. Not ninety-nine, not one hundred and one, but exactly one hundred. Understood?"

"Understood, Master," replied Mahir. "One hundred."

He glanced timidly at the cook, who realized that the boy wanted to tell him something. "Yes, Mahir?" the cook asked. "What is it?"

Mahir's voice was just as timid as his gaze. "Can I cook the rice?"

With difficulty, the cook stopped himself from refusing, which was what first came to mind. "Will you make it well?"

Mahir nodded. "I'm very good at it, Master."

The cook looked at him for a few moments. The boy seemed self-assured, but the cook had seen how inept he was. *Well, he can't make such a mess that I won't be able to put it right*, he thought. "Very well."

"Thank you, Master," he said with a smile, but his master was already rushing toward the Odalisques' Kitchen.

The cook arrived at the Odalisques' Kitchen to find that Master Bekir's assistants were almost halfway through the dinner preparations. Two huge cauldrons were boiling on the stove and six large pots of rice soaking in water had been placed on the table. Based on the scent of the steam filling the kitchen, the cook knew that lentils were boiling in the cauldrons.

One of the assistants saw him and said, "Welcome, Master. Master Bekir already explained the situation to us. We've begun as usual and had no problems."

The cook nodded. He lifted the lid of one of the pots. "Don't over-cook the lentils. As they cook, make sure you remove the foam from the top every few minutes. After taking them off the stove, run them under cold water to remove the skins."

"Yes, Master," the assistant said.

The cook replaced the lid of the cauldron and looked into the pots of rice. "When did you add the water?"

A young apprentice standing by the table answered, "Before the call to prayer, Master."

The cook nodded again, pleased with the situation. He had no desire to prepare the food there, because he had other matters on his mind. "Continue as you were," he said. "But make sure you tell me when you decide to cook the rice."

The assistants went back to work.

The cook spent the rest of the day shuttling back and forth between the two kitchens.

Everything proceeded smoothly at the Odalisque's Kitchen, and Mahir not only managed to cook the apples properly but also performed nothing short of a miracle by making a pot of rice with spinach. He boiled the spinach in a pan of water and strained it first through a sieve and then a piece of muslin cloth.

When the cook asked him how he'd learned how to cook rice so well, Mahir's eyes misted over. With a sigh he said, "My late father taught me." The cook was curious but decided to ask him more at a later time.

Seeing as the rice was done, the cook had little else to do. The meat for the stew was already cooked, and vermicelli soup was a dish he could make with one hand. Only the fruit blancmange was demanding, as he had to wait until it took on the right texture. Setting aside the pudding to cool, he drained the water from the pot of lamb and placed the meat in a hot oven. After it was properly seared, he cut it into thin slices and placed it on a porcelain plate, which he sprinkled with pepper, oregano, and cumin.

After preparing the Chief Sword Bearer's dinner, the cook began making palace fritters. When Mahir asked what the sweets were for, he got such a stern glare in reply that he regretted having opened his mouth to speak. Even so, he couldn't bring himself to leave the table as he enjoyed watching his master work: how he mixed the flour with whipped egg whites, tore off bits of dough with such precision, fried the bite-sized balls in sesame oil to perfection and dipped them in the honey that was simmering on the next stove. His master was so adept, and his hands moved with such magical grace, that it was impossible not be in awe of his skills. But his talent also aroused a strange feeling of mistrust, and even Mahir sensed that the cook had a talent that went far beyond hard work, aptitude, and experience.

Just as the cook finished frying the last three fritters and dipping them in honey, an assistant from the Odalisques' Kitchen appeared in the doorway. "The rice is ready, Master."

"I'll be there in a moment," the cook replied as he waited for the fritters to soak up the honey. Gesturing toward the Chief Sword

Bearer's dinner, he turned to Mahir and said, "If they come to get the food before I return, tell them to wait."

Mahir nodded. The cook removed the last fritters from the oil, placed them in a copper pan, and closed the lid. Then he took the apples Mahir had boiled with the cloves and made his way to the Odalisques' Kitchen.

The lentils and rice were ready.

The cook tasted both dishes. He could've mentioned dozens of faults, from the oil to the temperature, but kept quiet. "Well done," he told the assistants. They were all looking curiously at the plate of apples. The cook called an assistant and an apprentice over and told the others to start spooning out the lentils into smaller pots.

The cook set to work on the rice. He placed half an apple at the bottom of one of the large copper pans lined up on the table and told an assistant waiting with a massive spoon, "Put the rice over the apples."

Both the assistant and the apprentice, who was struggling to keep a firm grip on the cauldron which was nearly as large as himself, were dying of curiosity about the apples. However, they didn't dare ask any questions of that man whose talent had become the talk of the kitchen on the very first day he showed up.

As the assistant filled the first pot with rice, the cook moved on to the next, placing half an apple on the bottom of the pot. Once the rice was spooned into all the pots with half an apple concealed at the bottom of each, he told the assistants to put the lids on the pots and wait. Soon afterwards, eight meal-bearers led by a Black Eunuch entered the kitchen. The eunuch stood by the stoves and watched the men expressionlessly as they started gathering up the pots. After a while, he suddenly fixed his gaze on the cook. As luck would have it, right at that moment the cook looked at the eunuch. He had piqued the cook's interest not just because he was the largest man he had ever seen, but also because he worked in the Harem. He greeted the eunuch with a short nod.

After the meal-bearers had placed the pots on large metal trays which they balanced on their heads, the eunuch thanked the apprentices and left the kitchen.

Their work was complete. The cook turned to the assistants and apprentices and said, "Good work, everyone." Then he returned to his own kitchen, leaving their minds swirling with questions.

The Privy Chamber Page was waiting for him along with two other page boys. From their expressions he could tell they had been waiting a while.

"Forgive me for making you wait," the cook told them.

The page replied, "It's no matter," but his expression was dour. "You've had no trouble, I hope?"

The cook smiled. "No, Master. His Highness the Agha's food is ready. You may take it to him now."

The page gestured to the novices standing beside him. As the boys placed the porcelain dishes on a tray which they had brought to the kitchen, the cook approached the stove. "This is why I made you wait," he said as he picked up the pan of fritters. "A small gift for my brothers in the Privy Chamber. I hope it will please you."

The page opened the lid, a confused expression on his face. When he saw the golden fritters gleaming with honey, his eyes widened. The scent alone was enough to fill him with joy. He bit into one and exclaimed, "Oh, my! This is most kind of you. You shouldn't have gone to all this trouble!"

The cook bashfully looked away. "It's nothing really. Especially compared with how difficult your job is at the Inner Palace. If I can bring but a little sweetness into your lives, that would make me most happy."

The page's eyes were starting to fill with tears. He stammered, struggling to come up with a pompous expression of gratitude, but then gave up. In the end, he managed to say with profound sincerity, "Thank you very much."

"I hope you enjoy it," the cook replied. Then, lowering his voice, he added, "It would be better if His Highness the Agha did not hear of this. You know . . ."

The page closed the lid of the pan and said gravely, "Do not worry about that. I swear on behalf of all my brothers that this will remain a secret between us."

The cook thanked him. The page bowed to the cook and left the kitchen with the two novice pages.

Now there was nothing for the cook to do but wait. He knew how the food he sent to the Inner Palace would be received and that mattered little to him. But the dishes he sent to the Harem. . . . The more he thought about it, the more his stomach knotted up as he wondered if he would get the result he desired. He prepared himself for the worst but was determined to go through with what he had planned.

After performing his evening prayers at the cooks' masjid, he slipped downstairs and hid under the kitchen portico so he could hear what was happening at the Harem. As the sun set, the palace grew quiet. The cook waited, listening . . .

As the sky grew dark, a bright quarter moon emerged. The cook looked up at the moon, hoping it might inspire him with hope, but as soon as he did so, the sorrow he carried within became an arrow that struck his heart. "No," he muttered. "I'm not going to give in to despair this time." He refused to allow his pain to turn into anger and his yearning to turn into hatred. Still, the night was quiet, as if out of spite. "It's okay," he said to himself. "I'll try again tomorrow. I'll find another way."

Just as he decided to go back to the kitchen, he heard a voice for the briefest moment. The cook stopped. His heart seemed to have stopped as well. He listened carefully. The voice was very faint. His mind was asking, *Could it be?*, but his heart was certain. No matter how far away, only one voice on earth could make his heart beat so.

He emerged from the portico and proceeded on tiptoe. The voice was so faint that even the sound of the grass crunching under his feet roared in his ears. The cook stopped under the nearest tree and listened. The voice seemed to have fallen silent but then it rose again. It was a song, and the cook could make out the words:

What do the astrologer and the timekeeper know of the longest night—
Ask someone who is addicted to sorrow how long each night is . . .

The cook began to sob. He fell to his knees, tears streaming down his cheeks. "Thank God," he said. "Thank God."

It was her. He had never been so certain of anything in his life.

An angry voice interrupted the song and the singing stopped, as did the cook's tears. Jaw clenched, the cook looked beyond the Tower of Justice where the domes of the Harem could be seen. "Wait," he whispered between his teeth.

As he walked toward the lodgings, his heart was filled half with anger and half with joy, but his happiness grew with every step he took, washing away the fury and the pain. By the time he passed through the small vaulted gate and reached the courtyard in front of the lodgings, the cook was smiling.

Just as he was about to enter, a voice called after him: "Where have you been? I've been looking for you everywhere."

The cook turned and looked. It was Master Bekir. He was walking toward him, his arms open. "What a cook you are!" he exclaimed, embracing him. "What gave you the idea of putting apples under the rice?"

The cook smiled bashfully. "Did they like it?"

Master Bekir chuckled. "Like? They loved it! The whole Harem was talking about it. They say even Haseki Sultan asked for a portion of the concubines' rice, but I can't tell you whether that's really true. Now, tell me where you learned that trick."

The cook smiled. "It's a long story, Master, from my childhood. I'll tell you sometime."

4

The House of Pleasure

THAT DAY, MASTER Adem was surprised to see one of his old
assistants with a five-year-old boy asleep in his arms. When he
learned that it was İsfendiyar, another one of his old assistants,
who'd sent the boy, his surprise became curiosity.

Master Adem gently set the boy, who was still asleep and smelled of
rubbish, on some flour sacks in the corner and offered his old assistant
who'd traveled so far a bowl of yogurt soup and some moussaka left
over from the night before. As his old assistant ate, Master Adem tried
to find out more but his efforts were in vain. İsfendiyar had told the
man very little, only requesting that he take the boy to Master Adem,
who accepted the charge without thinking much about it. İsfendiyar
was one of the few men left in the world whose judgement he could
still trust.

He saw his old assistant out and returned to the kitchen, only to see
the boy had awoken and was nibbling on a piece of stale flatbread.
When the boy saw him, his eyes filled with fear and he sat there perfectly still, the piece of bread still in his mouth.

"Are you hungry, boy?" the master asked, smiling. The boy smiled back and continued gnawing on the bread. Then Master Adem called out to his assistant in the large kitchen: "Selman! Is the soup ready?"

His assistant called back, "It is, Master. I just seasoned it."

"Good. Bring me a bowl."

A few minutes later Selman entered the small kitchen carrying a steaming bowl. He was surprised to see a child there, but without saying a word he went back to work.

"Come!" Master Adem said to the child, pointing at the bowl. The boy stared at the bowl, sniffed the air a few times and then timidly approached the table, still clutching the piece of bread. Master Adam gave him the smallest spoon he could find. The boy sniffed the soup a few more times, glanced at the master, and then brought a spoonful of soup to his mouth. Immediately a grimace appeared on his face and he spat the soup out, looking at Master Adem all the while.

"What a little devil!" Master Adem said. "Don't you like tripe?"

The boy nodded but there was a certain meaningfulness in his refusal to eat. His gaze still locked on Master Adem, he stuck his finger into the bowl and traced the shape of an egg in the air.

The tips of Master Adem's long gray moustache quivered. "It can't be," he muttered to himself. "What could a child his age know about . . ."

He got up in a rage and went to the large kitchen, where he snapped at his assistant, "For God's sake, Selman, the seasoning of the soup is off again. Don't your hands know what they're doing? Do you not have brains in your head?"

He told Selman to empty the cauldron and start over. When he returned to the small kitchen, what he saw not only calmed his anger but also filled him with awe. The boy was standing in the middle of the kitchen holding out a bulb of garlic.

After gazing at the child for a few moments, Master Adem got down on his knees and stroked the boy's face. "Who are you?" The boy said nothing in response but merely held out his other hand which was locked in a fist. That's when Master Adem noticed the piece of paper the boy was holding. When he opened it, the smile on his face vanished: "The Pasha of Cuisine."

"Ah, İsfendiyar!" he muttered to himself. Now he understood why his old assistant hadn't told him anything about the boy's identity— because standing before him was a miracle. The boy had a unique talent, and his kind came into the world ever so rarely.

A legend every cook on earth had heard of but never seen . . . a living miracle! The Pasha of Cuisine was said to be in possession of the perfect palate, the ability to distinguish and wield power over every flavor down to the smallest detail, the blessed one of the culinary arts, the sovereign of every dish in the world.

And here he was, standing right in front of him.

His existence was important not just for himself, but for all the cooks in the world. It was said that the power of the Pasha of Cuisine would increase the skill of all cooks everywhere and render exquisite the flavor of every dish they made. Old tomes said that during eras in which Pashas of Cuisine lived, food went through golden ages. Not only food but fruits, vegetables, spices, and even meat became more flavorful, the tastiest crops grew, and the most abundant harvests were made. The light radiating from the Pasha of Cuisine spread across fields, gardens, orchards, and farms, and from there penetrated kitchens, the hands of cooks, and palates, beginning a new era of opulence, prosperity, joy, and health. In short, a new golden age of taste.

The child had to be taught.

Master Adem knew what he needed to do. He'd learned it from his master, and his master had learned it from his own master. He was part of a long line of cooks who had been waiting to train the next Pasha of Cuisine for generations. That sacred task was now his.

Master Adem never wondered about the boy's past and didn't ask İsfendiyar any questions about him during his rare visits. He gave the boy a new name and introduced him to the other cooks as his nephew.

The master gave the boy time to get used to being with him in his new surroundings. He could tell that his heart was filled with fear.

Whenever the boy seemed to be on the verge of falling asleep, he would awake with a jolt and open his eyes, looking around breathlessly. And when he did actually fall asleep, he would call out for his mother and wake up crying, drenched in sweat. Master Adem stayed by his side after every nightmare, and tried to calm him down.

As time went by, the nightmares became less frequent. Soon enough the boy got used to the people around him, and they got used to him being around. He was quiet and didn't fuss. On the rare occasion when he threw a tantrum, he would make up for it with a sweet smile. With his green eyes, gentle manner, and tenderness, he quickly became the darling of the entire House of Pleasure.

Master Adem was the head cook of the House of Pleasure, which had five mansions, one hammam, and lodgings for the servants. High walls ran around the House of Pleasure, sealing it off from the rest of the world.

True to its name, the House of Pleasure offered every kind of earthly delight, but it wasn't just a brothel, tavern, or opium den. In the five mansions, visitors had their own rooms where they could enjoy the purest opium and the best wine in the land, carouse at sumptuous banquets, enjoy the company of the most beautiful young women of Constantinople, listen to music, and dance with the sultriest female dancers. If they so desired, they could go downstairs and converse with the other visitors, listen to poetry, play dice, ride horses, stroll through the gardens, watch the most skilled of wrestlers, or go to the hammam to be bathed in rosewater and musk and take part in revelries.

That was the House of Pleasure. Anyone who knew how to open his purse strings could find a pleasure to suit his tastes there.

The owner was a woman by the name of Sirrah. The House of Pleasure was located on the far side of Bosphorus, two hours on horseback from Üsküdar in a secluded copse of woods behind a hill. From the outside, all that could be seen were the high stone walls which concealed the mansions and exquisite gardens and an iron gate that was often locked shut.

Sirrah had once been a dancer herself, so she was well aware of the importance of secrecy, and she assured her customers that all they experienced within those walls would remain a secret. But not everyone could get into the House of Pleasure. Before admitting anyone new into her house, Sirrah required that the newcomer to be vouched for by a reliable customer. Of course, all her clients were wealthy influential men, so much so that if their names were ever to be mentioned in reference to the House of Pleasure, Constantinople would be shaken to its foundations and heads would roll.

Sirrah would greet every customer at the door with four handsome servant boys by her side. With honeyed words dripping from her tongue, words that only became sweeter with age like wine, she would flatter her customers and inquire how long they would be staying, taking payment in full up front. The boys would then dress the newcomer in a long silken shirt embroidered with gold thread. They would lock all his possessions in a safe, the key for which the visitor would wear on a gold chain around his neck, and the customer would be seated on a chair with cushions of goose feather and carried by four muscled slaves to the hammam. There he would be bathed and pampered, and then the butler of the mansion where he was staying would see him to his room. The rest was up to his tastes and desires.

Unless something important happened, the visitor would see Sirrah again only at the end of his stay. Sirrah knew about everything that happened in her house, and when it was time for a visitor to leave, she would pay him a goodbye visit, bringing whatever it was she knew to be his favorite, be it a woman, wine, or opium, and tell him it was free of charge. Then the sweet talk would begin: "We've never seen the likes of you here," "We can't get enough of your company," "So-and-so singer still pines for you," and lastly, "Wouldn't you like to stay a few more days?"

Seasoned visitors of course did not fall for her trap, but newcomers would remove the golden key from around their necks and request that gold be taken from his purse to cover the cost of three or four more days' stay.

Regular visitors who vouched for the stay of a young relative or friend feared that final visit most of all. They would try to find out how many days the person they vouched for would be staying, and if they had not yet left by the time they said they would leave, they would try to recuse the poor man from Sirrah's clutches.

Sometimes, however, certain men, particularly merchants and politicians, would convince their rivals to agree to a stay at the House of Pleasure, and they would pay Sirrah extra to ensure that his reputation would be ruined before he could even step foot in the place.

All earthly sins could be found at the House of Pleasure and as such it had its dangers. It had caused the ruin of many a life, broken countless households, and devoured riches. So many men had lost their prestige, reputations, homes, and even themselves at the House of Pleasure. Master Adem was one of the latter.

The earliest memory the cook had about the House of Pleasure was the first cooking lesson he received from Master Adem.

The kitchens were located in the basement of a three-story building called the Great Mansion, which was located at the entrance to the House of Pleasure. It consisted of three sections. At the entrance there was the small kitchen, which was adjacent to the main building and extended a few paces from the wall. It was connected to the large kitchen, which took up most of the basement, by a narrow corridor a few meters in length, and another corridor running parallel to the large kitchen led to the lodgings of the cooks and assistants.

On the day of that lesson, the cook could not remember how long he had been there, but he supposed that it couldn't have been more than a couple of weeks. He was playing with some dried beans in the small kitchen and Master Adem was working at the table beneath the window. Master Adem called him over, picked him up, and sat him on a stool. On the counter was a pinch of salt, a small bowl of honey, half a lemon, and a small red pepper. The master asked him to taste each of them, which he did. The salt was salty, the lemon sour, the honey sweet, and the pepper spicy.

"These are the tastes that exist in the world," the master explained. Then he picked up a small carrot, peeled it, squeezed some lemon juice on it, and seasoned it with some salt. "Eat this," he said, handing him the carrot. As the boy nibbled on the carrot, the master cut two slices of cheese, daubing one with honey and putting the red pepper which he'd cut in half on the other. "Now eat these."

When the cook finished eating the cheese with pepper, Master Adem said, "Those are flavors. There are only four tastes, but the number of flavors is infinite."

The cook never forgot his first lesson. In his child's mind, the fact that the same cheese tasted different when combined with something sweet as opposed to something spicy seemed like magic to him, a miracle. As he sat on that stool, he fell in love with cooking.

Over the next two years, Master Adem and the boy only played games when it came to cooking. Everything in the huge kitchen, all the cookware, vegetables, fruits, cheeses, and sacks of grains, became his playthings.

His favorite game, and the one they played most often, was "What's too little? What's too much?" Master Adem would deliberately add too little or too much of a certain ingredient to a dish and ask him to guess what was wrong. The child had a natural talent for flavors, and he noticed mistakes straightaway. But that wasn't enough if he was going to become a true cook. He had to understand why something was wrong, and know exactly what was lacking or in excess. It wasn't a matter of natural talent—he had to acquire much knowledge and skill.

The young cook explored the flavors he was discovering. Carefully he tried to determine which parts of his mouth were affected by flavors, whether it be the tip or back of his tongue, the roof of his mouth, or the back of his throat.

He experimented, he discovered new things, he tasted everything, and he never forgot the earliest piece of advice his master gave him: "A good cook is never fussy. He isn't repulsed by anything. In fact, there are only two kinds of food in the world: good food and bad food. A cook might like a dish, or he might not. But he always tastes it first."

That's precisely what the young cook did. He mixed pickled cucumbers with honey, gnawed on raw mackerel, and seasoned a semolina cake with red pepper and cumin. Of course, a lot of the time he ended up ruining perfectly good foods and flavors. But that was also how he discovered many delectable doubles such as cumin and onions, parsley and pomegranate, cauliflower and green olives, and sesame halva and lemon, and by playing games he learned that onions could actually be sweet and that garlic had a different flavor when grilled compared to when it was fried in oil.

When he turned seven, Master Adem presented him with a knife suitable for a boy his size, and gave him another piece of advice: "A good cook only needs one knife. You can carve with the tip, slice with the middle, and peel with the bottom of the blade."

The young cook's official apprenticeship began with a slap on the back of his neck following that piece of advice. While he was disappointed that playtime was over, as an apprentice cook who was already in love with cooking, he quickly grew accustomed to his new responsibilities. He attended to all his tasks in the kitchen and listened carefully to his master's words: "What we call flavor has six layers. There are four main tastes: sweet, salty, spicy, and sour. These, separately or combined, form the main layer, the seed of the flavor. Then there is the matter of contact. Every flavor makes its own kind of contact with the mouth. Some flavors are full-bodied, while others are weak. Some make your teeth ache or your mouth water, yet others warm or cool your mouth. The third layer is the surface. That is, when contact combines with sounds. Some flavors are crunchy, some are crisp. Some are soft, and some are prickly. When the tongue tastes the flavor and the mouth discovers the surface, next comes the aroma. Aromas are very important, because flavors can be complete only with their scent. There is no such thing as a flavor without a smell. The fifth layer of flavor is the outer layer, the appearance. At this level, the flavor also appeals to the eyes, and satiates the eye as well as the stomach. Without the outer layer, no flavor can be complete. If the eye doesn't see, then the tongue, palate, and nose are also blind. Finally, the sixth layer, which exists at the deepest level, consists of sensations. Most people don't realize this, but every taste is related to a memory or an emotion. Flavors are part of a person's past, and are the translation of emotion into another language."

Master Adem paused, looking into the cook's eyes, which betrayed a certain amount of confusion, and asked him, "Have you ever thought why a person might hate or love a certain food?"

The cook shook his head.

"It's because they have a memory associated with it," the master said. "And every time people taste it, that memory comes back, along with the feelings it inspires. Remember that while taste may start in the mouth, it ends in the mind. You are talented enough to command all the secret feelings that flavors can awaken. It's not just about cooking meat at the correct temperature or making soup the right consistency. You must learn how to control the emotional aspect of taste."

The cook remembered how excited he had been when he heard those words, as well as nervous. "But how? How can I do that?" he asked.

Master Adem smiled and caressed his cheek. "You will learn how, but not from me. Such things are well beyond my knowledge. Still, I know the people who can teach you. But you mustn't rush. First you'll learn the art of cooking, and then you'll embark on a long journey. A very long journey . . ."

Those words echoed in his mind, becoming etched into his thoughts as the years went by. It was like they had become a dream—or to be more accurate, a dark nightmare—he had every time he went to sleep.

He didn't realize it in those days, but just as Master Adem had surmised, he was learning quickly. But what he was doing couldn't exactly be called learning. It was as if he'd known how to cook since the day he was born. He didn't have to think about how to make a certain dish. With his knife in hand, he took his place at the table and through intuition he cut, chopped, mixed, and stirred.

By the time he was nine years old, the cook could run an entire kitchen on his own. Nevertheless, Master Adem didn't give him free reign and forbade him from doing everything on his own. At times, this upset the cook, but the master knew the danger of giving him too much freedom. As he grew up, the cook's knowledge and skill increased. Still, his education wasn't complete and he wasn't yet able to control his extraordinary talent. The food he cooked on his own had the potential to have unpredictable effects on the denizens of the House of Pleasure. And so it did.

It was a busy day in the large kitchen. The cook was making *gülabiye*; first he placed some almond paste into a bowl of honey and stirred in some butter and starch, and then waited for it to set. He was excited, because soon he would be using nutmeg for the first time in a pudding. Just as he was about to remove the stopper of the small crystal bottle holding one of the most precious ingredients in the kitchen, Master Adem came in and pulled it from his hands.

Hurt, the young cook ran off to the small kitchen, eager to vent his anger. He noticed a pitcher full of cherry syrup, which Selman had brought for the sherbet, and a large bucket of snow. The cook decided to channel his fury into a batch of snow halva. He got the consistency just right and sprinkled fresh blackberries over it. Just then Master Adem summoned him to the large kitchen, so the cook left the halva as it was on the counter. A servant entered the kitchen and assumed that the halva was one of the cold desserts that were going to be served at the Green Mansion, so he took it there, setting into motion a disastrous chain of events. In no time at all, the walls of the House of Pleasure were echoing with angry shouts and swearing.

The servant placed the snow halva in front of four pleasure seekers who were listening to music and playing dice in one of the ground-floor rooms in the mansion. These four men, already intoxicated with opium and wine and longing for some refreshment, devoured the halva set before them. Soon, however, they began to glare at each other with hatred in their eyes.

The cook had infused the halva with such fury that all the anger the men had kept hidden away under a veneer of politeness rose to the surface. Every word and gesture irritated them to no end, leading to exchanges of dark looks, and when polite insinuations no longer sufficed, they turned to swear words so vile that all hell broke loose and one of the men cracked the solid silver halva bowl over the head of the man sitting next to him.

When the servants of the House of Pleasure rushed into the room, trying to ascertain the cause of the tumult, they didn't know whether to laugh or cry at the scene unfolding before them.

The poor musicians were huddled in a corner, watching the men in terror and astonishment.

The smallest of the four guests, the only son of a famous banker in Galata, had seized a tambour from one of the musicians when the scuffle broke out and was chasing one of his fellow revelers around the room with it. The poor tambour player watched helplessly as the instrument he had inherited from his father was smashed over the head of an aristocrat.

Another pleasure seeker who owned a jeweler's shop in the Grand Bazaar had pinned down and was throttling a leather merchant famous in his social circles for the way he said, "My dear fellow!" with an emphasis on "dear." As he choked the man, he shouted, "I'll shove your dear fellow up your backside!"

When the servants were overpowered by the erstwhile polite gentlemen, they called for Sirrah's slaves to help them. The burly slaves first tried to restrain the guests, but when that proved futile they had no choice but to beat them until they passed out.

No one ever found out why the fight broke out, and Sirrah had to spend sacks of gold to pay for the damage. That day remained a secret between Master Adem and the cook, one they would occasionally mention with a sly smile.

Thus the cook spent his days at the House of Pleasure, working and enjoying himself when he could.

By this time, he was eleven years of age. And one day, a day he would always remember, something happened when he was in the small kitchen.

It was late afternoon and Master Adem was making stuffed apples. The cook was gnawing on a piece of sour apple which Master Adem had given him.

The Great Mansion, with its barred windows, was located behind and above the kitchens. It was out of bounds for guests, as it housed the private apartments, harem, and rooms of the owner. That was where Sirrah kept her treasures and indulged in her share of the pleasures the house offered. The slaves she bought stayed there when they were still children and she trained each according to their abilities as a singer, actor, dancer, servant, or guard. She had long since abandoned emotions like compassion or affection, and that mansion was like a hidden house of pain within the House of Pleasure.

The quiet in the kitchen was suddenly interrupted by Sirrah's voice. She appeared in the doorway of the kitchen, her eyes flashing fire. Standing next to her was the most beautiful person the cook had seen in his brief life. The girl was about the same age as him and she had black hair that hung down to her waist and large, dark, almond-shaped eyes.

She was so thin that her dark blue dress was falling off her shoulders and her bare ankles looked like they were as fragile as wishbones. Her cheeks were sunken, and her jaw and tiny nose were sharply defined. But her eyes . . . they reflected a determination that even Sirrah's violence could not sway, a tenacity that no punishment or torture could bend.

The cook stood frozen, an unchewed piece of apple still in his mouth. The smell and taste of sour apple were so entwined with the magic of that moment that years later he would affectionately tell the girl that she was "apple scented."

Sirrah said, "Master Adem, for the love of God, I'm at my wits end. This girl is going to be the death of me."

Master Adem put down the apple he was cutting and asked, "What's the matter?"

Grabbing the girl by the arm and shoving her into the kitchen, Sirrah replied, "What do you mean what's the matter? Don't you see? She looks like a crow! She won't eat anything. How can I have her around the customers in a state like this?"

The tips of Master Adem's moustache quivered in indignation. "What customers, Sirrah?" he asked quietly. "She is far too young."

Sirrah shrieked, "Are you going to teach me how to do my job, Adem? When I was her age, I brought down the tavern walls with applause. She's only going to dance, it's not so hard!"

Master Adem, who'd placed himself under Sirrah's control years ago, could do nothing but remain silent. "Have some decency," he muttered as he prepared a plate of beans they'd cooked for themselves and put it on the table along with a spoon.

"Come over here," he said to the girl in a kindly voice.

The girl wouldn't budge. She turned her gaze away from the table and looked around. This enraged Sirrah even more. She took the girl by the shoulders, sat her down in front of the plate of beans and snapped, "Eat, girl!"

She refused. Her eyes fixed on nothing, she sat there in a display of absolute calm. She even seemed to be smiling ever so slightly but there was also an occasional flicker of anger in her eyes.

Grabbing the spoon and scooping up some beans, Sirrah squeezed the girl's cheeks with her thick fingers, forcing her to open her mouth, and shoved in the spoonful of beans. The spoon was too big and it clattered against the girl's teeth. A jolt of pain went through the cook's heart as he watched the girl squeeze her eyes shut in agony. *She's going to start crying*, he thought to himself, but he was wrong. Resuming an indifferent expression, she turned her head and looked at her mistress as she began to slowly chew her food. Sirrah smiled deviously as if she'd won a victory. "You see?" she said, turning to Master Adem. "You have to know how to speak their language."

Of course Sirrah knew how to speak anybody's language, but she was unaware that she had a lot more to learn about the girl who was sitting in front of her. As she was talking, the girl suddenly sprayed the contents of her mouth all over Sirrah's face. She cast a sidelong glance at the cook and gave him a brief smile as she awaited her fate.

The cook smiled, and let out a little chortle. But his joy was painfully short-lived. Sirrah's revenge was swift and so cruel that it pained the cook's heart for the rest of his life.

Sirrah flung the girl to the ground and kicked her twice. Then she pulled her up by her hair, slapped her to the ground again, dragged her into the hallway between the two kitchens, and threw her into the tiny windowless room they used for storage. The girl didn't cry once, but caught the cook's eye for the briefest moment.

After shouting, "You are not to feed her anything! Not even a piece of bread or a sip of water!" Sirrah left the room, making the floorboards creak as she stomped away, leaving the kitchen in a state of silent unease. Master Adem went back to stuffing the apples, head bowed. His teeth were still clenched in anger but the lines of his face reflected defeat.

The master's job was hard. He made difficult dishes for difficult customers. He'd fallen on hard times himself but having to suffer injustice in silence was unlike any other hardship he had endured.

The cook started placing the tops back on the apples his master had stuffed. His hands were occupied, but his mind and ears were focused on the dark doorway of the storeroom. That last look the girl had cast him was burned into his memory. The passing of time was torture. As he went between the two kitchens, he slowed down every time he walked past the storeroom door and listened carefully, but he heard no sound, no breath, or even the slightest movement.

Darkness fell and the House of Pleasure echoed with laughter and lascivious cries. The cook was still thinking about the girl. Every time he remembered how cold and dark the room was, he shuddered. Then a spark of idea flashed through his mind. He left his room on tiptoe, not even putting on his shoes, and made his way to the large kitchen. In the wan light of the moon trickling through the high windows, he felt his way forward until he found among the sacks of grains one containing chickpeas that was nearly empty, and after depositing its contents in a secluded corner and waiting for the sound of the chickpeas rolling across the floor to fall silent, he silently made his way toward the door in the dark.

Clutching the empty sack, the cook paused to listen. When he heard nothing, he placed his ear on the door, but there was still no sound. He was afraid. He had been afraid before, very much so, but this time it was an altogether different kind of fear. A shaky voice within him kept asking, *What if something happened to her?* He wanted to knock on the door, but he changed his mind when he realized how loud it would be. Feeling helpless, he started pushing the empty sack through the gap under the door. The hallway was so quiet that the coarse fabric scratching against the wooden floorboards grated on his ears.

He heard a quick gasp behind the door, followed by a few quiet thumps. Not knowing what to do, the cook tried to pull the sack back and then thought better of it. Leaning against the door, he whispered, "Don't be afraid, it's me."

Silence. The cook got down on his knees, placed his cheek against the floorboards, and tried to peer under the door. At first he could see nothing but pitch darkness, but after a few moments he could discern the movement of a shadow.

The girl whispered, "Who's there?"

The cook smiled. "It's me, from the kitchen this morning."

The girl didn't respond.

The cook said, "Here, wrap this around yourself. It's cold in there."

Again the girl said nothing. The cook felt as though cracks were opening in his heart. Then the girl started pulling the sack toward her. The sack disappeared under the door and silence descended once more.

The cook remained sitting on his knees in front of the door. He was a bit hurt by the girl's silence, but far from unhappy. While he knew that someone could walk in on him at any moment, he didn't want to leave. He struck upon an idea to give him an excuse to stay longer.

Leaning down toward the gap below the door, he asked, "Are you hungry?" He waited for an answer, and when none came, he repeated the question again slightly louder.

A few moments later he got a stubborn response: "No, I'm not."

The cook smiled again. Trying to make his absence unnoticed, he got up and walked toward the kitchen. He wasn't quite sure what to do. He knew that he couldn't light a lamp, and even if he could, he wouldn't be able to cook anything without making some noise. As he was thinking, he suddenly noticed the smell which had been filling his nostrils for some time: the smell of apples. His feet directed him to the counter. He reached out and touched the two small apples Master Adem had left behind.

He found a knife and quietly sliced the unpeeled apples and then wondered how he would carry them to the girl. There were a few plates he could use, but they were all far too large and wouldn't fit under the door. "If only there was a handkerchief, or a towel," he whispered to himself. Then another idea occurred to him. He picked up the knife and cut a piece of cloth from the hem of his nightshirt. Carefully he placed the apples on the fabric.

Just as he was about to return to the door, he stopped in his tracks. He felt that something was missing, but he wasn't sure what it was. His instincts, which always whispered to him in a strange language telling him what was wrong and what was right, were telling him that the apple alone simply would not do. The apple needed more flavor, a different scent, one that was spicy and burned the throat ever so slightly, but also smelled of calmness and joy, like the spring sun.

Mentally he went through all the scents he'd gotten to know, thinking about how difficult it was to translate his emotions into another language. None of them were quite right. Finally, the cook came upon the answer.

Running the risk of making some noise, he reached toward the jars of spices on the shelf and grabbed a pinch of cloves. Placing them on the piece of cloth, he crushed them with the handle of the knife. He sprinkled the crushed cloves over the apple slices and inhaled the smell: the sour scent of the apple mingled perfectly with the sharp but refreshing clove.

Quickly he went back, pushed the small bundle under the door, and sat down to wait. At first there was no movement. A little while later, he heard a brief crunch and he lay down on the floor to listen. He was not mistaken. He could hear the sound of chewing behind the door, and with increasing speed. A smile spread across his face.

He whispered, "What's your name?"

The crunching stopped. The girl replied, "None of your business."

Those quiet words slipped through the gap under the door and struck the cook like a slap across the face, wiping away his smile. He was frozen in place, kneeling as if he were bent down on a prayer rug. Then another whisper floated under the door, this time friendlier. The voice seemed to caress his face before reaching his ears. The cook closed his eyes and listened. He wanted the sound of her voice to echo for all eternity: "My name is Kamer."

Another whisper brought him to his senses. Her voice was slightly stern, perhaps because she was asking for the second time. "What's your name?"

The cook paused. He didn't know which one of his names to tell her. Master Adem had given him a new name and told him to forget the name his mother had given him. That was easy to say, but difficult to do. Years had passed and still he wasn't accustomed to his name.

But he knew that wasn't how a name should work. Your soul had to respond to it before your ears. He had thought about the fact that there were perhaps tens of thousands, hundreds of thousands of people on earth who shared the same name, but even though they consisted of the same syllables, every name was unique and merged with a particular soul. If you lost your name, it was like losing your soul.

The cook whispered his name under the door—his new name, the one everyone called him. The girl repeated his name. He heard her. Perhaps for the first time in all those years, he actually heard his new name. When the girl's lips whispered his name and it reached his ears, it took on its true meaning.

When people's names are spoken, it is just sound, and nothing else. Sometimes, though, someone comes along and says your name in such a way that both the speaker and the listener are moved. That utterance begins not in the mouth, nor does it end in the ear, but both begins and ends in the heart, freeing itself from the fetters of language, purifying itself and remaining a pure sound that echoes in the hearts of both people. When your name finally assumes its meaning, your soul is freed from being a mere ghost and settles into the body that is its shrine, sparkling inside the eyes which are its mirrors. That doesn't happen to everyone, but if it does, it means you have managed to live life a little more. And if you lose it, it means dying a little more.

On that day, as young as he was, the cook may not have realized all of that. Like so many others, he would realize what he had only after he lost it. But one thing was for certain: From that day onwards, the cook never felt like he was a stranger to his new name again.

Of course, that magical night didn't only change the cook; Kamer's soul also danced with life. Afterwards, she smiled more and started to eat. She knew that if she grew and became prettier, Sirrah would have her dancing in front of the guests all the sooner. But Kamer was no longer so afraid. Something inside of her always felt warm. However alone or helpless she felt, a part of her felt safe. She kept dreaming and didn't yet know that hope was the name of the unexplainable joy that pulsed inside her even during her darkest moments of despair.

Master Adem started preparing special dishes for the girl every day. That was on Sirrah's orders, of course. With her young but keen intellect, Kamer had figured out how much value her mistress placed on her and began to use it to her advantage. Every morning she would tell the kitchen what food she fancied that day, and the master would cook the dishes the young lady desired. That meant a little more work for the already busy kitchen, but Master Adem didn't mind, and the cook was thrilled.

In the first few days of this arrangement, the cook took advantage of the chaos of the kitchen and tried to prepare Kamer's food by himself, but Master Adem, who had one eye perpetually locked on him, noticed what he was trying to do and once again prevented him from making an entire dish on his own. He raised no objection to the cook preparing the finished meal for presentation, however, and that was all the opportunity the cook needed.

The cook had started placing small gifts for Kamer on the bottom of the plate before spooning in the food. At times it was a few walnuts he secretly boiled in sugar water, a few meatballs he cooked up when no one was looking, or if he was really pressed for time, a crushed bay leaf.

After every meal, Kamer would sing a song through the window of her prison-like room on the top floor of the mansion.

About ten days after the first night they had whispered their names to each other under the door, all hell broke loose on one of the floors above the kitchen. Sirrah was shouting again and then suddenly she appeared in the kitchen, face bright red, with Kamer in her clutches. No one dared ask what she had done wrong.

As the cook helplessly watched the familiar scene unfold once again, he saw Kamer cast him a mischievous grin. Her eyes spoke one sentence: "I've missed you!"

The smell of sour apples filled the cook's nostrils and his emotions were in turmoil; on the one hand, he felt joy, but on the other, despite everything, he felt rage, and there was also the terrible burden that such a sacrifice placed on his heart.

The cook waited impatiently for nightfall. When everyone withdrew, he once again made his way on tiptoe to the small room, lay down on the floor in front of the door, and whispered her name. They talked until morning; to be more precise, Kamer talked and the cook listened. And she told him so much: where she had been born, the house she'd grown up in, how she was sold to slave merchants, how she arrived at the House of Pleasure, Sirrah . . .

But in all truth the cook didn't hear much of it. Her voice was like a melody for him rather than a means of conveying ideas. As long as he heard her voice, it didn't matter to the cook what she was telling him. He wasn't old enough to realize that in addition to being a magical kind of joy, what he was experiencing was also a sinister curse. However, even as he got older he wouldn't be able to shake that off, and he didn't learn the error of his ways until years later when a woman finally told him; even then he didn't listen. If he could've released himself from the grip of that curse and actually listened, he would've been able to understand how much he mattered to her. He would learn far too late how precious the feeling of missing someone was for a girl who had never missed anything or anyone in her entire life.

After talking for hours on end, Kamer stopped and said, "Tell me about your life."

The cook returned from his reverie. He felt anxious, the cause of which he couldn't pin down. He muttered a few incoherent words like a child who had just awoken from a dream. He knew that he couldn't talk about his past. He couldn't have even if Master Adem hadn't told him to stay silent. Not because he was afraid of what would happen, but because he was afraid of the words themselves. He hadn't truly thought about what happened that night in the Harem. The idea of putting into words what he had experienced, what happened to his father, and especially what happened to his mother, caused a terrible fear to take hold of his heart. But he couldn't lie, either. Even though a voice deep within was screaming at him to make up a different past for himself, the cook couldn't risk lying, no matter how small the chance of the truth eventually coming out. Even if his young mind wasn't consciously aware that even the worst truth was more forgivable than a lie, he knew it in his heart.

"I'll tell you later," he replied.

Kamer's voice took on a sharper edge. "What do you mean?"

"I'll tell you later," the cook repeated, and added, "But you mustn't tell anyone."

Kamer's whispering voice was tinged with anger. "What is there to tell? You haven't told me anything!"

The cook's voice assumed an anxious seriousness. "Don't even tell anyone that. You mustn't tell anyone that I said I'll tell you about it later."

Kamer fell silent. She didn't broach the subject again until years later when the cook told her about his past.

That night, the cook stayed by the door until early morning. He didn't care that it was cold, nor did he feel the ache of having stayed on knees on the hard floor for hours on end. He started to miss Kamer the moment he went back to his own room. But he was also happy, because he knew Kamer would find a way to be sent to the storeroom room again.

Which is exactly what happened.

Not even a week had gone by before Kamer found another way to infuriate Sirrah, and she was locked up in the storeroom again to suffer her sweet punishment. The same pattern continued in the following weeks and seemed to be set to continue until someone noticed. But the cook had had enough and wanted to take matters into his own hands.

Of course, every night of punishment for Kamer meant a night of joy, but cruelty and pain were also a part of it. The cook could no longer endure the way she would be beaten. The torment grew with each day until it became insufferable. Knowing that Kamer's cheeks were still stinging with the pain of Sirrah's slaps hurt him, and talking with her knowing that she had suffered to be there with him wounded his pride.

For nights on end the cook tried to come up with a solution but his efforts were in vain, so he started to wander around looking for another way to be able to see her. The solution came to him, as it often did, in the form of the most obvious place: the roof of the kitchen.

The small kitchen was built up against the back of the Great Mansion. To ensure that the smoke from the four large chimneys on the roof didn't get into the mansion, there were no windows on that side of the building. Kamer's room was at the very top of the building, and he figured she could easily reach the rooftop from there.

The cook made two rather unsightly but sturdy ladders using some oak planks that were sent to the kitchen. One was for himself, so he could climb up to the roof of the kitchen, and the other was for Kamer, so she could climb down to the roof.

On their last night whispering to each other under the door, he explained his plan to Kamer, and he felt her heartbeat become one with the beating of his own heart.

"Will you be able to get down onto the roof?" he asked. She gave him a bright laugh in reply.

On the night they decided to meet up, the cook first climbed up to the roof using his own ladder and then he pulled Kamer's ladder up with a rope. He leaned it against the wall of the mansion. It was toward the end of April and there was a huge full moon. The cook waited breathlessly, his gaze fixed on the ladder as he prayed nothing would go wrong.

At last Kamer appeared on the edge of the roof. They looked at each other, one looking up from below, one looking down from above. They were free of Sirrah and Master Adem, and their time was their own. Kamer began to climb down the ladder. She was wearing a dark blue frock the cook had never seen before, and her hair was blowing in the gentle breeze.

In the cook's mind, Kamer looked like an angel who'd descended from the starry sky to the moonlit earth. She ran toward him and stopped a few paces away. She had pulled back her face veil and pinned it above her forehead, making her beautiful eyes even more stunning. The April wind blew a few strands of her carefully combed hair across her cheek. Her name meant "moon" and it was as if the moon was using all its light to illuminate its namesake on earth that night. The ivory light glowed on Kamer's fair skin, lighting up her cheeks, nervous smile, pearl hair pin, and the silver embroidery of her dress.

Neither of them said a word. No words existed that could suit such a moment, so they stood motionless, gazing at each other. The cook suddenly felt a warm, soft tingle in his fingertips and then his heart seemed to suddenly stop beating. But he could hear the wind and feel it caressing his skin. The scent of apples filled his nostrils and his fingertips were alive with that pleasant heat.

Later, he wouldn't be able to recall if he'd said anything. All he remembered was that they'd sat down with their backs against the chimney farthest from the mansion. Silently they watched the sky, occasionally glancing at each other, which made them break into shy smiles. That night, everything seemed to have been created for them alone. The moon had risen so they could watch it, the stars were there to decorate the sky above them, the House of Pleasure had been built so they could meet, and the roof was there so they could finally be together. Sirrah had bought the girl from a slave trader for that night, and the cook's mother had sacrificed herself so he could meet Kamer. All the suffering and joy in their lives, everything they had lived through, had happened for that night, so they could be together.

That was how the story of apples and cloves began.

The longer he spent working in the Imperial Kitchens, the quicker time seemed to pass.

The cook had been there for nearly four weeks and stores in the cellar were still dwindling. The idea of planning the dishes they would cook a week in advance hadn't worked as anticipated, and the people who suffered as a result were the lowest-ranking inhabitants of the palace. The concubines, palace guards, novices, and servants had to eat the same dishes at least three times a week, while those from the higher ranks continued to relay their requests to their personal cooks, not caring whether there was a shortage or not. As a result, the Imperial Kitchens had to keep borrowing from the Cooks' Union to make ends meet.

The fact that a new treasurer still had not been appointed made matters even worse. Sadık Agha, Halil Pasha's scribe, had been appointed as his successor, but he only lasted two days. After realizing the dire situation the Treasury was in, he begged the sultan to remove him from the post, even at the risk of losing his rank or possibly facing exile. The Interior Minister, Lütfü Pasha, was asked to step in. Everyone knew that he knew little about monetary matters. Master İsfendiyar explained it all very well when he said, "If he knew anything about handling money, he wouldn't have agreed to take the position in the first place." The defining quality of the new acting Treasurer was that he was one of the most loyal followers of the Grand Vizier, meaning it was unlikely he would quit.

As the world outside went about its business and matters of state unfolded, within the walls of the Imperial Kitchens the familiar routine continued in humdrum fashion.

Every morning with the morning call to prayer the stoves were lit, and the cooks emerged from their lodgings and got to work. Until lunchtime knives clattered and cauldrons boiled. After the lunch dishes were sent out, the apprentices would wash dishes and the masters would get started on preparations for dinner.

The cook was teaching Mahir everything from scratch as if he wasn't his assistant but an apprentice who was setting foot for the first time in the kitchen. The boy tried his best, but apart from his mysterious talent for making rice, he was hopeless when it came to anything else.

One afternoon, the cook was in the Odalisques' Kitchen again, helping prepare the food that would be sent to the Harem. The surprises he placed under the food had become a source of great entertainment for the concubines, as they led a dull, predictable life.

The cook tried his best to keep his notoriety at the Harem from spreading too far. He had already achieved what he wanted: the Black Eunuch who came to pick up the food every day was on friendly terms with him. He knew that if his fame spread any further, it could actually prove to be a hindrance.

The Black Eunuch who was responsible for picking up the concubines' food and returning the empty crockery was an Abyssinian slave named Neyyir. He was taller than three ells, and it was said that when they'd discovered a scale sturdy enough to weigh him, he weighed exactly one hundred and ten *oka*.

Since Neyyir Agha had been castrated at a very young age, there was a childish softness to his face and voice, which, coupled with his huge stature, gave him a striking appearance. The manners of speech that were common to all those who were trained at the palace seemed out of place when he used them, and even when he was being his politest, one couldn't help but wonder what would happen if that huge hand of his, gliding through the air like a swan, swung down with the intention of delivering a slap to the face.

Just like every day, after the food was portioned out and the lids of the pots were closed, Neyyir Agha arrived with the meal-bearers trailing behind him. Gravely, he watched the meal-bearers go about their work and once he was convinced that everything was perfectly arranged, he approached the cook in two huge strides and said with a smile, "I wonder what's at the bottom of the pots today?"

The cook had to crane his neck to look the eunuch in the face. Smiling in return he said, "Well, I supposed you'll have to eat down to the bottom to find out."

Neyyir Agha once again turned to the meal-bearers. His smile was gone, replaced by a haughty mask and courtly seriousness. He lingered by the cook, seemingly waiting for something.

When the meal-bearers put the cover on the last tray and securely fastened everything down with ropes, they lined up in front of the Black Eunuch, who nodded for them to pick up the trays. Then he said to them, "Wait for me in front of the Gate of Felicity."

After the last of the meal-bearers left the kitchen, Neyyir Agha said, "Well done to all," and followed them out. There was nothing out of the ordinary in his behavior apart from the fact that he lightly brushed against the cook as he walked by. Master Bekir told his assistants to tidy up and his apprentices to start cleaning. Picking up his grindstone, he sat down on a low stool to sharpen his knives, just as he did every evening.

The cook waited for a short while to make sure everyone was busy with their work before going into the courtyard. As he had guessed, Neyyir Agha was waiting for him on the corner of the porticos in front of the kitchen, watching the meal-bearers head off in various directions. The cook saw Firuz Agha and his entourage walking toward the Gate of Felicity. A boy behind Firuz Agha was carrying the Chief Sword Bearer's dinner. At the rear of the entourage there was a man carrying a sack of bread, and the cook knew that at the bottom of the sack was a porcelain bowl containing freshly fried sweets with cheese because he had put it there as a dessert for the page boys of the Privy Chamber.

When the courtyard was empty at last, the cook approached Neyyir Agha. Without taking his eyes off the meal-bearers who were waiting for him near the Gate of Felicity, he said to the cook, "Yet again you've done well, Master Effendi."

"Thank you," replied the cook. "But it's not over yet. Once everyone eats and we receive no complaints, only then can we feel at ease."

The Black Eunuch glanced at the cook. "You've nothing to worry about," he said. "After all, you cook for the Chief Sword Bearer, the most difficult person to please within the walls of this palace. The fact that His Highness the Agha is content with your cooking is known to everyone. If you don't receive any complaints from him, who could ever say a word against you?"

The cook replied, "Here, we are all one and the same. If one kitchen receives a complaint, we are all held responsible."

"I understand," Neyyir Agha responded, but his thoughts were elsewhere. Drawing a little closer, he continued, "But what I don't understand, Master Effendi, is why you want to help in the Odalisques' Kitchen as well, when your burden is as heavy as it is. Why create more work for yourself?"

If the Black Eunuch had been looking not into the cook's eyes but at his chest, he may have seen that his heart was pounding wildly. Despite this, the young cook's expression was impassive. He leaned toward

Neyyir Agha and said, "If you love your art, it becomes your life. For us, the rank of who we cook for matters nothing. The more palates a cook pleases, the happier he will feel. Besides, not everyone is lucky enough to work with a cook as talented as Master Bekir and learn from him. I'm not making life more difficult for myself but seizing the opportunities that come my way."

Neyyir Agha did not reply. He kept his eyes trained on the cook's face, trying to read his expression. The cook saw the agha's huge hand reaching into his cloak. His instincts told him to step away but he remained where he was and kept his eyes fixed on the agha's. "Then please accept this, Master Effendi," Neyyir Agha said, "as a reward for the love you feel for your work."

The cook looked at the large bottle Neyyir Agha was holding within the folds of his cloak. "Kandiye wine," the Black Eunuch continued. "It was taken from Haseki Sultan's personal cellar to be presented to you as a token of the odalisques' appreciation."

The cook was surprised. "That is most kind of them," he stammered. He wondered if Kamer had been one of the odalisques who sent the wine or even suggested the idea herself, but then he realized that she would never take such a risk.

Neyyir Agha handed him the wine, wishing him a pleasant evening as he did, and just as he was about to head toward the Gate of Felicity, the cook said, "Pardon my curiosity, but I have a question myself."

The Black Eunuch was intrigued, as the cook usually spoke very little. "But of course," he said.

The cook knew well the danger his question could put him in. But in the end his curiosity and longing overcame him. "I sometimes go out into the courtyard at night to get some fresh air," he explained, "and at certain times I hear the sound of singing coming from the Harem. Forgive me for my impertinence, but I was very curious because her voice is so lovely. Who sings those songs?"

Neyyir Agha smiled and answered without hesitation. "Who could it be? The Harem's greatest nuisance. Her name is Nur-i Leyl. You're right, she has a beautiful voice, but what use is that? I've been at the Harem for many years, and I've never seen a lady so obstinate, cross, or proud. She was supposedly given as a gift to the Harem so she could entertain Haseki Sultan and please her with her voice and dance, but there's no chance of that. Suppose there's a banquet and you tell her to sing—she won't open her mouth. But give her a lashing and she sings like a nightingale. You tell her to dance, and she stands as still as a statue. But if you throw her into the dungeon, she dances in her cell. So many haughty, headstrong girls have become meek and mild within the walls of the Imperial Harem, but that one has confounded us all. I myself don't know how we'll get rid of such a nuisance. Haseki Sultan keeps berating us for not having set her straight yet. God forbid we suffer for her disobedience in the end."

Neyyir Agha was breathless and his face was flushed. The cook was biting the insides of his cheeks to keep himself from laughing. "I see," he finally managed to say, sincerely adding, "May God make your work easier."

After bidding the cook farewell, the Black Eunuch strode toward the meal-bearers and the cook returned to the kitchen.

His emotions were wavering between anger, impatience, yearning, and determination, but above all he felt happy. For years he had kept Kamer alive in his mind as a dream, but now the ghost in his mind had at last taken on a bodily form. He no longer had to carry her within his memories, imagine her in idle daydreams, or see her in his dreams and nightmares and wonder if she was real.

The calm that settled over the kitchens at the end of the day also descended upon the Aghas' Kitchen. The cooks had left and the handful of assistants and apprentices who remained wearily placed the crockery and cutlery back on the shelves. The only person still bristling with energy was Mahir. He was sitting by the stove, wiping down chopping boards with a piece of cloth. The cook approached him quietly from behind and asked, "Almost finished?"

Startled, Mahir turned around. "Thank you, Master, yes," he said, getting up.

The cook looked over his assistant. He seemed nervous and his hands were shaking. "What's wrong?" he asked.

"You shouldn't have had me cook that dish," Mahir replied, tears welling up in his eyes. "I'm sure I got it wrong."

The cook smiled. Earlier that day, he had told his assistant that he could make one of the dishes for the Chief Sword Bearer's dinner himself, to the surprise of Mahir and the rest of the people in the kitchen. The dish in question was meat and celery root stew. Mahir had thought he was joking at first. When the cook repeated his request, Mahir protested. In the previous weeks, Mahir seemed to have gained some confidence, but he was still level-headed enough to know that he shouldn't cook anything that would be served to the Chief Sword Bearer by himself.

When the cook had loudly repeated his request for the third time, Mahir obediently took his place at the table and started sullenly pulling leaves off celery stalks.

The cook knew that meat and celery stew was a difficult dish to prepare. In addition, it was almost spring and the winter vegetables were no longer so fresh. But he was also certain of two things. First, Siyavuş Agha was no connoisseur of cuisine, contrary to what he wanted everyone to believe. Second, a single whisper from the Pasha of Cuisine would be powerful enough to make up for a thousand faults in a dish.

Mahir had made his first mistake by roasting the meat for too long, as it would cook again along with celery inside dove meat covered in dough, and by doing so, he spoiled not only the appearance of the dish but its taste.

The seasoning was an utter disaster. And because Mahir was incapable of learning how to measure out the spices, he had tried repeating the seasoning a second time, filling the kitchen with a rancid stench in the process. That was the only time the cook stepped in to help. With a few whispers, the stench had vanished and the dish became at least slightly more edible.

The cook looked at his apprentice, who was trembling as if an executioner's noose had been wound around his neck and asked, "Mahir, did you not taste the food you cooked?"

"I did, Master," Mahir stammered.

"And? Was there anything missing? Anything in excess? Were all the spices and the salt right?"

"It seemed right to me," Mahir replied.

Poor boy, he's hopeless, the cook thought.

Mahir continued, "But we're talking about the Chief Sword Bearer. Will he like it just as I did?"

The cook sighed. "Is it your hands you don't trust, or your palate? Suppose you know nothing of cooking or enjoying food. Did I not taste it?"

"You did, Master," Mahir replied, abashed.

"Did I tell you it was fine?"

"You did."

"Whose sense of taste do you trust more? Mine or the agha's?"

Mahir fixed his eyes on the ground. "Yours, Master. Of course."

"Well, there you have it!" said the cook. "I'm telling you for the last time, your cooking was fine."

After a pause, and with tears welling up in his eyes again, Mahir said, "But Master! We're talking about the Chief Sword Bearer. What if he doesn't like it? We'll be ruined."

The cook looked at Mahir, thinking how terrible it must be to be untalented, ambitious, and cowardly all at once. "Don't worry, Mahir," he replied. "We could open a soup shop in Galata if that were to happen. It's not the end of the world."

Mahir fell silent.

Just as the cook was about to leave, he turned around and asked, "Did the Privy Chamber Page say anything?"

After hesitating for a moment, Mahir replied, "He thanked you for the pastries, Master."

The cook fixed his eyes on his assistant. "Anything else?"

Mahir thought for a bit, looked at the apprentices milling around, stepped closer to his master and said in a near whisper, "He spoke ill of the Chief Sword Bearer again, Master. The other day he even swore about the agha. I pretended not to hear. It scares me, Master, you know the walls have ears."

The cook nodded. He knew that his assistant was quite right to be afraid because if Siyavuş Agha was to hear what the page was saying about him, he would bring to ruin not only who spoke those words but anyone who heard them. But he knew he had to take that risk, and in any case when the time was right, he would set matters straight.

Leaving his assistant to his worries and fears, the cook withdrew to the lodgings. He wanted to rest until the evening call to prayer and then, just like he did at the end of every day when he hid a surprise at the bottom of the pots, he planned to go and listen to Kamer sing.

He spent a few hours lying half-awake in bed thinking of Kamer. Then he went to the masjid before anyone else, quickly performed his prayers, and went downstairs. As he walked through the narrow passageway in front of the kitchens, he decided to go out into the courtyard and stand under the oak tree as he had done before. But when he saw a ladder propped up against the confectionery wall, he stopped, checked to make sure no one was around, and quickly returned to the lodgings. He took the bottle of wine he had hidden in his trunk and went back downstairs. No one was around. Quickly he walked through the Kitchens' Passageway and climbed up to the roof using the ladder. As soon as he reached the roof, he felt a sense of relief. He remembered how much he'd missed being alone. For weeks, from the moment he woke up until he went to bed at night, he'd been surrounded by people, which exhausted him. He breathed in the cool night air as if it were an elixir. Sitting down, he leaned back against one of the chimneys just as he had done years before at the House of Pleasure. Soon, Kamer would join him.

He removed the stopper of the bottle and smelled its contents. He took a small sip. It was exquisite, and he decided that it definitely merited a place in Haseki Sultan's cellar.

He thought about all that he heard during the day. Neyyir Agha had called Kamer "Nur-i Leyl," meaning "light of the night." He disliked the name, and muttered to himself, "What a farce! Couldn't they have come up with something better?"

As he sipped his wine, another thought occurred to him: Kamer had lost her name as well! No one else could better understand the trying times he'd been through. The cook made himself another promise: he was going to give Kamer her name back.

Just then, as if attesting to his promise, a song began to drift from the domes of the Harem up toward the sky. The words of the song were sad but her voice didn't sound as dejected as it had before. He assumed the cheer in her voice was due to none other than the crackers coated with *tulum* cheese and Kastamonu garlic which he had hidden at the bottom of the pots. The cook knew that cheese reminded one of home, love, and childhood, which was why it was the closest companion of bread, and the warm nature of garlic filled one with vivacity.

Kamer sang:

"No one but the fire in my heart burns for me,
No one but the morning wind opens my door . . ."

The cook listened with his eyes closed, hardly taking a breath. He didn't want to hear, see, or sense anything aside from her voice. His heart seemed to have stopped again and he was filled with silence. He felt as if Kamer was right beside him, sitting with her back to the chimney, as if he could touch her if he reached out.

The song ended and the spell was broken. The cook was alone with the night, with his yearning and despair.

And the sole remedy was wine.

The next day he couldn't quite remember how he got down the ladder or into bed. When he woke up in the morning, still feeling the effects of the wine, the first thing he did was check himself for injuries. *Thank God I didn't hurt myself,* he thought.

The day had started as usual and appeared set to continue in the same way. When he stepped into the kitchen, he found the Privy Chamber Page waiting for him just like every morning. But he sensed that something strange was happening. Master İsfendiyar and the Royal Kitchen's head cook were also standing next to the page.

The cook approached them with measured steps, nodded to the cooks, and bid them good morning. All three men were looking at him in silence. Master İsfendiyar turned to the Privy Chamber Page and said, "Go ahead."

Firuz Agha looked nervous. "Master Effendi," he began, "the praises of your name have reached the ears of Our Lord the Sultan. He wishes for you to cook for him."

The cook tried to conceal his excitement, but not because he wanted to make a show of modesty. He knew that he had to remain calm and keep his mind clear, because he was about to take a major step in his plan. That was precisely what he had been waiting for since the very beginning.

At the same time, he was internally cursing his luck. Because of a delay beyond his control, he wasn't prepared yet and he knew that he had to act quick. "Our gracious sultan's wish is my command," he replied, his voice steady. "I shall try to be worthy of the honor he has bestowed upon me."

"Doubtless you will," the page replied. His voice seemed sincere but his expression betrayed an unease that the cook could not understand. He continued, "Our sovereign will be having dinner with His Highness the Chief Sword Bearer in two days' time. You will create a single dish for their meal."

The cook bowed, saluting the ultan in absentia. "It will be my pleasure. Is there anything in particular our sovereign wishes to partake of?"

"You are free to choose to prepare whatever you like."

The Royal Kitchen's head cook cut in, glancing condescendingly at the cook, and said, "You shall cook in the Royal Kitchen. If there are any ingredients you require, you need only ask, and we shall bring them to you immediately. I would also like to offer my congratulations. You will be the youngest cook to step foot in the Royal Kitchen in the history of the Imperial Kitchens. Am I right, Master İsfendiyar?"

The master slowly nodded. He looked at the cook with concern in his eyes. "He's far too young."

The cook knew well why Master İsfendiyar was concerned and what he was trying to imply. "Please don't be troubled," he said. Then he turned to the Royal Kitchen's head cook and said, "I am aware of the gravity of the request made of me. I will endeavor to be worthy of it."

"God willing," the three men replied in unison. After casting one last glance at the cook, Master İsfendiyar left with the Royal Kitchens's head cook.

Checking to make sure that no one was eavesdropping, the cook lowered his voice and asked, "How did this happen? Do you have any idea?"

"Of course," the Privy Chamber Page replied. "The Chief Sword Bearer has sung your praises so often that he finally managed to even interest our sovereign."

The cook nodded. Neither the fact that the page did not refer to the Chief Sword Bearer as "His Highness" nor the anger that twisted his features each time he uttered the name had escaped his attention. "What's troubling you?" he asked. "You don't seem well. Is there a problem at the Inner Palace?"

The page was grinding his teeth. "How could there not be a problem, Master Effendi?" he asked, his voice trembling with rage. "The problem is right at the top of the Inner Palace before our very eyes!"

The cook feigned incomprehension. "What ever do you mean?"

The Privy Chamber Page sneered, "That Siyavuş Agha is out of control! As soon as he wakes up, he starts tormenting us. There's no one in the whole of the Inner Palace, including me, who he hasn't had beaten! And under such pretenses! I wouldn't be able to think one of them up if I thought about it for forty years. Once he has eaten, he calms down for a while, but then he starts up again. I swear to you, we all look forward to meal times, because we know we'll get a little respite. Master Effendi, sometimes, I think to myself . . ."

The page trailed off. The words he was about to utter frightened even him.

"Can't our sovereign do anything about it? If you were to mention something?" the cook asked, even though he knew what the answer would be.

The page would have laughed it off, but he felt compelled to reply out of respect. "You don't know what it's like at the Inner Palace, Master Effendi. We call Siyavuş Agha the 'Agha of Permission.' You can't even approach Our Lord the Sultan without him getting wind of it first. He constantly circles around our sovereign, never leaving his side. Let's say we could find a way and whispered in his ear . . ."

Firuz Agha lowered his voice even more. "Even our sovereign is afraid of Siyavuş Agha's malice. Think about it, he has heard your praises so many times, but didn't appoint you directly to the Royal Kitchen. Why? Because you are the agha's personal cook. Obviously he wouldn't dare take you from him."

"Please," the cook replied in astonishment, "how could that be? Our sovereign must be exceedingly pleased with his present cook so he wouldn't deign to appoint me in his place. How could a sultan who rules over half the world be intimidated by a mere agha? Your nerves must be frayed."

The page smiled bitterly. "You are right, my nerves are indeed frayed, but I speak the truth. No matter, may God grant a good end to us all."

"Amen," replied the cook. "What would His Highness the Agha like to eat today?"

The page opened his mouth to speak, then said, "God forgive me," and closed it again. Then he said, "For lunch he would like Davud Pasha meatballs and *levzine,* and for dinner he would like milk kebab."

"It will be my pleasure," the cook responded. He gave Firuz Agha a bow, and the Privy Chamber Page responded in kind. Before leaving, he asked one last question: "So, what will you cook for our sultan?"

The cook knew he had to think long on the matter. "I haven't decided yet."

As the page left, the cook grumbled to himself, "It's been weeks now, where have you been?"

After spending a few moments lost in thought, his features contorted in pain, he called for Mahir. His assistant had been milling around ever since he arrived that morning, waiting for the moment he would be needed. He ran up to his master, his eyes sparkling. With a big smile and a deep bow, he said, "My Master, may this bring you even more good fortune!"

"God willing, Mahir," the cook replied. "Now, what you need to do is—"

Mahir didn't appear to be hearing anything he was told. "Will I be able to come along as well, Master?" he excitedly asked.

"Come along where, Mahir?"

Mahir looked confused. "To the Royal Kitchen, Master."

"Are you not my assistant?" the cook scolded him playfully. "You go wherever I go."

Mahir grinned. "Thank you, Master."

The cook smiled back. "But leave tomorrow's business for tomorrow. Let's get through today first. We've a lot to do."

Mahir asked, "What did the Chief Sword Bearer request?"

When the cook told him, Mahir's eyes widened. The dishes Siyavuş Agha had requested were known as "meals of elegance," that is, dishes that were exceedingly difficult to make. Mahir couldn't have known that, of course, but they revealed much to the cook about the agha's state of mind.

"Start shelling some almonds, Mahir. Soak them in water and peel them, and then grind two handfuls in the mortar and put the rest through the mill. Then dry them in a pan. But make sure you don't roast them."

As Mahir went to the shelves to get the almonds, the cook grabbed a cleaver and started mincing the meat he was going to use for the meatballs.

A short while later Mahir returned with a small sack in his hand. "Is this enough almonds?" he asked.

The cook checked the contents of the sack and nodded. "You can get started."

Mahir filled a medium-sized bowl with water and soaked the almonds. The cook, who was working the meat with his knife, was thinking about Siyavuş Agha.

The dishes the agha requested were becoming increasingly complex. The cook surmised that the wounds in his soul were deepening and that the power and control he wielded no longer sufficed to ease his suffering or fill the void inside him. Helpless, he was reverting to old habits in the hope of rediscovering the peace of mind he had lost, habits based on pride and cruelty.

But the cook knew that what the agha didn't; that pride and cruelty, which he needed more of every day, would only worsen his agony, not alleviate it. He knew that because every day he ate the food that the cook prepared for him.

After the cook chopped the meat into a fine mince and mixed it with salt, pepper, cumin, and red pepper flakes, he started rolling out bite-sized balls from the mixture. He looked over and saw that Mahir had managed to dry the almonds without roasting them. As the cook ran his fingers through the almond flour, he instructed his assistant to fetch him some honey and water.

Mahir made his way back to the shelves and returned shortly after with a small pitcher of honey and a jug of water. Meanwhile, the cook put the almond flour into a deep pot which he placed over low heat.

"Listen carefully," he told his assistant. "As I stir the almonds, you pour in the honey. But do it carefully, so that the stream of honey is as thin as a thread. When I tell you to add water, do it slowly. Understand?"

Mahir nodded. The cook rolled up his sleeves and reminded Mahir one last time before starting, "Keep a steady hand!"

When he was sure his assistant understood, he started stirring the pot. As more honey was added, the thicker the almond flour became, and as more water was added, the thinner it became. As the cook stirred the mixture for the *levzine* more and more quickly, he was thinking about the milk kebab he would make for dinner. He knew he had to find good cuts of meat and fresh milk. He would first boil the meat in milk twice and then skewer it so he could roast it over low heat, pouring milk over the meat as it cooked. It wasn't extremely difficult but it took time and required careful attention, so he knew he couldn't leave it to Mahir.

The cook stirred the *levzine* until the heat in the kitchen made him break out in a sweat, but finally it took on the consistency he desired. He sampled the thick amber-colored mixture in the pot with the tip of his finger and decided that it wouldn't be necessary to whisper anything over it. He was saving that for the Davud Pasha meatballs.

"Pour it into a tray to cool it," he instructed his assistant.

"Shall I cook the rice afterwards?" Mahir asked.

The cook thought for a moment. "No," he replied, "I'll do it myself. You run along to the stewards' office and get me a piece of paper and a pen."

"Of course," Mahir replied, though he didn't see the point of the request.

As Mahir ran to the cellar, the cook began to thinly slice a large onion, which he fried in oil, and then he added the meatballs to the pan. Just as he had added some ground almonds and began to roast them, his assistant returned bearing a pen, paper, and a small inkwell. He stood to one side to await further orders.

When the meatballs were cooked and the almonds were ivory in color, the cook transferred the pot to a stove with a lower heat and squeezed in the juice of a lemon.

"Bring me the pen and paper," he told Mahir as he closed the lid. He took the pen, dipped it in the ink, and quickly wrote a few lines on the paper. He gave the piece of paper to Mahir and said, "Go to the Grand Bazaar and find Herbalist Naim Effendi's shop in the Lesser Saffron Market. Send him my greetings, pick up the items on the list, and come straight back."

Mahir glanced at the piece of paper. It was a simple list of herbs: Chinese cinnamon, Ashanti pepper, poppy seeds, aniseed, Indian mint.

"The cellar might have all these, Master," Mahir said. "Shall I check before I go?"

The cook looked at his assistant. "We're cooking for the sultan. Who knows how long the spices in the cellar have been there."

"You're right, Master," Mahir said. He checked the list once more and said, "Okay then, I will go now."

The cook grabbed him by the arm as he was about to run out. "Wait. If Naim Effendi tells you 'We're out of these,' tell him, 'My master needs as much as you've got, and he needs it all by tomorrow evening at the latest.' Do you understand?"

"I understand, Master."

The cook squeezed his arm a little tighter. "By tomorrow evening! As much as he can find. Got it?"

Mahir looked at his master's hand holding his arm. "I understand," he meekly replied and set off for the Grand Bazaar.

The cook approached the shelves, looking for rice for the saffron rice he was going to make. In the meanwhile, he was thinking about the following night. He could easily ask Master İsfendiyar for permission to leave, but he didn't know how long his business would take or how long he would need to wait. He knew that he might not be able to return to the palace until the next morning, meaning he had to come up with another solution. He decided that in the worst case he would leave after the evening prayers and return before dawn, but he didn't want to rouse any suspicions.

Then he thought of an idea which made him smile: *Why sneak off when I can walk out the gate? And who knows, maybe I'll get even more than I bargained for.*

It was almost time for the afternoon prayers. The cook had completed his work and Mahir was nowhere to be seen. Like every assistant sent on an errand to the outside world, he took his time returning. The cook wasn't upset. In fact, he enjoyed spending time without Mahir by his side. The only problem would be having to listen to his excuses for why he was late on his return. "I wish I'd given him the rest of the day off," he muttered to himself. Just then Firuz Agha and his retinue arrived to pick up the dishes he had prepared.

Avoiding small talk, the cook handed over the agha's food and apologized for not having been able to prepare dessert for the pages. "Forgive me, I sent my assistant to the market. I was alone the whole day."

"Of course, you're not obliged to give us something every single day," replied Firuz Agha, but disappointment tugged a crease between his eyebrows.

Of course, Mahir's absence was just an excuse. The cook wasn't pleased with the Privy Chamber Page's behavior in the morning, which was why he didn't make any sweets. It occurred to him that if Firuz Agha, who was one of the most respectful of the Inner Palace pages, was in such a state, the others must be much worse off. He knew that any untoward incidents could dash his plan completely.

After he sent Firuz Agha off with the food, he made his way toward the Odalisques' Kitchen. He'd only just stepped through the door when he saw Neyyir Agha striding toward him. Following palace etiquette, he stood aside and saluted the agha.

"I was just about to come and see you," Neyyir Agha said.

The cook smiled. "Likewise."

"I heard," the agha said, "that you'll be cooking for our sovereign. I would like to offer you my congratulations."

Racking his mind to find a lofty expression of gratitude, the cook merely thanked him in the end.

The agha asked, "Why did you wish to see me?"

"I wanted to thank you for the wine," the cook replied. "It was exquisite."

"I'm pleased to hear you enjoyed it," the Black Eunuch replied. Having worked at the Harem for so many years, he could understand with a glance when someone had something on their mind.

The cook, who knew this very well, straightaway said, "From what I can gather, you also enjoy culinary delights. As you well know, even in the Imperial Kitchens one gets bored of eating the same cook's food every day and fancies a change every so often. I have a friend who is a very good cook. His place is unique, far better than anywhere else. If I may be so bold, if you would allow me to have you as my guest there one night, I would be very pleased."

The Black Eunuch grinned. "Thank you very much. However, it is very difficult for us to leave the Harem at night."

"That's unfortunate," the cook said. "The place I was referring to is Fishmonger Bayram's place."

Neyyir Agha's expression suddenly changed. "Do you mean Mad Bayram?"

"The very same. Do you know him?"

"Everyone has heard of him. It is said that all the creatures in the sea swarm to his bait. I was under the impression he didn't have a place anymore, not since a while ago."

"You're right. But he just opened a new place. The location is secret; only his friends know about it. He and I have known each other a long time."

The cook knew that the agha was warming up to the idea. "Is Levon still with him?" the agha asked.

"Master Bayram thinks of Levon as a son," the cook replied. "He would never send him away." The cook added a final touch, saying "There's also a very nice wine cellar at his new place."

After a few moments of thought, the agha looked at the cook and asked, "When could we go?"

"Tomorrow night. As long as you can get permission."

"I'll speak to the Chief Eunuch."

"I'll await your glad tidings. I would be very pleased if you could come. The season is almost over, so we mustn't miss out."

"God willing," Neyyir Agha murmured. Master Bayram's fish and Levon's dishes were already filling his mind and teasing his palate.

Fishmonger Bayram, or "Mad Bayram," as he was also known, was considered the greatest fisherman not just of Istanbul, but of the Marmara Sea, the Aegean Sea, and the Black Sea, and even all seas around the world according to some. That wasn't the only thing he was famed for. He also knew how to cook the most exquisite fish dishes. Grilled, fried, steamed, smoked, pickled, salted . . . each was the stuff of legend. And, as his nickname implied, he was mad.

Years earlier, Master Bayram had owned a small place in Balat on the shores of the Golden Horn. It was actually a makeshift shack with two rooms he had built for himself and his adopted son Levon. He didn't care for running a tavern or making money. In fact he couldn't, since he disliked having to deal with people.

Still, he was a generous man. At his banquet tables he would share his catches with the poor in the neighborhood and he derived great pleasure from sharing the fish he caught with people he liked. Master Bayram hardly ever set foot in the Fishmongers' Market to sell his catch. Levon was young in those days and they had no need for money. He only went to the market when he encountered a problem, the solution of which was beyond his own means, his friends' help, or the sea's plenitude. He sold those fish he wouldn't deign serve to his friends for a handful of coins, and then went about his life as usual.

However, as is often the case, as Master Bayram withdrew from society, his fame spread. His fish and other dishes were spoken about all around the city. At the same time, Levon was growing up. He had to learn his craft as well, perhaps get a small boat of his own and at least one fishing net.

Worn down by worldly concerns, Master Bayram enlarged one of the two rooms in his shack, placed six or seven tables inside, and opened a tavern.

Master Bayram, who was in the habit of living as he pleased, ran the place in exactly the same way. He wouldn't let just anyone through the door. He particularly despised statesmen and men with bulging moneybags, and if anyone got rowdy in his tavern or didn't know how to handle their drink, he wouldn't admit them again even if he were presented with all the riches of the world.

There weren't any fixed prices for the food and drink at Bayram's tavern. He set the prices depending on how he felt and what he needed the next day. He could charge pennies for a plate of mackerel one day and three silver coins for the same dish the next day.

However, even if Master Bayram didn't set much store by them, there were laws, regulations, systems, and arrangements in place. The officials of the empire had set the upper prices of services and goods so that shopkeepers and merchants wouldn't upset the system, and they called this *narh*. What happened to Master Bayram happened because of those rules.

While Master Bayram was discerning when it came to admitting customers, sometimes he would make poor choices. On one such night when he was in need of money, a grouchy customer objected to the price he was charged. Master Bayram first gave the man a good beating and then threw him out, saying, "You son of a whore, it was fine last week when I didn't charge you anything. You walked out singing!" He had no way of knowing how serious things would get when the man, ashamed at having been given a public beating, rushed off to the local judge and lodged a complaint.

The following day, the judge visited Master Bayram's tavern along with his men and asked to hear his version of the story. If the master had said, "I didn't do anything of the sort, this is all made up," no one could have said otherwise, nor would the judge have dragged the matter out, but madness overcame him. Also, Master Bayram didn't know how to lie.

The judge asked: "Did you charge this man more than the *narh*?"

The master replied: "I don't know what a *narh* is. I just told him how much it cost."

The judge asked: "Fine. You also beat this man, is that true?"

The master said: "Yes. And it was a thorough beating, too!"

The judge ruled that the tavern had to remain closed for a week. The custom also allowed anyone who overstepped the *narh* to be given a lashing, but the master was a man of such high repute that it didn't even cross the judge's mind.

After the judge left, Master Bayram told everyone, all his close friends, loved ones, and even not-so-loved ones, that there would be a feast that night, and then he got in his boat and went fishing. Upon returning in the afternoon, he saw that a sizeable crowd had gathered around the tavern. He hauled in the crates of fish he had caught, left them in front of his guests, and then proceeded to set his tavern and home ablaze. "Here's a barbecue for you," he said. "Enjoy your fish!" Then he set off in his boat, rowing toward the Marmara Sea with his adopted son, and as the afternoon gave way to early evening with its reddening sky, he disappeared from sight.

That was how Master Bayram had done justice to his notoriety, and according to the story, no one ever saw him in the city again. But the story wasn't entirely correct. The master had returned about a year before with his son, delicious fish, and talented hands, and he opened a small new tavern in Karaköy. He only told a few friends whom he loved and trusted, and advised them that under no uncertain terms were they to tell anyone where it was located.

After sunset the cook, along with Mahir and Neyyir Agha, set out toward Master Bayram's new tavern.

Neyyir Agha had managed to obtain permission to leave for the night from the Chief Eunuch. The cook met him in front of the Gate of Salutation, which they passed through together, and they crossed the Golden Horn on a boat Mahir had arranged beforehand. After walking along the Karaköy shore, they turned left just before Tophane and began to climb the hill toward Galata.

The cook had found out about the location of the place from a friend, so they had to wander the narrow streets for a while before finally ending up at a black door at the end of a dead-end street that even the Devil himself would have been afraid to walk down alone.

The cook hesitantly knocked three times. He wasn't sure if the two-story house was the right place. He knew that knocking on the wrong door in that neighborhood after dark could lead to unsavory consequences, particularly for Neyyir Agha who, for reasons unknown, had decided to wear a garish red cloak with ivory adornments.

After a longish wait, the bolt of the door rattled, and the door opened slightly. A pair of large eyes which seemed to say "Go away!" appeared in the gap, darting from the cook, who was standing closest to the door, to Mahir and Neyyir Agha, whose faces were more difficult to make out in the darkness. A low voice said, "Well, look who it is," and the door opened a little further.

The cook saw Master Bayram in the dim light of the candles in the room, noticing that he had aged. The lines on his thin face were more prominent, and his tall, lanky body seemed to be slightly bent. His demeanor and expression, however, showed that he was as mad as ever. He playfully slapped the cook on his shoulder twice and then looked at his companions. It was obvious that Neyyir Agha was from the palace, and Master Bayram despised officials. But his guest was welcome, so he couldn't question who else had come along with him.

"Come in," Master Bayram said.

Once they were inside, the cook glanced around. Master Bayram's place lived up to his reputation: plain and modest, but unique in every regard.

The stove and the preparation table were on the left side of the room, which was fairly large. The rest of the space was taken up by six tables, on which were trays and pitchers, and there were four or five stools around each table. There was a large hearth in the middle of the room over which hung a large, boiling cauldron.

Since it was still early, the place was empty. The cook knew the customs of the place, so before Master Bayram could say anything, he approached the cauldron and lifted the lid, whereupon a thick cloud of steam rose upwards. The smell of fresh fish soup filled the room. The cook breathed in the steam and then filled one of the earthenware bowls lined up on the table next to him with soup. He passed the bowl to Neyyir Agha, who was intoxicated by the scent but hesitatingly looked at the bowl. It seemed strange to him to start eating without getting permission first.

"This is how things are done around here," the cook said to him to set his mind at ease. "Every newcomer gets his soup first and sits at a table."

Neyyir Agha took the bowl and sat at one of the tables in the corner. As the cook was filling his own bowl, the agha grabbed his spoon and sipped the soup even though it was scalding hot.

After handing the ladle to Mahir, the cook sat next to Neyyir Agha. He stirred his soup and smelled it, enjoying the slight tinge of envy that was sparked within him. Very few cooks had ever been able to invoke such feelings in him. The cook never saw anyone as a rival, and he wouldn't deign to sink so low as to compete with a fellow artisan. However, as far as Master Bayram and his fish dishes were concerned, even he would think twice about competing with him.

Fish soup was one of the two greatest soups in the world, and the pinnacle of fish dishes as it had to be made perfectly, just like anything else that was difficult. A fish soup could not be "so-so," "alright," or "passable." If done right, it would be soup; if done wrong, it would be rubbish, and that was that. It was one of the strangest dishes in the world. The more ingredients one added, the better it became. It did not have an absolute taste. The base flavor was fish, provided its smell was just right, but the soup changed taste with every spoonful. The first spoonful might be fish accompanied by celery stalk and carrot, the second might be onion and a small piece of fresh oregano, while the third could be the pure taste of fish scorched lovingly with the sweet taste of black pepper. This carnival of tastes continued until you finished the bowl. You could never guess what you would get with the next spoonful, and each sip was a surprise.

After swallowing his last mouthful of soup, the cook breathed a deep sigh, like the others had done, and leaned back on his stool. His sensitive palate had just undertaken an enjoyable test, but in the end the soup had triumphed. After a certain point, the cook gave up trying to figure out each of the flavors and gave himself over to blind pleasure. He knew that fish soup had to be made with at least twenty-two ingredients, but he guessed that there were many more in the cauldron.

After they had all finished their soup, Master Bayram approached them and placed bowls full of raw almonds, walnuts, and hazelnuts on the table and gathered up the empty soup bowls. Pointing toward the pitcher, he chided them, saying, "What, are you waiting for an invitation?" The cook shook off his soup-induced lethargy and began to fill the earthenware cups on the table with wine. The master turned to the cook and said, "I've been waiting for your visit for such a long time now."

"Fate wanted it to be tonight," the cook replied.

Master Bayram nodded. "Are you staying the night?"

"Indeed, we are your guests for the evening." Then he added, "That is, if it is acceptable for you."

Master Bayram called out, "Levon!" Before the echo of his voice died down, his adopted son appeared behind the counter. "Prepare three rooms upstairs," the master told him.

After welcoming the guests with a nod, Levon disappeared as quietly as he had appeared.

The agha, the assistant, and the cook sat at the table with the wine. The cook mused over the fact that the ruby-red contents of the pitcher were good enough to rival any bottle in Haseki Sultan's cellar. He couldn't help but think that if Master Bayram had put such good wine on the tables, he must have even better wine in his cellar. It was also a well-known fact that Master Bayram offered his best wine to his more influential guests, and Neyyir Agha assumed that the cook was such a guest.

There was only enough wine in the pitcher on the table to fill each of the three cups twice, but Levon rushed up and replaced it with a new one. The newly filled cups were already half empty when Master Bayram approached the table again, his hands laden with plates. The large flat plate he placed in the middle was heaped half with mackerel and half with barbel. The fish had been coated in flour and fried in oil, and they were still sizzling. Alongside the fish was a large bowl of salad. The green leaves of lettuce in the salad had been doused with lemon juice and glistened with pure olive oil, and there were sliced onions with plenty of sumac and parsley. Then he brought slices of freshly baked cornbread and chickpea bread in a basket covered with a piece of cloth. Now the feast was truly getting started.

Forgetting his Harem etiquette, Neyyir Agha dove into the fish. Mahir was already so engrossed in the food that he was oblivious to the world around him. There were only a few pieces of fish left when Levon brought out a plate of sizzling anchovy and haddock. Wherever Master Bayram had cast his net, he'd ended up with the last anchovies of the season and the thin haddocks were an additional gift from the sea.

When they were halfway through the second plate, the cook told Mahir, who was stuffing anchovies in his mouth in twos and threes, to slow down. To makes sure that his assistant, who sat there frozen with a mouthful of fish, wouldn't be offended, he added as an explanation, "There's much more coming. If you get full now, you'll be disappointed later."

His words also brought Neyyir Agha to his senses. He placed a haddock into his mouth, head, tail, and all, and gulped down the remaining wine in his cup in one go. The Black Eunuch's face gleamed with joy. "What else is there?" he asked, an even more childish smile than usual on his lips. "If I never eat fish for the rest of my life, let alone tonight, I would still be content."

The cook laughed. "As long as there's fish at the bottom of the sea and Master Bayram is in his boat, we'll be eating fish for a long while yet, Your Grace."

The Black Eunuch joined in the cook's laughter: "God willing, my Master, God willing!"

Just then, as if Neyyir Agha's prayer had been answered, Master Bayram approached again, carrying a large tray of variously sized plates. Swiftly he collected the dirty plates and replaced them with plates, bowls, and pots containing pan-fried mussels, calamari, and a steamed turbot on a bed of onion, garlic, carrots, and celery. The pan-fried mussels shared their plate with almonds, whilst the golden rings of fried calamari sat next to walnut sauce. The pickled anchovies were wrapped around seedless green olives, and the kipper was air dried, crushed, and seasoned with plenty of dill. There were large prawns and tiny octopus tentacles in the green salad this time. The slices of pickled fish looked as fresh as live fish and didn't come apart on the fork but melted like cream on the tongue.

The men at the table hadn't yet been able to shake off their astonishment at the first round of the banquet when Levon approached the table, this time with a smaller tray. First, he made room in the middle of the table for a large bluefish which had been sliced down the middle, grilled, and topped with onions. In between the plates, he placed bowls of hummus, fava beans, cold bean salad, stuffed mussels, and mashed roe. There was only room for one more plate on the table and Levon had obviously saved it for the best dish of all.

When he placed the last dish on the table, an exclamation of joy and appreciation arose from his guests: stuffed mackerel had graced the table with its presence, and like every experienced diner, they showed it the respect it deserved.

After the final drops of the Commandaria wine had run out, a pitcher of *meybuhter* wine, which was boiled and made stronger with the addition of honey, was brought to the table, making them feel properly light-headed, and eating was replaced with talking.

Mahir was the first to break the silence. Tripping over his words ever so slightly, he complained about the unfairness of fate and the difficulty of life, and then he launched into his life story, which the cook had been wondering about.

It turned out that Mahir's father had been a cook but a very bitter man. Mahir had wanted to follow in his footsteps, but since his skills didn't extend beyond making rice, he didn't remain as his father's apprentice for long. His father kicked him out of his kitchen so that he could find himself another trade while he was still young.

Because he was deeply offended, or perhaps because he was completely lacking in any other abilities, Mahir was unable to find any work. During his fourth apprenticeship, this time with a tailor, his father fell ill and died shortly afterwards. Since there was no one to run his shop, the debts grew day by day, and finally the shop, which was his grandfather's legacy, was sold for a song. Mahir's mother asked one of his father's influential friends to help, and he found her orphaned son a place in Istanbul in the Imperial Kitchens. Mahir saved some of his salary and sent it to his mother back home. His biggest dream was, in his own words, to become "a great man" and make sure his mother was comfortable in her old age.

The cook's heart ached as he listened to his assistant's tale, but inwardly he laughed at those final words. Mahir hadn't said "I want to become a great cook" or that he wanted to become great at something else. In fact, his heart wasn't really set on anything; if the opportunity arose, and if he could see any future in it, he would try his hand at becoming a tailor again, or even try becoming an ostler.

I chose just the right person, the cook thought. Then he said, "Don't worry, Mahir. If all goes well, your mother will be most comfortable."

Neyyir Agha was just as tipsy as Mahir, but because he'd been trained in the Harem, he initially approached the conversation in a more aloof manner. After feigning sympathy in response to Mahir's story, he began to talk, and the more he talked the more open he became, until finally he started to talk about the Harem. The cook was all ears. This time, though, he wanted to hear not about Kamer, but another woman. When Neyyir Agha finally began to talk about the sultan's chief consort and the mother of his son, Haseki Sultan, the cook listened even more attentively.

Haseki Sultan was even harder to approach than the sovereign himself, and very few little was known about her. The cook had included her in his plans long ago. She was the one who held the keys to the cook's goal and his ultimate aim.

Neyyir Agha said very little about her that the cook hadn't already heard before. But it was different to hear such things from someone who lived inside the Harem. Haseki Sultan was known to be one of the cleverest women the palace had ever seen. She had learned how to wield power over the sultan and the Harem at a very young age. She didn't like to share her power, and she was known for the swiftness with which she triumphed over her opponents. Rumors suggested that there was a quiet but pitched battle going on between her and Siyavuş Agha. It was said that the Chief Sword Bearer was fixated on Haseki Sultan and sought an opportunity to ensure her downfall.

After talking at length, Neyyir Agha realized that he was starting to reveal confidential information under the influence of the wine and he moved on to less important topics which nevertheless touched on the Harem and the palace. The cook had heard all he needed to hear. He leaned back a little and let the agha and Mahir go on talking. Only occasionally did he add to the conversation, and all the while keeping one eye on the door. More people had arrived after them, but apart from five people sitting at two tables, Master Bayram hadn't let anyone else inside.

Mahir and the Black Eunuch went on talking. Or to be more precise, Mahir kept bombarding Neyyir Agha with questions, and the latter, thoroughly drunk now, discoursed at length. The cook looked at his assistant from the corner of his eye. Mahir couldn't get enough of stories about life beyond the third gate of the palace. With his sparkling eyes and his half-open mouth, he seized upon the agha's every word, and then in his mind turned them into hard to attain but sweet dreams. He was, of course, aware that no male, apart from men in the sultan's family, could step into the Harem. But as a foolish person intoxicated by power, Mahir could begin to see that what was between his legs was a reasonable sacrifice to be closer to all that glamour, royalty, and, most importantly, power. The cook knew this very well, and that was partly why he had chosen Mahir as his assistant.

Neyyir Agha must have taken a liking to young Mahir with his shapely body, fair skin, and handsome face because he gave him endless advice, not forgetting to add that from now on he was his brother and he'd support him every step of the way. "It's not like you have to start from the Harem or the Inner Palace," Neyyir Agha instructed him. "Once you step foot inside any part of the palace, that's enough. If you have ambition and good friends to help you, you can always climb further!"

The cook was laughing inwardly as he listened to the hopes and dreams of his assistant, who considered sharing a bottle of wine with a Harem official of middling ranking to be a spectacular stroke of luck, when he heard a knock on the door. Without turning in the direction of the door, he listened attentively. Master Bayram cracked open the door as he always did, but instead of swearing and shutting the door in the newcomer's face, this time he invited him inside.

The cook waited for the new guest to get his soup and sit down. When the man sat down at the table on his right, he glanced at him. He was tallish with a sharp black beard. The man was wearing a white cloak with a black sash around his waist and a pointed black hat with the same black sash wrapped around it. Before digging into his soup, he filled his wine glass halfway and drank it down, giving a brief nod to the cook. The cook responded by looking at him at length and then he turned around.

"Finally," he muttered quietly.

He endured the conversation at the table for another hour before getting up and politely asking Neyyir Agha's permission to leave, citing the wine as an excuse. Neyyir Agha, himself quite drunk, and Mahir, who felt that he was one step closer to power, did not object to his departure. It appeared they would see dawn break before their conversation was over.

The cook went up to his room, lay down on the bed, and began to wait. There was only one candle to illuminate the room. In the dim light, he was praying that everything would go as smoothly as he hoped when there was a soft knock on the door. He jumped up and opened the door. Just as he expected, the man with the white cloak and black turban had come to see him.

The man greeted him: "Peace be upon you."

The cook noticed from the man's accent that he was an Arab. The cook asked, "Where have you been?"

The man smiled slightly and eyed the dark hallway behind him with suspicion. "It was difficult," he whispered. "It's not all ready yet, but when you sent word to bring over whatever I had, I did what I could."

The cook nodded. He could wait no longer, so he'd sent a coded message to the only person through which he could reach this man, that is, Herbalist Naim Effendi, asking him to bring whatever he could get his hands on.

"Did you get everything?" the cook asked. He was almost breathless with excitement.

With a brief smile the man pulled from his cloak a large bundle of leather-bound papers tied tightly together. "This is all I have," he said. "God willing, not too many are missing and they will serve your purpose."

"God willing," the cook repeated. "Thank you. I have caused you great trouble."

"Not at all." The man smiled. "A brothers' wish is my command."

Mention of the brothers made the cook's heart race. "Will you see them soon?" he asked.

"Not soon, but I will go to Baghdad in the summer," the man replied.

The cook grabbed him tightly by the arm. "Send them my greetings. Tell the brothers I miss them very much."

"Of course," the man said, and after a final salutation, disappeared from sight in the dark hallway.

After closing the door, the cook picked up the candle and sat cross-legged on the bed. Unfastening the pile of papers, he spread them out. He gazed at the papers as if he were looking upon a sacred treasure. Each of them depicted a large circle divided into twelve, and each of the twelve astrological signs from Aries to Pisces were marked in their place, as well as the positions of the seven main planets from Mercury to Saturn.

They were the horoscopes of all the important people who lived in the Imperial Palace.

Each page depicted the location of each planet and what sign they were under when the residents of the palace were born. For the uninitiated, the papers may have seemed like senseless diagrams, but someone who knew how to read the signs could learn about the person's fortunes and misfortunes, their skills and ineptitudes, what they liked and disliked, and even what they thought about or did not think about.

Quickly scanning through the pages, the cook set two of them aside, the ones he truly needed. One of the horoscopes was for the Chief Sword Bearer and the other was for the illustrious sovereign.

The cook read Siyavuş Agha's horoscope first. It was just as he expected, and he realized that he could've taken the right course of action without the horoscope. Then he perused the sultan's horoscope at length. He carefully studied the locations of the planets, which sign they were under, and their alignment with one another. He came up with an idea. After thinking for a while, he muttered to himself, "I'll tell the Market Steward to get some fowl tomorrow."

After checking the horoscope again, he looked at the others. He had the horoscopes of almost everyone in the palace, from the Grand Vizier to the Chief Gatekeeper. The amount of power at his fingertips made him shudder. Just then another horoscope caught his eye. As he picked it up to study it, his eyes widened in terror.

"My God!" the cook whispered to himself. The horoscope he was holding had been done for Haseki Sultan, and the zodiac confirmed what Neyyir Agha had just been saying about her.

The stars had graced Haseki Sultan with such intelligence, ability, and power that, had she been born a man, she could have conquered the whole world. The cook felt quite uneasy for the first time since he had come up with his plan. Haseki Sultan was indeed dangerous, but it was out of his hands now. There was no turning back.

After tidying up the horoscopes, placing them back in the leather binding, and stuffing them under his mattress, he blew out the candle. He knew that he should sleep, but he kept seeing visions of stars. It was as if he were gazing at the billions of stars that could be seen on a clear moonless night. A cool desert breeze enveloped his body and his mind wandered to the el-Haki brothers' house in Baghdad, where he had first learned about the art of the zodiac.

5

The Doctor and the Astrologer

THE COOK WAS seventeen years old at the time. In those days, everything in his life seemed to be shrouded in fog. When people spoke to him, their voices were either the slightest of hums or ear-splitting screams. Scents and flavors made no impression on him at all. Time seemed to have stopped; the difference between day and night was meaningless.

Just like his world, the cook was also quiet. Habitually he spoke little, but there had been no other time in his life when he had been silent for so long, and he didn't know whether there would be another. Notions about things such as the future meant nothing to the cook, nor did hopes, desires, or dreams. He was trapped in a cursed, turbid present lived out under the gloomy shadow of the past, merely breathing.

Before Master Adem turned to leave, they silently hugged. The cook remembered watching him walk over the hill, getting smaller with each step until he finally disappeared into the horizon. He recalled wondering if he would ever see him again. He remembered that because it was the only thought he had about the future in those days.

The cook wanted only one thing from life. He had a single hope and a single prayer: to forget.

Only by forgetting did he think he could be free of the acrid taste in his mouth and the gloom that weighed down on his chest.

What he desired was oblivion beyond death, as if he had never lived, never existed.

Even the sweetest memory pained his heart, as it was being torn from his chest, and mere mention of the future made his blood run cold because there was always the possibility he might experience the same pain yet again.

But oblivion never came. Kamer was always in his thoughts. He grew angry at himself and tried to banish such thoughts from his mind; he drank, he wept, but it was all in vain. He could neither stop the memories nor alleviate his anguish. He wondered if sleep could be his salvation, at least for a while, but the insidious darkness seeped into his dreams. He had nightmares every night and woke up drenched in sweat, breathless. Over time, the thought of sleep became terrifying.

Constant thinking, and getting lost in those thoughts, was comparably better since he at least had a modicum of control. Dreams, on the other hand, were cruel. Freed from his willpower, they went their own way, catching him unawares at his most vulnerable moments and inflicting still worse pain. He considered the idea that regardless of how silly it seemed, waking up in the middle of a story that was soothing yet brief and as deep as the ocean, then realizing it was naught but a dream must be one of the few things in the world that had the power to make a person feel utterly helpless, powerless, and pathetic.

He tried to figure out exactly when the world had started to go awry, but it was futile. He wondered if perhaps it had always been that way, if the happy memories he now barely remembered were also mere dreams.

His sole desire was to remain in that dream forever. Life could have gone on with all its fallacies without ever touching him. He and Kamer would have gone on living forever between the chimneys on the roof of the kitchen without ever growing up, without ever knowing unhappiness.

When the cook was fourteen and Kamer thirteen, they had met every night for a year on that roof, creating the happiest moments of their lives.

There had been a half-moon in the sky when Kamer's hair first touched his face, and a crescent moon when his hand brushed against hers, which sent a jolt of electricity through them. And there was a full moon when they realized that the song Kamer whispered into his ear described them perfectly, and that what they were experiencing was love.

He remembered that song, and would always remember it, as if he'd been forbidden to forget it:

So drunk am I,
I no longer comprehend the world.
Who am I?
Who is the cupbearer, where the wine?

And Kamer's dancing, which became more beautiful every day under the light of her namesake with her arms gliding above her head as if composing a new melody, her hair flying in the wind as if drawing a veil over the night, her steps caressing the ground, and her gaze— from which the cook couldn't take his eyes for a second—sometimes embarrassed, often mischievous, and occasionally aglow with a naïve flirtatiousness. Kamer was becoming more and more breathtakingly beautiful with each passing day, her dancing more elegant. Over time the cook began to worry that she would slip from his life like a stream of light, starting with her delicate swaying arms.

He also remembered the night when Kamer had danced so wildly. She circled around him with rhythmical steps, spinning on every third. The cook turned around and around, trying to keep up, but Kamer was feeling mischievous as usual and sped up. Since she was so used to dancing, she never missed a beat or felt light-headed, but the cook was already staggering and losing his balance. When Kamer began to spin even faster, he called out with a laugh, "Stop spinning!"

Kamer suddenly stopped and looked at the cook through her hair, which was blowing in the wind.

"I'm Kamer; spinning is what I do," she said coyly and spun ever faster.

The cook found it hard to even follow her with his gaze, but then his expression of awe was replaced by concern because with every turn, Kamer was getting closer to the edge of the roof. The cook called out to her again and again, but Kamer responded with a laugh and a small leap.

When he realized he couldn't stop her with words alone, the cook jumped forward and pulled her toward him. And as if his gesture was blessed by the night, she fell into the cook's arms with a small cry.

"What do you think you're doing?" she'd asked, mock anger in her voice. Still, she twined her arms around the cook's neck as if scared she might fall.

"You almost fell," he said, trying to appear annoyed. He had one hand on Kamer's arm and the other on her waist. Kamer was out of breath, and just watching her had exhausted the cook as well. Sweat was beading up on their foreheads as they stood there together.

"I wasn't going to fall," Kamer objected.

"You were," the cook insisted. "You were on the edge of—"

Kamer interrupted him with a smile. "I wasn't going to fall. You were there, you wouldn't have let me."

The cook's heart seemed to stop beating once again. He couldn't feel his legs and at that moment he felt as though he would never breathe again. He was looking into Kamer's eyes, trying to find the right thing to say. She leaned forward and put her head on his shoulder, rendering all words pointless. The sole meaning of all existence at that moment was to feel Kamer's hands on his shoulders, her eyelashes on his neck, and the warmth of her breasts on his chest. He caressed her hair and looked up at the sky, longing for the moment to go on forever. But then from the corner of his eye he saw disaster approaching.

One of Sirrah's slaves was at the top of the ladder.

But the cook didn't care, and he wasn't afraid in the slightest. His only concern was the fact that Kamer, whose head was still on his shoulder, would be upset. He glared at the slave with such ferocity that he quickly disappeared from sight.

Later he wouldn't be able to remember how much longer they'd stayed there that night. But before they parted, he told Kamer they'd been caught.

Kamer laughed. "Of course the slave will tell Sirrah, but we haven't really been caught. Only people doing something bad, or running away, can get caught."

The cook fell even more in love with her when she said that.

The disaster they had been expecting did not happen the next day, nor in the days that followed. Sirrah was a clever woman, and she knew Kamer. If she put any pressure on her, or forbade her from doing anything, she knew Kamer would become even more obstinate, so she made do with small precautions. Even when there were no customers, she would send Kamer from one mansion to the next, and during the rest of the day had her practice until she was exhausted. Her door was doubly locked, and all the passageways leading up to the roof were barred.

It fell to Master Adem to warn the cook. He constantly reminded him that the House of Pleasure was a temporary stop for him, that he would become a great cook one day, the greatest cook of all time, and that he must remember it was his destiny and dedicate his life to the art. The cook wearied of listening to the sermon, but out of respect for his master he remained silent and nodded in agreement. But when Master Adem made a disparaging remark about Kamer, the words pierced his heart and made his blood boil. His master repeated, "Has anyone decent ever come out of the House of Pleasure? Do you think you deserve an ordinary dancer?" The cook clenched his teeth and prayed for patience.

Of course, neither Sirrah's precautions nor Master Adem's words were enough to keep them from seeing each other.

Either the cook, who was discovering the power of the dishes he prepared, would convince one of the slaves or customers to help him, or Kamer would sweet talk or force one of Sirrah's servant girls to arrange a place for them to meet. If that failed, the cook would send messages to Kamer through the dishes he cooked. When her longing grew too strong, Kamer would sing so loud the windows rattled, and the cook, whether he was working or tossing and turning in bed, would feel the despair within him dissolve only to be replaced by an urge to both laugh and cry.

Weeks and months passed. Their small moments of joy were like mirages in the desert, offering only the slightest comfort. They had never broached the issue, but they both knew that things would not—could not—go on forever. And they knew that they needed a future to look forward to, no matter how distant or difficult to attain. However, they weren't the only ones thinking about their futures. The years ahead of them had already been pledged to the House of Pleasure.

The cook went downstairs to the kitchen one morning and saw Master Adem sitting with two men he'd never seen before. His master did not introduce his guests, and the cook was too shy to ask. The men carefully watched him work from morning till noon, and after tasting the dishes he'd prepared, they had a brief conversation with Master Adem outside the door and left. The cook wondered what was in store for him, and soon enough he would find out.

Master Adem woke him a few days later at the crack of dawn, even before the call to prayer. He offered no explanation, but merely told him to get dressed. The cook did as he was told and followed Master Adem outside. They walked to Üsküdar and made the rather long journey to Unkapanı by rowboat. Once ashore they began to walk up the hill toward Etmeydanı. On the way there, the cook glanced at Master Adem and noticed that his face was pale, as if he was feeling uneasy.

At one point they turned right, entering a street where there were shops selling kebab, tripe, liver, boiled sheep's head, halva, and pickles. Master Adam knocked on a small door between the halva maker's shop and the kebab seller. Shortly afterwards the door opened. The cook recognized the man who invited them inside as one of the two men who'd visited the House of Pleasure to watch him work a few days earlier.

After passing through a short corridor they entered a large room. When the cook saw an elderly man sitting on a sheepskin rug draped across a bedstead in the corner of the room, he surmised that they were at the cooks' guild. He guessed that the elderly man was the guild's sheikh, the man on his right was the registrar, and the other, the man who had gone to the House of Pleasure's kitchen to watch him, was the scout.

The cook had never given a thought to achieving the rank of master until that day. But despite his age, he was already a superb cook, a fact to which his own master attested as well as anyone who tasted his cooking, even the cruel Sirrah. All the same, he was excited, and his heart was pounding. But he sensed that something was amiss. As far as he knew, the ceremony for awarding mastery took place in the spring with the Guild Council, with all the members of the guild, and even the Judge and the Chief Constable of the district, in attendance. Master Adem's anxious expression had been replaced with a look of morbidity and he avoided locking eyes with anyone in the room. He introduced himself to the members of the council and vouched for the cook, whereupon the agent attested to having witnessed the cook's abilities. The guild sheikh then declared him to have obtained the rank of master. The registrar handed Master Adem a red apron, which he tied around the cook's waist with trembling hands, and the agent handed the cook his certificate. There were no prayers, and contrary to centuries of tradition, the sheikh made no comments. Thus the cook attained his rank at perhaps the strangest ceremony the guild had held in its thousand-year history.

They were about to leave as quickly as they'd arrived when the sheikh called out to Master Adem. He hesitated for a moment but guild tradition forced him to turn around. "Wait for me outside," he told the cook.

"Of course, Master." The cook left the room, but his curiosity won out at the last moment, so he stood just outside the door so he could hear what they were saying.

"Haven't all these years of self-imposed suffering been enough?" he heard the sheikh tell Master Adem. "Let us pay your remaining debt out of the Guild Fund so you can return to our ranks."

"That I cannot do," Master Adem replied. "I must reap what I've sown. I can't make the guild pay for my erring ways."

The sheikh insisted, "Think about it, my son. If you have no pity for yourself, then have pity on your skill as a cook. The world has never seen the likes of you."

"Soon it will see better, God willing," Master Adem replied.

After leaving the guild, they quickly retraced their steps back to Unkapanı, and as they drew closer to the sea, Master Adem's anxiety seemed to lessen. As they were passing by a *boza* shop, he stopped.

"Come," he said to the cook. "Let's sit down for a while."

The *boza* shop was small and dusty. In front of the shop was a charcoal stove on which a few meat kebabs were sizzling and a few wicker stools. Sitting down, Master Adem asked, "Albanian or Circassian?"

The cook smiled shyly. "You decide, Master."

Circassian *boza* was the ordinary fermented millet drink, while Albanian *boza* was slightly alcoholic and was sold underneath the counter. Master Adem called out to the shopkeeper standing behind a table topped with large wooden barrels. "Two Albanians!"

The shopkeeper came to their table a short while later with two earthenware mugs. As he placed the mugs on the table, he caught sight of the brand-new apron around the cook's waist and the certificate with the red stamp which he had rolled up and tucked into his sash. "My congratulations," he said. "May God make you proud."

"Amen," the cook and Master Adem replied in unison. After the shopkeeper left, Master Adem smiled for the first time that day and congratulated him once again.

"Thank you, Master," the cook replied. "It's all thanks to you."

The master looked at his old assistant at length. The cook knew that proud gaze. His master had looked at him the same way once when he had taken a perfectly prepared dish off the stove. "No," Master Adem replied after a while, "it's all because of your skills. I didn't do much at all, and there is nothing more I can do."

The cook was confused. Master Adem continued, "Son, I no longer have anything to teach you. You already knew from birth many of the intricacies of the art of cooking. It's in your blood, in your soul. I only added what I could. But saying that I've got nothing left to teach you does not mean you have nothing left to learn. Do you understand what I am trying to say?"

The cook nodded and looked away. His expression was glum, as he knew what was coming next. Lowering his voice, Master Adem said, "You are the Pasha of Cuisine! There's a long road ahead of you, and you're not even halfway down it yet. What I've taught you is merely a few drops in the ocean. There are great scholars, many learned men, who await your arrival. You must visit them and receive their teachings. You've a lot to learn before you can truly become the Pasha of Cuisine. Son, you must leave!"

At that moment, the cook felt like he was bearing the weight of the world on his shoulders. Master Adem had told him that one day he would have to embark on long journeys. But the cook had taken it to be nothing more than a distant story and shrugged it off because taking it seriously would have meant leaving Kamer, which was the cook's greatest fear.

He took a deep breath, summoned all his courage and, with his eyes fixed on the mug before him from which he'd only taken two sips, he murmured, "Master, I don't want to leave."

Master Adem responded with a long silence. After a while he asked, "Why?" When the cook didn't answer, he asked with the utmost frankness, "Is it because of Kamer?"

The cook merely nodded, still looking down.

"Look at me," Master Adem said. His voice betrayed concern. His master repeated, "Look at me!"

This time the cook did as he was told and his gaze was met with a look of disappointment and anger. "The House of Pleasure is not the place for you," he said. "Neither the women nor the men there are trustworthy. In the end you'll be disappointed, son. The women there aren't for you."

The cook pursed his lips, trying to bite back the words that were on the tip of his tongue, and contented himself with saying, "Kamer is different, Master."

Master Adem chuckled in response. "Look," he said, "do you know who is sitting here across from you?" A distant look came into his eyes, a look marked by bitterness and disappointment. After a pause, he said, "I was once the greatest cook in the whole of Istanbul and my place had three floors. It was packed morning and night. We had to turn customers away because there was no room. Pashas and gentlemen begged me to cook for their feasts. I would return home with my arms filled with gifts and my pockets filled with gold. I can't remember how many times the Kitchen Chamberlain visited me to try to convince me to work in the Imperial Kitchens, saying that I would start in the Royal Kitchen. I refused and sent İsfendiyar in my stead. Even though he was just my assistant, they took him in immediately. I was the best in the art of cooking, I was happy, I had a sterling reputation. I had fame and enough money to last even my grandchildren. And then . . ."

Master Adem stopped to take a breath. Quickly wiping away a tear, he continued, "One day, I ended up at the House of Pleasure. Not because I was overly fond of drinking or lovemaking, but because I'd heard good things about their cook. I was only going to try the food and go back home. But I had no idea that it was a cursed place. First, Sirrah's tongue poisoned me. I stayed five days when I should've returned on the same day I visited, and that was with the help of my assistant and my friends. I did manage to get out, but my mind kept wandering back to the House of Pleasure. I was filled with passion."

The master averted his eyes. Swallowing with difficulty as if there was a stone stuck in his throat, he went on: "I met her on the third night I was there. She played the lute and sang. She was indescribably beautiful, so much so that no mortal could ever describe her. I was enthralled and couldn't get her out of my thoughts. I couldn't even eat a bite of food, let alone cook. Unable to bear it any longer, I sent her a letter. I received a reply the next day. And what a reply it was! I was swept off my feet. I didn't charge anyone for the food that day, and the next day I was at the gates of the House of Pleasure once again. For ten days, I had the time of my life with her. She was in love with me, too. I was sure of it. Money, work, and fame meant nothing to me anymore. I wanted to spend all my time with her. In less than a year we had to close down my place. But I didn't care because I could find work anywhere I wanted. I started cooking at the House of Pleasure. Over time, it started to bother me that she sang for other customers and attended revelries and banquets in the mansions. I wanted to be the only person who listened to her songs, the only person she played the lute for, but my desires meant money. After all, the girl was Sirrah's property. I paid on behalf of every customer so she wouldn't perform for him. That was how my fortune vanished. And I became indebted to Sirrah by buying the girl's freedom. She set her free, but the girl ran off with a rich aristocrat. She left me, son. She left me."

Master Adem paused and, looking at the cook with tears in his eyes, said his last words on the matter: "Don't think Kamer will stay with you. Don't be fooled by fantasies. She's been poisoned by the House of Pleasure. She will leave you, too."

The cook's hands began to tremble, and the wave of fury building up within him washed away the sorrow he'd felt for his master. Still, he tried to remain calm. "Kamer is different, Master," he said. "She really is different."

Master Adem laughed. "You're right," he replied, "Kamer is different. She's different, because she's still young. She hasn't seen anything of the world yet. She knows nothing of wealth or extravagance. She thinks you and I and the House of Pleasure are all there is to life. But mark my words, she will discover the truth soon enough."

The cook didn't open his mouth, fearing what would come out of it next. But with one look, Master Adem could tell exactly what the cook was thinking. "Be as angry as you like," he told him, "but that is the truth. You have a talent that comes around only once in a thousand years. Don't waste it. You have to leave."

Through clenched teeth, the cook replied, "I'm not going anywhere!"

After that day, no mention was made of Kamer or traveling, and the matter was consigned to time and silence. The cook went over Master Adem's story in his mind. Of course, hearing his story saddened him, and he couldn't quite believe the man he called his master could have been so foolish. But he could neither put Kamer in the place of the girl in the story, nor liken himself to Master Adem. At that moment, his faith in Kamer was unshaken. But the seed of malady known as suspicion had been planted in his mind.

Even for the wise, it can be hard to tell when the curse of suspicion has become rooted in their minds, so for the young cook, it was impossible for him to know that when he got up from the *boza* shop, he was a different person. Suspicion insidiously wormed its way into his thoughts, gnawing at him from within. People who are untouched by suspicion and firm in their faith do not constantly need to remind themselves of what they believe in. But just as a man of religion whose faith has been shaken begins to pray more fervently, the cook kept telling himself that Kamer would never leave him, that she loved him, and that they'd spend the rest of their lives together. But suspicion, feeding on that litany, seeped from his thoughts into his vision day by day.

The cook didn't know if it was just his imagination, but Kamer seemed to grow more beautiful with each passing day. The mischievous young girl was slowly taking on the figure of a gorgeous woman. Sirrah, of course, noticed as well and did all she could to add to the beauty of her new favorite. She had dresses of rare fabrics made for her and adorned the girl's hair, neck, and arms with the most valuable of jewels.

The cook also wanted to celebrate Kamer's beauty. He saved up the allowance Master Adem gave him and the tips he got from the customers. He got permission to leave the House of Pleasure for half a day so he could go to the Grand Bazaar. Once there, he found a jeweler who agreed to make a gold necklace with a small pendant in the shape of an apple. He only had enough money to pay for gold of the lowest quality so the necklace didn't sparkle like the ones Sirrah gave Kamer, but he didn't mind. The sparkle in Kamer's eyes on the night when he gave the necklace to her, in a secluded corner of the large gardens at the House of Pleasure, outshone all the jewels in the world for him. Her hands were shaking so much that she dropped the necklace twice as she was trying to put it on, and in the end she asked the cook to put it on for her. However, the cook's hands were shaking as well, and the clasp was so small it would have been difficult even with steady hands. When the necklace fell to the ground for the third time, they laughed. As they kneeled down to pick up the necklace, their hands touched on the ground, and the cook's heart seemed to stop again.

After the necklace was finally around Kamer's neck, they sat down with their backs against an ancient oak tree, watching the night sky and the stars through the leaves. Kamer rested her head against the cook's shoulder. She held his hand with one hand and grasped the apple pendant with the other. After she finished the song, she was whispering into his ear, she said, "I'm never going to take this off."

The cook squeezed her hand. "One day," he said, "I'll buy you an even nicer one."

Kamer said nothing in reply, and the cook understood that her silence wasn't the silence of bliss. A shiver ran down his spine and a cold sweat broke on his back as he realized that even the mere mention of the future filled Kamer with dread.

He was also concerned about what Sirrah was planning, as she knew that Kamer met up with him at every opportunity. Had he listened more carefully to Master Adem's story, he would have noticed that the cunning woman was in fact plotting to take him in as a new cook and keep him bound for the rest of his life. Just as she hadn't taken Master Adem seriously before, she didn't think that the cook would dare try to take Kamer away from the House of Pleasure. By pretending to not see what was happening, she was waiting for her prospective cook to sink deeper into her clutches. Sirrah was a lucky woman and clever as well.

Then an incident occurred which made her realize that things wouldn't be as easy as she supposed.

Kamer may have become Sirrah's favorite, but she was kept on a tight leash. She was, however, just as obstinate as she had been in her childhood and even more outspoken, meaning that she was so adept at getting on Sirrah's nerves that the older woman had difficulty handling her on her own. Whenever she had to teach Kamer a lesson in obedience, she had to get help from her slaves, and then all hell would break loose. Kamer would throw whatever she could get her hands on at the slaves, and her screams and curses would echo through the mansion. Of course, the cook could hear her, and he was tormented by the sound of her cries. A few times on such occasions he reached for the meat cleaver, but Master Adem managed to hold him in check.

One day, he was alone in the kitchen as Kamer's screams began echoing through the halls again. The cook prayed for patience, but Kamer let out such a pained scream that he lost control. He stormed upstairs with the cleaver, shoving aside the servants who tried to stop him, until he reached the room where two slaves were lashing Kamer. Using the back of the blade, he broke the arm of one of the slaves and gashed the forehead of the other. He turned to Sirrah and growled, "If you hurt her again, I'll take your life."

Of course, that wasn't the first time Sirrah had seen a man brandishing a meat cleaver. She had dealt with thousands of threats that were a thousand times more serious from men who were a thousand times more dangerous. She shot the cook a contemptuous look and then turned to Kamer, ordering her out. Kamer hesitated, unsure of what she should do. After seeing the two lovers glance at each other, Sirrah snapped, "Kamer! I told you to leave!"

There was such an insidious threat in her mistress's voice that Kamer was truly afraid of her for the first time in her life. After she left, Sirrah turned her most condescending smile on the cook, and then gesturing toward the large full-length mirror on the wall, she said, "Cook! Take a look at yourself."

Had the wise people he would come to know later in life been there, they would have shouted, "Don't look!" But the cook was alone. With his naivety, his love sinking deeper into sorrow day by day, and the demon of suspicion constantly whispering within him, he turned around to look in the mirror.

Just as Sirrah wanted, he didn't like what he saw. His clothes were stained and his hands were covered with burns and cuts. Cuts could heal and clothes could be washed, but he was unsure about his future. He knew that even if he were the Pasha of Cuisine, he was after all only a cook and would remain one forever. The more he looked in the mirror, the more he saw his handsome face as hideous, and his talent as a curse that was tightening around his neck.

At the same time, he thought of Kamer and how beautiful she was, which made him think that she deserved to live a splendorous life. As he slaved away in the stuffy kitchen, Kamer danced in lavishly decorated rooms, showered with the compliments of pashas and aristocrats, and slaves and servants fawned over her, doing whatever she wanted.

"It's so difficult," the cook muttered to himself. And when he said that, a dark fog settled over all the dreams he'd had until that day.

From that moment on, everything seemed to be a twist of fate to the cook. It was as if the world was conspiring against him, trying to shatter his dreams and destroy his future. To make matters worse, he could no longer meet up with Kamer as often as he had before, as Sirrah had started to watch over her like a hawk. Sirrah had been able to perceive what the cook could not—namely, the fact that what was happening was no passing fancy but genuine love, and that the cook was nothing like Master Adem, just as Kamer was nothing like the girl he loved. Sirrah could tell when someone was ready to risk everything, and she was afraid that the couple would elope, so she had her slaves keep a close eye on Kamer.

The cook, however, was in no state to rationally analyze the situation. No matter how hard he tried to stave off his dark thoughts, part of his mind kept whispering that Kamer no longer wanted to see him as often as she had in the past. The less he saw her, the more concerned he became; the more he concerned he became, the more he thought; and the more he thought, the more his mind gave way to morbid visions. He wondered if perhaps she no longer loved him, if she'd been hoodwinked by one of the guests, or had fallen in love with another man but hadn't told him so as not to break his heart. The cook thought constantly, and sank deeper and deeper into despair.

It was at this time that Mahmud Bey, the elder son of the renowned Darıcızade family from Alexandria, decided to visit Istanbul. The Darıcızade family was very wealthy and just as powerful. They owned so much land that the harvests from their fields affected grain prices not just in Istanbul but in the entirety of the Ottoman Empire.

Mahmud Bey's arrival in Istanbul, replete with three galleys, was greeted with great fanfare. He moved into a mansion on the shores of the Bosphorus and his entourage settled into two other mansions. He was received by the Grand Vizier who gave a feast in his honor, and the merchants of the city lined up at his door to secure an audience with him.

Of course, Mahmud Bey couldn't visit Istanbul without hearing about the House of Pleasure—Sirrah made sure of that.

His arrival at the House of Pleasure was an event in itself.

Preparations had begun a week in advance. All the other guests were sent away, the mansions were cleaned and repaired from top to bottom, and all the servants were given new outfits.

The kitchen had never been so busy. Every ingredient was purchased anew even though the cellar was stocked, and the freshest and rarest of foodstuffs were bought.

But the cook's mind was elsewhere. A dark mood had descended on him when he'd heard Kamer would be the lead dancer at the reception to be held in Mahmud Bey's honor. Naturally, Sirrah had decided to present such an important guest with her best dancer. The cook had already envisioned what would happen days before Mahmud Bey arrived at the House of Pleasure. In his mind, Mahmud Bey would be awestruck by Kamer, prolong his stay just for her sake, and, unable to endure being separated from her for too long, return shortly afterwards to invite Kamer to his home.

Even his despairing mind did not permit him to imagine what would follow.

Whether it truly was a twist of fate, or whether because imagining something so many times suffices to make it happen, as the old proverb says, things transpired just as the cook had imagined they would.

The Darıcızade heir returned to the House of Pleasure a few days after his departure, this time at night. His second arrival wasn't as grand as the first. He only brought a few servants with him, took up a room like an ordinary customer, and requested neither drink nor services. He wanted only one thing, and that was Kamer.

It wasn't unheard of for someone who had visited the House of Pleasure to return. There had been others who paid the house a visit just to watch Kamer dance, but the fact that Mahmud Bey invited the girl to his mansion the following morning was a true exception.

It was no small matter to take a girl outside the mansion, and few customers dared make such a request. Sirrah only accorded this privilege to her most influential customers, and in exchange she asked for an exorbitant payment.

But Mahmud Bey had plenty of influence and just as much money.

Of course, the cook heard about it, as everyone at the House of Pleasure was talking about what had happened. Some went so far as to suggest that Mahmud Bey was desperately in love with Kamer, that he'd prolonged his stay in Istanbul just for her, and that he was in talks with Sirrah to take her back to Alexandria with him. According to rumors, the amount of money he'd promised in exchange for Kamer was enough to buy the entire House of Pleasure and all the slaves living there.

The cook tried everything so he could see Kamer one last time before she went off to the Darıcızade mansion, but all his efforts failed.

Neither the bribes he offered nor his pleading had any effect, and he watched helplessly as Kamer left the House of Pleasure in a carriage drawn by six horses.

He spent that night tossing and turning in bed, drenched in sweat. Just before dawn there was a knock on his door. It was one of the girls who accompanied Kamer. "She's waiting for you in the garden," she whispered.

The cook quickly got dressed. When he saw Kamer waiting for him under the oak tree, all the gloom he had been carrying inside vanished—but just for a moment. As he got closer, darkness seized him once again. He was overcome by such fury and disappointment that he was blind to the smile and sparkling eyes of his beloved whom he had not seen for almost a month.

The cook stood at a cold distance from her, staring at her large necklace adorned with diamonds and emeralds.

She stammered, "I just got here. I haven't even been to my room yet." Then she leaned forward to embrace the cook.

Stiffly, he said, "Don't go there again."

Kamer longed to linger in his embrace but a shudder ran through her soul. "I don't want to go back," she said.

"Then don't go."

"But I have no choice."

"Don't . . ."

Feeling the pain of the bitter truth she was about to utter, she replied, "I belong to Sirrah. I have to go."

The cook fell silent. There was only one thing left for him to say, something he'd often thought about. "Let's go. . . . Let's get away from here."

Kamer's eyes sparkled for a moment. "But how?" she asked. "What will we do?"

The cook had no answer.

As they gazed at each other in the darkness, someone whispered Kamer's name from the darkness. It was the girl who had summoned the cook. "Sirrah is awake," she warned them.

Kamer quickly kissed the cook's cheek and he watched as she disappeared into the darkness of the trees.

That was the last time he saw her.

He didn't hear from Kamer for weeks. According to rumors, she was going to visit the Darıcızade mansion again, but no one knew for sure. One day, Master Adem said he had business to attend to and wouldn't be back that evening, leaving the cook to handle everything. Burdened by his worries and the work of the kitchen, the cook felt overwhelmed. One of Sirrah's slaves stopped by the kitchen and handed the cook a small folded piece of paper.

When he unfolded it, he felt something drop on his foot.

It was a short letter from Kamer, saying that she was going to Alexandria with Darıcızade Mahmud Bey, and bidding him farewell.

The cook read the letter again and again.

When he set it aside, he saw the necklace with the small apple pendant lying by his foot.

When Master Adem left him at the gates of the el-Haki brothers' home, the cook suddenly felt a sense of solitude which soothed his mind.

The el-Haki brothers were twins, and they were identical in every way, from their demeanor to their manner of speech and from the color of their eyes to their beards. But it was easy for him to tell Sa'd el-Haki from Sadr el-Haki.

Sa'd el-Haki was an astrologer, and because he spent most his time gazing at the sky, he walked around with his head held high.

Because Sadr el-Haki pored over books and leaned over as he tended to his patients, he usually walked around with his head bowed down.

The cook met Sa'd first. The house's servant, Fadıl, who was deaf as a post, did not hear the knock on the door and at the time Sadr was preparing an ointment for a patient. Sa'd opened the door, looked the cook up and down, and muttered, "Hmm, either an Aquarius or Gemini."

When the cook was a child, his mother had told him, "Never tell anybody your star sign." He didn't know why, but he'd always followed her advice. During the two years he spent with the el-Haki brothers, he would come to understand why she was right.

When the cook didn't reply, Sa'd invited him in and started walking toward the observatory. "Come, let's have a look. Perhaps we already have your horoscope."

Feeling uneasy, the cook followed him, wondering how he could have got his hands on his astrological chart. However, when he stepped into the observatory behind Sa'd el-Haki, all the questions in his mind vanished.

The interior of the observatory, which seemed modest from the outside, was splendorous. It had a large dome rising above exterior walls that were as tall as eight men. On the east side of the dome there was an opening which started at the point of the horizon and rose up to the sky. The pointed tip of a huge astrolabe rising up from the floor to the ceiling extended toward the heavens through the opening. When night fell, the stars would come out and Sa'd would take his place at the astrolabe, watching their movements and calculating their angles.

All four walls of the observatory were lined from top to bottom with shelves packed with books and manuscripts. Above the shelves were drawings of the twelve astrological signs and the seven ancient stars.

When he entered the room, Sa'd moved a ladder leaning against a bookshelf slightly to the left and quickly climbed up. After shuffling through some manuscripts, he announced, "Here it is!" Still on the ladder, he first looked at the yellowed piece of parchment in his hand and then at the cook. Smiling, he said, "I was right. You're an Aquarius."

"That's right," the cook replied coolly.

It was only then that Sa'd realized his guest was feeling uneasy, and he offered an explanation. "Don't be alarmed," he said as he climbed down the ladder. "We have to know everything about the people who come to this house. Master Adem told us everything about your past."

"I see," he replied. "How about the horoscope? How did you know that?"

Sa'd grinned. "A horoscope is created for every child born in the palace. We astrologers know each other and it is an honor to share the information we possess."

After a pause, Sa'd el-Haki said, "I see that you are tired. Do you have any ailments? Pains, aches?"

The cook shook his head. "No, my health is fine."

"In that case, all is well," Brother Sa'd replied. "The most important thing is health. All the rest can be sorted out." Then he looked at the astrological chart he was holding and continued, "The stars say that what ails you is not a financial matter. Could it be a matter of the heart?"

The cook laughed bitterly. "The nature of that 'matter,' as you say, is not that important. Do the stars also say when it will pass?"

Sa'd did not respond but sat down on a small divan sandwiched between two bookshelves and gestured for the cook to sit down beside him. "The stars don't tell us what will happen," he said. "They tell us how we might feel, or what we might think. The state of our emotions determines our actions and our choices, and the sum of that is called destiny, my young master. For example, Venus is the star of love, enjoyment, and pleasure. If I were to tell you that tomorrow Venus will be shining under your star, it would not mean that you will meet the love of your life or find joy. It would, however, stoke your desire for love and enjoyment, which in turn would be reflected in your behavior, words, and even how you look at the world, whether you realize it or not. Don't such things determine what sort of a day you'll have?"

The cook thought for a moment, intrigued. For the next two years, that look of intrigue would never leave his eyes.

Sa'd knew all the secrets of the sky, and whenever he explained the twelve astrological signs, the seven stars, and the relationship of the stars to each other, as well as the signs, the signs' houses, and their angles, retreats, conjunctions, and eclipses, the cook was awestruck by the divine mathematics which repeated itself with unfailing order, but never in the same manner twice, and his outlook on destiny, order, the world, and humanity changed every day.

"Look at the sky," Sa'd told him one hot summer night as they sat on a divan in the courtyard. He pointed to a cluster of stars just above the horizon to the east. "Mercury is in its home, Gemini, peaceful and at ease. Jupiter is three steps away in Libra. It's in harmony with Mercury. This is beneficial for all signs, but particularly for water and fire signs. Mercury is the sign of words, speech, and trade. Right now, it is in repose, benefitting from Jupiter's abundance. You should watch out for Saturn, however. It is four houses away from Jupiter, warning everyone against excess. This is only what three stars in three signs tell us. We haven't even looked at the other four: the moon, the sun, Venus, or Mars. We haven't talked about the phases of the moon, its waxing and waning, or the signs that are on the ascent and those on the descent. What's more, these are only the things in the sky at this moment tonight, my young master. Now, close your eyes, wait a second, and then open them again. You'll see that the sky has changed. Mercury will be in the same sign, but it will have moved one thousandth of a degree, and even this difference which cannot be seen with the eye will affect many things. Remember this: the sky is like a flowing river. No moment resembles the next. Everything is constantly changing. This is why people are so different, even identical twins."

Sa'd was indeed right, and the greatest proof of his claim was the existence of his twin brother, Sadr el-Haki. Only a few minutes had passed between their births but they were strikingly different, the most apparent difference being that Sa'd el-Haki was friendly and easygoing while his twin was distant and disciplined.

The cook met Sadr el-Haki a week after he arrived at the house. As he was listening to Sa'd talk about the movements of the moon and sun through the signs, Sadr walked in, introduced himself, and apologized for the delay in meeting him, briefly explaining that he had been searching for a cure for a patient with a rare illness. "Tomorrow we will begin our lessons," he said, "and every second day we'll continue. Come to my room at lunchtime."

Sadr left the observatory just as he had come in, head bowed down.

Sa'd had not mentioned anything about the timing of their "lessons" or things of that sort. Their discussions were nothing like lessons; rather, Sa'd chatted about the signs and the stars, told stories, and asked questions. Noticing that the cook was surprised, Brother Sa'd let out a small laugh and said, "Yes, he really is my brother."

When he went to Sadr's room the next day, the doctor was waiting for him beside two low tables facing each other. There was a bundle of paper on one of the tables and a small inkwell with a pen.

"Please sit down," Sadr el-Haki said, pointing to one of the tables. The cook quietly walked in and sat cross-legged on a cushion in front of the table.

After scrutinizing his face for a moment, Brother Sadr got up from his cushion and inspected the cook's eyelids, asked him to look up and down, and checked his pulse.

"You're sitting still, but your heart is beating fast," he said after letting go of the cook's wrist. "Do you have a headache?"

"No," the cook responded.

"Do you suffer from sleeplessness?"

"Yes, a little."

"Difficulty gathering your thoughts? An inability to concentrate or converse at length?"

The cook paused to think before answering, which gave Sadr all the answers he needed. "I see," he said. Just as he was about to offer his diagnosis, the cook, like many people who suffer from spiritual ill-health, attempted to prove his well-being by saying, "Master Sa'd told me I was in good health."

After casting an annoyed look at the cook, Sadr el-Haki sat down and said, "Please don't be confused by the fact we're twins. He is not the doctor, I am."

The cook fell silent. Assured that the young man sitting across from him had learned his very first lesson, Brother Sadr began to lecture him on the actual subject of the lesson.

"Master Fuzuli says that the favorite place in the land of the body is the city of the heart," he began, casting a meaningful glance at his new pupil. "This city has three allies and three enemies. Its allies are relief, friendship, and hope, while its enemies are spite, fear, and sorrow.

"Each of these have allies of their own. The allies of spite are dishonesty, animosity, and ill-will, while the allies of fear are confusion, terror, and boredom. The allies of sorrow are trouble, deprivation, and longing.

"As for the allies of the city of the heart, the ally of relief is beauty, the ally of friendship is love, and the ally of hope is intellect.

"As you can see, the enemies have more allies than the friends, which makes the city of the heart the most sensitive area of the land of the body. If it gets ill, so does the body, and this condition of ill-health is called 'disease' by the science of medicine.

"That which we call the body is made up of four elements, just like nature itself and the sky. These elements are air, water, fire, and earth, and what we call good health is the harmony and balance between these four elements.

"The element of air is related to blood, and its location is the spleen.

"The element of water is located in the lungs, but it also concerns the stomach, and therefore digestion.

"The location of the element of fire is the gallbladder. It concerns the fitness of the body, the color of the skin, and the brightness of the eyes.

"The element of earth is located in the heart and the mind. It concerns diseases of the heart, and mental and spiritual sicknesses.

"A decrease or increase of any one of these four elements, which in turn causes the increase or decrease of the other three, leads to the deterioration of health.

"Master Fuzuli says, 'Disease enters the land of the body through food.' He is quite right. However, not only what we eat, but what we see, what we hear, what we smell, what we touch, and even what we experience can cause us to become unwell.

"Regardless of the means by which disease enters the body, there are only three ways one can banish it: diet, medicine, and surgery.

"Diet is the most important one, firstly because it is the most natural means of treatment, and secondly because it not only eliminates disease but also helps to protect one's health. If diet doesn't work, then medicine is used. If medicine doesn't work, surgery is the last resort.

"My young master, while you're here, we'll work on the issue of foods. Now, tell me. You already know about the four elements of nature. Do you know about the nature of these elements?"

The cook shook his head.

"Then please take notes," Sadr el-Haki said, pointing at the sheaf of paper in front of him.

The cook wasn't accustomed to writing. He reached toward the pen timidly, carefully dipped it into the inkwell, and began to write.

"Air," began Sadr el-Haki, "is warm and moist in nature.

"Water is cold and moist in nature.

"Fire is warm and dry in nature.

"Earth is cold and dry in nature.

"My young master, you will not only memorize the natures of the four elements, but grasp them with your entire being. Just as your art is founded on the four tastes, the science of medicine is founded on the nature of these elements. Your art of cooking and our science intersect just at that point, at the nature of the elements. Do you understand?"

Brother Sadr looked at the cook's uncomprehending expression for a few moments, and smiled imperceptibly. "You will see, my young master. That's why you're here. Let's continue with examples. Please write this down: Garlic is a food which is warm in the second degree and also dry in the second degree. Its star is Mars."

Pen in hand, the cook paused in confusion. Sadr nodded as if he had been expecting him to react that way and continued: "Not only humans, but plants, animals, and even the stones and minerals in the earth have natures and stars. Think about what I said: Health is the harmony of the four elements in the human body. If that harmony is disrupted, the body falls ill. For example, if you visit a doctor complaining of exhaustion, a dry mouth, pain in your joints, and your skin is pale yellow, this shows that there is an excess of the fire element in the body. We know that fire is warm and dry in nature. We've also seen that garlic is warm and dry in nature. Now, here is my question: What would happen if this patient were to eat garlic?"

The cook replied, "The dry and warm element in the body would increase."

"Yes, and therefore the sickness would worsen." Then he asked, "What should you do then?"

"Consume cold and moist foods."

"Correct. And what must we do in the case of your complaints?"

The cook started to look through the pieces of paper in front of him. He knew that Sadr had said that matters of the heart were caused by an excess of the earth element in the body. Earth was cold and dry in nature, so he concluded that in order restore balance, warm and moist foods were needed.

After a lengthy silence he gave his answer, and once again Sadr replied that it was correct. Seeing that the cook was beginning to understand, he continued, "Let's move on to degrees. What did I say? Garlic is warm and dry in the second degree.

"Let's imagine a body in which the elements are in harmony. Any outside interference with this body, including the ingestion of food, will disrupt the balance, and the body will immediately begin to work to restore it. Degrees tell us how long it will take before the body regains its equilibrium.

"Garlic is a food whose nature is in the second degree, which means that the balance in the body of someone who eats garlic will return to normal in two hours at most. The higher the degree, the longer the period of time needed to reach equilibrium. Foods of the third and fourth degree are ones we commonly call 'heavy.' Those that are of the fifth degree and upward are poisonous. For serious illnesses, doctors recommend high-degree foods and make medicines prepared from them. For example, in the case of a deep spiritual ailment, we recommend third- and even fourth-degree foods that are warm and moist, depending on the course of the illness, or medicines made from high-degree spices, such as *mesir* paste.

"Here is my last question: Suppose that a certain dish or paste is being prepared for a patient. The apothecary has chosen medium-degree foods and spices. Just as the paste is being mixed, you enter the room and become involved in the process. Can you imagine what would happen?"

The cook looked at his teacher, unable to answer. Sadr el-Haki asked, "Can you imagine what would happen if the Pasha of Cuisine touched that pot?"

It wasn't difficult for him to imagine what could happen, but again he remained silent. His was the silence of someone who was just discovering the extent of his power, who was perhaps for the first time in his life taking it seriously, and trying to acquaint himself with and believe in it.

Sadr continued as if he could read the cook's mind: "My young master, you possess great power. You could reward someone with health, or strike them down with death. We only have one hope, and that is for you to use your power for good. You will learn the secrets of the body and of foods from me, and you'll learn the secret language of the sky from my brother. If you were to make a mistake, or if for one second you gave in to evil and used your power for malice, we as your teachers shall be held responsible. I hope you realize the enormity of the responsibility that you place on our shoulders."

The cook nodded, but he had a strong desire to rush off to the library in the observatory, pick out a book at random, and start to read. An overwhelming sense of curiosity seized him along with the awareness of his own power. The feeling was one of such enormous appetite that he longed to devour all the secrets on earth.

At the same time, he wondered if he had found a solution for the trouble in his soul. He thought that by immersing himself in books and devoting his mind to the intricacies of the sciences of medicine and astronomy, he could cast off his gloomy thoughts or at least put them aside for a while.

From that day onward, the cook spent the majority of his time at his table in Sadr's room, among the shelves in the observatory, and sitting on a bench in the garden, writing, reading, and memorizing.

From Sadr el-Haki, he learnt the secrets of meat, vegetables, fruits, roots, grains, and legumes, as well as their natures and their stars. From Sa'd el-Haki, he learned about the stars wandering the heavens, distant and slow or close by and swift; about Venus the "composer," Mercury the "scribe," Mars the "*seraskier*," Jupiter the "treasurer," and the sun, which was the "sultan of the universe," and its "vizier," the moon. He learned how they changed in property and nature as they moved through the signs and their houses while retaining their essence; how Venus, the star of pleasure, beauty, and love, could be frivolous under Libra, its home, but serious under Sagittarius, which was an earth sign. He also learned how to determine how a person born under Mercury in the second house of Leo would be affected in terms of financial matters as Mercury moved from sign to sign.

The cook studied as a way to banish the pain in his heart and silence the noise whirling in his mind. But every time he became exhausted and looked up at the heavens for relief, he saw her.

He had been fond of looking into Kamer's dark eyes, which widened to become as vast as the night sky. Sparkling stars would appear, each one a sign of hope, love, and passion.

In her absence, he looked up at the night sky when he missed her. The sky would become her eyes, and then one by one the stars would disappear, condemning the night to the pitch-blackness of longing.

That was how the cook learned about the stars and the secrets of the senses.

Before deciding on what he was going to cook for His Highness the Sultan, he carefully studied the sovereign's astrological chart and managed to seize on the opportunity the skies afforded him amongst all those complex calculations which could be interpreted in a thousand different ways.

Three days had passed since the dishes the cook had prepared were presented to the sultan, but things were still quiet and not a single word had reached him from beyond the Gate of Felicity.

They were going about their usual tasks in the kitchen. Mahir was standing next to him by the table, dicing meat for a dish called Sultan's Rice that they were planning on making for dinner that evening. Without looking up from his work, he murmured, "No news yet, Master?"

The cook sighed. "God give me strength." His eyes were fixed on the water dripping from the sack of washed rice which they had hung from a hook. The rice had to be properly drained to make Sultan's Rice. Ordinarily, the dish was never cooked outside of the Royal Kitchen, and because it was one of the dishes assumed to be reserved for the sultan alone, no one ever dared request it. But the Chief Sword Bearer had had the audacity to ask for it. The cook felt assured that the agha was at his breaking point and the die had been cast.

"No news yet," he responded.

Mahir put down his knife and looked at his master with tear-filled eyes. "I don't just mean compliments," he said. "Hasn't he said anything about what was wrong?"

The cook glared at Mahir, eyes flashing with anger and disappointment. "The sovereign is presented with thirty-four dishes at every meal, Mahir. Surely he has better things to do than list their faults!" He pointed to the rice on the hook. "Take down the rice. It's time to start cooking it."

He knew exactly which of his assistant's dreams had been shattered, and he enjoyed that awareness. Mahir had taken to dreaming about the Royal Kitchen. In his mind, the sultan should have been quite pleased with their dishes and requested that the cook be appointed to the Royal Kitchen, along with his assistant, of course.

It was a pleasant dream. However, for Mahir, being sent to that kitchen was not so much about his desire to become a cook, but to take one step closer to the source of power, under whose shadow he could find good fortune as well as a future. His plan was to get into the Royal Kitchen and make his name heard at the Harem through Neyyir Agha. He figured that he could then get into the good graces of Haseki Sultan herself and secure himself a rank and a title either at the Inner Palace or, by means of sacrificing certain parts of his anatomy, in the Harem. After all, he figured, it had happened before.

Nothing had gone how Mahir had planned, however. From what he heard, the sultan only took two bites of the dish the cook prepared, and then ordered his servants to bring in truffles roasted in butter and yogurt with thistle.

Mahir couldn't believe that their dish had been brushed aside for mere roasted truffles and yoghurt. And how excited he had been when he had heard which dish the cook had in mind for the sovereign's table: wrapped kebab made from fowl.

His initial excitement had now turned into anger. "Why did he choose such a difficult dish?" he kept grumbling to himself. The dish was known for being the most difficult kebab to make, and it involved wrapping strips of turkey, chicken, duck, and quail around each other. First the various meats had to be boiled separately for just the right amount of time before being placed on a single skewer and roasted over an open fire. It demanded the utmost of patience and skill rather than knowledge and art, and the slightest carelessness could ruin the whole dish.

In his mind, the cook had gone too far by using game birds, which were tastier but more difficult to cook. Under the surprised gazes of the Royal Kitchen cooks, he had boiled the meat of a wild goose, a large pheasant, a partridge, and a quail and then rubbed the meat with spices before placing it on a skewer and roasting it over a fire for hours. When the meat was ready, he placed it on a plate with some roasted vegetables and then poured a sauce of hot citrus and pomegranate juice over the whole dish.

The cook may not have been able to gain the sultan's praise but he had become the talk of not just the Royal Kitchen but the entirety of the Imperial Kitchens. Some thought that he had just tried to show off and was suffering the consequences, while others commended his courage and admired his attempt to bring a never-before-tried flavor to an already difficult dish.

But only the cook knew why he had cooked that particular dish.

He had made his decision when he'd looked at the sultan's horoscope and saw that the star of Mars was favoring the sovereign's sign. He'd also seen that the star would be in the same place when he would cook the dish. Mars was known to heighten the emotions when it traversed a sign and Venus was also winking on the other side, an invitation to turn fervor into pleasure.

The cook had used meat from game birds that were warm in the third degree and dry in the second degree for the base of the food, heightening the effect of Mars, which was a fiery star, and the spices and vegetables he used had added to Venus's thirst. It didn't matter whether the sultan had taken one bite or two from the dish. Even inhaling its scent would have been enough for his plan. The cook was completely sure of himself, which was why he patiently waited for the news he would eventually hear.

As he was roasting pistachios and raisins, he watched his assistant, who sliced the last remaining piece of meat in half. Placing the wooden spoon he was holding in Mahir's hand, he pointed at the pan on the stove and said, "Put the meat in the pan and roast it with the pistachios."

As Mahir attended to the meat, the cook added spices over his shoulder. He added plenty of ground black pepper and tossed in a few whole peppercorns. Just as he was about to reach for the jar of coriander, Mahir said, "Master, please permit me to divulge a personal matter to you."

The cook looked at his assistant in surprise. Never before had he heard Mahir speak so formally.

"What is it?" he asked.

"When can I attain the rank of master?"

The cooked paused to think.

But he wasn't thinking about whether Mahir would become a master or not. He was thinking that in another life, he would have done all he could for him, or even told him to change professions while he still had the time. But the cook knew that Mahir was going to play an important role in his plan and that he needed him.

"Why? Are you bored of working with me already?" he asked with a smile.

Mahir blushed. "No, Master. I've been working for so many years . . . and I'm getting older, too, as you know."

The cook's smile broadened. He had decided that giving his assistant a little hope might help him in the near future. "Let me think about it," he replied.

That was enough for Mahir. His eyes welled up with tears. He was as happy as if he had been told he would be donning the red apron the very next day. "Thank you, Master, I—" he began, but he was cut off by a commotion outside, which was getting louder second by second.

"Expedition!" the stone walls echoed. "Expedition! Our sovereign has called for an Imperial Expedition!"

The cooks and assistants stopped what they were doing and listened. Some, overcome by curiosity, dashed outside to see what was going on, and asked passersby, "What's happening? Are we going to war?"

Master İsfendiyar entered the kitchen through the middle gate, accompanied by the Chamberlain of the Kitchen, Şakir Effendi, and a Council Sergeant. He appeared tense, and the Chamberlain, who was standing at the very rear behind the Council Sergeant, appeared to be lost in thought.

Master İsfendiyar stopped at the threshold of the Royal Kitchen along with his retinue. He surveyed the crowd which had quickly gathered around and gestured toward the Council Sergeant. "Effendi has an announcement to make."

All the eyes and ears of the denizens of the Imperial Kitchens were fixed on the Council Sergeant, who had taken a step forward. As per custom, the Sergeant struck his staff on the ground three times and then stated, "Our sovereign has declared that he will be having a hunting expedition in Rumelia. Our sultan will set off toward Edirne after tomorrow morning's prayers and the hunting attendants will complete their preparations as soon as possible and leave within two days. The Imperial Council orders that six cooks from the Royal Kitchen and the cooks and assistants of the Chief Privy Chamber Page, Chief Sword Bearer, Chief Tailor, Chief Butler, Chief Cellar Steward, and Chief Treasurer, as well as thirty cooks and their assistants from the Inner Palace Servants' Kitchen and the Imperial Council Kitchen, join the expedition."

When he was finished, the Sergeant marched out of the kitchen. The moment he walked out, pandemonium broke out in the kitchen.

"Why the rush?"

"How can we prepare for an expedition so soon?"

"Is this the time for a hunting expedition, when the coffers are empty?"

"Has he lost his mind?"

The tangled yarn of whisperings unraveled when Master İsfendiyar shouted, "Silence!" His stern gaze was fixed on the cook, who was standing in a far corner of the kitchen.

"Everyone back to work!" Master İsfendiyar boomed.

After the crowd dispersed, Master İsfendiyar approached the cook. "Come with me," he whispered.

The cook followed a few steps behind Master İsfendiyar. When they walked through the door of the lodgings into the dimly lit entryway, the master turned around and looked angrily at the cook.

"Master, what's wrong?" the cook began to ask, but he was cut short when the master struck him in the chest with his cane. When he doubled over, Master İsfendiyar pushed him against the wall, pinning him there with his cane.

The master growled, "What in heaven's name do you think you're doing?"

The cook barely managed a hoarse whisper in reply.

The master continued, "Are you trying to bankrupt the empire? Is that your plan?"

The master pushed hard on the cane, which he was now holding against the cook's neck. Drawing on all his strength, the cook shoved his master away and coughed a few times. "What are you doing, Master?" he asked.

Master İsfendiyar stepped toward him again, still in a rage. "Wrapped kebab, eh?" he said in a low voice. "I thought you had it in for the sultan's health, but you've gone even further than that. You made him long to go hunting with the dish you made! You know how much a hunting expedition costs the Treasury, don't you? Of course you do. You know it full well!"

"I know, Master," the cook replied. There wasn't a trace of regret or shame in his expression.

Master İsfendiyar pointed his cane at the cook. "The Treasury is already in dire straits. Now the coffers will be completely wiped out. In ten days' time, salaries will have to be paid. You know that too, right? When the Janissaries don't get their payment, they will revolt. The sovereign will be away and there will be no one to defend the throne. When the revolt begins, heads will roll, the palace will be plunged into turmoil, and in that chaos you will take what you want from the Harem, won't you?"

"Master, listen for a second," the cook tried to say, but the cane tapping on his neck silenced him.

"The sultan will probably be overthrown," Master İsfendiyar continued, "and you know what the new sultan will do. All those young boys will be sent to the noose because of you. But what do you care? You don't even care about the girl; all you want is to get revenge on the palace and the empire!"

"I want neither revenge nor to bring harm to the empire, my master," the cook said. "Yes, you're right, the Treasury will have a difficult time and the Janissaries will grumble, but don't worry. I don't mean to bring harm to anyone."

Master İsfendiyar smiled wryly. "You fool! When the Janissaries revolt, what then? You're not thinking straight. Didn't you realize that the Chief Sword Bearer would go on the expedition with the sultan? You idiot, couldn't you figure out that much? Now you stand there and tell me that no harm will come to anyone. You'll be on the expedition along with the agha. What are you going to do? Do you think you can make matters right with your cooking?"

A self-assured smile appeared on the cook's face. "Siyavuş Agha is still in the palace," he whispered. "How do you know he'll go on the expedition?"

Master İsfendiyar was a little afraid of the man standing before him. Still, he pressed his cane against the cook's neck again and said, "If the empire suffers because of this, I will place your head in front of the Gate of Felicity with my own two hands! Do you understand?"

The cook nodded. "I understand, Master. Please don't worry. Whatever I might have become, I still have royal blood running through my veins. Our sovereign and his children are my relatives. If I bring harm to the state or the royal family, I will gladly sacrifice my life to set matters right."

Master İsfendiyar silently lowered his cane. After casting the cook a final glance, he turned and walked away.

The cook stepped outside and saw the Chamberlain of the Kitchen, Şakir Effendi, making his way toward his quarters along with a few other men. He saluted them as they passed by.

He guessed that the men walking with him were the deputies responsible for the expedition. Together they would sit down and meticulously calculate where the *sekban* regiment, falconers, hound-keepers, messengers, guards, and Inner Palace residents would stay, where the Imperial Tent would be pitched, what the members of the expedition—about six hundred in number—would eat for two months, and how all the horses, cows, mules, and hounds would be fed.

That wasn't in itself a problem. The state had etiquette to follow and its subjects had experience. They could draw the route, calculate the amount of supplies needed, prepare them, and set out on the road in a single day. But the cellar, which Şakir Effendi had meticulously put back into order, would be emptied again, and the sudden expedition would siphon off a great deal of the money from the Treasury, which meant it would be even harder to replace the supplies that were going to run out.

Şakir Effendi had been a public servant for many years and he could foresee the approaching storm. Thinking about the Janissaries' payment made his hair stand on end, but even that wasn't the most pressing matter. He knew that if he couldn't somehow find a way to feed the remainder of the palace residents after the expedition, he might be removed from his post before the payment had to be made to the Janissaries. *Who knows*, he thought, *perhaps that was the best thing that could happen to me, all things considered.*

When the cook returned to the kitchen, he saw that all was calm save for a few cooks who were whispering to each other. Silence hung heavily in the air in the Aghas' Kitchen. Many of the assistants were nowhere to be seen. He guessed that they had been instructed to begin the preparations.

All the masters were dejected, as they knew that the hardships of the expedition would be a heavy burden on them as they tried to please the aghas, pashas, and the sovereign as they cooked in a makeshift kitchen under a half-open tent.

The only person who seemed to be pleased was Mahir, who was rubbing ash on a dirty pot to clean it, whispering a cheerful tune as he dreamed of the days he would spend in close quarters with the palace elite.

When Mahir saw the cook, he put down the pot and smiled. "Look, Master," he said, wiping ash from his hands, "fortune is on our side again. Our sovereign will ask for another dish from us. This time we won't embarrass ourselves."

The cook studied his assistant for a moment. If these had been ordinary times and they had been living in an ordinary place, he would have punished Mahir for his impertinence, or at the very least said, "If there is an embarrassment in this kitchen, Mahir, it's you!" But he knew that it wasn't the time or the place, and it suited him for his assistant to be lost in dreams.

"God willing," he said. "God willing . . ." He picked up a small pan and said, "Now run along and bring me some pastry flour, eggs, butter, a little yogurt, and sesame oil."

"Straightaway, Master," Mahir replied, but he didn't move. "Are you going to make fritters again?"

The cook nodded.

"For the Privy Chamber?" Mahir asked.

"They should have something sweet to eat before the expedition," the cook replied, running out of patience. "They won't have any such treats while they're gone."

Mahir was surprised. "But Master, won't we be with them? Can't you cook desserts during the expedition?"

The cook bit his tongue, unsure of whether he should be angry with himself or with his assistant. He snapped, "Don't ask so many questions! Now run along."

"Straightaway, Master," Mahir said and ran off. He got the butter, eggs, and yogurt from the shelves in the kitchen and then made his way to the cellar to get the pastry flour and sesame oil. Returning not long after, he was carrying not only a sack of flour and a pitcher of oil, but also a large bowl. With a smile he said, "You forgot to tell me to bring honey, but I brought it anyway." The smile fell from his lips when he saw the cook holding a large paper cone.

"Is that . . . ceremonial sugar, Master?" he stammered, gazing at the large clear crystals of sugar that glimmered even in the dim light of the kitchen. The best honey in the capital cost sixteen or twenty silver coins per *oka*, but sugar sold for a hundred silver coins for the same amount. Few households could afford that kind of sugar. Desserts and sherbets that were served to the sovereign used sugar instead of honey, but even then ceremonial sugar was only used on special occasions such as royal weddings or ceremonies held in honor of newborn heirs.

"Where did you get it, Master?" Mahir asked. "Is that what you'll use for the fritters?" He wanted to ask other questions but clamped his mouth shut when he saw the cook looking at him, his index finger pressed to his lips. The cook looked around to see if anyone was watching them. After all, there was no way he could explain why he was using sugar for a sweet he was going to secretly send to the Privy Chamber as a gift.

The cook said, "You go get a little rest."

Mahir was crestfallen. "Don't you want any help, Master?" he asked.

"No," the cook replied without looking at him. "Go on."

"Very well, Master," Mahir replied and shuffled toward the door. The pitiful tone of his voice pained the cook's heart. *I'm sorry, Mahir,* he thought, and then set to work on the fritters.

First he put away the yogurt and the eggs, as they weren't necessary. He put the flour into the pan and made a small hollow atop the mound of flour with his fist. He looked around again and saw that everybody was engrossed in their work. He took out a small glass bottle that was tucked into his sash and slowly uncorked it. When he poured the thick yellow-green liquid into the pan, the pungent smell of linden rose into the air. The cook took the lid off of a boiling pot of soup to mask the scent.

He planned on making fritters with fermented dough, which was why he had prepared the linden mixture. As he whispered over the pot, the linden mixture congealed and was now ready to raise the dough. It would give the fritters a soft, full texture, and, most importantly, create the mysterious essence at their center.

Everyone knew that linden naturally brought on a feeling of calmness, and when fermented, that effect was heightened. Some religious scholars stated that fermented linden was an intoxicating substance that Muslims were prohibited from consuming, and in some territories of the empire, judges had even had forbidden people from fermenting it.

Such religious scholars may have been slightly overzealous in condemning that beautifully scented flower, but if they were to have tasted a pastry made with the linden fermented by the Pasha of Cuisine, they wouldn't have just advised against its consumption but banned it outright. In the hands of the Pasha of Cuisine, the innocent fermentation created a substance that tore down the barriers of logic which held back strong emotions and did away with all self-control. And that was exactly what the cook desired. Whoever ate the fritters would forget about fear and loyalty, discarding tradition and rules in the process.

The void created by the fermented linden would be filled with the sugar, the taste of which would be heightened by the sesame oil. The cook knew that sweet, one of the four basic tastes, was coupled with the element of fire, which was famed for its violence.

The cook fried the round fritters, and, after soaking them in a bowl of sugar water prepared with a little lemon, he placed them in a porcelain bowl shaped like a gondola. He didn't put a lid on the bowl to make sure they stayed crisp. As the scent of the fritters filled the air, everyone in the kitchen glanced at the bowl on the counter; it was only the cook's aloof disposition which prevented them from asking for a taste.

The cook pretended to clean his knives as he waited for Firuz Agha. When he saw a silhouette pass through the doorway, he thought Firuz Agha had finally arrived, but it was Mahir.

Mahir approached with his head bowed and a sullen expression on his face. He walked slowly toward the table where the cook was standing and silently stood two paces away. "So," the cook said, "is something amiss?"

"Neyyir Agha came," Mahir replied.

"I see," the cook murmured. After a pause he asked, "Is he well?"

"He was in high spirits."

"For good reason, I suppose?"

"I asked but he didn't tell me why. He only said 'We're getting rid of our troubles.' But he said that it was too early to say anything."

The cook frowned, thinking that if a discreet agha from the Harem was openly being cheerful, something serious must have transpired. A feeling of unease took hold of him. *I have to find out what's happening*, he thought. He was about to make a decisive step in his plan, and he knew that he couldn't leave anything to chance.

The cook was lost in thought, thinking about how he could speak to Neyyir Agha and ask him what had happened. As his mind raced, he saw a hand reaching toward the bowl of fritters. At first, he didn't mind but when he remembered what he had put in them, he shouted, "No!"

In his panic, he had shouted so loudly that every head in the kitchen turned toward him. Mahir stood there, frozen. His hand was hovering above the bowl and he looked at his master with resentment and fear in his eyes.

"They're still hot," the cook offered, but it was too late to mend Mahir's hurt feelings. One of the nearby assistants in the kitchen could hold it back no longer and let out a hearty laugh. On the verge of tears, Mahir stormed out of the kitchen.

The cook felt bad for him, but the thought of Mahir acting without loyalty and fear was too much to bear.

He knew Mahir was angry at him and that he would become angrier yet. Very soon, when the time was right, the cook would give his assistant the opportunity to take his revenge and cool his burning heart. That was Mahir's purpose, and that was why he needed him, just like the others, including Treasurer Halil Pasha, Neyyir Agha, Privy Chamber Page Firuz Agha, Chief Sword Bearer Siyavuş Agha, the sovereign, and Haseki Sultan.

For months he had been setting the stage with meticulous care and the play was about to begin. The gondola-shaped bowl by his elbow would begin its journey toward the Inner Palace along with the Chief Sword Bearer's meal.

And the next day, nothing would be the same at the palace.

When the cook withdrew to his lodgings that night, he knew very well he wouldn't get a wink of sleep. Throughout the night, he feigned sleep and listened for any sounds that were out of the ordinary. The next morning just after the prayers, a farewell ceremony was going to be held for the sultan with all the residents of the palace in attendance. In the morning, the more experienced assistants would teach the apprentices how to behave during the ceremony. The cooks would get dressed, put on their finest attire along with embroidered handkerchiefs and spotless blue and red aprons, wind their turbans, comb their moustaches, and trim their beards.

Around midnight the palace fell silent. The cook closed his eyes, slowed down his breathing, and gave himself over to his thoughts. Time passed with agonizing slowness, and having to pretend to be asleep while his mind was occupied only increased the tediousness of waiting, which in itself was tantamount to torture.

In fact, the cook knew very well what was going to happen.

But he wondered how the events would transpire. He tried to clear his mind of doubts, but they kept coming back. As each scene unfolded before his eyes, his conscience recoiled in pain, and he had to stoke the flames of his anger to suppress the guilt he felt. And every time he felt angry, he found himself wandering among the painful memories of his past.

It was as if he possessed two hearts, one of which was quick-tempered and stern, while the other wise and compassionate.

An hour before the morning call to prayer, the cook heard what he was waiting for. Hasty footsteps made their way toward the kitchens from the Gate of Felicity; based on the sound of the steps, the cook surmised that they belonged to a page boy. He heard the footsteps enter the Royal Kitchen, make their way toward the lodgings via the passageway, and pause for a moment in the courtyard. Clearly whoever it was did not want to enter the lodgings alone. Then he heard another pair of feet slowly approaching. The cook thought, *It's probably the cellar guard*. After a brief exchange of whispers, the guard became agitated. They walked toward the lodgings together and began to climb the steps.

The lodging guard met the newcomers at the top of the stairs, and after receiving the news he circled the cook's bed a few times, considering waking him, but then made his way toward Master İsfendiyar. A few of the cooks woke up and sleepily murmured, "What's the matter? What happened?" As more of them woke up, the cook heard the sound of other footsteps approaching from the direction of the Gate of

Felicity and he was certain he heard the heavy footsteps of Firuz Agha approaching the kitchen.

The cook did not stir until Master İsfendiyar approached him with his limping gait and poked him in the shoulder with his cane. The cook opened his eyes, feigning surprise, and looked up. "What is the matter, Master?" Master İsfendiyar's eyes were filled with anger and concern, but the cook thought that he saw a little admiration as well. "Firuz Agha is downstairs," he said. "He's waiting for you."

The cook clambered out of bed, muttering, "What does he want at this hour?" Ignoring the cooks who had gathered around his bed, he put on his shirt and rushed downstairs.

Firuz Agha was waiting for him in the courtyard a few paces from the gate which led to the lodgings. There were two other pages with him. The cook assumed that the one who was out of breath must have been the one who'd rushed ahead to deliver the news.

The cook approached Firuz Agha and greeted him. Before asking anything, he waited for the curious cooks who had followed him to congregate within earshot. From what he had heard while he was in bed, news had already spread around the lodgings, and now everyone was waiting for the Privy Chamber Page to make an official announcement.

After the sound of footsteps fell silent, the cook looked into the agha's eyes and asked, "What is all this commotion about?"

It may have seemed like an innocent question, but he made no effort to conceal in his voice what he already knew.

After glancing at the cook, Firuz Agha bowed his head in a contrived expression of grief. "His Highness the Chief Sword Bearer has passed away," he said.

The cook was shaken, but not because he felt pity or sorrow or guilt. On the contrary, he was surprised by how unmoved his conscience was. A strange dark sense of relief, which he was ashamed to feel, swept over him. Part of his heart felt light as a feather, but the other was filled with the dregs of fury and still felt heavy as lead. He was a novice when it came to revenge and was tasting it for the first time. He was just learning that rather than erasing fury, revenge only made it a permanent part of one's heart, just like words inscribed in stone.

Without waiting for the insincere mutterings from the crowd behind him to quiet, he replied, "My condolences. How did it happen?"

"A terrible accident," the Privy Chamber Page responded. "His Highness the Agha wanted to visit the hammam. He felt he should perform his ablutions before seeing off our sovereign on his expedition in the morning. The late agha was quite a hasty person, as you know. He was walking quickly through the hammam and slipped, hitting his head on the corner of the basin. God must have willed it so."

"So be the will of God," the cook murmured. They glanced into each other's eyes knowingly.

The lie may have slipped from Firuz Agha's lips, but the flames of the truth burned in his eyes. Firuz Agha knew he had to remain silent, and perhaps would have to do so for many years to come. But one day he would talk about it. The cook knew as well that Firuz Agha would one day tell someone in detail what had taken place a few hours earlier that night inside the Inner Palace hammam.

He would begin by talking about Siyavuş Agha. He would explain at length what a cruel, tyrannical, vindictive, and cursed man he had been. Then he would talk about that night. How Siyavuş Agha had bellowed for all the novice pages to get up and get dressed, how he ordered the hammam fire to be stoked, how he poured a hand basin full of hot water over the furnace attendant's head just because he wanted the water to be hotter, how he soaped and washed himself for hours, not caring about the poor novice boys drenched in sweat, waiting hand and foot on him in all that heat and humidity while dressed in full ceremonial attire as per his orders, how he began to beat the novice boy who was responsible for his laundry with a silk towel he'd doused in cold water because the towel offered to him to dry himself was not soft enough, and how a large lad who could not stand to watch his friend get beaten grabbed Siyavuş Agha's tiny head and slammed it against the corner of the washbasin. He would tell everything, filled with anger which would still remain as fresh as it had been on that night.

The cook knew this because one day he would do the same.

How he wormed his way into Siyavuş Agha's dreams by cooking the food he hated the most so that he would be appointed to the Imperial Kitchens, how he multiplied the agha's conceit and cruelty with the food he cooked, how he turned the page boys' hatred and spite into violence drop by drop with the sweets he kept sending them, and how he cleared the path toward his goal by getting rid of the agha who wielded such power over the palace as well as the Harem.

He would of course also say that there were hundreds of other ways he could've gotten rid of the Chief Sword Bearer without killing him. He could've confined him to his bed, just like he had done with Treasurer Halil Pasha, or driven him mad so that he would spend the rest of his days under lock and key.

"The agha could have still been alive," the cook would admit.

It was true. Neither his cruel treatment of the page boys nor his influence at the palace was reason enough to warrant the Chief Sword Bearer's demise.

Had Siyavuş Agha not been so fond of retelling in detail the story about how he caught an odalisque running for her life on the previous sultan's enthronement night and how, on the roof of the Harem, just next to the Tower of Justice, he had slipped a noose around her neck and flung the still-conscious woman into the sea inside a sack on the shores of Sarayburnu, he may have still been alive. He told that story at every banquet table as if it was the peak of his career.

And the cook remembered quite well the woman who was caught on the roof of the Harem that night. It was his mother.

Siyavuş Agha shared that fate with so many other cruel people—his death had been sudden, and it was quickly forgotten. Contrary to what was expected, His Highness the Sultan did not cancel his expedition but merely postponed his departure from morning to noon.

The agha was given a quick burial following the noon prayers as if he had been a nuisance to be rid of, and before his coffin had left through the first gate, the denizens of the palace had already congregated in the Second Courtyard to bid the sultan farewell.

The sultan's departure from the palace was even swifter than Siyavuş Agha's funeral. He was filled with a burning desire to go hunting, a desire which he didn't quite understand himself, and he had ordered for there to be no farewell ceremony. Such an act was unheard of in the history of the Ottoman Empire. Even when the sovereign went from one room of the palace to another he was accompanied by ceremony, so setting out on an expedition without a farewell ceremony was unprecedented. While the public servants bowed to the sultan's wishes, they still ordered the residents of the entire palace to gather in the Second Courtyard so there would be a small crowd to set their minds at ease. But even that didn't slow the sultan down. He spurred his horse on and disappeared from sight with his entourage. So quickly did he leave that the Grand Vizier and other pashas' salutations were left hanging in the air and his regiment of guards had to run after him in their ceremonial armor.

Questions remained behind in the sovereign's absence. His state of mind was mysterious of course, but the most pressing question concerned who would be appointed as the new Chief Sword Bearer. The sultan hadn't yet hinted at whom he might appoint as he knew it would only cause more turmoil.

The cooks in the Aghas' Kitchen were the most curious, followed by those of the Inner Palace and Harem. If the sultan ordered that the successor be appointed from the ranks, the Treasurer, Chief Equerry, Chief Footman, or Chief Cellar Attendant would move up a step in the ranks, as would their cooks. If the sultan appointed a Chief Sword Bearer from outside the ranks, nothing would change and the only sticking point of curiosity would be about who the new Chief Sword Bearer would choose as his personal cook.

News was delivered to the palace by messenger after the evening call to prayer, reaching the kitchens at lightning speed.

When the cook entered the stewards' office, having been summoned to receive notification of the decision, he saw that Master İsfendiyar, Kitchen Chamberlain Şakir Effendi, and other high-ranking cooks from the Imperial Kitchens were seated around a table. The mixture of pitying and derisive gazes that greeted him as soon as he walked in gave him a clue as to what the sovereign's decision was.

"You sent for me. What is your wish?" he said, looking at Master İsfendiyar.

Master İsfendiyar took a sip from a silver chalice in front of him and said, "Our Sovereign has decided that the successor be appointed according to rank. His Highness the Chief Equerry has risen to the rank of Chief Sword Bearer. His personal cook will also resume his duties."

"The order is from Our Lord the Sovereign, and the desire is that of His Highness the Agha," the cook replied, trying to conceal his disappointment. "What are your orders for me?"

Master İsfendiyar took another slow sip. "Truth be told," he began, "we have more cooks than we need. However, Master Bekir requested your services, and I couldn't say no."

The cook turned to Master Bekir, who was seated next to Master İsfendiyar, and gave a grateful bow. "I thank you."

"It is my pleasure," Master Bekir replied. "It would be a waste to send away a cook of your talents."

"You are too kind," the cook replied.

Master Bekir let out a paternal laugh. "No need for blushes, you are among family here." He shifted on the bench toward Master İsfendiyar and gestured at the gap beside him. "Come, sit down. We were just bidding our brothers farewell, the ones who will be going on the expedition."

The cook sat down next to Master Bekir after casting a glance at Master İsfendiyar and noting his approval. Master Bekir placed a glass in front of him and began to fill it up as the chatter around the table continued. The subject was, of course, matters of state. Just like at many other tables all around the capital just then, the stewards' office rang with talk about the sultan's present state and his sudden hunting expedition.

Master İsfendiyar turned to the Chief Privy Chamber Page's personal cook, who was seated two places to his left. "Sorry, Master Kerim," he said. "We've interrupted you."

"Not at all," Kerim Usta replied, continuing, "As I was just saying, we mustn't find too great a fault with the sovereign. He was almost a child when he acceded to the throne. He didn't even have any experience even of ruling over a province—"

Chief Confectioner Master Bilal, who was sitting across from him, cut him off. "So this is what the Ottoman state has come to! How could a man rule over the whole empire without having ruled over a province yet? A prince without experience can't lead. It's not just a matter of getting the right education."

"Master Bilal is right," concurred Master Bekir. "His inexperience is a bigger concern than his youth. A prince isn't sent to a province just so he can learn about matters of state. He also learns how to behave toward his subjects. He rules over his own harem and his own pages. Now, look at the sultan. He didn't have many people around him to begin with. When his grandmother moved to the Old Palace, the Harem was left empty."

"You're right, Aghas," Master İsfendiyar joined in. "But isn't there a single man left in the whole of the empire who can tell the sultan what's right and what's wrong?" His voice had an angry edge. "I don't just mean the Inner Palace aghas. What does the Grand Vizier do? What are his teachers and advisors for?"

Şakir Effendi laughed softly. "Master İsfendiyar, you can be so amusing sometimes. One would think you had never lived in the palace. Do you not know what kind of place this is?"

"It suits the Grand Vizier just fine," Mater Kerim added. "He's glad to see the sultan off on an expedition so he can control things as he wishes. Don't even mention the Inner Palace. They all put their futures before the state's. They say that the new Haseki Sultan is a very intelligent and capable lady, but . . ."

The cook, who was lost in thought until then, pricked up his ears when he heard Haseki Sultan's name. But the Chief Confectioner concluded the matter by saying, "That Harem has ruined many a capable lady, don't you know, Master?"

A gloomy silence fell over the table, and it fell to Master İsfendiyar to bring in some cheer. "Well, that is that, and this is this," he said. "There's no remedy for one who has died, that's for sure. As long as this hunting expedition doesn't bring us to ruin, the rest can be sorted out later. What do you think, Chamberlain Effendi? What is the situation?"

All eyes were fixed on the Chamberlain of the Kitchen. As his duties required, he often had dealings with administrative staff so naturally he knew what was afoot. "Bad," Şakir Effendi said curtly. "The Treasury is cleared out. They can't even pull together the Janissaries' salaries according to what I've heard."

Dismayed cries echoed around the table. "The payments are due in less than ten days!" Master Bekir exclaimed. "The Janissaries will revolt!"

"There's more," Chamberlain Effendi went on to say. "Treasurer Lütfi Pasha requested that he be excused from his post, but the Grand Vizier refused. He even posted a soldier by his door so that he wouldn't try to sneak off."

"Lütfi Pasha asked to be removed from his post?" Master Bekir asked incredulously. "He's the closest ally of the Grand Vizier. He wouldn't take one step before getting his approval, let alone sneak off."

"Well, he values his own life," Master Kerim explained. "If their salaries come up short, the Janissaries will be after his head."

Casting a sideways glance at the cook, Master İsfendiyar grumbled, "This is unbelievable. What was His Highness the Grand Vizier thinking? Why hasn't he talked our sovereign out of this expedition? Does he think he will save himself by sacrificing the Treasurer's head?"

Master İsfendiyar was quite right, and the Grand Vizier's nonchalance was incomprehensible. As the cooks murmured to each other,

Master Hayri, the personal cook of the Chief Eunuch, started laughing softly. After making sure all eyes were on him, he said, "That matter has already been attended to."

Everyone was astonished, but none more than the Kitchen Chamberlain. "How so?" he asked, sitting up.

Master Hayri savored the sweet taste of the secret only he possessed by staying silent for a few more moments, and then he explained, "Don't tell anyone you've heard it from me. No one outside the Harem knows about this aside from the Grand Vizier. One of Haseki Sultan's personal attendants in the Harem, a concubine, has been promised to Darıcızade Mahmud Bey."

Among the surprised exclamations, a voice boomed out: "Promised to whom?"

Master Hayri looked at the ashen face of the cook uncomprehendingly, and replied, "Darıcızade Mahmud, the son of a wealthy Alexandrian family. Haven't you ever heard of them? Well, it's not an easy task, being a bridegroom to a woman from the Harem. Mahmud Bey loosened his purse strings as far as they could go. The Janissaries' payment will be made on time and in its entirety. Master Kerim is quite right. Haseki Sultan is a very clever lady. She solved the problem by herself."

The cook was deaf to the chatter around him. He couldn't even decide what to feel upset about, let alone think clearly, and a sense of defeat seized his soul. "Please excuse me," he muttered with difficulty, getting up from the table. He left the stewards' office as if an entire army was hunting him down.

Master İsfendiyar also couldn't believe what he had heard. The more the Chief Eunuch's cook repeated the name "Darıcızade," the more he felt like someone was twisting a knife in his stomach. After listening to the conversation for a while longer, he said, "Let me go and see if the assistants have finished their cleaning," and left the table. He went down the stairs, walked into the courtyard, and found the cook exactly where he thought he would be, in a secluded corner under the porticos, gazing at the Harem.

The cook appeared so motionless that it was difficult to tell him apart from the stone columns holding up the porticos. He was gazing at the Harem, his eyes filled with a piercing coldness.

Master İsfendiyar walked up and placed his hand on his shoulder. "Look," he said.

But the cook was beyond consolation. "What sort of fate is this, Master?" the cook muttered.

Master İsfendiyar shook him slightly. "Hold on, son. We don't know who the Darıcızade heir will be taking for his wife. The Harem is filled with odalisques."

The cook said nothing. He knew just as well as Master İsfendiyar that Mahmud Bey would want no one but Kamer.

"Listen to me for a moment," Master İsfendiyar continued. "Let's discover the truth of the matter first. I had an old assistant; he now works at the Inner Palace. He is quick to hear about such things. I'll ask him what he knows."

The cook nodded, still silent.

"I beg of you, wait for me here. Don't do anything before I come back," Master İsfendiyar said, and then he began to hobble toward the Gate of Felicity as quickly as he could.

The cook was left alone in the impending night, his soul frozen with defeat and his mind refusing to think. "What sort of fate is this?" he muttered once more. He was right in a way. The man who had appeared out of thin air all those years ago and coveted the light of his night, the one who had awakened the devil within him and caused him to fall into suspicion, the man who had caused him to err, had reappeared. And just at the moment when he was but a few steps away from getting Kamer back, he had shattered his plans. He really did wonder if it was just a twist of fate.

Suddenly the voice of a woman echoed in his mind, saying, "Don't blame fate for your own ineptitude!"

His thoughts drifted back to a few years before.

The voice howled in his head once more, and a woman's large, kohl-framed eyes appeared in his mind's eye, glaring at him with disdain and disappointment. Then their owner repeated that simple but crucial question she had asked the cook all those years ago: "And what have you done?"

The cook lost track of time between Master İsfendiyar's departure and return. He didn't see or hear him come back, but only realized he was standing next to him when he felt his hand on his shoulder again.

The master was out of breath and sweating, unsure of how he should broach the subject. After grappling with it for a while longer, he finally blurted, "It's true. Kamer has been promised to Darıcızade Mahmud Bey."

The cook didn't say a word. His eyes were still fixed on the Harem.

"Son," Master İsfendiyar continued, his voice sounding as if he was trying to console someone on his deathbed. "Sometimes it just doesn't work. Sometimes destiny gets in the way. There's nothing to do now. There's no other way."

Master İsfendiyar's platitudes sounded asinine even to his own ears. The cook slowly turned to look at him. The defeated expression on the master's face froze and then vanished entirely, because the cook was looking at him with his customary self-assurance and wild sense of willpower.

He had been thinking of how he could see yet again the woman whose eyes had appeared in his mind. If they were to meet again and if she asked him once more, "And what have you done?" he decided that rather than fixing his eyes on the ground in silence like he had done years before, he would look her in the eye and tell her a wondrous story filled with adventure, even if it might end in sorrow.

The cook placed his hand over Master İsfendiyar's hand on his shoulder and said, "Oh, but there is a way, Master."

6

The Lady of Essences

B Y THE END of the two years he had spent with the el-Haki brothers, the cook had learned how to wield his power over his lot of the infinite number of secrets of the earth and the sky, and he was almost fluent in the language of the stars and the plants.

The wheel of astrological signs and stars had replaced the calendar and clock for him. When Brother Sa'd said, "We'll leave when the moon is freed from the abyss and enters Scorpio," he could understand that he meant the following afternoon, or when he said, "Remember when Venus was retreating under Taurus?" he knew he was referring to the previous spring.

He could identify plants even as two-leafed sprouts and rattle off which star and sign their leaves, fruit, roots, and flowers fell under, as well as their degrees and natures.

The cook tried hard to apply his learnings to his art. But not all worked out as he had planned.

The problem was not that the house's kitchen could be called worse than modest. After all, he had been trained by Master Adem, and he could create four different dishes using two ingredients and a single pot.

The first problem was that the house's residents suffered from a poverty of appetite. He had seen Feridun, the house's servant, eat only once or twice while he was there, and he began to wonder how that tall, slender, big-boned man managed to stay alive.

But that hadn't bothered him so much either. He began to prepare dinners with as many dishes as the kitchen and ingredients at hand would allow him, for the evenings were the only time of day when Brother Sa'd, who began to watch the stars after sunset and only went to bed after dawn, and Brother Sadr, who woke up with dawn and went to bed shortly after evening prayers, would come together. He cooked dishes that would help Brother Astrologer stay alert during the hours he worked and dishes that would soothe Brother Doctor in his sleep. He made two different meals for each dinner, but that wasn't the only problem.

First of all, Brother Sadr was incredibly picky about such things and he tried to keep everyone on a strict regime.

Brother Sa'd's dishes, on the other hand, had to be in absolute harmony with the skies.

The cook saw during their dinners how the science of medicine and the science of astrology, which seemed at first glance to support each other and even intertwine at certain points, could often clash terribly.

The biggest arguments between the brothers broke out concerning the elements and the natures of foods. One evening when Brother Sadr advised his twin, who was suffering from a slight headache, to stay away from warm and moist foods and that even taking a bite from the stew in front of him, which was laden with coriander, would make his affliction worse and God forbid confine him to his bed, Brother Sa'd retorted that despite coriander and lamb being warm and moist in nature, coriander was under the star of Mars, and Mars was in descent according to the present condition of the stars and his horoscope, which meant that was why he was feeling poorly and that eating a lot of coriander would do him good.

The argument stretched on and on, with Brother Sadr trying to convince his twin by providing proof from books he retrieved from his study and the words of great medicinal scholars, and Brother Sa'd using plates and glasses to create a map of stars on the table. In the ensuing chaos, of course, the food went cold.

The cook then understood why Feridun hardly ever ate. The poor man, having lived with the twin brothers for years, must have been confused as to exactly what he was allowed to eat and found the solution in eating very little.

Thankfully the cook was soon divested of the task of preparing dinner. The el-Haki brothers, always extremely conscious of their physical and mental health, were hesitant to eat anything the cook prepared for them as his talent increased in proportion to his knowledge, and finally one day they requested that Feridun prepare dinner from that day on, as he had once done.

The more he read and the more he learned, the more skilled the cook became. During one of his visits to a Baghdad hospital alongside Brother Sadr, he was allowed to cook for some of the patients in accordance with their regimens. The result stunned even the cook himself. The patients, each of whom suffered from a different ailment, began to get better and respond well to the medicines they were taking. Yet that was the first and last time the cook prepared food for a sick person. "I only let you do it this once so you could bear witness to the extent of your power," Brother Sadr explained. "However, consistency is what matters in treatment. Regardless of how good a remedy might be, if you don't repeat it, you must not use it. It will cause more harm than good. And also remember this: You are a cook, not a doctor or an apothecary."

The days and nights at the el-Haki brothers' house passed with reading, writing, and learning, and when the cook could answer questions such as, "If, in a person's horoscope, Saturn is in Libra, Jupiter is in Cancer, Mercury is retrograde in Virgo, and the sun is in Leo, and at the time of question, the Moon is in Taurus, and Saturn is in retrograde in Scorpio, what will this person's state of mind and mental outlook be like, and if said person has a congenial heart condition on his father's side, in which circumstances regarding the movement of the stars should he watch out for the health of his heart and which sort of regimen should he follow?" Brother Sa'd and Brother Sadr decided that he would only be wasting his time by staying with them any longer and politely requested him to start getting ready for the next step in his journey of knowledge.

They hadn't told him until his last night where he would be going. When the time came to bid each other farewell, they asked him to cook dishes that would cheer them up.

The cook rose to the occasion magnificently. Thanks to that dinner, the el-Haki brothers' house enjoyed its most cheerful and enjoyable night, and the brothers did not bicker. Rather, each told anecdotes and jokes regarding their fields, and as the hours ticked away, the conversation turned to their past, as far back as their childhood.

Hours after the evening prayer, with Brother Sadr yawning, the cook could no longer restrain his impatience and he asked where he would be going. Brother Sa'd cast a sidelong glance at his twin and, with a wry smile on his lips, he said, "Do you want to know where you'll be going or what you'll be learning?"

The cook thought it best to keep silent. Brother Sa'd continued, "From here, you'll go south toward the Persian Gulf. When you reach the city of Basra, you'll see a small ship with black sails docked at the harbor. Its captain is named Behrengi. He will take you to Hormuz Island. When you reach the island, do not tarry in the city but walk straight along with the sea on your right. After passing along a long beach with reddish sand, you'll see some boulders. Climb over them and after scaling two hills, you'll see a beach with a large pier and a stone mansion hidden between some outcroppings. Knock on the door and say you wish to speak to the Lady of Essences. She will teach you about spices."

Along with the sweet fear of taking a step into the unknown, the cook was also seized by excitement. Spices had been a mysterious riddle for him ever since he first started practicing his art. For as long as he'd been aware, cooking, blending flavors together, and imagining how the result would taste before even putting the pot over the stove had been quite easy. But when it came to spices, everything was different. He was in awe of the fact that even the smallest pinch of spice could change a food's taste, and his mind balked at how a spice that was used in the same quantity for the same dish could create a different taste every single time.

In short, the cook's clockwork logic faltered when it came to spices, and even his vast store of often arrogant skills had to retreat. "Is it not too soon?" he was about to ask, but he held his tongue and said, "Let's hope for the best."

During the final hours of their last night together, Brother Sadr could no longer resist the pull of sleep and bade the cook farewell before retiring to bed, even giving him a hug in a rare display of affection. Brother Sa'd made his way toward his observatory, and the cook, now alone, went to pack his belongings.

Brother Sa'd knocked on his door toward dawn. "Venus is almost rising," he said. The cook left with his bundle on his back, and, after looking at that sacred star burning on the horizon toward the east with a yellowish gleam, he embraced Brother Sa'd.

"What you have learned here will always be of use to you," Brother Astrologer said. "My wish is for you to use everything we have taught you for the sake of good. If the day comes when you are in need of the science of the stars, no matter where you might be in the world, talk to the first astrologer you find and mention our names. Whatever information you desire will be handed to you."

The cook thanked him.

He began to walk south toward the Gulf of Persia. When he turned around for the last time, he saw Brother Sa'd going back into the house.

The journey from Baghdad toward the city of Basra was an unexpectedly nightmarish one. Alone and far away from the house and the brothers, so far from his books and the learning which had occupied his mind for months, all the memories he thought he had forgotten began to emerge one by one, and the gloomy thoughts he once believed he had cast off began to occupy his mind and his soul even more painfully than before.

The cook could not remember ever having felt so helpless and alone. Kamer was always in his thoughts: during the day when he tried to take shelter from the scorching sun in the shadows of an outcropping at a dingy *caravanserai* or in the corner of a loud inn, or at night as he walked on a deserted path in the cool desert air or rested next to an oasis with a caravan group he was following. After all the time that had passed, it was now even more painful to think about her. Now he had questions, endless unanswerable questions that multiplied, as deep and endless as the remediless suffering that had seized his soul: where was she, what was she doing, was she hungry, was she cold, was she a wife, was she a mother, did she still dance, was she happy, did she regret anything, did she sometimes think of the past or did gloomy thoughts occupy her mind with even one thousandth of the strength that they occupied the mind of this Majnun traipsing across the desert, or . . . had she forgotten him long ago?

He wondered if she had, and, if that was the case, as terrible as that possibility was, it at least offered a consolation: that thing called forgetting might be possible.

The cook's mind was hopelessly mired in questions when he arrived at Basra harbor. The trip across the water did him well; he helped the sailors, aided the helmsmen by using the stars as a compass, and found solace in the captain's endless tales.

After four nights and five days, the small ship cast anchor in the harbor of Hormuz. The cook left the city and began walking along the shore with the sea on his right. He longed to find his new master and lose himself in knowledge, learning, and memorizing again.

He climbed the boulders and, just as Brother Sa'd had told him, he saw the small pier and the stone mansion in a small cove further down. It was quiet and calm. The rocky peaks blocked the wind and the crescent-shaped bay sheltered the beach from the waves of the open sea.

Perhaps alerted to his presence by the noise of the stones clattering under his feet as he walked down toward the sea, someone had opened the door of the large, two-story mansion before he arrived. Standing in the doorway was a tall, strikingly handsome man with olive skin. The cook climbed the four steps to the door and announced that he wanted to see the Lady of Essences.

"Did you come here from the el-Haki brothers' house?" the man asked him.

When the cook nodded, the man stepped aside and invited him in.

As he took his first step into the mansion, the cook first thought his mind was playing tricks on him. The door opened into a large room packed with all manner of spices. Men and women were seated at tables placed in rows in the middle of the room, and they pressed, ground, sorted, and sifted dried spices, roots, seeds, flowers, pips, and mastic from the large and small sacks, jars, containers, and bottles by their feet. After weighing the items out on tiny scales, they placed them in velvet pouches with the Lady's seal on them or put them in porcelain containers. They performed their tasks in absolute quiet and calm, as if they'd been intoxicated by the thousands of scents filling the room.

When the cook began to walk toward the middle of the room, enchanted by the smells filling his nostrils, some of which were completely new to him, the man who greeted him at the door politely took him by the arm and said, "The Lady is upstairs, on the terrace." Together they ascended the stairs next to the left wall of the room, and after walking down a long, dim, rather cool corridor with doors on each side, they arrived at the bottom of yet another staircase.

"Please, go on," the man said, standing aside. The cook began to climb the stairs. The light sea breeze drifting in from upstairs began to clear his thoughts, and the clearer his mind became, the more he thought about certain strange details that he had seen downstairs. All the women and the men in the Lady's mansion were surprisingly beautiful or handsome. They were all barefoot, and they all were wearing long white gowns, obviously of silk, which left their shoulders and arms bare. They were wearing silver belts which consisted of links in the shape of flowers.

He thought it may have been a trick of the light or perhaps his confusion, but what was even more striking was that they all resembled one another. The cook knew he had seen men and women downstairs, but when he stopped and thought about it, he couldn't recall who had been female or who had been male apart from the man who greeted him.

The cook's confusion fell from his thoughts when he stepped out onto the terrace. The Lady of Essences was standing toward the edge of the balcony with her back toward him, her hands resting on the stone railing as she looked out at the sea.

She was wearing the same white dress and silver floral belt as the people downstairs and her black hair fell in waves over her shoulders. The red rays of the setting sun pierced through the dress, illuminating the Lady of Essences's naked body underneath the thin fabric; her smooth back, her thin waist, her hips which seemed to have been carved from an ebony tree, the two dimples on her lower back, her shapely legs. . . . It was a silhouette of such perfection that the cook felt compelled to worship rather than lust.

When the Lady of Essences turned around, her breasts and stomach visible beneath the fluttering cloth of her dress, the cook didn't know what to say or where to look. He found the solution in bowing his head.

"Raise your head," the Lady of Essences said as she approached him. "Such shame only befits evil eyes."

After hearing those words, the cook had a singular desire: to withdraw into a shell like a tortoise. He finally looked up and gazed into her eyes, which were like those of the statues of female goddesses that ancient civilizations once raised, eyes that he would never forget for the rest of his days.

"I am the Lady of Essences," she said, standing a few steps away, her wavy black hair blowing in the breeze. "The best of all the rarest essences, leaves, roots, flowers, and resins are delivered to my home, and from here they are sent all around the world. This is my work, my science. Now, tell me. Who are you and why have you come?"

"I am the Pasha of Cuisine," the cook managed to murmur. "I am here to learn about spices."

The Lady of Essences took two graceful steps forward. Fixing her gaze on the cook's eyes, she repeated, "Why are you here?"

He realized that she had seen through his words. The way she looked at him compelled him to utter not just the truth, but the simplest piece of honesty that could be expressed in two words unsullied by languishing in the labyrinths of language.

"To forget," the cook said.

The Lady of Essences pursed her lips and nodded. "Perhaps it's not right for you to be here," she said thoughtfully. "Perhaps I should send you directly to the Master of Oblivion." When he heard those words, the cook's eyes glittered with childish gullibility. "Would you like that?" the Lady of Essences asked.

The cook faltered. Knowing that it would be uncouth to say "Yes," he said, "I have never heard of him. But I wonder . . . where can he be found?"

The Lady of Essences looked away and said, "Once upon a time, I sent a lad like you to him. He, too, had a burning desire to forget. Only the master could help him, because he is surely the only person on earth who knows all the secrets of the science of forgetting."

The cook's curiosity was piqued. "And was he able to find the master?"

The Lady looked toward the sea and said, "He did, but it was very difficult. He crossed snowy mountains, traversed dark forests and empty deserts, but finally he found him. The Master of Oblivion was sitting on the shore of a lake. The young man went up to him, introduced himself, and said that he wanted to forget, that he wanted to condemn everything that caused him pain and suffering to oblivion, that he never wanted to recall them again. 'If you teach me the secrets of this science,' the young man said, 'I will do anything you like, even be your servant until the end of my life.' The master was modest. He said he would teach the lad everything he knew, without asking for anything in return. 'However,' the master said, 'there's a small problem.'" The Lady of Essences paused and turned around to face the cook, who was listening raptly, and said, "'I've forgotten the secrets of my science, too!'"

Suddenly realizing she was teasing him, the cook blushed. The Lady laughed, but then with earnest seriousness, she added, "There's no such thing as forgetting. No matter how hard you try, you only think you've forgotten, and over time the things you think you have forgotten emerge again under another guise and tear into your soul. Understand this: whoever says they have forgotten have merely condemned themselves to an endless repetition of the same event until the end of their lives."

The Lady of Essences was circling around him as she spoke, running her hand along a string of seashells hanging by the doorway as she moved, making them jingle. Each time she passed by, she made them jingle even louder. After a pause, she snapped, "Do you see what I'm getting at?"

The truth of the matter was that the cook did not understand, or rather, could not. Finding the bare truth suddenly laid out before him, he was consumed by denial and rebellion. He searched for a reply but could find none. When he finally did hit upon something, he didn't have the courage to speak the words out loud, not so much out of respect but because he was afraid of the harshness of what she might say—he knew he couldn't bear another blow of truth.

The cook was saved from his predicament when five residents who must have heard the sound of the seashells ran up to see what was happening. They lined up by the doorway, awaiting the Lady's instructions.

"We have a guest," the Lady of Essences said. "He has come to our home to learn about spices. Prepare the hammam straightaway. We need to rescue his body from exhaustion and his mind from confusion. We'll see to his soul later."

The cook looked at the people standing on each side of the door, inviting him downstairs with a bow. Only after a few moments did he realize that three of them were female. Habitually uneasy, his soul was suddenly filled with a sense of peace that surprised even himself.

As they descended the stairs and walked toward the hammam at the end of the hallway, the Lady of Essences continued to give brisk orders: "First rub him down with saffron, camphor, and musk, and prepare the censers. Burn a lot of sage, some hemp, and a pinch of wormwood. Let's see if his troubles are in his mind or hidden even deeper. Scatter rose leaves over the warm pool, along with lilac, jasmine, and Indian hyacinth. Pour only ambergris into the cold pool."

Later the cook would think about how those five pairs of hands undressed him so gently yet quickly. When they undid the sash on his waist a small wave of embarrassment washed over him, but the five pairs of eyes looked at him so guilelessly that the feeling fell away. The smoke rising from the censers cleared his mind until he thought only of the scents filling his nostrils, the sensations on his skin, and the quiet melodies drifting through the air.

They had the cook lie face down on the warm marble slab in the middle of the hammam, and hands began to wander over his back, his neck, and his legs.

He recognized the scent of saffron, one of the rarest ingredients in every kitchen. And there was the scent of musk from his childhood, from the Harem rooms filled with scents of perfume. Those two scents brought back the purest memories of his childhood. But the scent of camphor which followed, though not necessarily unpleasant, was so strong it seemed to cover every possible malodor. By virtue of its very nature, it made the cook think of death, rotting, and putrefaction, reminding him that the thorns of life were still very real.

Later, the cook dreamed he was lying in a garden full of flowers, a pleasant warmth enveloping his body as if the sun was shining down on him from all sides. He inhaled the scents one by one and in twos and threes, pursuing a dream inside his dream, walking toward infinity in a land of bright hues and a murmur of songs. He almost woke up when he felt a slight cold pricking his body all over like thousands of tiny needles, but then he drifted back to sleep, a deep, uninterrupted sleep that embraced pain as well as pleasure and calm.

When he awoke, the cook found himself lying naked on a large downy bed. There was nothing in the room apart from a small bedside table with a small earthenware pitcher on top. The only smell was the scent of clean sea air gently blowing in through the open window. Next to his bed he saw one of the white silk gowns everyone at the mansion was wearing with a silver floral belt draped over it.

He put them on and walked downstairs. He felt vulnerable and naked wearing the thin gown, but he also felt a peculiar lightness, as if his soul had donned the same outfit. He ascribed the feeling to the incense he had breathed in at the hammam and the skilled hands of the Lady's attendants. In those days, he was so naïve that he didn't realize that many of our woes are imaginary and the chains we forge for ourselves become heavier the longer we carry them.

Everyone at the mansion was already awake, calmly going about their tasks. Their hands were deft but unhurried, and their faces showed none of the strain of stress. The cook approached one of them, who was putting black pepper grains through a grinder, and asked him where the Lady was. He received a simple answer: "I don't know."

The cook would soon realize that no one in the house was required to be aware of anything except for themselves because the presence of others was not a prerequisite for another's existence, and a person's absence did not lessen another's presence. No one in the house told anyone else what to do or not to do. Together they carried in the sacks of spices brought in by ships, and they loaded the ships in the same way after the spices had been sorted. When they got hungry, they would put any spice they desired into a bowl of olive oil and dip a piece of bread into it. When they got tired or bored, they withdrew to their rooms or whiled away the hours in conversation, listening to music, or sometimes delving into love.

Everyone spoke in quiet murmurs. Apart from the waves, the wind, and the clinking of jars, the only sounds were songs, musical instruments, lines by the poets Firdevsî, Fuzûlî, and Ruhi of Baghdad, or anecdotes by Zarri who had not yet changed his name to Nef'i.

Of course, there was also the Lady of Essences's voice, which rang out at the most unexpected times. Only she was granted the privilege of being able to speak loudly in the mansion, and only she could disrupt the seemingly infinite peace to remind them that the world was still turning with all the burdens it carried.

The cook did not see the Lady of Essences that day, nor the day after, nor the day after that.

When they encountered each other on the morning of his fourth day there, the Lady only asked him how he felt and then withdrew to her room. The next day, the cook learned that she had set off on a journey to buy spices and wouldn't be back for at least three weeks. When the Lady returned, nothing changed. She would be there one minute and absent the next, and the lessons the cook was eagerly awaiting never seemed to begin.

Despite feeling a deep respect for the way of life at the mansion and all its residents, the cook was becoming impatient. His desire to cook shriveled when he realized that there wasn't even a proper stove at the mansion, let alone a kitchen, so he was forced to turn his attention to the processing of the spices, the carrying of loads, and tidying up. He listened to the poems recited at night on the terrace and joined the singing, but he couldn't keep his mind occupied. He was bored, and as his boredom increased, the sorrow within him swelled, filling the void left behind. With each passing day he felt more and more trapped, and he began to despise the calm of the mansion, the peacefulness of the people there, the spices, and the scents.

After almost a month, the cook could stand it no longer. He waited in front of the Lady's room, and when she came out he asked when his lessons would begin. She gave him an odd look, as if she seemed to be hearing such a question for the first time in her life. The cook tried to frame his question another way: "You were going to teach me about spices. That's what I was told."

After looking at him for a few more moments with the same blank expression, the Lady of Essences smiled pointedly. "Do you want to learn about spices?"

The cook nodded.

"Come with me," the Lady said, and together they went downstairs. They walked past the rows of people working with sieves and mortars, and then stopped in front of a shelf, from which the Lady selected a jar at random. She opened the lid, quickly checked its contents, and shoved it into the cook's hand. "Here's some sesame. It's a secret miracle. By itself it tastes almost of nothing, but adds density and a light oil to food. Smells slightly burnt after being cooked. There's also sesame oil, which is another matter entirely. I'll explain that later."

As the cook stared at the jar of sesame seeds in bewilderment, the Lady reached toward another shelf. "And here are nigella seeds. They also taste burnt at first, but then take on a sharp taste like aniseed. They burn brightly, but only for a moment. They don't have that much power over the palate. Actually, never mind these. We should find something that'll be useful to you. Let's see . . ."

After sniffing around the shelf in front of her for a moment, the Lady of Essences opened a large earthenware jar, took out a pinch of its contents, and tossed them into the air. The scent belonged to a spice that every cook knew well. "Cumin," the Lady announced. "It's one of the most capable spices. It changes the mood of whatever you cook. Its scent is what matters, not its taste. It doesn't blend into food as well as black pepper or cinnamon, but when its scent blends into the scent of the dish, it creates an appetizing, lustful, inviting smell. Cumin calls out to you, lusty and enticing."

Just as the Lady was about to make her way to another shelf, the cook asked, "And what is its nature?"

Again the Lady of Essences appeared surprised.

The cook went on: "Is it warm, for example? Or moist?"

"I don't know," the Lady curtly answered. "I'm not a doctor."

The cook was taken aback but said nothing. He thought they had begun their lessons at last and he longed for anything to occupy his thoughts.

"May I have a pen and some paper?" he asked.

The Lady burst into laughter. She pointed to the rows of shelves and the hundreds of jars, bowls, and pots that were on them. "What will you do, memorize them all?" she asked.

Before the cook could open his mouth to reply, she went on to say, "Which ones are you going to memorize, and more importantly, what exactly will you be memorizing? Cinnamon, for example. It goes with sweet, savory, sour, and bitter. Here is ginger: you can cook it with meat or use it to make pickles or jam. What about cinnamon or ginger will you memorize? The taste of coriander for one person is not the same as for another. Oregano tastes very different when used in two dishes made by two different cooks. You can't memorize spices, you can't learn them. You can only understand them."

The Lady of Essences walked toward the cook and placed her finger in the center of his forehead and said, "Spices are not related to intelligence, but to emotions." Then she pointed at his heart. "It is meaningless to know what spices are, whether they come from trees or roots or bark, or to memorize their natures, as it won't be of any use to you. You should be able to inhale the scent of garlic and write two verses of poetry, compose an epic about the basil and mastic combining in your mouth, and extol the virtues of myrrh and a pinch of rosemary. Only then can you tell me that you've learned about spices. You should look into the eyes of the person you want to mesmerize with your food and see into their heart and soul, and at the same time be able to go through all the scents you know in your mind and decide which ones will either dampen or whet the appetite of their soul. Only then can I say that you've become the true Pasha of Cuisine."

The Lady of Essences took a breath and turned those eyes of hers, eyes which seemed to be mirrors of truth, to the cook's once more before saying, "In order to do all that, you have to learn what it means to be human. To get to know humanity, you must first be aware of your own existence. As long as you try to run away from your own feelings as if they are ghosts, try to bury and destroy your memories as if they are worthless, I see no way forward for you. But I can give you a small piece of advice, for what it's worth: stop fighting yourself. Break the chains of your memories. Let them flow. You only stop and think, but you need to think in the right way. Not just with your mind but with your heart, too."

At first, the cook thought she was making fun of him as she often did. It made no sense to him. Why would she suggest thinking to someone whose biggest problem was thinking and whose greatest desire was to stop his mind and keep his thoughts under control?

Out of desperation, he went along with the Lady's advice, trying to come to terms with himself by quieting his busy mind. If he didn't feel like doing anything, he merely stood there; sometimes he would join in with the work and grind cinnamon for hours on end, and sometimes he would spend a whole day on the terrace staring at the sea.

As the months went by, winter began to loom on the horizon and the winds began to blow stronger. One day the cook found himself doing exactly what the Lady had advised him to do: thinking.

He had come to the conclusion that it was useless to force himself not to think, to try and banish the darkness from his soul and the memories from his mind. From the moment he began to think about everything he had been through, all the happiness and pain, all his dreams and nightmares, they became more manageable, and in time almost ceased being fears altogether.

As he started to genuinely and truthfully think, and to bravely think, he also began to feel again, and he realized that he had crippled his soul so he wouldn't suffer. Just as the night was a natural part of the day, pain, suffering, and gloom were parts of the heart, and trying to get rid of them did not bring peace but on the contrary left one's spirit broken and devoid of feeling.

Thinking about what had happened, thinking about Kamer and what could happen in the future, still filled his heart with an indescribable pain, but he no longer felt like a lifeless empty shell. Darkness wasn't comparable to living in the void. It left a taste in one's throat, no matter how sour; it smelled of longing and its fruit was tears.

The cook wept. After all those years, he could finally cry.

He had tried to hold himself back, terrified of what might happen if he let himself go. He had thought if he were to cry, his last defense would crumble and the ensuing darkness would fill his heart, making him its prisoner forever, condemning him to endless suffering.

What he had really been frightened of was remembering. And crying meant remembering.

The more he thought, the more he could see the truth of the matter. But he perceived his memories and his dreams not through eyes filled with fury and anguish as before, but as if he were an angel floating in the sky, aware that memories are left in the past and dreams never happen. He could see it all from outside, from up above: his childhood, the palace, the House of Pleasure, Master Adem, Sirrah, and Kamer. Most importantly, he could see himself. He could perceive his own life with all its what-ifs, if-onlys, truths, mistakes, hopes, worries, and everything he had done or not been able to do. Finally he could do nothing but admit one inescapable truth: he was still madly in love with Kamer.

On one of those nights when he abandoned himself to the sound of the tumbling waves and the moon in the sky, murmuring a song he had once heard Kamer sing, he felt a gentle hand wipe away a tear that had started coursing down his cheek.

The cook was startled. He turned and saw the Lady of Essences standing next to him.

"Tears are the lifeblood of withered souls," the Lady said, looking at the droplet on her fingertip. Then she sat down next to him. "Tell me. Tell me what happened."

It was the cook's turn to be surprised. He had never imagined putting the thoughts in his mind into words until that day, let alone telling his entire story. It occurred to him that he hadn't ever truly spoken to anyone in all his life apart from Kamer, and that even with her he had been secretive. The Lady of Essences had revealed his absolute solitude to him.

To tell his story and put an end to the deathly silence with his own voice, he began with the first sentence that came to mind, which was perhaps the purest: "I was born in the palace . . ."

At first he was ashamed of what he was doing. Somehow it felt pathetic. But as the words flowed, the knots came undone and the burden in his heart slowly began to lighten.

After a while the cook had become not only the speaker but also the listener. He listened to himself as if he were someone else and saw with astonishment how the thoughts that had circled in his mind for all those years transformed when they came into contact with his tongue. What he had thought to be hopelessly complicated turned out to be simple, and what he had thought to be certain was actually doubtful. When he saw that a memory or dream he would spend entire nights mulling over took only three sentences to describe in words, he could do nothing but smile in confusion. Most of the time he couldn't bring himself to lie, but sometimes he didn't have the courage to speak of painful heavy truths exactly as they were, so he pruned and shaped his words before allowing them to venture forth.

The cook talked all night, stopping only when dawn was about to break. The wind had subsided, the waves had calmed, and the sea had turned into a massive mirror waiting to add more color to the redness of the dawn which was about to break.

The last words the cook uttered were, "It's difficult."

The Lady of Essences replied with a short laugh. "Difficult? You think your life has been hard?"

The cook could not reply. He merely looked at her.

The Lady said, "Yes, bad things have happened to you, but your life couldn't exactly be called hard. You know nothing of what hardship is. You were born in the palace and your parents doted on you. When you lost your family, you were welcomed by your masters, and they took care of you. You did not suffer as an apprentice nor toil as an assistant. Thanks to your God-given talent, you don't even know what it means to compete. You have never lost! Because you have never lost, you haven't learned how to win, how to fight and work to win. Only once were you met with a true challenge, and you failed at that."

The cook felt uneasy. Part of him wanted to grab the Lady and fling her into the sea, while another part said he should get down on his knees and kiss the hem of her skirt.

The Lady went on: "You've told me all about your dreams. Kamer this and Kamer that. If a person wants something, dreaming is not enough. You have to have faith in your heart. If, instead of all those dreams, you'd had a drop of faith in love, you wouldn't be in this state today. Now tell me. Kamer sent you that letter, fine, but what have you done? Besides crying and leaving your home, what else? Did you find her and ask her to say those words that were written in that letter? Were you afraid? Did your love made of dreams vanish when your dreams shattered? Did you follow her? Did you bring that pasha's mansion down on his head? Did you set fire to the whole of Alexandria? Were a piece of paper and a few drops of ink the sum of your love? Tell me, young man. What have you done?"

The cook bowed his head, the Lady's voice echoing shrilly in his ears. He couldn't bring himself to look her in the eye. He knew her eyes would seek out an answer, and there was only one answer the cook could give: "Nothing."

That was how the cook discovered that the worst kind of shame arises not from what you do or what you fail at, but from what you don't carry out to completion. He saw that empty, irrelevant, futile, or even evil actions could have a truthfulness and pride of their own.

That day, as he looked at the Harem and felt Kamer slipping through his fingers, the cook could not justify standing there helplessly and giving in to fate.

"There is a way, Master," the cook repeated.

"Son . . ." Master İsfendiyar replied, stammering. "Haseki Sultan has already seen to their engagement, and our sovereign has given his permission. The wedding can't be prevented."

The cook laughed. "I know of something, Master, which listens to neither willpower nor edicts."

Concern flashed in the master's eyes. "Only Darıcızade's death could stop this wedding," he said. "And we can't even get close to him. He's protected by an army of guards. Even if we were able to get into his chamber, we would never be able to get out. Suppose we could get out, what then? It would be certain death. I'm not afraid for my sake, but you're still trying to—"

"I said there was a way," the cook interrupted him. He took a step closer to Master İsfendiyar. "But I need some help."

The master's lips moved silently for a few moments as if he was praying. "Tell me."

"I need cooks. Three or four of them, good enough to create a feast, and they must be discreet. Can you do that?"

"Easily. What else?"

"I need to leave the palace tonight without anyone seeing me. There's someone I must speak with. Could you open the rear gate for me?"

"That's easy as well. What else?"

"That is all for now, Master. I will be back before the morning prayers, don't worry."

"Good. Wait here. I'm going to send an assistant to tell you that I've summoned you, which means the gate is open."

"Thank you, Master."

"When you return, don't go up to the dormitory. Go to the Odalisques' Kitchen, no matter what time it is. I will be waiting for you there."

"But why?"

"Just do as I say," Master İsfendiyar replied, and then he disappeared into the darkness.

When the cook returned to the palace, he knew he would have to wait a few hours for the morning call to prayer. He had paid a short visit to Mad Bayram's tavern, explained the situation in brief, and received a promise of help. Master Bayram was an astute and rather uncurious person. He merely said, "Don't you worry, my boy. We will take care of this."

The cook padded toward the kitchen after closing and latching the rear gate of the Imperial Kitchens. To reach the kitchen, he had to pass by the stewards' office, the cellar, and the lodgings. He hid in a corner and waited for the guard to finish his rounds. After he was sure there was no one around, he quickly walked across the courtyard. The night was so dark that the stars seemed blindingly bright. Placing his right hand on the wall, he felt his way along the Kitchens' Passageway and entered through the first door he came upon. He could see a dim light coming from the Odalisques' Kitchen. The single candle burning there revealed the silhouette of a man, but it wasn't Master İsfendiyar. This man was taller and larger. When he noticed the movement of a few more shadows behind the silhouette, the cook panicked. Just as he was about to slink back the way he had come, a voice said, "It's me, brother. Don't worry."

He recognized the voice. "Master Bekir?"

"Yes."

The cook took a few more steps toward the candle. Master Bekir was standing in the middle of the kitchen with his usual friendly grin. His six assistants were lined up behind him.

"I . . . I couldn't sleep," the cook said.

But Master Bekir laughed. "We were waiting for you. Master İsfendiyar said you would be coming. I know everything."

A cold sweat ran down the cook's back. "What did he tell you?" he asked, trying to keep his voice from trembling.

"He said the Pasha of Cuisine needed our help," Master Bekir replied.

A familiar voice arose from the darkest corner of the kitchen: "That's exactly what I said."

There was the tapping of a walking stick and then Master İsfendiyar appeared in the dim light. "You wanted capable cooks? Well, here are some capable cooks. Eight of them, in fact. Does that suffice?"

"It does, Master," the cook said. "But, Master Bekir . . . how long has he known?"

Master Bekir himself answered. "Right from the start. Master İsfendiyar told me the day you walked into the kitchen. He wanted me to watch out for you."

The cook glanced at Master İsfendiyar.

"Now, leave off such useless questions," Master İsfendiyar said, "and tell us, how may we help you?"

"With your cooking of course, Master," the cook replied. "We have to prepare a magnificent banquet. One that will please the eye before the mouth."

"Nothing we haven't done before. How many people will the banquet be for?"

"One person."

"And where will this banquet be?"

The cook smiled. "At the House of Pleasure."

"Understood." Master İsfendiyar nodded. "But will they let us use the kitchen?"

"We'll need some help with that," the cook said. "But I have arranged for a few friends of mine to take care of such matters."

When Master İsfendiyar heaved a worried sigh, Master Bekir pulled a large knife from the sash around his waist. "Don't trouble yourself, Master İsfendiyar," he said. "You know, this isn't only good for slicing onions! Aside from the fact that he is the pasha of our art, when a brother from the kitchens tells us his troubles and asks for our help, we'll put our lives on the line if need be."

"Well said," Master İsfendiyar murmured, which was echoed by the six assistants behind Master Bekir.

The cook was at a loss for words. In the end, he merely said, "Thank you."

Master İsfendiyar got up, tapping his cane on the ground. "That's it then, let us pray for success. When are we leaving?"

"Tomorrow, before dawn," the cook replied. "The boats will be waiting for us. We'll leave the palace separately and meet up at the boaters' pier in Kasımpaşa."

Master İsfendiyar nodded and said, "Very well," and started to walk away. Master Bekir picked up the candle and headed out.

The cook caught up with Master İsfendiyar, who was about to disappear into the darkness, and took his arm. "What is it now?" the master asked.

After waiting for Master Bekir and his assistants to leave, the cook said, "Master, you asked whether eight cooks would suffice."

"And?"

"Eight is too many. Seven is enough."

Master İsfendiyar turned toward the cook. As the light of the receding candle grew dimmer, the anger in the master's eyes seemed to grow brighter. "What ever do you mean?" he hissed.

"You need to stay here," the cook replied.

"No chance! I can't send you away on your own."

"For God's sake, listen to me!" the cook pleaded, tightening his grip on his arm. "You have to stay here because there are a few more things I need you to do after I'm gone."

"What do you mean, after you're gone?"

"I'm not going to come back to the kitchens," the cook said. He pulled a small flask from his sash and placed it in Master İsfendiyar's hand. "Keep this safe. When Master Bekir returns and tells you all is well, mix the contents of this bottle with a glass of tamarind juice and have Mahir drink it. That same night, visit him while he's sleeping and whisper into his ear my true identity and everything I've done here. Don't worry, he won't remember your voice. He will think everything you tell him was his own sudden realization. A few days will pass and the palace guards will come looking for me, but I will be at the bachelors' lodgings on Melekgirmez Street. You are to report me anonymously. Do you understand?"

Master İsfendiyar swallowed a few times. "Then what will happen?"

"Only God knows," the cook replied. "If everything goes as planned, I'll have to do a few more things here, so I will come back. If things don't go as planned . . . please remember me with kindness."

"Of course I will, son, but—"

"There are no buts, Master! Either I will claim Kamer, or this palace will claim my life."

A tear gleamed in the corner of Master İsfendiyar's eye.

They embraced.

When he returned to the lodgings, the cook quietly opened the chest by his bedside and took out the horoscopes and the two books. After grabbing one of his spare towels, he went out again and sat down beneath one of the oil lamps burning on the stairs.

He quickly rifled through the pages of the black book. "Sorry, Master," he murmured as he tore off the three pages he would need and tucked them into his sash, and then he wrapped the books and the horoscopes in the towel.

Now ready, he went back to bed and placed the bundle under his mattress. The morning call to prayer was but moments away, so sleeping would be pointless, but the cook lay back and closed his eyes anyway.

The day got off to a swift start as the cooks and assistants going on the expedition prepared for the journey. There was a small ceremony in the courtyard outside the lodgings and they said their farewells with prayers.

Amidst the bustle, the Privy Chamber Page found a chance to bid the cook farewell. He expressed his condolences for the cook's removal from the Aghas' Kitchen and asked if he wanted him to bring him anything back from Edirne.

"I shall definitely let you know if I think of anything," the cook replied. Regardless of how fondly he would remember Firuz Agha, he swore to himself that he would never request anything from a denizen of the palace for as long as he lived.

After the ceremony, everything quickly went back to normal in the kitchens, and the centuries-old wheels of the kitchens began turning in faultless fashion once again.

That day, the unhappiest person not just in the Imperial Kitchens, but the entirety of the palace itself, was undoubtedly Mahir. He was deeply offended that they had been moved from the Aghas' Kitchen to the Odalisques' Kitchen. He wandered around, a restless soul whose future and dreams had been wrested from his tentative grip. He gazed with disgust and disdain at the bulky iron cauldrons of the kitchen, the copper pots, the ordinary dishes, and the assistants who poured food straight from the pots into serving bowls

And then there was the way his master said "As you wish" to Master Bekir's every request. It tore at Mahir's heart.

When Neyyir Agha arrived to pick up the food, Mahir cornered the huge eunuch and whispered his troubles to him. That young assistant, who had long since abandoned himself to the clutches of ambition, was so engrossed in his own problems that he didn't even notice the myriad gestures and whispers around him that day, nor the fact that Master İsfendiyar had visited the kitchen a few too many times.

As Mahir built up in his mind a distant and imaginary future, the cook, Master Bekir, and the six assistants had already laid the foundations of a future that was already at hand. Master İsfendiyar prepared documents for the cook and three assistants so they would be able to exit the gate. They were to leave the palace at sunset and Master Bekir and the other assistants would go through the back door late at night when no one was around.

The cook left the kitchen without his assistant, who was still talking to Neyyir Agha, and went to the lodgings, sat down on his bed, and waited. Exhaustion was pulling at his eyelids but soon enough he heard his assistant's plodding footsteps.

Opening his eyes, he sat up. "Come over here."

Mahir approached the bed and crouched down. The cook reached under his pillow and removed the bundle. "Take this," he said.

After staring at the bundle for a few moments, Mahir took it. "What is this, Master?"

"Let's just say that there are some very important things inside," the cook replied. "I will be gone for a few days. I'm entrusting them to you. Whatever you do, don't look inside."

"I won't, Master," Mahir promised.

The cook smiled and closed his eyes again, but his assistant remained by the bed. "Is there anything else?" he asked, eyes still closed.

"I spoke to Neyyir Agha," he said. "If I could become a master, he said that he'd try to have me reassigned to the Inner Palace. What do you think? I know I asked only recently, but . . . have you thought about the possibility of me becoming a master?"

The cook opened his eyes and looked at Mahir. "Still thinking about that?"

Mahir nodded. "Yes, and you told me you would consider it."

"I did think about it," the cook replied. "It depends on you, actually. What I mean to say is that the sooner you can eat forty ovens' worth of bread in one sitting, the quicker you'll advance."

He closed his eyes again. His heart couldn't bear the expression on his assistant's face. Mahir was already walking toward the door, not dragging his feet but stomping out of rage.

After drinking the tamarind juice mixed with fermented violets, Mahir himself would be surprised at the thoughts teeming in his mind and the courage filling his heart, and he would quickly sever the last ties he had with his master.

Mahir would do it even if he didn't want to because he was going to open the door that would lead to the Harem.

The cook spent an hour in bed, resisting sleep, before getting up and leaving the palace. First, he stopped at a soup restaurant near Tahtakale and ate, and then he headed down toward the sea. He saw a large inn near the pier in Unkapanı and took a room so he could get some sleep.

When he opened his eyes, the *muezzins* were reciting the call to prayer, which said that prayer was holier than sleep. Quickly he got up and went down to the pier, weaving his way along back alleys. He woke up the oarsman of the first boat he came across and asked him to take him to Kasımpaşa.

As they swiftly glided over the still waters of the Golden Horn, a galley docked at the Imperial Shipyard caught the cook's eye. It was a huge ship with three masts, two decks, and fifty-eight cannons. It looked ghostly in the twilight. But as the rays of the rising sun illuminated the scene, he imagined the ship taking on bodily form and becoming a sea dragon yearning to get back to the open sea.

The cook saw Master Bekir and his six assistants waiting for him. He paid the oarsman and joined them. They greeted each other with nods. "Your men are running late," Master Bekir murmured. The cook turned his gaze in the direction of Kasımpaşa.

As his patience dwindled, time seemed to move ever so slowly. At last, the silhouette of Mad Bayram appeared on one of the streets leading down to the shore. Levon was with him, as always, and a few paces behind them were about half a dozen men with peculiar gaits. One was limping, another stopped after every few steps and turned around, one seemed to walk sideways like a crab, and one walked leaning forward as if he was going to start running any second.

The cook was displeased, not because of the strange appearance of the men but because he wasn't sure if there was enough of them. As he greeted each with a nod, he cast a pointed look at Master Bayram, who understood what the look meant. He grinned and blew a shrill whistle. When the high-pitched sound echoed across the water, five rowboats took to the waters of the Golden Horn, rowing toward the shore.

As the five pairs of oars silently cut through the water, Master Bayram introduced the shortest of the men whom he'd brought along to the cook: "This is Tekir."

The cook's eyes lit up. He had never seen him in person, but he'd heard much about Tekir. A swift and silent thief, he had burgled the House of Pleasure twice.

"Do you know the Great Mansion?" the cook asked.

Tekir grinned. "Like the back of my hand."

"The lodgings of the guards, Sirrah's room?"

"One needn't know where Sirrah's room is, sir. Follow the scent of gold and it shall lead you there."

"Good," said the cook. "Then you can show our friends here the way. Once the Great Mansion falls, the House of Pleasure is ours. There's only one condition: Sirrah must not be harmed in any way. After the deed is done, you can take whatever you like."

Tekir bowed his head in gratitude and placed his hand over his half-naked chest. In the meantime, the rowboats had reached the shore. The oarsmen stepped ashore and lashed the painters of their boats to the rocks. Two of them looked very similar, and just as Master Bayram had said, they were a pair of tall, well-built young men, strikingly handsome.

"Are these the Slow Brothers?" the cook asked.

Master Bayram nodded. "Don't be fooled by their looks. They are wanted in nine different provinces."

The cook looked at the Slow Brothers. Truly, with their solemn handsome faces worthy of palaces, they stuck out amid that crowd of degenerates. "In that case, let's go," he said quietly.

As the men were making their way toward the rowboats, Master Bayram's voice froze them in their tracks. "Whatever my brother here says," he said, pointing at the cook, "do it!"

The men placed their hands over their hearts and then they all set off in the boats. Master Bayram watched the five boats move away from the shore as they steered toward the mouth of the Bosphorus toward Üsküdar at the mouth of the Golden Horn.

They arrived in Üsküdar and started walking. After passing by a few fields, they crossed a small stream and then, as they reached the middle of the woods, they quietly approached the House of Pleasure.

The cook hid under a tree and looked up at the towering wall. On instinct he turned and saw Tekir standing beside him with a small bundle on his back. *So,* the cook thought, *the rumors were right. He walks so quietly that his feet don't seem to even touch the ground.*

From his bundle, Tekir pulled a long length of rope with a hook attached to one end and, after a quick glance around, he flung the rope over the wall. It landed with an audible clang but the hook set. Tekir scaled the wall and disappeared in a matter of seconds.

The cook and the others waited a safe distance from the entrance. About five minutes later, they heard a sound like the call of a nightingale—that was the sign.

Trying to walk as silently as he could across the leaf-strewn ground, the cook made his way toward the entrance and saw that the massive iron gate was ajar. At that time of day, the House of Pleasure, which lived and breathed at night, was at its quietest. The cook and the others approached Tekir and as they passed through the gate, they saw two guards lying face down on the ground.

They gathered in two groups on each side of the gate. Master Bekir and his assistants were standing behind the cook, while Master Bayram's men were standing behind Tekir.

"We'll meet in the kitchen," the cook said. Tekir nodded.

As Tekir gave his final instructions to his men, the cooks slowly made their way toward the kitchens. The cook was seized by bittersweet excitement. When one of the assistants lifted the latch on the kitchen door and pushed it open, the cook felt a pang in his heart as memories washed over him.

The cook quickly composed himself, knowing that it was not the time for emotions. He walked toward the small kitchen and motioned to the others to follow him.

Quietly, they walked through the kitchens and reached the hallway which led to the lodgings. After showing the assistants how many people slept in each room with his fingers, the cook approached Master Adem's room. Master Bekir and one of his assistants were standing beside him, each with his knife at the ready.

After exchanging the briefest of glances with the cook, Master Bekir pushed the door open. Master Adem was asleep in bed. He had aged; the lines around his eyes were much deeper, and his hair and moustache were almost completely white.

As the cook looked at his master, he was overcome by a mixture of emotions. On the one hand, he wanted to grab the knife Master Bekir was holding, while on the other hand he wanted to throw his arms around Master Adem's neck. However, timing and the events unfolding at the mansion allowed the cook to do neither of those things as his old master was stirred awake by the muffled screams coming from the other rooms. Just as he was about to open his eyes, Master Bekir and his assistant jumped on him. As the assistant pinned him down, the master covered his mouth tightly with his hand.

After struggling with all his might for a few moments, Master Adem realized he was fighting in vain and he lay back. Eyes filled with surprise and fear, he looked at the cook, who was approaching his bedside, and for a second his features were twisted with an expression of regret.

The cook whispered, "Don't be afraid. I have no intention of taking your life. Just keep quiet."

He nodded meekly. After the sounds of tumult coming from the other rooms had died down, Master Bekir removed his hand.

Master Adem shakily said, "Son . . ."

"Don't say a word," the cook said. "Get up and come with me."

They helped him to his feet and together went up to the large kitchen. The assistants joined them one by one. "Any problems?" Master Bekir asked.

The highest-ranking assistant said, "No, Master. We put the lot of them in that room in the corner."

There were a few short screams upstairs and then the mansion was plunged into silence. A few moments later Tekir appeared in the doorway along with the Slow Brothers. Sirrah was standing between the brothers, her hair tousled. She wasn't wearing any makeup and her face was pale with fear. They had tied her hands behind her back and stuffed one corner of her veil into her mouth.

The Slow Brothers pulled Sirrah toward the cook.

"How are you, Sirrah?" the cook asked. Like anyone who thinks they are untouchable, she could not believe the brazenness of the person standing before her.

After a few moments she regained her usual composure and spat out the cloth. "What do *you* want?" she sneered.

The cook took a few steps toward her and said, "Your tongue. I need your sweet-talking tongue, Sirrah. Will you give it to me?"

"What do you want?" Sirrah repeated. She was a woman of the world and knew when her life was in danger and when it wasn't.

The cook cut to the chase: "The Darıcızade heir is in Istanbul. You will entertain him at the House of Pleasure tonight."

Sirrah narrowed her eyes. "He won't come," she said. "He's busy. Preparing for a wedding."

When she realized what she had just said, it was too late.

"He will come," the cook said between clenched teeth. "You will go to the Darıcızade mansion with Master Adem. You will ask, beg, do whatever it takes to get that bastard to come here tonight. The Slow Brothers will come with you. If you can't convince him, if you try anything underhanded, they will cut your throats on the spot. Do you understand?"

Sirrah shifted her gaze to the two blades gleaming in the hands of the two men on either side of her. The cook turned toward the Slow Brothers and said, "Take her upstairs so she can get ready. Find yourselves something to wear as well."

After the Slow Brothers left with Sirrah, it was time to deal with Master Adem. "Master Adem," the cook said. "Go and get changed."

In about an hour, the seven were ready: the Slow Brothers in servants' uniforms of green velvet, the three robbers disguised as guards, Master Adem, and Sirrah. They left the House of Pleasure in a fancy carriage drawn by four horses.

Tekir and the rest of his men who remained behind roamed through the Great Mansion's rooms, collecting their spoils, while Master Bekir, his assistants, and the cook were in the kitchen nervously waiting for news from the Darıcızade mansion. Only the cook was standing. He was looking at his hands, examining the scars on his fingers and palms, each the relic of a memory rooted in that kitchen.

The deep crescent-shaped scar in the middle of his left palm was from when he was nine years old. He had been cutting a quince as he was preparing a dessert, and as he pressed down on the knife, the point cut into his palm and the blood gushed forth. He'd screamed. Master Adem had run in, squeezed his wrist tightly, and covered the wound with a pinch of salt. After bandaging his hand with a cloth, his master had pointed at the half of the quince on the floor and told him to go on with his work. That was how the cook learned that as long as his hands and his fingers were working, a cook had to finish whatever he started.

The burn scar running across his right palm came about as the result of a large pan. He was eleven or twelve at the time. Master Adem had asked him to lightly fry some pieces of aubergine. After the cook put the pan on the stove, he'd turned his attention back to the meat he was mincing and had only realized what was happening when he caught the scent of the aubergine. He'd known that if he left them for a second longer, they'd be overdone and there wasn't a single piece of cloth nearby, so out of instinct he'd grabbed the iron handle of the pan with his bare hand. He may have saved the dish, but he was rewarded with a scar that would stay with him for the rest of his life, reminding him that even the slightest absentmindedness could result in disaster.

The deep scars on the middle and index fingers of his right hand could be thought of as Kamer's doing. One day the cook was grating some lemon peels when Kamer started singing, and when he heard her voice, his thoughts wandered. He noticed he had finished grating the lemon peels and had moved on to his fingers only when she stopped singing. Thankfully Kamer had sung a short song, and he hadn't felt any pain at all.

He stood there in the middle of the kitchen, lost in his reminiscing. Master Bekir tried to strike up a conversation once or twice, but the cook responded curtly each time as he examined every pot, every knife, every corner of the kitchen, trying to remember each moment he had spent in that house.

What he was doing struck him as being somewhat silly and brought him more sorrow than joy, but he felt that he had no choice. Some of the things he remembered may have pierced his heart like a thousand thorns, but that was the only place he could call home, with all its good and bad; after all, it was proof of his past.

He did have a past, whether it lay in ruins or not, and he knew he had to reclaim it.

The cook snapped out of his reverie when the main gate clattered and he heard the sound of horses' hooves on the stony path.

Master Bekir and his assistants leapt to their feet and they all went outside.

Master Adem emerged from the carriage first, followed by Sirrah and the Slow Brothers. The cook approached Sirrah.

"It has been arranged," she said. "He will come tonight."

The expression on Sirrah's face betrayed, perhaps for the first time in her life, a sense of defeat at having accomplished something.

The cook looked at the Slow Brothers for confirmation.

"Don't worry, my Master," the larger of the two said. "Darıcızade will be here tonight."

The tense expression on the cook's face softened. "Thank you," he told them. "Now I have one final request."

The Slow Brothers nodded.

"Bring all the women of the House of Pleasure into the garden. Musicians, dancers . . . the whole lot of them."

Then he turned to Master Bekir and his assistants and said, "Let's go, Aghas," he said. "It's time to get to work."

They went to the kitchen.

"We're done with the worst of it. Now it's time for us to show what we can do. We must prepare a banquet that will put the Royal Kitchen to shame."

Master Bekir thought for a moment and said, "In that case, saffron rice is a must. Do they have good saffron here?"

The cook nodded. "The best, Master. Sirrah isn't stingy with the ingredients. What else shall we cook?"

One of the more experienced assistants offered, "Since there's saffron, if we can get fresh bass from Üsküdar, I could roast it."

Another assistant piped up, "Whoever is going to Üsküdar should buy some prawns, too. I'll make a cold salad with them; it will go well with the rest."

The cook silently nodded his approval when he found a suggestion sensible and brushed off those he did not like with a sour look. The banquet for Darıcızade was slowly coming together: "Hummus, almond soup, goose kebab, chicken with pomegranate syrup, mutton leg over cherry rice, guards' stew, and *mahmudiye*."

The cook gave his approval to a brave suggestion put forward by an assistant: minced meat with sauce over rye bread. He turned to Master Bekir. "What shall we do for dessert?"

"Baklava, of course," the master replied without hesitation.

The cook was unsure. "Will it stay fresh?"

Master Bekir smiled. "But of course."

"That's good," said the cook. "But we should have something light as well. All these dishes are quite rich."

Master Bekir was likely thinking the same thing, because he came up with a solution: "In that case, let's make *helatiye*. The cold fruit with syrup will be refreshing."

"So be it," the cook said. Then he looked out into the garden through the open door.

In the meanwhile, Master Bekir asked the question everybody had been wanting to ask: "And what will you cook?"

The cook smiled. He was listening to the nervous murmurings coming from outside. "I'll decide in a moment," he replied and stepped outside.

The Slow Brothers had brought all the women of the House of Pleasure into the garden, nearly thirty of them altogether.

The cook looked at the gathering of women at length, and sent about twenty of them back to their rooms. He told the others to line up in a row in front of him, and he approached the girl on the leftmost side, standing close as he looked at her at length. He closed his eyes and secretly breathed in her scent.

Scents of spring stirred in his mind, like the newly flowered branches of plum and almond trees swaying in the breeze. *Too innocent*, he thought and moved on to the next girl.

She had a sharper scent, but many of the aromas were bitter and sharp: black pepper, cinnamon, mustard, and an undertone of coriander. He moved on to the next girl.

Under the uneasy gaze of the women, he had almost made it halfway through the line in this manner, eyes closed. He liked a few of the girls with crisp scents, like fresh mint or basil, but they were either too dull to be any use to him, or the bouquet of their scents was too complex. Some of them evoked scents that were completely unremarkable compared with their remarkable physical beauty. The cook was about to pick a lesser of two evils when a scent filled him and brought back his cheer.

That scent was a blend of dozens but managed to work as one, as if expertly created from a hundred thousand spices. Unique, hot, and prickly, yet soothing and enticing. As one of the Pashas of Cuisine, he knew the word for that scent, and the moment he repeated its name to himself, the scent was transformed into a taste he could feel first on his tongue and then on his palate; it then became a feeling that worked its way from his heart to his stomach and from there to his groin. Quickly he banished the fantasies crowding his mind and repeated the name of the scent once more. The result was the same. It was the right scent and the right woman.

The cook was momentarily stunned when he opened his eyes because the woman standing in front of him resembled a young version of Sirrah. Pleased by this turn of events, he asked the young woman what her name was.

"Nihan," she replied.

When he looked into her eyes, he saw the timidity of youth and little more.

The cook repeated softly, "Nihan." Then he said, "Darıcızade Mahmud Bey will be visiting the House of Pleasure tonight. Were you aware of this?"

"No," she replied.

"Well, now you know. And you will be his favorite. You will dance for him and serve him. So dress for the role."

The young woman's eyes gleamed with a sparkle of ambition that sent chills down the cook's spine. Just then a woman's voice behind him said, "No, not her."

It was Sirrah. She was wise in the ways of the world, and she sensed impending danger. Perhaps she didn't know exactly what would transpire, but she sensed something was amiss. Rushing up to the cook she repeated, "Not her!"

"Why not?" the cook asked.

Sirrah paused and then said in a low voice, "There's something sinister about her. People call her the wrecker of mansions."

The cook looked at the young woman. He had no doubt she would live up to her reputation. He reached out, plucked a strand of her hair, and told her to get ready. Then he quickly made his way to the kitchen.

By the time the others caught up with him, the cook had already placed the strand of hair at the bottom of a pot and was preparing the ingredients he would need.

Master Bekir looked at the cook's table piled with lamb neck, shallots, truffles, a small beet, a handful of chestnuts, some dried plums, fresh ginger, basil, rosemary, and oregano. He asked the cook, "Are you going to make *gerdaniye?*"

The cook smiled. "Yes, something like that."

Master Bekir turned to his assistants and said, "Take up your knives!"

At his command, the kitchen was suddenly filled with a flurry of action. Knives were sharpened, pots and pans clattered, and sacks, bags, and baskets were carried up from the cellar into the kitchen. The cook was lost in that culinary symphony he loved so passionately, and as he was rubbing freshly ground ginger and rosemary into the meat on the table, he heard Tekir's voice on his left: "What shall we do with these two?"

The cook turned around, first looking at Tekir and then at Sirrah and Master Adem, both of whom were awaiting their fates as they stood between the Slow Brothers.

Putting down the piece of meat, he told them to follow him.

He walked toward the small, windowless, cold, dark room between the two kitchens.

The room in which Sirrah had kept Kamer locked up all those years ago.

He opened the door and looked inside. An image of Kamer appeared in his mind. She was sitting there surrounded by sacks of coal and planks of wood with her knees pulled up to her chest. Without taking his eyes from room, the cook said, "Put them inside."

Sirrah walked into the room without waiting to be pushed in, but Master Adem stood at the threshold, looked at the cook, and said, "Listen to me—"

The cook interrupted him: "That's enough from you, Master."

But Master Adem was insistent. "Whatever I did, I did it for you. I did it for the name you bear, so that you could become the true Pasha of Cuisine and live up to your title."

The cook scowled. He was hurt, almost on the verge of tears. "Master," he began, "the Pasha of Cuisine is a title, but it is not my name."

7

The Power of Names

AFTER THE COOK had spent more than a year at that stone mansion on the shores of Hormuz Island, he set out on a long sea voyage with the Lady of Essences.

He had spent the previous year doing almost nothing, or to put it more precisely, doing nothing different from what the other residents of the mansion did: he worked at the spice storehouse, read books, thought, remembered, and talked.

During all that time, talking was probably what helped him the most. He was surprised to find that the people whom he couldn't tell apart when he first arrived at the mansion soon became distinct individuals the more he spoke to them and got to know them. By taking them as seriously as they took him, he learned that he could only become close with others if they allowed him to do so.

Every September, the Lady of Essences would set out on a journey, as did all the merchants in the region. That was when the rains abated and the merchants rode the monsoon winds still blowing in from the sea and set sail for the coast of India and islands further east.

Around the middle of September that year, the Lady of Essences told the cook to get ready for a journey. She offered no explanation, keeping her thoughts to herself as she always did. Perhaps she wanted to expand the cook's knowledge and experience, or perhaps she thought a change of scenery would do his soul good. The cook did not ask any questions. He had learned long ago to not question the Lady's wisdom.

A few days later a familiar ship docked at the pier in front of the stone mansion: Captain Behrengi's black-sailed ship. The residents of the mansion helped them load the ship with provisions, spices to be sold and traded, and the Lady's pearl-inlaid chest. They bade the two farewell on the pier. As the ship set sail, they sang the ancient farewell song of those who remained behind. The ship glided over the calm sea, passed through the straits, and before sailing out into the open ocean they veered to the southwest toward the harbor of Muscat, which was their first destination.

Muscat was one of the most enthralling cities the cook had ever seen. They spent two nights in that small bustling harbor town where every kind of spice imaginable was bought and sold, filling the ship's hold with various spices, particularly frankincense, myrrh, and mastic.

The cook watched in astonishment as the Lady of Essences bought a small jar of Mecca balsam, paying twice its weight in silver without even bothering to haggle. Later, when he brought up the subject, the Lady laughed and said, "You should feel lucky we found any pure balsam at all." As she sold the very same jar for its weight in gold to a Portuguese merchant at a market near the Bay of Bengal, she winked at the cook.

After Muscat, they traveled to the Island of Ceylon, where the Lady of Essences wanted to buy a large amount of cinnamon. After mooring their ship, they traveled inland for half a day with some of the sailors until they reached the cinnamon groves in the middle of the forest. Since the owner of the groves did not protest when the Lady asked for certain trees to be marked for cutting, the cook assumed he must have had an abiding respect for the renowned customer gracing the island.

But that wasn't the Lady's only condition and desire. The sailors were to oversee the peeling of the trees and wait until the bark had dried, becoming sticks of cinnamon. The payment was to be made after the Lady completed the rest of her journey and stopped by on her return trip, whereupon the price would be calculated based on the weight of the dried cinnamon.

After leaving the Isle of Ceylon, they steered toward the Bay of Bengal. The cook thought they would continue hence until they reached the Indian coast, but when he woke up one morning and went up on deck, he saw that the ship had dropped anchor off the coast of a mysterious island.

The ocean, which was calm enough where they were anchored, churned wildly along the rocky shores of the island, and giant waves pounded the stone coast.

When the cook saw that the Lady of Essences was getting ready to go ashore with two sailors who were carrying her chest, his face went white with fear. It seemed impossible to him that the ship's small rowboat could stand up to the waves crashing along the coast. Even if the boat didn't capsize, the waves would smash the boat against the rocks.

In the end, none of the boats were lowered into the water. The Lady of Essences remained on deck with the sailors, watching the island impatiently. Minutes later, a few shadowy shapes appeared among the waves and started to approach the ship. As they drew nearer, the cook saw that they were long narrow canoes. Each was paddled by four men, and as their short oars sliced at the water as if taming a beast, the canoes slipped through the waves rather than fighting against them.

The canoes easily navigated the rocky shore, and when they reached the calm open water, they shot forward, appearing at the side of the ship in what seemed like seconds.

The Lady of Essences ordered the sailors carrying her chest down into one of the canoes, and as she climbed down the rope ladder, she gestured for the cook to follow her.

The cook had no choice but to comply. As he sat there among the islanders—whose language he didn't speak and whose religion he knew nothing of—he looked at their dark skin adorned with white tattoos and their unfriendly faces. He prayed silently all the way to the island.

But his fears proved unfounded. The men were fluent in the language of the ocean, and when the waves rose up around them, they rowed slower, letting the heaving water carry them forward, and smoothly they made their way toward the shore.

The cook realized that what he had thought to be one island was actually a collection of hundreds of stony outcrops which the oarsmen deftly navigated. When they reached the actual island by traversing a lagoon, the cook was stunned by the beauty of the place.

The still water was clearer and brighter than any he had ever seen, neither blue nor green, but clear enough to see not only the fish swimming around but even the grains of sand at the bottom.

The landscape had changed so suddenly that the terrifying din of the waves beating wildly against the rocks along the rocky reef seemed imaginary, nothing more than a frightening story told on a calm summer evening. The white sand of the seafloor gently rose up until it became a narrow beach which wound around the coast of the island like a pearly belt. Coconut trees grew along the shore, their fronds hanging low over the sand, contrasting with the blue of the sky and white of the beach with the softest shade of green.

As if in a dream the cook stepped ashore. There was nothing in his mind but the sand shuffling under his feet, the wind caressing his face, the scent of the sea, and the coconut fronds in the sunlight. In the distance he could hear the sound of the waves. When the Lady called out to him he snapped out of his reverie. She was standing up the beach a little ways, about forty or fifty paces inland. The cook ran over to her. The canoes had been pulled up to the shore but at some point the oarsmen had disappeared into the underbrush. The Lady of Essences pointed to some simple twig baskets which had been placed at the edge of the water. The cook was baffled at first, so the Lady picked up one of the baskets and raised it to his nose. Inside was a peculiar shapeless object, covered in a layer of gray-white slime. It smelled foul, like a bucketful of fish left under the sun all day.

"What is that?" the cook asked, scowling.

The Lady smiled. "Don't you recognize it?"

The first words to come to his mind to describe the smell were filth and carrion. But he held his tongue and merely shook his head. Just then, the oarsmen who had rowed them to the island appeared again from among the trees. Two of them were carrying a large basket, each holding one handle.

The Lady of Essences met them in the middle of the beach and began speaking in a language the cook had never heard before. As he approached them, he may not have been able to understand what they were saying to each other, but he could tell that they were passionately haggling. The cook's eyes were fixed on the shapeless objects in the basket, the smallest being the size of his palm and the biggest as large as a coconut. He realized they were dried versions of the things he had seen in the basket on the beach, but he still had no idea what they were.

The Lady pointed to the grayish-yellow ones in the basket and frowned, expressing her dissatisfaction with clipped words. Then she pointed to some other ones which were much darker in hue and counted on her fingers how much she would pay for the lot of them.

The islanders seemed to disagree with the amount the Lady proposed. As they grumbled in unison, one of them picked up two of the darkest-colored objects and offered a small piece to the Lady and the cook.

When the cook raised it to his nose, he smelled a mixture of rotten seaweed and manure. Anyone else may have been repulsed and tossed it aside, but the cook's nose was trained in scents, and it discerned the base aroma which had emerged from the depths and became stronger as he inhaled the smell. He was so surprised he let out a short laugh: it was ambergris!

He had experience of how seemingly foul-smelling things could bring zest to a dish. For example, the resin asafetida smelt not unlike rotten onions, which at first had made him approach it cautiously. Unsure of what the result would be, he'd only used a pea-sized amount to grease a pot once before cooking a dish. But the taste that had ensued cleared his mind of all prejudices. The asafetida added a quietly zingy flavor to the dish, like a few slices of salted onion or a baby leek.

But ambergris was entirely different. It was used in very small amounts, and only for certain sherbets and puddings. The cook also knew that the strange odoriferous was crucial for perfume producers. He had heard that it came from sperm whales, but he'd laughed it off as a silly rumor. Now, however, the truth was before him. The foul-smelling things he'd seen on the beach, placed among the waves to be washed and matured, were dried in the sun for years on end, whereupon they became ambergris, which made up the base scent of many perfumes and acted as a stabilizer for others. And it was valuable enough to lighten the Lady's treasure chest significantly.

During that journey, with each passing day the cook encountered something new, and something that astonished him even more than ambergris was musk.

After a long journey, they arrived in Calcutta, where they met with a Chinese merchant at one of the city's innumerable spice bazaars. Until that day, they had been met punctually and had been respectfully received at every harbor and market. But that particular merchant kept them waiting for a long time, and when he finally did show up, he greeted the Lady in an overfamiliar manner and proceeded with the transaction immediately, as if there was a queue of customers waiting behind them.

The merchant's attitude angered the cook. Never before had he seen anyone talk down to the Lady of Essences in such a way, and he'd also never seen a merchant talk of money without even showing the goods he was selling first.

What perplexed the cook even more was the Lady's attitude. Just as she had done when she'd bought the Mecca balsam, she did not haggle and immediately agreed to the price he was asking.

After the deal was made, the Chinese merchant took a small bundle out of his bag. He removed the cloth, revealing an elegant long-necked vial with a spout so small, it was little more than a slit.

As if he was about to perform a magic trick, the merchant dramatically pulled a needle out of his pocket and stuck it into the wax stopper on the bottle until it touched the liquid. The merchant then removed the needle and waved it in the air a few times, making the wide dragon-embroidered cuffs of his silk shirt billow.

Just as the cook was becoming thoroughly fed up with the merchant's antics and airs, something suddenly took his breath away. And not metaphorically, but literally. The thick scent of the musk hanging in the air was making it difficult for him to breathe. Of course the cook recognized the smell; like everyone who had been born in the Harem, it was one of the first scents he'd ever breathed in. But that was the first time he smelled it in its purest form, and it was unlike anything he could have imagined. After a few gasps he was able to breathe again, and what he experienced next left him astonished; in the middle of that bazaar, the dozens and dozens of scents lingering in the air seemed to be frozen in time. The musk did not block out the other scents but rather made them all the more pronounced, and what was even more intriguing was that it did not allow even one smell to mask another. In short, it had done away with the temporal, spatial, and tonal differences between them. The scent of a pepper plant carried by a merchant who had walked past a minute earlier, the piper *cubeba* in the stall next to them, and the sandalwood at the other end of the market all had the same intensity.

The cook put aside all other thoughts and let himself enjoy the peculiar bouquet. As he breathed, taking in all that he could, he saw from the corner of his eye that the Lady of Essences was paying the merchant twice the vial's weight in gold. He wasn't surprised in the least.

As his journey went on, the cook felt that he was getting closer to attaining peace and happiness for the first time in his life.

His old life seemed so distant. Now he was surrounded by people and the shouts of the sailors, there was always work to be done on the ship, the sea kept him on his toes, and the harbors were enthralling. He may not have had much time to think, but even on those brief occasions when he was alone, it seemed to him that his mind was calmer. The pain, melancholy, and longing were still there, but they were not transformed into the fits of suffering that tore at his heart.

The only thing that bothered him was the Lady of Essences.

For some reason he could not fathom, she would not let him forget. Not that the word actually existed in her vocabulary, but she was trying to prevent him from concealing things behind a veil of fog in the back of his mind, or at the very least she discouraged him from pretending he had forgotten.

At every opportunity the Lady reminded the cook of his past and Kamer, even at the most inopportune times such as when the cook was lost in thought, gazing at the sea, the sky, or the moon, or when he was organizing the goods in the hold and sorting out the spices. She would start talking and then deftly weave Kamer, the House of Pleasure, and any other painful topic into the conversation. And she seemed to enjoy it. She would repeat the stories he had told her, laughing.

The cook could do nothing but laugh along, but anger still welled up within him. The Lady of Essences's idea of fun, however, was much more than an idle pastime. Every time the cook listened to his own stories told by the Lady, he would grasp a truth that he had been blind to before or misunderstood. He was well aware by this time that "destiny" had not taken Kamer from his life. Just as the Lady of Essences said, what was called "destiny" was the mathematics of the "divine disorder," and humanity's biggest mistake was to regard it simply as a creator of consequences. But destiny encompassed not only what a person does but also what they don't do, what they choose and what they disregard, what they become and what they cannot become. It wasn't a linear line stretching through time, beginning in the past and extending toward the future. Destiny was a cycle, filled with beginnings as well as endings. It contained unseen, secret causes in addition to consequences. The only thing that mattered was being able to interpret destiny. What the cook and many other people in the world did was merely look at one facet of destiny and then get trapped in a whirlpool. The important thing was to look at the whole cycle, to see the imprints left on times, places, people, and events. Being able to do so revealed the equations hidden within divine mathematics and made clear the opportunities available and those that had been missed.

On a night when their journey was at a crossroads, they weren't talking about such things. Rather, they were talking about travel, trade, and other cities.

The Lady of Essences told him about golden cities hidden in the mountains of China, the glorious ancient capital city of Rome, Venice and Geneva, which became rising stars after the fall of the Romans, and the stunning harbors of Algeria, Tripoli, and Tunisia, which lined the coast of North Africa like a string of pearls.

When the subject turned to Alexandria, she became quiet and turned to look at the cook. "Whenever Alexandria is mentioned, you think of a city of darkness, don't you?" she asked.

It was true; the cook had always imagined Alexandria to be a city of shadows, a nightmarish city that had a dark, painful beauty.

"But that's not the case at all," the Lady of Essences said and then spoke at length about Alexandria. But as she spoke, her voice became more subdued. Her thoughts seemed to be elsewhere. Then she paused, muttered "Alexandria" one more time, and fell silent. She took a few steps away, the wooden deck squeaking beneath her feet, and then returned, gazing into the cook's eyes as if seeking out the final solution to a puzzle.

"Alexandria is your final stop," she murmured. "But you have a long way to go yet. After you leave here, you will study with other masters and learn other secrets, until at last you travel to Alexandria, just like all the other Pashas of Cuisine have done before you. There you will complete your education and learn the greatest secret of your art, and only then will you be the master of every taste in the world."

The cook stared at her blankly. The look in the Lady of Essences's eyes betrayed a slight sense of hopelessness and confusion. "But you," she said, "I'm afraid you may never become the Pasha of Cuisine.

Because . . . your soul is incomplete. You're alone. You're completely alone, and as long as you can't mend the void within your soul, you'll remain alone. Having people around you, whether they adore you or hate you, cannot change that fact. That is why you cannot become the Pasha of Cuisine. People with incomplete souls cannot attain completion in anything, in any art or science. What I mean to say is perhaps we've been looking at it wrong all along. We thought that becoming the Pasha of Cuisine would save your soul. But that's not it! Becoming the Pasha of Cuisine will not make your soul whole again. On the contrary, you will only be deserving of that title once you heal your soul. To do that, you have to get rid of that loneliness, which curses you. So complete your adventure, find Kamer, and discover the truth. You have to hear your name fall from Kamer's lips. Otherwise your adventure will never end and it will drag you into nothingness."

"Alexandria?" the cook murmured. Of everything she'd said, that was the only word that stuck in his mind. A misty vision of that city which he had never seen was taking him in its grip like a nightmare, and the fear in his eyes was visible even in the darkness of night.

"I'm not sure," the Lady of Essences replied. Her expression wavered between joy and sorrow, and her gaze seemed to be fixed on an invisible realm beyond this world.

"I'm not sure," she repeated. "It's complicated. But from what I can see, it seems that your fate has become tangled just so it can be untangled in Alexandria. A future with Kamer did not exist in your past; you couldn't have stayed with her as an ordinary cook. But you couldn't have stayed with her as the Pasha of Cuisine either. You had to leave her so you could take on that title, which is what you did. And now, only by becoming the Pasha of Cuisine can you take her back. If you go to Alexandria, if you can learn the greatest secret of your art—you can begin to hold sway over flavors, and through them you can learn to control emotions and people. Then you will have truly mastered your powers, the greatest on earth. You could take Kamer back. Or perhaps not; perhaps you must not. Maybe then you would become something else altogether. I don't know. I can't see that far ahead."

The words Lady of Essences was murmuring became less and less distinct, finally giving way to a silence that enveloped the ship and the night, leaving only the soft splashes of small waves and the creaking of the parbuckle to be heard. The Lady suddenly took a few decisive strides toward the wheelhouse and shouted, "Captain Behrengi! Weigh anchor! Hoist the sail! Toward the Red Sea!"

The captain leaped to action, the officers took their places, and the sailors, who were used to receiving orders at all hours of the night, emerged from their places of slumber and started hauling in the anchor and unfurling the sails.

The Lady's expression was half playful, half serious. "I may have given you a future tonight," she said, looking at the cook. "But it's also possible that I've taken your past from you. Maybe I've granted you Heaven on Earth, or drawn the apocalypse ever nearer. I don't know. My job was to act as your guide and I have done what I could. If I have made the wrong decision, I am ready to suffer the consequences. The rest is up to you."

The wind filled the sails with a snap and the ship lurched forward. The cook, who had been listening to the Lady in stunned silence, raised his head to look at the sky and the stars. He turned to the Lady of Essences in a panic. "What am I supposed to do?"

The Lady laughed and touched the cook's face. "You're going to go to Alexandria and find the Master Librarian. And you're going to ask him to teach you the greatest secret of what it means to be the Pasha of Cuisine."

The cook was even more uneasy. He could barely hear the words coming out of his own mouth: "What on earth is the greatest secret?"

The Lady of Essences held his face between her hands. "It's a mystery that the master has shared only with Pashas of Cuisine since the beginning of time. Like any mystery, it is simple in essence, but incredibly powerful. But remember, the work ahead of you will be difficult because you are going to your final destination, to the Master Librarian, much earlier than all the others before you. You should have spent many more years studying and learning. You have not even met half of the masters who would have guided you. But you must succeed. No matter what you do, you must learn the secret because you only get one chance at it. Every Pasha of Cuisine only gets to see the Master Librarian once in his lifetime. You can stay with him for as long as you like. You can try anything to convince him to tell you the secret. But if you give up and leave Alexandria, that will be the end of it. You will never be able to find him again, you will never be able to become a true Pasha of Cuisine, and you'll be destined to remain incomplete for the rest of your life. Do you understand what I am saying?"

The cook said nothing but merely looked at the Lady of Essences, his eyes full of questions.

She pulled her hands away and said, "No, I know nothing about the great secret. I have never seen the Master. I don't want to confuse you with rumors and hearsay. So, no. Don't expect me to tell you anything. But don't forget: if you don't complete your training, that does not mean you're still a novice. Experience is not acquired merely through charts and books. Maturity means knowing yourself. That is why you must look inward, learn more about your art, and see your art in yourself and yourself in your art. Think about what you're doing, how you're doing it, why you're doing it. Great mysteries are ancient. They remain in place perpetually and wait for those who can see them. You should search for the secret within yourself, not in the Master Librarian's words."

The cook was in no state to decide whether or not he actually understood what the Lady was telling him. He felt as though the ship had set sail for a land of fairy tales: *The Master and the Great Secret.* The more he thought about it, the more he wanted to laugh. He knew he was good at what he did. In fact, he was better at it than anyone he'd ever known. But it had always struck him as being quite ordinary. Cooking was to him was what flying was to a bird. What always surprised him was not his creations but the inability of others to create the same. That night, however, he discovered that the essence of his talent contained an otherworldly truth, which was why everything seemed so unreal and distant.

Yet the more he thought about Kamer, the deeper his mind seemed to sink into a quagmire and questions raced through his mind. According to what the Lady had been telling him, if he'd understood correctly, he was going to go to Alexandria, find Kamer, and hear the truth from her. But what was he supposed to say? What was he going to ask her? Would Kamer be able to understand what he was telling her? Did someone named Kamer really exist? Had she been alive; was she alive now? He understood better than ever why Majnun had asked Layla, "Who are you?" after meeting her in the desert. He had seen Kamer so often in his dreams that he had forgotten she actually existed in the world.

He decided that the Lady was right. The truth was not what Kamer would say. The truth was Kamer herself. And as long as he was encountering visions of her in his dreams rather than seeing the woman herself, the world would not turn for the cook. That was why he had to leave.

The Lady of Essences did not leave her cabin for the next four days. The cook knew that she was hiding from him and his questions. She had nothing more to say and no answers to give. That was only the inevitable consequence of an inevitable situation: for the first time in his life, and in every sense of the word, the cook was truly alone.

The cook had been ready long before the ship approached the harbor of Suez and the sailors lowered the gangplank onto the pier. But he did not disembark at first. He knew that the Lady, who had been avoiding him for days, would come to bid him farewell. After a while she emerged from her cabin, smiling—but her smile betrayed confusion. She approached the cook, stroked his cheek with her palm, and said, "Good luck."

"Thank you," the cook replied. Hundreds of questions were filling his mind, but he brushed them aside. "Thank you," he repeated, "for everything you've done for me."

He turned to leave, thinking that the Lady had nothing more to say. But he was wrong.

"Don't forget," the Lady said, her voice as warm as her palm on his cheek, "loneliness is what you feel when you miss someone calling out your name."

The cook strode down the gangplank onto the pier. When he turned around after a dozen or so steps, he heard the Lady's voice again: "Weigh anchor!"

The cook listened to the clamor of the sailors as he walked away, and then the noise of the harbor, the shouting of porters, the calls of merchants, and the cries of touters from a nearby market drowned out their voices. When he stepped through the large gate of the wall separating the harbor and the city, Captain Behrengi's black-sailed ship disappeared into the realm of silence.

During his journey to Cairo along the banks of the River Nile, the cook recalled how he had walked under the scorching heat of the sun and over barren earth to reach its shores. As he got closer to the river, the baked earth gave way to greenery, but the heat remained the same. The waters of the Nile gave life to the desert, but rather than cooling the air, the river filled it with humidity so intense that the cook found it suffocating. But he walked on, without waiting to run into a caravan, guide, or fellow traveler, without stopping unless he had to, asking for directions along the way.

After five days of walking through fields, gardens, and vineyards, the cook saw the sea, and to the left he saw the city of Alexandria abutting seemingly infinite green fields. The city was surrounded by walls, behind which white buildings and minarets rose up into the air. Perhaps it was indeed as beautiful as the Lady had said it was, but the darkness in the cook's soul was able to devour the whiteness of the city even from a distance.

He might have been in denial about it in the moment, but in truth the cook was thinking about giving up. Cairo was behind him now, and the harbor of Suez was even further back. He knew that the Lady of Essences was probably on the open seas by then—either travelling back home or continuing on her journey—and that going back to her home would be the worst thing he could possibly do, as he knew he wouldn't be able to look her in the eye.

Up ahead on his right, where the green came to an end, a desert began, one that stretched all the way to the land of Nubia. The Mediterranean stretched out in the distance. The cook considered going back home. But what would happen if he did? Would he spend the rest of his life cooking for the House of Pleasure, just like Master Adem, and cursing his past just like him, too?

The cook was terrified, and his sole desire was to run away. But it seemed to him that the world was only as big as the landscape that spread out before him. Apart from the sea, the desert, and distant unknown lands, only Alexandria seemed to exist in the world, and that was the only place he could go.

He kept walking.

When he entered the city, he began to follow the Lady's somewhat odd instructions. "Walk toward the sea, toward the Eastern Harbor," she had told him. "Walk on the streets that look out onto the western tip of the island of Faros. You'll find the Master's shop eventually."

That was it. There was no mention of the name of a square or a street, or anything else.

Soon enough he found the streets she had mentioned and began to walk along them. They were modest streets, lined with buildings that had shops on the ground floor and apartments on the upper floors. As the cook wandered around, he stumbled upon what he was looking for on his right, between a grindery and a tinsmith: the Master Librarian's bookshop. He peered through the window. It was fairly large inside, but it was hard to tell just how large because the rear of the shop was shrouded in darkness.

As he hesitantly pushed the door open, light streamed into the shop, revealing more of its depths. In the farthest corner past some book-shelves, there was a large desk, and a thin figure was sitting in a large chair behind it.

The cook stepped through the doorway and, as he walked toward the figure, he was surprised to see that with each step he was leaving deep footprints on the floor. The dust was so thick that it seemed that no one had been there in centuries.

When he was finally standing in front of the figure, the cook real-ized that the man was also looking back at him. A shiver ran down his spine. The man had the oldest face he had ever seen in his life. The deep wrinkles on his face made him look so ancient that even death himself would have seemed young compared to him. The hood of the man's worn cloak was pulled over his head, but the cook could see his honey-colored eyes, which gleamed with the vigor of a young man.

"I'm looking for the Master Librarian," the cook said.

"I am he," the man replied in a clear voice that was remarkably youthful.

It occurred to the cook that the man seated before him was very much like the books in the shop: ancient, yellowed, but very much there and alive.

"I bring you greetings from the Lady of Essences," the cook said.

The Master Librarian searched his face, a hint of bemused surprise in his expression, and replied, "I have not heard from her for a long time. But I do know that the Lady wouldn't send just anyone to bring her greetings."

The cook averted his eyes and nodded. As he went over one ques-tion, turning it over and over in his mind, the master said, "You're still quite young. Would you be so kind as to tell me which masters you studied with before coming here?"

The cook understood that the question was the first link in a chain of questions, and saw where it was going. "Before staying at the Lady's house, I was the guest of the el-Haki brothers," he said, somewhat abashed. "I know, it's not nearly enough, but—"

The master interrupted him. "You can't know that," he said. "Yes, you're only at the beginning of a long road. You've not yet learnt the secrets of dough and baking bread from Master Kirkovyan, or the power of fire and the intricacies of cooking from Master Elşad. You've not yet visited Turkistan. You don't know anything about the language of animals or the science of meat, let alone the miracles of milk. You're only a beginner when it comes to the art of wielding a knife. You know little of wine or olives and their oil, what grows in fields and what grows on trees in the wild, or what can be found in the seas and waters of the world, not to mention your ignorance of water itself and much else. But, you're here! That is what concerns us. Tell me, why did the Lady of Essences send you here?"

It seemed that the Master Librarian wanted to hear the cook say what was truly on his mind. The cook could resist no longer and replied, "I am here to learn the great secret of my art from you, so that I can become the Pasha of Cuisine."

The Master Librarian's eyes filled with mischief. "Yes," he said, nodding slowly. "You have to learn the secret to become a Pasha of Cuisine. Seeing as the Lady thinks the time is right, go on then, ask me your question."

The cook was confused. He didn't know what it was he should be asking, and the enthusiasm in the master's eyes seemed to be fading. "Do you not have a question?" he asked.

The cook blurted, "What is the great secret of my art? Please teach me." But before he could even complete his questions, the master's eyes dimmed even further.

"Is that your question?" he asked.

The cook lapsed into silence and as he did so, the master slowly turned his gaze from the cook's face.

"So that's your question," he said after a long pause. "If that's the case, this is very sad indeed. It's sad to realize that the Lady was wrong."

The cook felt as if he'd turned a corner only to find himself on a dead-end street. His voice full of contempt, the Master Librarian said, "You're still immature. More so than a complete novice. You haven't asked anything at all. You haven't even managed to ask the wrong question properly. You have no idea about which facet of your art carries the great secret. If an apprentice who had thought at least a little about his profession had been standing in your place, he would have at least said, 'Teach me the secrets of the knife,' 'Teach me the secrets of fire,' or 'Teach me the secrets of cooking.' Because even in his novice's mind he would have been able to realize that the great secret of his art lies hidden in one of those things. He would have been wrong, obviously. But at least he would have had something of an idea regarding his art and over time, that idea would grow, helping him understand the mistakes he was making and leading the apprentice to the right question one day. Such an apprentice would never have come up to me and asked, 'Teach me the great secret of my art' as if he were a neophyte who knew nothing about his art."

The cook managed only a pathetic whimper in response. If he had been able to unknot his tongue, he would have begged the master to help him and show him the way, but before he could get a word out, the Master Librarian silenced him by raising two fingers in the air.

"I'm here to help whoever is worthy of it," the master said. "As long as you remain in Alexandria, my door is open to you. You have all the time you want and as many chances as you want to ask the right question. But, as you've been told, if you give up and leave Alexandria, you will never find me again."

The Master Librarian closed his eyes. The bookshop was suddenly enveloped in an ancient, parched silence, and the cook had no choice but to leave.

In the following days he spent in Alexandria, the cook thought about what the Lady and the master had told him. The question nagged at him: truly, what was the secret to his profession? When he was being taught by Brother Sa'd at the el-Haki brothers' house, he was almost convinced that the greatest secret to cooking was the stars. But what Brother Sadr had taught him was also important. The secrets of medicine that were revealed to him made the stars seem a little duller as a result. And then at the Lady's mansion everything changed again. That time, spices took the foreground and pushed what he had learned until then into the shadows. The cook was only just starting to realize what his journey was about. It wasn't merely a matter of learning. At the place he would have gone after the Lady's mansion, he would have learned about fire, meat, or some other aspect of cooking, and he would have been astounded yet again by what he learned, but each time, what he learned would make what had learned before seem like ordinary knowledge rather than a mystery, and the cook would finally see that the secret truth which set him apart from other cooks was not hidden in what he learned or what he knew, and that he would have to search elsewhere for it, in places that were deeper and more internal.

The cook finally understood why his journey was so important, but that understanding trapped him in such a hopeless state of mind even his journey started to lose meaning. As soon as he left Alexandria, the master would disappear, and it wouldn't make any difference afterwards if he had struck upon the right question. For the time being, Alexandria was his entire world. It was both his prison and his only salvation. There was only one thing he could do, even if it took him until the end of time: he had to stay where he was and search for the right question.

After spending three nights walking the empty streets of Alexandria by the city walls and the ruins on the harbor, one early morning the cook found himself on a hilltop observing a large mansion just outside the city.

He wasn't sure why or how he ended up there. It was almost as if he had woken up on the small hill on which he was standing. He hadn't asked anybody anything, nor had anyone told him to go there, but somehow the cook knew where she was. The red rays of the rising sun were gleaming on the walls of the Darıcızade mansion.

The cook was feeling the frightening pleasure of being so close to Kamer after so long. With each passing day, his desire to see her grew. The Kamer of his dreams was slowly returning to reality.

The cook looked at the tall thick walls surrounding the mansion. They seemed insurmountable, but the cook knew what he had to do:

he had to enter the mansion as a flavor, as a scent which could seep in through the gaps under doors and the cracks in the walls. He had to interpret feelings, find weaknesses, and replace feelings with other emotions and servile desires. He knew that was the only way he would ever get into the mansion. The cook knew very well what he had to do, but he couldn't do it. He hadn't yet become the Pasha of Cuisine.

The cook did the only thing he could do, which was wait. He knew Kamer would go out sooner or later and he was waiting for that time. Once it came, he would find a way to stand before her even if it cost him his life. Perhaps they wouldn't even have a minute to talk, perhaps the guards would grab their daggers as soon as they saw him. But it didn't matter. The cook did not need much time. A moment, just a moment so he could look into Kamer's eyes—because the truth was brief, and it lay in Kamer's eyes.

But Kamer was nowhere to be seen.

Heart pounding, he watched each group of people leave the mansion. He would wait on top of the hill until they approached the city's southern wall and then he'd quickly run down, entering the city through the southwestern gate which used to be called the Sun Gate, and follow them. The women of the Darıcızade mansion traveled to the city on sedan chairs. Aside from the slaves who carried the chairs on their shoulders, there were also around a dozen guards accompanying each group. Half of those surrounded the sedan chair at the front, while the other half guarded the concubines, maids, and eunuchs who followed behind, which made it impossible for the cook to get any closer than ten paces. But still, he watched. Buoyed by the hope of actually seeing Kamer, he searched for even a mere trace of her, a crack in the wall.

Months went by this way. The possibility of seeing Kamer again made everything else pale in comparison. With each passing day, he thought less and less about the Master Librarian. He told himself that if he could only be reunited with Kamer, there wouldn't be a problem on earth he couldn't solve. But he couldn't find her. The walls of the Darıcızade mansion were not only high but silent. Not a whisper escaped them. Even the residents of the city knew nothing of the Darıcızade family and the cook almost started to think that their existence was a figment of his imagination.

But then a coincidence saved him.

Once again he had followed a group of people who had left the mansion and were headed for the market. The group of women, who were out to do some shopping, was larger than usual. Even though they were surrounded by twice the usual number of eunuchs and guards, the women were unstoppable as they scattered around the market, looking at fabrics. The cook watched them carefully. It was the first time he'd been able to get so close to the women from the mansion, and his heart was pounding. He listened to the conversations of every woman he could get close to, hoping to hear Kamer's name or a whisper about her, while at the same time keeping an eye on the guards.

Just then a breeze brought him a miracle that made his heart beat so fast it hurt.

The breeze had blown back the thin green silver-embroidered veil of a woman standing in front of the stall next to him. The cook only saw her face for the briefest of moments, but it was enough for him to be certain. He recognized the face he saw. The woman's name was Şehandan. She had once played the lute and sang at the House of Pleasure, and she was one of the twelve girls gifted to the Darıcızade heir by Sirrah. The cook knew she had traveled there with Kamer, so she would undoubtedly know where she was or what she was doing. He decided that he had to ask her.

The cook didn't have enough time to be subtle, and so he did the first thing that came to mind. The market was crowded and noisy, so the cook suddenly sprang forward, took her by the arm, and pulled her into a narrow gap between two stalls that was concealed behind some fabric. Şehandan was terrified. At first she opened her mouth to scream, but when she realized she was face to face with the cook, she gasped.

"Where is Kamer?" the cook asked her. She said nothing, so he asked again, "Where is Kamer?"

Again she said nothing, but not because she was hiding anything or trying to think up a lie. Rather, she didn't seem to know how to tell him the truth. The cook's trembling hand started sliding from her arm to her neck. Şehandan said in a low whisper, "She's not here."

That possibility had never occurred to the cook and he looked at her in confusion.

"She's not here," Şehandan repeated. "Kamer never came to Alexandria."

Then she began to explain.

When the girl's whispering howl of truth concluded, nothing was left of the cook but a lonely, faded shadow. He felt like the vapor of a potion in an uncorked bottle. His mind and soul were suddenly so empty and his very being was lost in a void so great that if he were to dissolve into the molecules that made up his body and blow away, it would have meant nothing to him.

Şehandan told him:

How Kamer never traveled to Alexandria, because she never left Istanbul.

How it was all a ruse devised by Sirrah.

How Kamer was locked up for days so that the cook would think she had left, how she was beaten and forced to write that farewell letter.

How one of the authors of that farce had been Sirrah, and the other was Master Adem.

That which caused both Sirrah and Master Adem to have sleepless nights was one and the same: the love affair between the cook and Kamer.

Sirrah was certain that her most valuable girl would slip from her grasp all for the sake of a cook because Kamer had screamed the truth in her face, saying she was in love with the cook and would elope with him the first chance she got.

As for Master Adem, he was afraid he would lose his Pasha of Cuisine. He knew that as long as he was enamored of Kamer, the cook would never set out on his journey of learning and thus never become the Pasha of Cuisine, who was the last hope of an old cook who had squandered his life and his talent.

Darıcızade Mahmud Bey had descended upon the House of Pleasure like a savior. The plan was that Sirrah would receive a sizeable payment in exchange for her favorite girl, and the cook would set out on his travels after a few days of mourning. They were both still young, young enough to forget each other and fall in love again. Kamer did not want to go to Alexandria, but that was a trivial detail for Sirrah.

However, Mahmud Bey's dear old father had put his foot down. He made it clear in no uncertain terms that he would not accept a daughter-in-law who came from the House of Pleasure, especially a dancer. Mahmud Bey apologized to Sirrah again and again, purchasing a dozen girls for his harem from the House of Pleasure to soothe his disappointment and have something to take his mind off Kamer while he was in Alexandria, and then he went back home.

That was when Sirrah devised the ruse. First, she locked Kamer up and told everyone that she would be going off to Alexandria with Mahmud Bey. The only remaining detail was to get Kamer to write the letter, but she resisted. She was beaten for days on end and still refused to write it. Just as Sirrah was about to give up, Master Adem stepped in. "If you don't write that letter," he told Kamer, "I will hack him to pieces in his bed tonight! I raised him myself, but that won't stop me! He is going to become the greatest in the world. I won't have him throw his life away for a harlot from the House of Pleasure like I did!"

Kamer looked into Master Adem's eyes.

She looked into his eyes and she was frightened.

She was frightened and she wrote the letter.

That was how the cook discovered the truth he had been seeking, between two market stalls at the bazaar in Alexandria. He did not feel anything, because nothing was left in his life. Kamer was not there, but hidden away inside another unknown. The great secret of his art remained a mystery. And worst of all, Master Adem was gone from his life. And with him, the only place he could return to and call home had disappeared. He was alone again, and every time he ended up alone, he felt that he was in a place that was so much more desolate than the one before. Such a poisonous dejection had taken root within him that even getting angry was an arduous task. Only by thinking of Master Adem could he invoke any real feeling inside himself, and even that wasn't pure anger; rather, it was mixed with disappointment and smelled terribly of fear, the fear of loneliness, the fear of losing his past, the fear of betrayal.

He spent the next day and the days that followed seeking an answer to the one important question in his mind: what could he do?

He had no one to turn to for advice, and he would have even settled for Master Adem's platitudes. If he continued to chase after Kamer, he would have to leave Alexandria and lose the Master Librarian as well. But if he stayed put and tried to attain the great secret. . . . He didn't even know whether he would ultimately become successful, let alone how long it would take.

That day at dawn, as he lay sprawled in a hovel by the city walls, the cook considered his position as those thoughts rushed through his mind. He had spent two nights in the ruin to escape the heat. He was covered in so much dust and dirt that he couldn't even see the color of his clothes. His shoes were in tatters from running back and forth from the city to the hill. His beard and hair were long and scraggly. He couldn't remember the last time he'd slept in a bed or had a proper meal. When he realized that he could stay in those ruins forever, or until he died of starvation, thirst, sickness, or until someone came and murdered him, he got to his feet. He finally managed to murmur to himself, "I won't die like this!"

He bought a new set of clothes and something to eat with the last of his money, went to the hammam, and then made his way to the harbor. Finding a ship headed to Istanbul would not be a problem. The real problem was finding a ship that was sailing to Istanbul and also needed a cook.

Thanks to his patience and luck, he managed to find a place for himself on a twenty-six-oar cargo galley headed to Istanbul with its hold full of wheat. According to the captain, the previous cook had gotten fed up with preparing food for all the oarsmen and sailors in the narrow galley of the ship and had disappeared in Alexandria. It didn't take long for the cook to convince the captain to take him on; all he had to do was work a little magic with some calamari stew that the crew members were trying to cook up.

The cook enjoyed being appreciated, even if it was the appreciation of the crew of a small galley. At the same time, he was experiencing the bittersweet relief of having made a decision. He had decided to leave the Master Librarian and the great secret behind in Alexandria forever so he could find Kamer. He didn't know what would happen afterwards, and he didn't care. Even the prospect of spending the rest of his life as a ship's cook did not bother him much.

Over the next few days he bought provisions for the ship with the captain, organized the kitchen, and bought the rest of the equipment he needed.

Going back to cooking cleared his mind. Once again his thoughts were filled with meats, vegetables, spices, measures, pots, and knives, and he dreamt of the dishes he could make with what they had in the ship's hold while trying to come up with dishes that the captain and the crew would enjoy. What the cook was actually doing was trying to remember what it was like to follow his calling in life. Along with his own identity, he had forgotten the simplest thing that made him who he was: cooking.

At last the day of departure arrived. The crew gathered at the harbor and loaded the last of the provisions on the galley. They were to set sail before sunset.

The cook had picked up his sharpened knives from the grindery and was returning back to ship, thinking about a recipe for the vermicelli soup he was planning on making that night. When he arrived at the pier, he saw the captain and two officers eating and drinking at a table they had set up in a spot on the quay. As he greeted them, the captain asked, "You bought lots of cheese, didn't you?"

The captain was extremely fond of cheese and had asked the same question before. The cook was about to reply, "We've cheese of every type, sir, don't worry" when the captain said with a childish expression of joy on his face, "The old cook used to crush some white cheese, add some basil to it, and roll it into little balls. He added lots of other spices, too. He fried them so that they would be as soft as cotton on the inside and crispy on the outside. Ah, what a scent! I don't know how to describe it, but it was like eating spring flowers. As if . . ."

With a somewhat condescending look on his face, the cook was listening to the captain's pathetic attempt to describe a certain flavor when he suddenly froze.

He had just realized something quite odd. Something he did all the time without knowing he was doing it, like breathing. He knew what the captain was trying to describe. The flavor he wanted to describe had appeared in the cook's mind as a whispered word. That wasn't just the case for that particular flavor. Regardless of whether he had tasted it himself, every taste and every smell on earth, and every mixture therein, had a meaningful equivalent in his mind. Those words, which existed as whispers in his mind, usually became nonsensical sounds when he said them aloud, but those words existed as a mysterious language that described flavors. And the words in his mind weren't only created by the flavors. When he whispered them out loud, a reflection of the corresponding flavor also appeared in his mind. In that way, even if there was no food to be had, a flavor could exist as a purely cognitive taste.

The cook realized just then, a few steps from the ship, that he had been doing that for a very long time. That was the biggest secret he had discovered about himself in his entire life. He thought and thought, and then those words spoken by the Lady of Essences echoed in his mind: "Loneliness is what you feel when you miss someone calling out your name."

Was he certain? Not in the least. Was it worth trying? By all means.

The cook started to run. With every step he prayed that the Master Librarian's shop would be where he had left it. He hadn't yet left Alexandria exactly, but the closer he got, the more worried he became.

When he saw the bookshop across the street, he paused and breathed a sigh of relief. After catching his breath, he walked through the door. The footprints he'd left on his previous visit were barely visible. Stepping over them, he walked toward the rear of the shop. The master was behind the large desk, just as he had left him, as motionless as the books on the shelves.

The cook approached the master and, trying to keep his voice from shaking, said, "Teach me the names of flavors."

There was no need for him to wait for an answer. As soon as he made his request, a sparkle of hope appeared in the Master Librarian's eyes, which told him everything he needed to know.

As the master slowly got up, his garments made rustling sounds like the pages of a book. He pushed open a door behind him, which was hidden behind some shelves, and stepped through the doorway into the secret depths of the shop. The cook followed behind him. The place was almost pitch dark, save for the weak light given off by oil lamps placed intermittently above the shelves which stretched the length of the two walls of the passageway and seemed to go on forever. There was no darkness at the end of the passageway, nor any light, only shelves and books extending into infinity and the pervading smell of books.

The master asked in his youthful voice, "Have you ever noticed how few names flavors have? Think of the languages you know. Everything has a name: air, wind, rain, snow, colors, sounds. But flavors have so few names: sweet, salty, spicy, sour, bitter, burnt, acrid. . . . How many others can you list? There are no more than a dozen. That is why people always explain tastes by making half-complete comparisons. They say, for example, 'This tastes like onions.' But 'onion' is not the name of a flavor, it is only the name of the plant. As the saying goes, 'Taste begins in the mouth, but has no language.' Or rather, that's true for most people in the world. But a Pasha of Cuisine would laugh at such a statement, because he knows that flavors have a language all their own. He has learned that every flavor in the world can be described by its name. That is the greatest talent of the Pasha of Cuisine; it's why he is a better cook than anyone else. He can understand flavors, and in time he learns how to communicate with them. He makes tastes docile. He raises them up and lowers them down. He toys with them. As he creates new flavors, he learns and discovers new names."

The Master Librarian suddenly stopped and reached toward the shelf on his left. He took out a thick book bound in green leather and gave it to the cook. "This is for you," he said.

The book was heavy. When the cook opened its cover, he saw that it was very old. The paper was so worn that it seemed it would disintegrate if he were to touch it. He looked in confusion at the small pictures inked on the page. At the time, he did not know that they were the hieroglyphs of ancient Egypt.

As he turned the pages, both the paper and the writing changed. The cook recognized the Greek and Latin letters on a page that was yellowed but in better condition than the others. He kept turning the pages until he found a page he could actually read, one written in the Arabic script, and read the first word he saw in a low voice. The word meant nothing to his ears, but it made a familiar taste appear on his palate. It was the taste of raw dough, properly fermented, ready to be shaped and placed in the oven; a slightly sour, rich smell. The word beneath it was the name of freshly baked bread. It manifested not only in taste and smell, but also with a warm crunchiness. The names went on for pages and pages, and with every word he pronounced, another flavor acquired meaning and became etched in his mind. It was as if the cook was bringing to completion the souls and existence of all the flavors in the world by whispering their names. There were no words to describe the pleasure and joy he felt. If he could have, he would have read the whole book straight through in that narrow hallway until he memorized all the names.

Pointing at the book in the cook's hand, the Master Librarian said, "*The Names of Flavors*. The first Pashas of Cuisine in the world wrote down the names of flavors in this book. Time passed. Flavors merged into one another: they changed, were transformed, and became other flavors. They took on new names and new meanings. The Pashas of Cuisine who came before you added each new name they discovered to those pages. Now it's your turn to add a few names of your own."

"Can I keep it?" the cook asked hopefully.

"Yes, for now," the master said. "And don't worry about returning it. When the time comes, the book will find its way back to me."

As the cook was searching for the right words to describe his gratitude, the master pulled out another book from the opposite shelf. "Take this, too," he said with a meaningful look. "You'll need it."

The cook opened the worn black cover which had nothing written on it, and looked at a few pages. A mischievous smile tugged at his lips. The master was right. The book, which contained recipes from previous Pashas of Cuisine, would be very useful to him, very useful indeed.

Before he left, he looked at the master's deeply wrinkled face and sparkling honey-colored eyes one last time, knowing that he would never see him, or his shop, again for the rest of his life. Pressing the books to his chest, he bowed and thanked him.

"You who will add life to the lives of flavors," the Master Librarian said. "May your path be clear and pure!"

The cook noticed a hint of warning in those parting words, as well as the fire of excitement that was slowly beginning to burn within him. He now had a great power, and he knew he had to use that power to overcome every obstacle that he might come across during the adventure he was about to undertake. He knew it would be no trouble at all to keep his path clear, but to keep it pure, he would have to be as careful as humanly possible.

He left the bookshop and dashed back to the pier, brushing aside the captain's confused looks and curious questions with a few expertly crafted lies. That evening, the ship set sail for Istanbul.

The cook spent the first few days making rather ordinary dishes that were easy to prepare so he could spend the rest of his time shut up in the galley, reading the books.

At the end of the third day, he made a few dishes based on the recipes from the book for the captain and his officers, and what ensued surprised him. He already knew that flavors could affect people's emotions. Whispering the name of a flavor made it more intense, but how a flavor affected an individual depended on the person's past and their state of mind. For example, the deck officer, who was known for being a gentle-natured person, attempted to strike up a mutiny after eating a plate of the cook's *borani*. But the word that the cook whispered as he made poached eggs in boiling water had an almost uniform effect on the entire crew. Everyone felt more energized, particularly the oarsmen, and despite the strong wind blowing over the bow of the ship, they traveled twice the distance they normally would have.

Whispering the names of flavors was like rolling dice. The cook realized that only with time and practice could he gain complete power over their names and effects. He would try and he would fail, but finally he would manage to isolate those flavors which had the same effect on almost everyone, just like the Pashas of Cuisine before him had done. That was why the second book the master had given him was so important. The recipes on those pages contained combinations of flavors shaped by the pashas' experiences, and their effects were universal. Those who came before him had written in great detail about which tastes were to be combined, which names whispered, and which flavors brought to the forefront, and they had forged a path that began with absolute tastes and ended in absolute emotional responses. It sounded fairly easy, but the mechanism they discovered was in fact exceedingly complex. Rice, for example, had a basic taste and a basic name. But when it was steamed with oil and salt, its taste and name changed, and therefore the emotions it represented also changed. When it came to entire dishes, matters got even more complicated. A plate of stuffed vine leaves, for example, was not solely vine leaves or stuffing or mint or onion. It wasn't any of those things in isolation but all of them at once. That was where the Pasha of Cuisine's talent came into play. Just as a conductor wields power over all sections of an orchestra and introduces subtle changes according to the audience's mood without interfering with the basics of the music, a Pasha of Cuisine had to adjust the intensity of the basic tastes in a dish while still maintaining its overall flavor.

By the time the ship passed the island of Rhodes and entered the Aegean Sea, the cook grew worried about the consequences of what he was doing. The oarsmen were still rowing vigorously, but the captain had become enamored with the idea of those lands to the west of the Great Sea which were said to have been newly discovered, so much so that he tried to steer the ship toward the strait of Gibraltar once. Thankfully, the Chief Captain, an experienced elderly seaman, stepped in and managed to talk the captain out of it.

The navigator was in the worst state of them all. The cook never understood exactly what he had used in excess in a dish of couscous he had cooked for the burly man, but the resulting situation became more and more precarious with each passing day. The navigator seemed to have fallen in love with the cook. He visited him in the kitchen every other day and told him how, "if he so wished," he would immediately slit the throats of the captain and the other officers, seize control of the ship, and steer them toward whichever destination their hearts desired. Needless to say, the cook was in a difficult position. He tried to keep the man's wits about him by carefully choosing his words and steering his mind from the passions that burned in his breast, and at the same time he pored over the book of recipes, looking for a remedy to quench the raging fire he had ignited.

The journey soon came to an end thanks to the vigor of the oarsmen. As soon as the ship approached the pier at Unkapanı, the cook did not even wait for the gangplank to be lowered and jumped off the deck, disappearing into the crowd as the captain and navigator called out after him.

It hadn't been difficult for him to get news of Kamer. Through conversations he had with a few regular customers of the House of Pleasure with whom he was acquainted, he found out that she had been sold off to the owner of the Zümrützade mansion. They explained with astonishment how suddenly the light had gone out in that beautiful young woman's eyes, and neither her dancing nor singing had their previous allure. As she fell out of favor with the customers, Sirrah had no choice but to get rid of her as quickly as possible.

After his stay in Alexandria, the cook set his sights on a wealthy mansion once again. But this time his eyes had a different glow. He had a plan.

It was easy enough for him to get on friendly terms with a few of the servants working at the mansion. Through those new acquaintances he challenged the Zümrützade cook to a contest. Naturally the cook won the contest, which was held at a small kebab shop near Sirkeci, by the unanimous vote of a jury; not only that, but he also managed to make the Zümrützade cook decide to set out on a long journey. One of the dishes he chose to prepare for the contest was the priest's stew he had cooked for the captain of the ship that had brought him to Istanbul.

The rest simply fell into place. When the kitchen was left without a cook, his new acquaintances recommended him to the patriarch of the mansion, Hüsnü Bey. Faced with such pressure, Hüsnü Bey did not know what to do, and one day he let the cook make just one dish for lunch. Of course, before the dirty plates could be put away, he sent word to the cook waiting in the courtyard that he had decided to employ him with a daily salary of five silver coins.

Another disappointment, rather than Kamer, awaited him at the Zümrützade mansion. She had been sent to the Imperial Harem as a gift.

According to whispered rumors, Zümrützade Hüsnü Bey had gifted Kamer, who had destroyed the peace and quiet of the mansion when she arrived, to the Chief Gatekeeper of the Imperial Palace. The Chief Gatekeeper was an educated but rather naïve man, and unaware of the animosity Zümrützade Hüsnü Bey felt for him, he accepted the present. He in turn was planning to give the odalisque with a penchant for dancing and a voice like a nightingale to the Harem, and thereby heal the rift between himself and Haseki Sultan. But things didn't go as planned. Soon enough it came to light what a handful Kamer was, and the poor Chief Gatekeeper was sacked from the post he had worked all his life to attain.

The cook listened to all these stories with a smile. He didn't ascribe it to cruel fate that Kamer seemed to be hidden behind higher and more insurmountable walls each time she vanished, nor did he despair or feel even the slightest hint of dejection. "This is it," he said to himself. "That is her final destination. She can't go any further."

The cook devised his plan with meticulous care as he worked in the kitchen of the Zümrützade mansion. The owner and the palace were on amicable terms, and the rustling of a leaf in the Inner Palace, or the sound of a pearl dropping onto the floor of the Harem, would echo in the Zümrützade mansion. He listened intently, crafting his plan by molding his ideas with his science, knowledge, and art.

Then it was time to take his final step on that path.

The cook had been hiding out in a dingy room at a bachelors' lodging house at the far end of Melekgirmez Street for three days. Hiding out was perhaps not the best term. For three days and nights he had been wandering around, drinking at taverns, playing dice at gambling dens, and, contrary to his usual habit, talking to people he happened to meet and telling them that he used to work as a cook at the Imperial Kitchens until recently, but quit because he'd had an argument with the Head Cook and planned on leaving the country to go to Venice on a ship passing through Morea in two days' time.

He also listened.

Constantinople was shaken by an endless string of rumors. The fact that Darıcızade Mahmud Bey changed his mind at the last minute and abandoned the idea of marrying a woman from the Imperial Harem shook the capital to its core, as if a thousand cannonballs had been volleyed at the city at once. Hearsay abounded, and those with at least a little common sense said that Mahmud Bey had been offended at being presented with an odalisque from the Harem as a bride when he was expecting at least a second-generation member of the royal family, and that was why he broke off the engagement.

Those with a bit more cunning said that the doge of Venice had talked Mahmud Bey out of the marriage, either with direct threats or by promising him privileges in trade, thus preventing the groom-to-be from making a massive contribution to the Treasury and plunging the Imperial Treasury into even worse circumstances.

Some said that the Darıcızade heir had fallen in love at first sight with a young woman named Nihan, also known by the nickname "wrecker of mansions," who hailed from the House of Pleasure, and ultimately went back on his promise to the palace because of his new-found love; it was said that as soon as he'd bought the girl from Sirrah, he'd set off to Alexandria with her. No matter how many times they swore up and down that the rumor was true, people who told that story were inevitably subjected to the condescending looks of their audience. No one could believe that a member of an aristocratic family like Mahmud Bey would risk drawing the ire of the great Imperial Palace just for the sake of a woman from the House of Pleasure.

As varied and effervescent as the rumors were, truths were few, yet as strong as the walls that had surrounded the city since ancient times.

Seeing how Mahmud Bey had broken his promise and his money had gone back to Alexandria with him, the Treasury, which had been on the verge of collapse since Treasurer Halil Pasha had fallen ill, was in an even worse state than before. The Janissaries' salaries, which were due in three days' time, would not be paid in full unless a miracle occurred. Rumors of an uprising spread like wildfire. Those with con-nections to the Janissaries' Guild spoke of how members of the Janissaries had already started to polish their symbolic copper caul-drons. On the day of payment, they would touch neither the bags of money given to them nor the saffron rice laid out for them, and then they would gather in Et Meydanı and raise their cauldrons above their heads in a gesture of defiance. Many heads would roll, the Grand Vizier being the prime target, and even the sovereign's throne would be under threat during such an earthquake of a rebellion.

The capital was on edge and shrouded in gray, as if a veil of gloom had been pulled over it. The dark clouds blanketing the skies for days hadn't turned into rain or been blown away by the wind. Everyone was in a state of quiet panic, commoners, aristocrats, and merchants alike. The bankers of Galata had stopped lending money and were collecting their debts one by one. Because of this shortage of cash, interest rates soared, and ships carrying provisions to Istanbul anchored off shore beyond the harbor as the captains heard rumors that there might be an uprising. Vendors stopped selling goods on credit—even if the customer was a member of their own family—and locked up their goods in secure storehouses. In short, everyone was waiting for the day when the payment would be made, whispering prayers and asking for God's mercy through clenched teeth.

The cook's inner voice told him that he would achieve the result he desired very soon. It was almost dusk, and he made his way toward a kebab shop near his lodgings. Despite the chilly weather, he asked for a small table to be brought outside so he could sit there and eat. The apprentice who brought the table outside—and who happened to be about the same size as the table he was carrying—asked him what he wanted, and the cook replied, "Kebab with vegetables, and some roasted liver on the side. Bring some *ayran*, too, but with lots of coriander in it. Add some pepper to the liver after it's done cooking, and don't forget to bring some sumac and oregano."

The apprentice went in, muttering the order to himself so he wouldn't forget, and returned after a while with two large plates. On one of the plates there were some roasted onions and garlic as well as sautéed red peppers, and the other was heaped with slices of bread. The sizzling of the peppers caressed the cook's ears like a soothing memory. He ate one of them. It was just the right spiciness. It withdrew without occupying his palate for too long, and left its flavor and the remnants of its spiciness only at the back of his throat. He took a large clove of roasted garlic and spread it onto a slice of bread. The garlic seemed hard on the outside, but inside it was as soft as paste. When he took his first bite, the cook was surprised; it was as if he was relishing such a taste for the very first time. The garlic seemed to be in love with heat; as soon as it was introduced to those hot, fireless, smokeless cinders, it melted on the inside, abandoning its sharpness and assuming a soft, mild, almost sweet taste.

He drank down the *ayran* with coriander, which was brought to his table at the same time as the kebabs, in a single gulp and asked for another. He then proceeded to eat slowly, as if he were having his last meal. By the time he had mopped up the last of the cumin and oregano soaked in olive oil at the bottom of the copper plate with a slice of bread and swallowed his last bite, the sun had already set, and the red veil of dusk was pulled over Melekgirmez Street, which was always busy but never safe.

The cook made his way back to his room. He fastened the flimsy door latch and lay down on the bed without undressing. He wasn't tired, and he did not intend to sleep. He listened to the sounds coming from the street and the floors below. Everything was as it should be. Darkness settled down over the city and the night owls started to hoot: a drunken man's shout, the shrill clink of castanets accompanying music from a tavern farther away, flirtatious laughter that made one's heart skip a beat, and footsteps, some timid, some hurried.

Then he heard the sound of other footsteps approaching, but they were foreign to the street. They were determined, severe. As they advanced, the other sounds seemed to fall silent, scamper away, or stand aside. He took a deep breath but kept his eyes closed. The foot-steps stopped under his window. A voice firmly but quietly asked the elderly doorman—who was sitting, as always, in a chair in front of the building—a few questions. The cook heard his name among the whis-perings. When the doorman replied in a shaky voice, the wooden staircase of the building began to creak. The sound of footsteps got louder and paused in front of his door, and then a kick sent the latch of the door flying off its hinges.

The cook quickly sat up as if he was going to try to run away or put up a fight. Two huge palace guards immediately threw themselves at him. Standing behind them was the Chief Palace Guard himself. The guards took hold of his arms and as he was dragged to his feet, the cook put up some slight resistance, to which the response was swift. The Chief Palace Guard slapped him so hard that a white flash appeared before his eyes, leaving him blind for a few moments, and then all went dark as the Chief Palace Guard pulled a black sack over the cook's head.

He was dragged downstairs, his feet barely touching the floor, and thrown facedown into the back of a carriage waiting at the end of the street. One of the guards pressed a foot into his back and tied his hands behind him, and the carriage began to move. The cook could tell by the sound of the hooves that the carriage was drawn by four horses, and judging by the fact that the coachman kept shouting "Stand aside!" he surmised they were in a hurry. The cook knew that so long as something unexpected hadn't occurred, they were headed straight for the palace.

After proceeding alongside the city walls for a while, the carriage turned right, toward the Hagia Sophia. The particular rattling produced by the large stones paving that road which lead straight to the Gate of Felicity was familiar to anyone who had grown up in the capital. But the cook did not think it likely that they would enter the palace through the main gate, and he was right. Just as he was thinking they must have been approaching the Hagia Sophia, the carriage suddenly veered left and entered a side street. The streets may have been complicated to navigate, but the cook's mind was clear and he knew they were headed toward one of the dozens of smaller, more clandestine gates that had been hewn into the Sultan's Wall. Just when he thought that they were somewhere near the Troops' Manor, the carriage ground to a halt. The cook heard the Chief Palace Guard, who immediately jumped out, bang his fist against an iron gate three times in quick succession. A muffled voice from behind the door asked, "Who is it?"

"Open the gate!" the Chief Palace Guard commanded. The chains of the gate rattled and it swung open with a creak.

The carriage was now proceeding more slowly as the coachman kept the horses at an ambling gait in the quiet of the night. The cook could hear the sound of the carriage wheels grinding across fine gravel and the small pebbles scattered by the horses' hooves.

They proceeded along for a while until the coachman pulled on the reins. As soon as the carriage stopped, strong hands grabbed the cook again. Quickly they guided him along, a palace guard on each side of the cook, holding his arms. While the sack over his head didn't let any light through, the cook could smell the scents around him: earth and fresh leaves. It hadn't rained recently, which the cook inferred to mean that both sides of the path must have been freshly hoed and watered. He rightly guessed that he was passing through a well-kept garden, and in fact it was the Royal Gardens.

The pebbled path suddenly gave way to cobblestones, and then they passed through a short passageway and climbed eight or nine steps up. They then turned left and proceeded through an open door. As soon as they entered the room, the guards forced the cook to his knees. It was bitterly cold. The cold of the marble floor and the voices echoing against the high walls made the cook feel that chill in both body and soul.

Footsteps approached from the left. They weren't clad in heavy boots like the guards but soft palace shoes. Then, from the right, probably from the next room or from behind a wooden panel, came a stern female voice: "Get out! And close the door behind you."

The cook imagined the guards backing out of the room, and then he heard the sound of the massive door slamming shut. After the din died down, a ponderous silence reigned over the room. The same female voice that had just ordered the guards out said in the cook's ear, "Who are you?"

Naturally, the cook was somewhat frightened. A woman who could tread softly enough to not be heard by keen ears but whose voice seethed with anger always meant trouble. Still, he managed to keep his composure and reply, "Remove the sack from my head."

There was a brief silence, and the cook could hear the woman next to him grinding her teeth. "Neyyir Agha!" the woman hissed, and then a resounding slap sent the cook sprawling to the floor. His cheek instantly went numb, and the force of the blow left his neck aching. He could barely make out the sound of the woman's voice over the ringing in his ears. "Raise him up."

As the agha brought him back to his knees, the woman said, "You swine, do you think you can lay your wretched gaze on someone like me? Have you any idea where you are, who you're kneeling before?"

"I do," the cook responded in the calmest tone he could muster. "We're inside the Tiled Mansion. And you are Haseki Sultan."

The woman was grinding her teeth again. She reached down and grabbed the cook by the hair through the sack and began to ask in stern whispers, "Who are you? Who sent you? What are your intentions? Do you wish to bring harm to our sovereign or bring the Ottoman Empire to ruin? Answer me! Answer, or I will flay you with my nails until you do!"

"Remove the sack," the cook repeated, "so you can see who I am!"

Haseki Sultan yanked the sack from the cook's head so roughly that she pulled out a tuft of hair along with it. The cook's eyes watered from the pain and the sudden light. The vestibule was illuminated only by two large oil lamps, but the light reflected off the blue and green tiles on the walls, becoming a thousandfold brighter.

The cook first looked to his left. There stood Mahir, hands clasped in front of him, head bowed. He couldn't decide whether Mahir looked more afraid or ashamed. Neyyir Agha looked straight at the cook, his eyes filled with hatred as he awaited new orders with clenched fists.

After the cook's eyes adjusted to the light, he raised his head and looked at Haseki Sultan. Her thin eyebrows were furrowed and her plump cheeks were red with rage. As she pressed her small but shapely lips together, her plump jaw quivered. The cook wasn't at all surprised to see that she seemed older than she was. The Harem was not a child's playground. Everybody there had to grow up quickly.

The cook summoned all his courage and looked her straight in the eye. She was taken aback and the tension in her expression gave way to barely perceptible bewilderment. His wasn't just any stare, it was a hidden message, the meaning of which only a few people in the world could discern. Haseki Sultan was quite familiar with it, having entered the Harem as a concubine and knowing that she would remain so regardless of the power she held until her son acceded to the throne and she became the Valide Sultan. She knew that only a member of the royal family could look into a concubine's eyes with such thinly veiled contempt.

Without giving her the chance to collect herself, the cook said, "You must have read the books Mahir sent you."

"I did," Haseki Sultan replied. The fury had faded from her expression but her voice was still stern. "You've written down all your achievements. The food you used to paralyze the Treasurer, how you killed Siyavuş Agha. You're a sorcerer and a murderer. You know what your sentence will be? You won't even get to die on the gallows. They'll string you up on a pike and leave you to die a slow death."

The cook ignored her threats and picked up from where he had left off: "If you looked carefully, you probably noticed that one of the books was missing three pages."

She was even more perplexed by this comment, but her quick intellect warned her that the conversation was taking an unexpected, perhaps dangerous, course. The cook persisted: "Did you not notice?"

Haseki Sultan nodded, almost imperceptibly. The cook lowered his voice and said, "There are some things we need to talk about," and then he glanced at Mahir and Neyyir Agha, who were standing in the corner. "Send them away first, if you like. Believe me, you'll want our conversation to be kept a secret. It's your choice, but don't go around murdering poor creatures like them just because they happened to overhear something they shouldn't have."

Haseki Sultan weighed the cook's suggestion and turned to Neyyir Agha and Mahir. "Stand outside!"

Mahir was more than happy to leave. Without waiting for the agha, he shuffled off, and Neyyir Agha cast the cook a spiteful look before leaving.

When the echoes of their footsteps died down, the cook slowly stood up, his gaze still fixed on Haseki Sultan's eyes. With his hands still tied together, he reached into the sash tied around his waist and took out the three missing pages. "That book contained the things I have done," he said, holding the pages toward her, "and these are the things I could do."

Haseki Sultan unfolded the pieces of paper and started to read the first one. It was a recipe, and its title, written in red ink, was "Stew of Health."

"I could use that to make the Treasurer healthier than ever before," the cook said, "Both his mind and body would be sprightlier than they ever have been. You could save the Treasury from inept minds."

Without waiting for a response, he moved on to the second page. It was titled "Rice of Obedience."

He explained, "The Janissaries who eat of this rice would not complain even if their money bags contained pebbles. And its effects are long-lasting."

Haseki Sultan remained silent. But when she turned to the next page, she couldn't conceal her fascination. Without raising her head from the page, she looked at the cook.

"You've read it correctly," the cook said. "The Sherbet of Power. Just one sip would make you the most powerful woman of the Ottoman royal family who ever lived. Neither another Haseki nor a Valide Sultan could ever compete with you. You'll have absolute power, and enjoy it for as long as you live."

Without taking her eyes from his, Haseki Sultan folded the papers and stuffed them back into the cook's sash. "And in return for all this, I'm going to have mercy on your lowly life, is that so?" she asked.

The cook smiled briefly. "You will have mercy on my life regardless. That isn't even one of the terms of our deal."

Haseki Sultan was lost in thought. "So what do you want?"

The cook's reply had long been at the ready. "I'm giving you three things. I want three things in return."

Haseki Sultan was no longer looking straight at him, but instead directing her gaze toward the marble floor. With a hand gesture typical of Harem women, she motioned for him to go on.

"One," the cook began, "you will forget I ever existed. You won't search for me, you won't ask after me, you won't even think about me. No matter where I am, you'll have nothing to do with me or those around me. Two, you will take all the children in this palace under your personal protection. For as long as you live, neither for the sake of the empire nor for personal gain, will a single child will be harmed."

Haseki Sultan looked up at the cook. She seemed to be considering asking "Why?" but then thought better of it.

"Three," the cook was about to say, when he was overcome by nervousness and excitement. He paused, gulped, and then said, "You have a concubine in the Harem. She . . . you will set her free."

There was a brief period of silence, and then Haseki Sultan burst out laughing. "Now I understand," she finally said. "So all of this was for the sake of an odalisque. For love."

She turned her gaze toward the cook again, but this time the astonishment in her eyes was mixed with genuine admiration. "Which girl is it?" she asked. "What's her name?"

After a brief hesitation, the cook whispered, "Kamer."

Haseki Sultan had to think about the name for a while, but soon her eyes filled with astonishment again. "Kamer?" she asked, laughing again. "Well, you've got yourself a troublemaker there!" Then she continued, as if talking to herself, "Love! Look at what love can do. My darling sovereign's reign was almost brought to ruin all because of love, as it turns out. Love almost put an end to the Ottoman Empire. The poets were right—the fires of love could burn the whole world down if given the chance."

The look in Haseki Sultan's eyes softened. Slowly she reached under her kaftan and took out a small dagger with a jewel-encrusted hilt. "But I can burn things, too," she said as she stepped slowly behind the cook. "I don't know if you have realized this, but you're looking into the eyes of someone who is as madly in love as you. If anyone dared touch my sovereign, I would become a raging fire! If anyone dare lay their hands on my child, I would become a storm! Now go. Raise the

Treasurer from his sick bed, calm the Janissaries, and prepare the sherbet for me. If you try any more tricks, or if you fail, I swear to you I will tear out that girl's heart before your very eyes and throw it at your feet, and I will make sure you live with that for the rest of your life. Go!"

The cook felt cold steel against his arm. Haseki Sultan cut the cloth binding his wrists and left the vestibule as quickly and silently as she had arrived.

Three days later, at dawn, the cook was in the Odalisques' Kitchen, looking nervously at a dozen huge cauldrons at the ready on the stoves. He was surrounded by sacks of rice as well as buckets of butter and pitchers full of honey.

Standing to his right, Master İsfendiyar asked him, seemingly just as nervous, "Do you think you'll be able to manage?"

"I won't lie to you, Master," the cook replied. "I've never cooked so much at once, but I think I can do it."

Master Bekir, who was standing to his left, slapped his shoulder. "And why on earth wouldn't you be able to? Does it matter whether it's one cauldron or a dozen? Aren't they all the same?"

"We'll never know until we try," the cook replied. Turning to the assistants waiting behind them, he said, "Get to work."

The more experienced of the young assistants picked up the sacks of rice and carried them to the massive pitchers of water hanging from the wall, as the rice had to be washed before it could be cooked. The younger assistants took their places by the stoves, holding buckets of cinder, sacks of coal, and bellows, waiting for the command to stoke the fires.

The cook set to work adding pinches of pure saffron to the dozen large vessels of water in front of him. He rubbed the saffron so that it would dissolve evenly, while at the same time whispering the names of the flavors that would turn the rice into the Rice of Obedience. Soon, he would ask for water to be poured into the cauldrons, boil the dissolved saffron with honey, and finally add the rice that the assistants had washed and steamed. Lastly, he would add some wheat starch, again dissolved in water, and leave it to boil until it took on the right consistency. That would be no problem at all if he was only cooking with one cauldron, but the cook had to perform each step a dozen times in a row and whisper the right names at the right time with the right intensity. His eyes were half-closed as he focused on the names in his mind and the saffron between his fingertips. Already he was exhausted, as he had been in the kitchen ever since returning from his negotiations with Haseki Sultan. First he had visited Master İsfendiyar, who he had found in the Odalisques' Kitchen, sitting gloomily with Master Bekir. When Master İsfendiyar saw the cook standing before him, his eyes had filled with tears and he'd stood up to embrace the cook. He'd then asked him about the bruise on the left side of his face. Hearing that it was Neyyir Agha's doing, he'd said with a smile, "Be grateful, you got off lightly."

The first dish the cook prepared was the one for Treasurer Halil Pasha. He worked all morning, and the Stew of Health was ready by lunchtime. The news that followed was good. Halil Pasha opened his eyes that same afternoon, and when he was able to talk toward evening, his first words were, "Are the payments for the Janissaries ready?" According to hearsay, the Treasurer had attempted to get out of bed as soon as he heard what was happening, but because he had been bedridden for days, he could not summon the energy and laid his head back on his pillow, tears coursing down his cheeks. Some said that Haseki Sultan had sent her personal physicians to Halil Pasha's house. It was rumored that Haseki Sultan was given the joyful news that the pasha would be able to return to his post in a week at most and was in a much better state.

After getting that out of the way, the cook locked himself away in the confectionery for two full days. He sent everyone out—even the Chief Confectioner—locked the doors, and made the sherbet for Haseki Sultan with berries he had handpicked one by one. It was almost ready. All it needed now was a single whisper from the lips of the Pasha of Cuisine.

As usual, the most difficult task was left for last: cooking the Rice of Obedience for the Janissaries.

It was a tradition to serve rice to the Janissaries who went to the palace to collect their earnings on payment day. Thousands of plates would be set before the Janissaries and the cavalry packed into the Second Courtyard. But it wasn't any ordinary meal. Most often, it was a chance for the sultan and the empire to display their splendor. Important foreign guests and ambassadors from the capital would be invited to the palace, and the military march would be performed by the Janissaries, driven on as they were by the excitement of payment day, making hearts quiver with fear and admiration. Before the bags of money were presented to each of the soldiers beneath the dome, every soldier would eat the rice, which represented the compliments of the sovereign. However, if the soldiers were disgruntled, not a single one of them would touch the food set before them, and that would be the final silence before the approaching storm. And when the cavalry refused to touch the food, everyone knew rebellion was imminent. Usually, either in the next few minutes when the Grand Vizier and members of the Imperial Council emerged from the dome, or at the very least the next day, all hell would break loose.

That was the threat the cook was faced with when preparing those cauldrons of rice. The burden on his shoulders was, needless to say, quite heavy, because he was the one who set the first steps of the rebellion into motion.

After the dozen cauldrons had been removed from the stoves and the rice was dished out, the Odalisques' Kitchen was filled from floor to ceiling with thousands of plates. They were placed on trays, and the trays were stacked on top of each other in rows of ten, with two wooden blocks separating each tray from the next.

The cook looked at the steaming plates with suspicion. "I wonder if it will work?" he murmured to himself. He had taken the utmost care each step of the way. He went over what he had done time and time again and could find no fault, but the thought that he had made even the smallest mistake gnawed at him.

Master Bekir, perhaps to break the tension more than anything else, turned to Master İsfendiyar and said with a laugh, "Master, why don't you try some? Let's see if it works."

"I'm already an obedient man," Master İsfendiyar said irritably. "You wouldn't be able to tell the difference." After thinking for a moment, he turned to one of the assistants in the rear of the kitchen and said, "Why don't you go and call Master Sıtkı over here?"

As the assistant ran out of the kitchen, Master Bekir exclaimed, "Good thinking! If it works on him, it will work on anyone."

A few minutes later, Master Sıtkı, the cook for the Imperial Council who was known throughout the kitchens for his ill temper, sour demeanor, and miserliness, walked into the kitchen. He had been making rice for the next day's ceremony since midnight and he was already in a foul mood. "What's the matter, Master?" he asked, approaching Master İsfendiyar.

"Is the rice ready?"

Master Sıtkı snapped, "It'll be ready soon enough."

"Is it good?"

Master Sıtkı seemed to be on the brink of an explosion of rage. "It's rice; it's the way it's always been. It won't make any difference if it's any good, because no one's going to have a bite of it. It's not worth the money we've spent cooking it!"

Master İsfendiyar nodded slowly and pointed to a plate of saffron rice on a table. "Why don't you have a taste of that?"

Master Sıtkı was taken aback. "The saffron rice?"

"The saffron rice, what else!" Master İsfendiyar sneered. "Do you see anything else in this room that you might be able to taste?"

Master Sıtkı could not understand why he was suddenly being chastised, but his right eye was twitching with anger. He grabbed a spoon from a rack on the wall and plunged it into the saffron rice. After eating his first spoonful, initially it seemed as if he might toss the spoon aside, but his hand hung motionless in the air. His eyes glazed over. In slow motion, as if he were sleepwalking, he clutched the plate and wolfed down the rice.

After swallowing his last mouthful, he smacked his lips and said in admiration, "Well done. It's so light and tasty, the butter and honey are just right. The consistency is exactly as it should be, not too starchy, the best of saffron."

"Alright, alright," Master İsfendiyar said, interrupting the lengthening litany of compliments. Then he suddenly extended his palm toward the poor man and said, "Give us a silver coin."

Master Sıtkı was surprised again, but still smiling. "What for?" he asked.

"Well, for the saffron rice, of course," Master İsfendiyar replied.

Master Sıtkı could make neither head nor tail of the situation, but for some inexplicable reason he couldn't find it in himself to protest. He reached toward his waistband and took out a silver coin, which he placed on Master İsfendiyar's palm, a silly smile still on his lips.

"Go on then, off with you," Master İsfendiyar said. "I hope you enjoyed the rice."

Master Sıtkı began to walk back toward his own kitchen, still smacking his lips. He didn't neglect to congratulate them one last time before leaving the kitchen.

Master Bekir and his assistants had to cover their mouths with their hands so their howls of laughter would not echo down the hallways of the kitchens. Master İsfendiyar placed the silver coin in the cook's hand with a flourish, and said, "Well, that's that. Let's hope it all ends well."

The mood in the Odalisques' Kitchen became lighter. As the intermittent laughter continued, the morning call to prayer rang out from the Hagia Sophia.

Silence descended upon the kitchen once more. The call meant that the payment ceremony would begin soon, as the members of the Imperial Council and the Janissaries would come to the palace following the morning prayers.

Master İsfendiyar told the assistants, "Ready the trays and go out when I give the sign."

The assistants stood around the trays in twos, one to carry the tray and the other to distribute the plates. The cook, along with Master

İsfendiyar and Master Bekir, left the kitchen and started heading toward the Tinsmiths' Lodge lodgings on the other side of the Kitchens' Passageway. They ascended to the second floor. There was only one good thing about the long, narrow lodgings which were shared by the tinsmiths and their apprentices, and that was the fact that they faced the Second Courtyard where the ceremony was to be held.

They raised the thick curtain and looked out through the latticed window. There was no one in the courtyard yet. A light spring breeze was blowing, at times rustling the grass and the leaves on the trees. They waited quietly.

After what seemed like a lifetime, they heard footsteps approaching from The Gate of Salutation. First, the two ceremonial battalions of the Janissaries slowly entered the courtyard. Their flat caps were decorated with long, snow-white tassels. Afterwards, the Chief Janissary's imposing figure appeared by the gate, followed by the guild's twelve highest-ranking officers. After the ceremonial troops and the troop aghas led by the Chief Janissary took their positions, foot soldiers began to fill the courtyard. Led by their commanders, the soldiers who came to the palace to represent their regiments entered the gate according to how many troops there were, and they lined up behind the troop aghas who were waiting single file across from the dome.

The courtyard was soon completely full. With their red robes and white headgear, the Janissaries stood completely still, and the deafening silence of that crowd numbering in the thousands was unnerving.

The silence was interrupted by the Gate of Felicity's Chief Gatekeeper when he shouted, "Attention!" which meant that the Grand Vizier and members of the Imperial Council would soon be passing through the gate. The Grand Vizier appeared, followed by other state officials. The cook was surprised to see the Grand Vizier walk in such a self-assured manner, his head held high. He looked at the others. Even the Treasurer, who was walking behind the Viziers of the Dome, seemed rather dignified. The cook attributed their poise to the statesmanship that had become ingrained in them. After all, each of them had vast experience, and none would dare show their fear, even to their executioners.

The Grand Vizier received the Janissaries' greetings and as soon as he took his place under the dome with the members of the Imperial Council and the troop aghas, Master İsfendiyar gave the sign to Master Bekir: "It's time!"

Master Bekir rushed downstairs. Kitchen assistants bearing trays poured out of the three gates of the Imperial Kitchens toward the Janissaries.

The cook watched the saffron rice being distributed while also keeping an eye on the dome. He was nervous. According to custom, as the foot soldiers ate their meal outside, a gathering would be held inside. Nothing of importance would be discussed at the gathering, but the Chief Janissary and the troop aghas would kiss the hem of the Grand Vizier's skirt, and upon the Grand Vizier's command the soldiers' payments would be carried from the Treasury chamber into the courtyard. Afterwards, the meal would be over, and one of the troop aghas, the Chief Lieutenant, would go out and direct the military march, after which the payments would be distributed. Of course, nothing would follow tradition that day, and what frightened the cook the most was the possibility of an early rebellion, that is, one that broke out before the Janissaries could eat the saffron rice.

Thankfully, the cook's fears were unfounded. The assistants finished distributing all the plates and returned to the kitchens in the same order they had emerged. The deathly silence in the Second Courtyard continued. No one moved. Not even the Janissaries.

That was when the cook realized he had overlooked a small detail. That oversight had proven to be a deadly mistake. And now, alas, it was too late.

Master Bekir must have noticed the same thing, because he whispered, "They're not eating." And then he added, "They won't eat."

The cook's oversight had to do with the Janissary Guild's tradition. He had forgotten about the soldiers' loyalty to one another and their obedience to their commanders. If the guild had decided that no one would touch their food, no force on earth could compel any of the soldiers to eat even one spoonful of the rice. Besides, the food was already cold, its inviting steam long gone.

Master İsfendiyar clutched the cook's shirt and whispered, "Run, quick! The capital will be thrown into confusion for a few days, so they won't come after you. Run, save yourself!"

The cook couldn't reply, because he didn't hear what the master was saying. A voice howled in his mind, shouting, "You have killed Kamer. You have killed her while trying to save her!"

Soon the Grand Vizier would come out to ask why the offended soldiers were refusing the palace's offering, and then the tumult would commence. The Janissaries would demand to see heads roll. The cook couldn't imagine what would happen after that; no one could. The one thing he knew was that Haseki Sultan would keep her word. He remembered the look in her eyes, and he knew Haseki Sultan would do exactly what she said she would do. She would tear out Kamer's heart, throw it at his feet, and make sure he lived with the memory of that moment.

The last thing the cook saw was the opening of the dome's gate. The officials were stepping outside. He closed his eyes and waited. There was nothing he could do but await his fate.

Suddenly, a voice rang out in the Second Courtyard. "Aghas!" it announced. "Your payments will be made in full. Eat up!"

The cook opened his eyes. The person who made the announcement was none other than the Chief Janissary. He surveyed his troops in the courtyard.

A high-ranking member of the cavalry summoned the courage to stand up. "My lord," he called out. "This is not about whether the payment will be made in full. The condition of the state is obvious. For a long time now—"

The Chief Janissary interrupted him with a roar: "Aghas! The payment will be made. The empire will endure hardship just as well as it has enjoyed abundance. The lot that falls to us, the subjects of the empire, is to stand by the state in these hard times. Cast off your impudence!"

His fiery stare was directed at every soldier congregated in the court-yard, and he repeated a final time: "Eat up!"

The Second Courtyard repeated in unison: "Thanks be to God!"

The soldiers' loyalty to their guild and officers had triumphed. The Janissaries in the courtyard removed their spoons from their field bags and started to eat. Unable to stand on his feet any longer, the cook slouched down. Master İsfendiyar's fingers were still curled around his arm. Tears welled up in his eyes.

The cook sat beneath that window for hours. He listened to the prayers of gratitude the Janissaries recited after they finished eating as they vowed their dedication to the Ottoman Empire, the officials of state, the sovereign, and Haseki Sultan. Even after the ceremony was over and the palace returned to its usual daily routine, he did not get up. He didn't know what would happen, nor could he tell whether he had succeeded or ruined everything. The cook could not think. He couldn't imagine what would happen if something went wrong, because he did not have the strength to fix anything anymore.

Shortly after the afternoon call to prayer, the door to the Tinsmiths' Lodge opened, and a large shadow fell across the room. "Haseki Sultan awaits you in the same place after sunset," Neyyir Agha announced from the doorway. He glared at the cook like one would look down on a cornered insect.

The cook nodded weakly.

After the evening call to prayer, he made his way to the confection-ery. He didn't know whether Haseki Sultan would want it or not, but he took the sherbet with him just in case and began making his way toward the Tiled Mansion.

She was waiting for him in the same place where they had parted ways three days earlier. The door to the mansion was open. Light from the newly risen moon illuminated the marble of the courtyard, filling the landing and the vestibule covered in tiles with an icy blue light.

As the cook approached, Haseki Sultan was smiling mockingly, triumphantly. "You failed," she said, stepping toward him. "And what is to happen now?"

The cook said nothing.

She said, "You've roused the Treasurer from his sickbed, which is all well and good. But the Janissaries? You couldn't stop them. Thankfully, the Chief Janissary and I have an understanding. It has cost me dearly, and I would have preferred that your plan succeed instead. But you failed!"

The cook had no reply to offer. Haseki Sultan's smile faded as she sneered, "I am the master of an art that is much more powerful than yours. I am a master of politics! I have no need of your rice to calm disgruntled troops. And I do not need your sherbet to have power, believe me."

She paused, looked at the cook at length, and asked again, "So tell me. What is to happen now?"

She was sure he would not reply, so she continued, "Tell me, what shall I do to you? Shall I force you to your knees and make you beg? Shall I make you my slave for forty years in exchange for a single look at Kamer once a year? No. . . . There are many people around me to whom I can do such things, and I wouldn't want you to become one of them. Do you know why? Not because I need you or because I am fearful of your art, but because I have respect for your love, for your intellect, and for your travails. I don't care if you're the Pasha of Cuisine, but your love is admirable. That is why I am going to be fair to you."

Haseki Sultan took a deep breath and began to recite her decree: "You asked me for three things in exchange for three promises. You failed at one of yours. But I shall not go back on my word. For two of your services, I shall grant two of your wishes. Is that fair?"

The cook nodded.

"Forget about us not seeing each other ever again," Haseki Sultan said. "You can go and live wherever you like, and for as long as I live you will not be harmed. But you will come to me every time I summon you and you will be at my service. Do you understand?"

"I understand," the cook replied quietly.

"The other two promises still hold," Haseke Sultan continued. "Now, do whatever it is you said you would do!"

The cook pulled the velvet cover from the silver pitcher of sherbet that was sitting by his right foot. "It's not ready yet," he said as he raised the pitcher. "I haven't whispered one of the names over it yet. You will drink it from my hands. Each sip will be a sworn seal to your promises."

Haseki Sultan approached the cook and brought her lips to the pitcher, which he was holding up.

The cook spoke gravely, as if he was performing a religious ritual. "Are you aware that this sherbet will course through your veins as poison if you ever go back on your word, be it today or in the future?"

"I am," she replied.

The cook asked, "From today onwards, do you swear to ensure that no children will be murdered within the walls of this palace and to never issue a decree commanding the death of a child, no matter what the cause?"

"I do," she said, taking a sip from the pitcher.

The cook moved on to the second promise, trying to keep his voice from shaking. "Do you swear . . ." he stammered, "to give Kamer to me before sunrise?"

She smiled. "I do."

After Haseki Sultan took a sip to seal her final vow, the cook handed the pitcher to her. He felt that at that moment it wasn't only his own fortunes and story that were changing, but the fortunes and stories of the entire Ottoman royal family, even the world. He wasn't entirely wrong. That intelligent and ambitious woman, who truly did not need much of the Pasha of Cuisine's art to acquire power in the first place, was now drinking deep of the Sherbet of Power.

When she pulled the empty pitcher from her lips, a strange look came into her eyes. She looked around, as if nothing in the world mattered to her anymore. She trained the same cold stare on the cook. "Wait here," she said and, leaving the pitcher by his feet, left the room.

When he could no longer hear the footsteps of Haseki Sultan and her retinue, the cook stepped outside. The full moon was now high in the sky. He began to pace up and down in the courtyard, his shoes clacking on the marble paving stones washed by the white rays of moonlight. He felt like he was dreaming. "Wait," Haseki Sultan had told him, and she had sworn.

The only thing that told his mind, which was experiencing an altogether different kind of drunkenness, that what was happening was real was a terrible tightening in his chest. It was so powerful that he could barely breathe.

He walked toward the left corner of the courtyard and looked up at the Harem. He knew that Kamer would be approaching from that side, but when? His soul could not endure such waiting. Even the ceiling of the portico high above began to feel suffocating. Unable to bear waiting any longer, he went down the steps and walked in the direction of the Harem. The closer he got, the more clearly he could make out the outlines of the palace. The cook looked at the dark shadows of the walls, the latticed windows, the minarets, and the domes rising up, their roofs gleaming in the moonlight. The sight of the Harem frightened him. Yet that was where he had been born. He had learned to walk and talk on the other side of those walls. He had never dreamed he would return to that place where he had nearly lost his life, but life had tough wiles. Once again he was on the palace grounds, all these years later, on another day as important as the day he was born.

Once upon a time, he had been there, and now the past was embedded within the present.

The cook remembered. He remembered the Harem, his father, his mother, compassion, fear, Master İsfendiyar, the House of Pleasure, Master Adem, Sirrah, love, betrayal, hatred, and loyalty. He remembered separation. Longing, nightmares, endless roads, Brother Sadr and Brother Sa'd, stars, books . . .

He would never forget the Lady of Essences, nor would he ever forget Master Bayram and Levon.

Mahir, Neyyir Agha, the Privy Chamber Page, the late Siyavuş Agha, Master Bekir and his assistants . . . he would never forget any of them.

The cook had become the master of remembering, and the only person he had always remembered and would always remember was coming toward him from the Harem like a light piercing the darkness.

He was stricken. All he could do was blink. Nothing had changed. She was there, she was Kamer, and she was walking toward him. She was wearing an ivory dress. Her black hair fell in waves to her shoulders beneath a white silk veil held in place with a silver headband.

As she got closer, he could see her face more clearly. Her dark brown almond-shaped eyes, her strong jawline. She was still beautiful. She had grown up, and perhaps life had graced her face with a few thin lines, but what did it matter? She was eternally Kamer, and she would always remain so, regardless of time.

He saw her trembling lips, and as she took the final two steps toward him, the moonlight sparkled in her damp eyes.

Kamer embraced him. Without saying a word, without a pause, without a look.

Even that sharp line dividing life and death no longer meant anything to the cook. His nostrils filled with the scent of apples and clover. Kamer's hands clutched his back tightly, her hair brushed his face, her tears fell on his shoulder.

With the last of his strength the cook hugged her and said, "Forgive me."

Kamer replied with a sound that was something between a laugh and a sob. "I was never angry at you," she said in a frail, trembling voice. "I always missed you."

The cook wanted to say something. His mind raced. There were a thousand words in his thoughts, but all the sentences in the world, all the words, and even all the meanings and ideas ended up translating themselves into the name of the girl who was now in his arms.

It was the only word that existed for the cook now, representing every other word and all meanings. The cook whispered that name which for him sufficed to express everything in his life: "Kamer."

Then he fell silent.

He had said the one thing he knew, the one thing he could utter. He'd done everything he could, and that was the final step. He waited.

Then he heard a whisper. Not just any whisper, but the one he had been yearning for all those years. He had heard it millions of times both when Kamer was there and in her absence, but hearing it fall from her lips. . . . It reminded him of his own existence, it spoke of the fact that he was alive, breathing, that his heart was beating. It told him of a past, promised a future, reminded him of hope. It was joy and pleasure, a single sound. Just one name. His name.

Kamer's voice started to complete the missing part of his soul which had been wandering incomplete for so long.

Kamer whispered once more, "Cihan."

8

And So It All Comes to an End

AND ONCE THE story was over . . .

Cihan did not tarry long in Istanbul. Being in the capital had become unbearable for him. He and Kamer settled down not too far away, but the farthest they could go while remaining close, or the closest they could remain while going afar. They moved to Antakya on the eastern coast of the Mediterranean and opened a small kebab house just outside the city. A few years later, Master İsfendiyar retired and joined them. Together they cooked, they ate, and they sang, enjoying a content life together.

Kamer and Cihan had two children, a boy and a girl. Neither of them inherited even the slightest trace of either parent's talents.

Their son was extremely fond of books. When he turned fourteen, the cook sent him to the el-Haki Brothers' house. The boy liked Brother Sa'd but had a fondness for medicine, so he became Brother Sadr's student.

Their daughter was also talented in her own way. At the age of six, she was able to look after the restaurant by herself, and by the time she was eight she haggled with merchants like the best of traders. The cook took her to the Lady of Essences's mansion. The Lady was pleased and trained her as if she were her own daughter, teaching her about spices and trade.

Cihan also kept his promise to Haseki Sultan. Every time she summoned him, he went to the capital and helped her in her political wiles with his dishes and enchanted whispers. And soon enough she became renowned throughout the world. However, over time Haseki Sultan began to forget about the cook. She had reached such heights and attained such power that she refused to stoop so low as to ask for anyone's help.

Haseki Sultan enjoyed a reign that was longer and more powerful than many sultans'. When her son acceded to the throne at a young age, she ruled over the empire herself for fourteen years as regent. The promises she had made while drinking the Sherbet of Power were always in her thoughts, and not once did she break any of them. She even convinced the sovereign to annul the fratricide law. Not a single child of the palace was killed during her reign. That is until one day, thirty-five years later, when Haseki Sultan fell victim to her own greed and wrote a decree commanding the murder of a child, her seven-year-old grandson.

The cook had warned her. Oaths taken with the Sherbet of Power were lasting and cruel.

On the night she broke her promise, Haseki Sultan was strangled by a greased noose in the place where she felt the safest: the Harem.

On one of his final visits to Istanbul, the cook got news that Master Adem was on his deathbed and had asked for him. The cook knew he couldn't refuse. After all, he was Master Adem, the man who had raised him.

He found Master Adem on his deathbed in an abandoned building outside Üsküdar. He was gravely ill, and had only one final wish: to die with the most wondrous of flavors lingering on his palate.

The cook first boiled a few belladonna seeds and had the master drink the concoction. Afterwards, when Master Adem's mind was lost in peculiar dreams and hallucinations, the cook began to whisper the names of flavors into his ear. Master Adem left this world with thousands of flavors playing upon his mind.

The cook received other news, too.

He heard that Sirrah's slaves had rebelled and strangled her in her sleep, looted her treasure, and set the House of Pleasure ablaze.

Neyyir Agha found favor with Haseki Sultan and, during her reign, he became a pasha and climbed his way up the ranks to the Imperial Council. Unfortunately, Neyyir Agha did not see his retirement; the day after Haseki Sultan was strangled in the Harem, he lost his head to an executioner.

Privy Chamber Page Firuz Agha became a governor and left the Inner Palace, and after serving in various provinces throughout Rumelia, he became the Governor of Chios, after which he retired. He settled on the island with his wife and children, and lived a happy, peaceful life.

Darıcızade Mahmud Bey met a swift end. The young woman he met and fell in love with at the House of Pleasure, Nihan, "the wrecker of mansions," lived up to her reputation and within two years the great Darıcızade dynasty was bankrupt. People said that Mahmud Bey couldn't hang himself because he did not have enough money to buy a rope, so he had put an end to his sorrowful life by jumping off a cliff.

Master Bayram did not remain long in Istanbul either. After having an argument with a few customers, he packed up his stuff, got in his boat, and left. The cook did not hear news of him for a very long time, until one day he was making *topik* and could not get the consistency right, and he thought of Levon. He asked around and at last got news of the tragic story. Master Bayram had moved to Thessaloniki and opened a restaurant there. One day, two officers who had had a bit too much to drink got into a scuffle, and the knives they pulled ended up being plunged into Levon's chest as he tried to separate them.

Witnesses described how Master Bayram placed Levon's lifeless body in his boat and rowed off toward the horizon.

After that day, the fish and mezes never tasted the same again.

The happiest news the cook received was about Mahir.

Mahir had also risen alongside Haseki Sultan and he returned home as a governor. At last he had become "a great man," and his dear mother became the mother of a bey.

The cook was delighted for him. He felt as if a huge weight had been lifted from his shoulders.

And so it was . . .

Some died, some lived, and some left.

The cook spent the rest of his life in happiness and peace, filled with delicious flavors, and he loved Kamer with the same intensity of that very first day. He no longer asked big questions of life, nor did he expect great answers. He put all he had into his art. Seeing as he was born as a Pasha of Cuisine, he decided that he had to do justice to his title. And that is precisely what he did. He never tried to make a name for himself, and he worked to better not just the flavors he created but those created by other cooks as well. He traveled and lent his divine talent to anyone who needed or desired it. Under his enchanted hands, flavors became wondrous, and just like the legend says, the best dishes were made and the greatest cooks were trained in those days. So much so that those familiar with the legend of the Pasha of Cuisine say that the light of the last Pasha of Cuisine still burns and the lands upon which he breathed his last are still renowned for their cuisine, even today.

Who knows?

THE END